PANDORA'S SISTERS

Also by Michael Stephen Fuchs

The Manuscript

MICHAEL STEPHEN FUCHS

PANDORA'S SISTERS

MACMILLAN NEW WRITING

First published 2007 by Macmillan New Writing
an imprint of Pan Macmillan Ltd
Pan Macmillan, 20 New Wharf Road, London N1 9RR
Basingstoke and Oxford
Associated companies throughout the world
www.panmacmillan.com

ISBN 978-0-230-01828-0

1 3 5 7 9 8 6 4 2

A CIP catalogue record for this book is available from
the British Library.

Typeset by Intype London Ltd
Printed and bound in Great Britain by
MPG Books Ltd, Bodmin, Cornwall

Visit **www.panmacmillan.com** to read more about all our books
and to buy them. You will also find features, author interviews and
news of any author events, and you can sign up for e-newsletters
so that you're always first to hear about our new releases.

For SNAFU, D, and Tiny E

With great steaming piles of thanks to: My editor Will Atkins (for saving me from sounding like an American bloke, and not to mention from the Pope), Sophie Portas, Maria Rejt and Caitriona Row at Macmillan; Pops, for always encouraging me to carry on; Mum, for being eternally lovely; Grandpa, for saving civilization in the twentieth century and thus making all this possible; my mates, for all buying copies of the first book; all the other legions of people who so graciously and energetically supported the first one (see http://www. michaelfuchs.org/razorsedge/?story=2006-08-15); David at Goldsboro Books, for the discreet whispers and beer; Joeboy for setting me straight re monkeys v. chimps; Steven Pinker, Daniel Dennett, Robert Wright, Richard Dawkins, Steven Johnson, Alexander M. Heublein, Ryan Canolty, Scott Christensen and Dana Pitely for all the applecart-upsetting ideas I stole from them; and most especially to Mark Pitely – for the garret, the air-conditioned conference room with fast Ethernet, the steady diet of things worth reading, and the first principles.

Alone of species, all alone! we try to understand ourselves and the world. We become rebels or patriots or martyrs on the basis of ideas. We build Chartres and computers, write poems and tensor equations, play chess and quartets, sail ships to other planets and listen in to other galaxies . . . The yearning for certainty which grails the scientist, the aching beauty which harasses the artist, the sweet thorn of justice which fierces the rebel from the eases of life, or the thrill of exultation with which we hear of true acts of that now difficult virtue of courage, of cheerful endurance of hopeless suffering – are these really derivable from matter? The intellectual life of man, his culture and history and religion and science, is different from anything else we know of in the universe. That is fact. It is as if all life evolved to a certain point, and then in ourselves turned at a right angle and simply exploded in a different direction.

– Julian Jaynes, *The Origin of Consciousness in the Breakdown of the Bicameral Mind*

One

I'm kneeling before the hundred-foot altar in the centre of St Peter's Cathedral in Rome, my hands pressed together before me as if in prayer. Only, between my two hands, I am clutching two whole other hands. A second pair, with very slim fingers, and cool to the touch. This is because they are made out of bronze.

Also, a Swiss Guard – and I mean a really burly, no-nonsense son of a bitch, despite the Bavarian schoolgirl outfit – is holding a halberd to my neck. This is not a playtime halberd; this is a no-shit, take-you-off-your-horse, send-your-head-on-its-merry-way sort of halberd.

And I've got an unshakeable feeling the next few minutes are going to suck.

On the upside, my friend Helen has an extremely large-calibre handgun trained on the Swiss guy's melon.

It is getting toward midnight. So even though we're smack in the middle of Easter Week, St Pete's is not doing any business. The whole Vatican is asleep – including, presumably, His Holiness, who's sacked out probably not three hundred yards from where I'm kneeling.

'She dies, you die,' says Helen. The Swiss guy ratchets his scowl in response.

'I'd take that at face value,' I say, without moving my head. 'She's a behavioural geneticist. She knows what a worthless pile of pre-programmed amino acids you are.'

I'm perceiving a deep and fundamental irony about where this is all coming to a head. You want to know who gave you your soul? You want a personal relationship with God? Well, we found God. We're all up in God. We've got God's private number.

And so do you. Imprinted something in the order of a hundred trillion times – once in every living cell in your big dripping corpus.

1

Of course, you can't tell the religionists this kind of thing. They'll have your head. On a halberd, evidently.

Did I mention the religionists? The cabal of Qabbalists? The horde of Hindu Naga cultists? They're all here, too, in Christendom's grandest church, flitting furtively around all the ornate pillars, the statues of the saints – and the shadows. Shadows like you wouldn't believe. The Jewish and Hindu kids are on the home turf of the Papists, and so they're a little edgy, right? But, you know what, in my book, the God guys are all reading from the same script.

The wrong one, as it happens. Only Helen and her very close friends get to look at the real Holy Text. Electron microscopes. Mass spectrometers. Shotgun gene sequencers. God's infinite grace in a double helix. Word.

Yet somehow Helen has ended up wielding a very different sort of tool on this night. I can see the hammer of her nickel-plated .44 hauled back like a snake strike that's all over but the nervous-system shutdown; and she's distributing her gaze coolly around the room. This makes a stark contrast to the night I met her – when she was tearing up a nightclub in San Francisco, drunk, flirting with everyone. Including with me. And including with my monkey. That was three weeks ago.

Back up.

Two

From: A'hib Khouri <ahib@genenw.com>
To: keq@ctake.com
Cc: Helen Dolan <helen@genenw.com>
Subject: change of plans
Date: Sat, 15 Apr 2006 03:38:42 (PST)

Listen. What we agreed on. It's all changed now. Those
men, the same men you described, they're on to me
now. I saw the same black sedan. And when I went home
last night, one was sitting in my living room – I saw him
through the window. I ran for it, and went back to the
office.

I'm starting to believe the sequence, the pattern we've
found, is a HUGE deal. That it really means something.
And that these people want it from us. Look, I'm
attaching a zip file, ok? It's got the HGP identifier of the
specific genome we used, details on the sequencing
method, and, mainly, the exact location of the sequence
on the genome. I've DES encrypted the whole thing
using the first 128 bits in the pattern (triplet values) as a
key. You should easily be able to decrypt it – but
whoever's been snooping our mail won't. DON'T LET
ANYTHING HAPPEN TO THIS.

I'm going to get out of the country, at least for a while,
back home. If you don't hear from me . . . actually, I have
no idea what to tell you to do with this. But I for one am
going to keep trying to decode it. Just somewhere safer.

– A'hib

Hold on. I hadn't seen this mail yet. Helen hadn't seen it yet. We
didn't yet know A'hib was dead. Correction – we didn't yet *think*
A'hib was dead.

Back up.

3

Three

Smack my bitch up.

Yeah, that's it – right about there. I remember The Prodigy was playing. That song always makes me think of San Francisco. It was still big when I moved out there.

Swinging star-flashes, liquid sweat-diamonds arcing in strobe motion. Two hundred bodies heaving like thrown pistons. A club in the Mission District, I don't even think it's open any more. I don't know if it was open the following weekend.

But they had a liberal monkey-policy, which made the joint just all right by me.

Don't leap ahead and get all anthropomorphic, though. The monkey isn't a club kid. The monkey doesn't even really dance. But he does enjoy a good groove. Usually, he stakes out a table or a bit of sofa, while I'm off shaking my bits, where he'll squat and sway a little – and smile. Big smile. Happy guy. I *love* my monkey. Don't fuck with the monkey. Do not fuck with the monkey.

The monkey's name, and by which he should probably henceforth be referred, is Erasmus D. And Erasmus, in all fairness, and just for the record, isn't even really a monkey. He's a chimpanzee – specifically, a bonobo chimp, humankind's nearest living relative. An eye-blink six million years of evolution, and the merest handful of genomic base pairs, separates Erasmus from your mother. (Or, more aptly, your father. But you take my point.)

Helen hit it off with Erasmus like the kissing cousins that they are.

In fact, that night in the Mission, when I'd dripped a glorious sweat trail back to the table where I'd left him, I barged in on Erasmus and Helen kissing. Nothing kinky. (And you just never know with bonobos, who are the unrivalled booty monsters of the primate

4

world.) Just an exchange of grandmotherly cheek pecks. Sweet, it was.

And that's my initial, and enduring, image of Helen Dolan.

Kissing my chimp.

About Helen Dolan

Twenty-nine years old. American. Holds advanced degrees in behavioural genetics and biomedical informatics. Reserved, mysterious, garment-rendingly complex; got that icy professionalism/too-cool-for-school thing nailed. Unreasonably hot. Unreasonably. Dark, dark, dark – lots of Afro-Caribbean blood. Head full of wild creature curls, a moonless midnight thicket. Legs to next leap year. Waist you want to tape-measure.

Works for GenenW, another Silicon Valley biotechnology revolution in corporate form. (The W reportedly stands for 'Whatever'.) Takes her work, which is heart-attack serious, seriously. Otherwise, doesn't give a fuck. Just doesn't give a fuck.

About Me (While We're At It)

Twenty-seven years old. British. Terminal degree in cognitive science from Cal Berkeley, undergrad in computer science from Stanford. Came to the States for the universities, stayed in the Bay Area for the parodically perfect weather and the BPs (beautiful people). Red-headed, also curl-stricken, with defenceless English skin and melanomas-to-be in freckle form. Not too bad to look at. Figure oscillates between slim and slinky, but with well-inflected curves on the right surfaces. Pretend I don't give a fuck.

Work for a video game software company called Complete & Total Ass-Kicking Entertainment, Inc. My job there mainly involves architecting and implementing advanced strong AI in the context of NPC bots for use in . . . but, then again, who gives a damn about work right now.

5

Me And Helen Going Home Together The Night We Met And, Kind of Inexplicably, Winding Up In Bed

'I'm not really gay,' I told her at five in the morning when she woke me up sneaking out. (I left out the '. . . but you're just so fucking hot' bit.)

'Hey, who is?' she drolled, pouring herself back into her club outfit. After a brief-but-visible internal debate, she came back and kissed me – on the forehead.

That was when I knew we were only going to be friends.

But it was when she kissed Erasmus goodbye that I figured we were going to be *good* friends.

Mucho Mas On The Monkey

Handsome and self-possessed pygmy (aka bonobo) chimp, weight eighty pounds, stands two-and-a-half feet short. Black fur with a white tail splotch, wears his hair parted down the middle. Comic-book creature ears, but for all that with the solemn and serene gaze of a many-millennia-old soul. Biological age probably about the same as mine, at a guess, which has him flirting with monkey middle age.

Serene and self-directed. Can be left alone in the house for indefinite stretches as long as I stock the fridge. Watches cable, sleeps in his own bed, and flushes as appropriate. Even feeds the fish – when he's not fucking with them by tapping on the glass, making goofy faces, etc.

Get this: only monkey ever to escape from the SF Zoo. Subsequently shown on local news (via heli-cam) climbing the westernmost span of the Golden Gate Bridge, evading capture. Shot on home video four days later terrorizing art vendors in Union Square. Where he wasn't caught on film: in a tree out front of my place busting into a bird-feeder. How I lured him inside: made him a better offer (bananas).

Why I had to have him: A month earlier I'd been to the zoo with my co-worker Thaddeus and his two small children. In the monkey house we found the older one, the girl, who is called Kennedy, frozen in place, staring at one of the chimps. The chimp sat staring back. Thad came up behind her.

'Hey, Kennedy. You okay?'

The little girl bit her fist. 'Why is he here, Daddy?' she asked.

'What do you mean, honey? He lives here.'

She paused again, maintaining eye contact with that disturbingly expressive set of eyes. 'Does he know why he's here? *Why* is he here? Why does he *look* like that?'

'Like what, honey?'

'Like . . . like he's not supposed to *be* here.'

It turned out later that this episode got to Thad like you wouldn't believe. Me too, in honesty. Though I've no way of knowing if Kennedy's monkey was Erasmus.

Why he's called Erasmus D: possibly too obvious to belabour, but let's just recapitulate Wordsworth's suggestion that the child is the father of the man.

What This Story Is About

The origin of subjective higher consciousness on Earth. (Hint: It didn't come from any of the places you might have been in the habit of thinking it did. Just a friendly heads-up.)

Four

It's axiomatic that you have no idea how hard something actually is until you try to teach a computer how to do it. Famously, Marvin Minsky was working on one of his early robotics experiments when he assigned a graduate student the following as a summer project: *Vision*. Forty years later, we still don't have machines that can reliably make out that the kettle is boiling over.

Computer science sheds an awful lot of light on brain science, and vice versa – so much so that people in the two fields watch each other like unhinged hawks. Try and construct a mechanical thinking machine (a smart computer) and you get a pointed lesson in the real, and staggeringly complex, requirements of cognition. On the other hand, poke around at a *working* thinking machine (a human brain) and you slowly illuminate how Mother Nature, in the form of evolution, actually met those requirements. In other words, the AI guys are trying to build an intelligent device; and the neuroscience guys are taking one apart. You can see the synergies here.

But the funny thing is this: tasks which for humans are a piece of cake, computers get their thinking caps singed right off even attempting – and the other way around, as well. Just try factoring a twelve-digit number some lazy afternoon and you'll soon long for the job of watching the kettle. And the computer will gladly let you have it. Hence the other old rule of thumb in AI: hard things are easy and easy things are hard.

It's because I spend my days trying to get computers to do tasks any four-year-old could knock off with a snort before nap-time that I know a little something about human consciousness. And about the stark anomaly of such a baroque and staggeringly complex phenomenon spontaneously turning up in a band of gawky hairless hominids out on the African savannah. Folks who were pretty much minding their own business – hunting, gathering, reproducing, trying to avoid becoming a hot lunch for the local predators.

And then one day, perhaps it was a Tuesday, around teatime . . . they all turned up with profound *self-awareness* – which was a complete newcomer in 3.5 billion years of evolution. In the days that followed, they used that self-awareness to build a little something called civilization. Which also really shook things up in the old biosphere. Suffice it to say we're still really vague on how that happened – and on how evolution could possibly account for any of it.

But enough about the gaping hole in what's still the single best idea anybody ever had (Darwin's). I certainly wasn't going to get my head around it today – not with a head that felt three sizes too small for my brain, and the brain in question sort of dramatically throbbing inside of it. I was padding back to my carpet-walled cube with a quad espresso and a fistful of 500mg Tylenol, looking like a woman with a thorax-wringing hangover, which I was, when Thaddeus Gottlieb hailed me over.

'Clubbing again?' he asked, without a grin.

'Yeah, mate.'

'Walkage?' he asked seriously.

'Yeah,' I managed, after a big gulp of analgesics with a coffee chaser. 'A spot of fresh air with you and I'll be a new woman. Or, at least, the same old woman.'

Workday walks with Thad are key.

What's So Bloody Fascinating About Thad – And Get This:

He's battling his way in earnest through a full-blown, no-holds-barred, Iron-Cage-Texas-Deathmatch *Existential Crisis*. No kidding. No posturing. The full meal deal. The yawning void. The ravening maw of bottomlessly pointless mortality. The Big Nothing.

The rap sheet on Thad is that he's thirty-eight, married with two small and extremely winning children, former full back for the Division I Notre Dame football team, former military officer (about which service he talks very little indeed), now a database

9

administrator – quite a good one – here at Complete & Total Ass-Kicking Entertainment.

And he's a lapsed Catholic. A recently lapsed Catholic.

Flash Back To Walk With Thad v1.0

So I'd been working at the company for about five and a half minutes when Thad first stuck his nose into my cubicle and invited me on our inaugural walk, a tour around the corporate campus. Thad's outgoing and earnest. I'm pliable. Being dropped down in an adjacent cube is, it turns out, a fine way to make a swords-crossed lifelong friend (or foe).

So the first thing about C&TAKE is that it's not your big brother's video game company – nor his late-nineties Internet startup. You know the ones, with the dedicated rumpus rooms and running Nerf missile-launcher battles in the hallways. I mean, yeah, sure, the atmosphere's pretty relaxed, and we have a few amenities (café on the ground floor, a TV lounge with comfy couches). But on the other hand, the US$12 billion video game business has all the laid-back camaraderie and sangfroid of a World Cup final – and our share-holders have this enduring hang-up about making money. So, the pressure builds, and one occasionally wants to pop smoke and call for extraction. The best twenty-minute pressure release is a turn around the grounds, which are green and manicured enough to fool you into thinking you've gone somewhere real.

And so at about the halfway point of our very first lap around the local Love Canal, and this was nearly a year ago, I happened to let slip to Thad that I'd studied a bit of philosophy as part of my cognitive science degree. (Cog-sci, which is to do principally with how thought happens, lives at the unholy intersection of philosophy, psychology, artificial intelligence, neuroscience, linguistics, and anthropology.) And before you can shout 'Incoming! Nihilism!' Thad had set up this saturation-fire field of mortar-shell questions like 'If there's no God dictating morality – the rules of proper behaviour – then what does it matter *what* I do?' and 'If I don't believe in

Heaven any more, then at the end of all this, do I just end up staring up at the inside of a pine box?' and of course the grand old slavering matriarch of this brood: 'And if so, then what the hell is the point? Of any of this? Why bother?'

Sigh. I told the dear afflicted boy straight away that he needed to understand two very important things: (1) That what he thinks of as his immortal soul is really just a massively parallel protein computer; and, (2), We're only here at all because we're the output of a very long-running – and extraordinarily bloody – equation.

I can't claim that this was precisely calibrated to make Thad feel better, you know, not right off the bat. In point of fact, it was intended to break the back of his romantic notions – with a mighty snap. The quicker you do it, the less total pain.

He and I have taken a lot of walks since that first one.

On this particular walk, the one with the blistering hangover, we had the garden path to ourselves – and as well a rare couple of clouds had snuck into California airspace, thus mercifully keeping the solar radiation off. We walked in silence, tracing the curve of the man-made lake, hardwoods to our right, a breeze at our backs. As we rounded a bend, a grey squirrel jumped out right in our path, like a crossing guard. We all stopped and regarded one another.

'So take this little guy,' I said, segueing from nothing. My head felt better, so I figured I'd resume my normal avocation of making Thad's hurt. 'Just like us, he's got an incredibly complex onboard information-processing system. He can do differential calculus – taking into account constants like gravitational acceleration and atmospheric friction – for leaping from one branch to another. He can work out a complex route to a suspended bird feeder, or bury nuts in three hundred places and save a location map.' I gave the squirrel an approving wink. 'We can't remotely build systems like that. I certainly can't program bots that smart.'

Thad nodded gravely. The squirrel considered all this, flicked his tail noncommittally, and moved on.

'But here's the thing,' I said, as we resumed our rambling.

'The squirrel has no "soul"?' Thad suggested.

'Exactly,' I said. This was a not-unusual topic for us. 'No self-consciousness, no subjectivity, no higher-order awareness. Definitely no art, no culture, no language. Never mind figurative language.' I squinted at the pavement scrolling smoothly under our feet. 'It's really almost a qualitative difference of computation. Rather than one of degree.'

Thad had his hands in his pockets, his shoulders rounded. He wore spiky hair, round-framed glasses (with much darker-tinted lenses stuck on the front for out-of-doors use), and a red-shot van Dyke beard. Thad always struck me as palpably, pleasingly, American – he believed in progress.

'So now you're going to explain to me,' he optimistically predicted, 'where we humans got all that cool higher-order processing? Consciousness and culture?'

I looked up to find we'd come back around to our building. I held open the swinging glass door for him. I took a look back over my shoulder for our squirrelly friend. But he had gone.

'No,' I said quietly, following him into the dim and cool interior. 'No, I'm not.'

Five

It was because of the whole existential crisis thing that I originally introduced Thad to the Retard. That was also a few months back.

Oh, and it's the Rootin' Tootin' Retard to you, mate.

And, no, I don't actually know the RTR myself. Not in the flesh. Not as such.

The name's a dodge, I reckon. A self-deprecation, as it were. Because the Retard is the single wisest person to whom I've ever been exposed (even obliquely, over the Net). The Retard haemorrhages good ideas and right thinking. The Retard drains the deserts and waters the swamps. The Retard seems to live everywhere and nowhere – writing from net-cafés in Budapest and Belize City, Cape Town and Cairns.

Never twice in a place.

I did the usual routine, sure, firing off some clever web searches, trying to chase down a bit trail on the Retard. (Virtually everyone with any virtual life to speak of leaves a bit trail.) But I got nada. No real name. No employer. Definitely no picture. (Which is, honestly, the lurid grail we're always looking for when we do this.)

Today, back at my desk, plugged into my machine for the day, I got serious: I caught up with mail. (Priorities: coffee, walk, mail, lunch, work. Anytime before lunch is always too soon before lunch to do work.) And I found some mail from the Retard.

The Retard appeared to be writing from the Seychelles, on this occasion. I thought, you know, I thought I'd escaped by coming here. California, U S of A, land of sunshine and dreams. And all like that. But it's as Buckaroo Banzai said. Wherever you go, there you are. And escape is where you aren't.

Freedom is what the other guy has.

Here's what the Retard originally had to say when I introduced him to Thad:

From: Kafe 19 <kafe19@kafe.santorini.gr>
To: keq@ctake.com
Cc: thad@ctake.com
Subject: Re: Meet Thad
Date: Tues, 6 Dec 2005 23:53:44 -0500 (GMT +2)

Salaam, Thad. You know what? The more one considers it, the more convinced one is that 'existential crisis' is the default state of homo sapiens sapiens. Consider: Here we are, these extremely sensitive creatures (however unlikely it is for us to have gotten this way). And we squat here on this wet, mossy boulder, hurtling in circles through an otherwise barren cosmos.

What are we meant to do with that? How are we supposed to react? We should sit here and come up with some meaningful way to live out our three score and ten? Or just run the clock out gracefully? And with NO help or advice whatsoever forthcoming from above? Just ringing silence? Brother, the universe cares so little about us you can taste it all coppery in your mouth.

Nonetheless, may you find peace, my friend.

After taking a cold couple of hours to digest that, Thad wheeled into my cube, buttonholed me, and said:

'Okay, I'll bite. Is the Rootin' Tootin' Retard a boy or a girl?'

I cocked my head, parted my lips – and stared wordlessly into Thad's thick chest. He got my drift and went back to his cube.

I stayed in today and ate more espresso for lunch, as I planned to duck out early. I had a date. I also called home a little past noon to try and convey to Erasmus that I'd be late. It's genuinely difficult to tell for sure how much English he understands. But not none, I can tell you that. And, yes, he does often pick up the phone – though usually after screening. He hates telemarketers. Naturally, I wish he'd take the telemarketing calls. That'd wake those guys up in the morning.

I intuited from his curt snorting that he got my drift – and wasn't pleased I'd be out late. So I gave him permission to pay-per-view a skin flick. Here's the thing you've got to understand about bonobos: they're the randiest primates walking. Just no contest. They're the only great ape species to have invented French kissing, mutual masturbation – *and* oral sex. I mean, yeah, we invented all those things. But humans never indulged them so often. Bonobo social life pretty much revolves around shagging. Shagging for fun. Shagging for food or favours. Sympathy shags.

Which may be why violence is virtually unknown in bonobo society.

And which is also why I feel such gnawing guilt for keeping him out of that society. But I guess you get used to anything. And there's always pay-per-view.

A little after 2 pm, my mobile phone beeped its chirpy little you've-got-voicemail-and-I'm-going-to-carry-on-beeping-at-you-until-you-fucking-check-it beep. Needing a break from code-slinging anyway, I dialled in – and the familiar creepy feminine voicemail voice welcomed me back to its little world. It alerted me that I had . one new message and three old ones. It asked me if I cared to listen to my new message. The message, which involved mainly clicking and banging noises, was pretty clearly from Erasmus – just giving me additional grief about tonight.

I deleted the message. The voicemail voice recited its litany of familiar options. I've found I have to listen to the litany and exit properly – or voicemail doesn't inform the phone that I've gotten my message, and that it can stop beeping at me.

The phone suggested a button I could press to listen to my old messages.

And another one I might press to change my personal options.

And a further one I should consider if I wanted to send a message.

A penultimate, meta-option button would provide further options.

And, finally, blessedly, the button I could press 'to quit – *while you're ahead.*'

There was no way I heard that right. It was the latent hangover talking. Or I was going mad. Luckily, either of those explanations was perfectly plausible.

I chose to quit.

At the stroke of 5 pm I ducked out (literally ducking, with my hand over my head) and took the back stairs. I swung out of the emergency exit. I loped through our parking lot, shrugging on my biker jacket, reviewing familiar vanity licence-plates (mostly valid Unix commands), sun-bleached QuakeWorld window stickers, and inexplicable dangly things under rearview mirrors. One of our programmers hates Bay Area traffic so much he has a bumper sticker that says: 'I'd Rather Be Sucking Cock'. (And, no, he's not gay.)

The bumper sticker on Helen's car, I'd shortly discover, says: 'Darwin Found God'.

I jumped on my Ducati – black, Supersport, 2005 – and blasted her up.

I roared out of the lot and nosed it toward the sea.

Six

The first most important thing to know about how civilized the Bay Area is that it only rains during certain specially designated periods: January and February. Otherwise, you can get up on a given morning and know you're not going to get pissed on. January and February are the rainy season.

And don't make of it a bigger deal than it is, either. People say, Oh, watch out for the rainy season! Yeah, right. I did the research before I came out. During the so-called rainy season, you get as much rainfall as you get year-round in most places. And never mind in the British Isles, which come to think of it, is kind of civilized in its own way – you also know what you're going to get everyday, weather-wise: Shit.

Anyway, after the rainy season gets out of the way, that's pretty much it for rain for the year. After that, it's pretty much going to be 68.4°, sunny, breezy, and delightful for the next ten months. Bay Area natives stop noticing this. I can tell you I don't. One minor downside, hardly worth mentioning really, is that after April or so, anything you want to stay green you have to personally water. They've solved this problem though – with terminology. After April, we say the hills turn 'golden.'

I rode over these hills – the endless, gentle bulges that pad the Bay Area from the rest of California – on my way to meet Helen, my pulse kind of racing about all that actually. As I rode along, I mentally recounted, for no reason that sprang right to mind, the conversation I had with Thad where I properly introduced him to Important Thing #1.

Flash Back To, Oh, I Don't Know, Probably Our Second Or Third Walk

'So you said,' Thad said to me, out on the garden path, 'that I needed to understand two very important things.'

'Before you're going to make any progress, yes.'

'The first thing you said,' he said, 'was you said that . . . that my soul is really just a massively parallel computer.'

'Yes. I'm sorry to be the one to tell you.'

'Are you the mad scientist?' he asked. 'Did you set all this up?'

'No,' I said. 'Don't worry. You're really here. All of this,' and I gestured expansively at the mirrored glass office buildings and the man-made lake, 'is real.' I paused to consider what I meant by that. I decided to carry on.

'It's just this, really: It's just that your mind, everything you think of as yourself, all your feelings and experience and beliefs . . . consist of nothing more, nor less, than the physical activity, electrical and chemical, of the brain. That's it.'

'Okay,' he said, monitoring the path, striding with hands in pockets. 'I think I'm okay with that.'

'Good for you,' I said. 'Because, historically, from Descartes . . . to your mother-in-law . . . to the Pope . . . most people haven't been. They've mostly got really attached to the idea that their essential selves actually consist of some kind of mysterious soul stuff. Some kind of luminous God-granted goop, some *élan vital*, that grants personhood, that allows free will, that assures immortality. They see, on the one hand, a physical universe of trees, rocks, and billiard balls bouncing mechanistically off one another. And, on the other hand, they see these mystical spirit creatures, namely us, created by God, and endowed with agency.' I paused for a breath, and to tug at my inseam. '"Agency" being a technical philosophical term meaning we are "uncaused causers". That is, we can create effects in the universe, but nothing causes our actions. We are different. We are free.'

'I can see where that would be kind of comforting,' Thad said.

'Yes, funny how it's always the real whoppers that are. I mean, people started suspecting that this idea was bunk hundreds of years ago – when the logical inconsistencies of metaphysical dualism started getting hard to ignore.'

'What sort of inconsistencies?'

'Well, it's what we call the mind–body problem. For instance, if you and I are non-material protoplasm, or spirit stuff . . . then how the hell do we push around cue sticks that subsequently push the billiard balls around? That is to say, if we aren't part of the chain of cause and effect of a mechanical universe, then that certainly insulates us from being effects. But it also insulates us from being causes! Descartes had this idea that the pineal gland, a little nubbin of flesh in the middle of the brain, served as the gateway between the spirit and the body. But that just pushes the problem around, it doesn't solve it.'

I paused to kick an acorn down the path. 'It also shows you how direly a lack of decent science – in this case, neuroscience – can hamper philosophy.'

'So the soul is a non-starter?' Thad asked.

'Totally,' I said. 'The soul's out.'

'What's in?'

'Massively parallel protein-based computer. Organic information processor. Let's put it in computer terms – which are good terms in which to put it, just because computer science gives us such an apt vocabulary to discuss psychology. In fact, some say we should stop referring to "artificial intelligence" and start referring to "natural computing". Anyway, to put it in computer terms, your brain is slower than your old Apple][e. It only runs at about a hundred sequential operations per second – or a ten thousandth of a megahertz. But it's massively parallel. We've each got about a hundred billion neurons, and each neuron has about a thousand connections to its neighbours. That means a hundred trillion connections, and thus a theoretical ten quadrillion operations per second, total. Not bad for three and half pounds of spongy meat, eh?'

Thad nodded thoughtfully, squinting behind his darkened

glasses. 'It also sounds about like what you'd expect, maybe, to drive something as complex as a human mind. So maybe you don't even need a soul to explain things?'

'Precisely! Nonetheless, it's a huge leap for most people to get from the hunk of meat – however many synaptic connections – to reading a bedtime story, or programming a VCR . . . never mind to Bach, Michelangelo, Einstein . . . and especially to higher values like morality, meaning, love. They just can't find their way from there to here.'

'But they've got to get over it?'

'Yes. The mind simply is the physical operation of the brain. If you don't believe me, I've got neurosurgeon buddies up at Berkeley who can crack your skull – while you're still awake – start poking around with little pokers, and make you raise your leg, laugh out loud, see a patch of blue, hear celestial music . . .'

By this point, we had looped nearly back around to our building. And there was our squirrel friend in our path again. (Or a pretty close relation.) He had stopped, and was regarding us again. I looked over at Thad and saw his lips part.

'Go ahead,' I said.

He closed his mouth and swallowed. He said: 'Can the neurosurgeons make me fall in love? Or be more honourable? Or start liking classical music?'

We actually had to step around the squirrel this time.

I downshifted, stopped daydreaming, and rolled the Ducati off the highway when I got to where I was going – namely, the beach at Fort Funston. I found I had done most of the driving with that one-hemisphere-on-autopilot thing where you don't have any consciousness of it. I don't know how good an idea that is on a motorcycle.

I parked, hopped off, and looked for Helen.

Seven

Fort Funston, in South San Francisco, serves mainly as a local dog-walker's Mecca. Helen informed me (via email, when setting this up) that she refuses to own one – but has regular dog-walking gigs for a half-dozen friends and neighbours. By this means, she keeps herself in dogs, but out of dependents (and commitment).

This was our first 'date'.

I parked on one end of the large sandy lot. I'd been here once or twice before. Trails wind around either side of a set of dunes, and another path leads down to a rocky beach. Depending on the time of day, you might find as many as a hundred canines leading their humans around while obeying (more or less faithfully) an elaborate set of off-leash etiquette conventions.

Paragliders also usually hover overhead, after having jumped off one of the many suitable cliffs nearby.

It's all really very northern California.

Helen rolled up fifteen minutes late in her black Special Edition Miata, top down and a large Alsatian with paws hanging over the passenger-side door. She parked on the other side of the lot, not having spotted me yet. I shuffled over while she and the pooch climbed out.

She turned around and greeted me from behind sunglasses that looked, if anything, darker than mine. (Mine have my prescription in them and are exactly as dark as the optometrist would make them without actually having me sign a waiver.)

The dog jumped on me.

'This is Alfred,' Helen said. 'Al lives in my building.'

I started to pet Al hello but he leapt off toward the dunes.

'Wait for us!' Helen shouted after him. He did, standing tensely at the trailhead, shifting from paw to paw. Helen and I caught up and the three of us moved out.

Nobody said anything for a minute or two. Finally, Helen asked:

'So tell me what you do again?'

I'd actually never told her the one time. Moreover, I'm not a big fan of the question. I employed my normal riposte:

'You mean – for money?'

'Yeah,' she said, looking out toward the sea as it came into view. 'For money.'

'I do artificial intelligence,' I said, looking out with her at the water. The dunes were flatter and we'd paused to peer through them. 'AI, in the vitally important context of gratuitously bloody first-person shooter video games.'

'Which first-person shooter?' she asked.

'Ours is called GibletWorld,' I said. I always blush when I have to say this.

'That's evocative,' she said.

'Yes,' I said. We started off again. Alfred hadn't waited. 'So's our corporate tagline: "Bring Mops".'

Helen wore ragged jeans that hugged what little she had in the way of hips, pointy-toed brown boots that kicked a lot of sand around, and a thigh-length, brown leather jacket (with flaring sleeves). The wind off the water kept it chilly here.

'Bring mops to GibletWorld? That would seem to go without saying.'

'Yes,' I agreed. 'And the last people you want to risk boring are sixteen- to thirty-five-year-old boys. But marketing's not my deal.' She arched a thin dark brow by way of asking what my deal was. I said: 'I get paid for programming non-player characters in the game – bots – to behave convincingly as if they were player characters. Or, really, to behave as if they were apocalyptically clad and tremendously muscular men and women fighting balls-out with implausibly destructive weapons in ill-lit tunnels and Roman-style arenas.'

Helen squeezed her hands into her jeans pockets and turned toward me. 'And how exactly does an apocalyptically clad and tremendously muscular man or woman fighting balls-out with implausibly destructive weapons in ill-lit tunnels and Roman-style arenas behave?' This was one of my first clues as to how, and how well, Helen's mind works.

'Surprisingly subtly,' I answered. 'I mean, there are levels and levels of behaviour. At the beginning of the day, there's the stuff any competent code slinger can program. Like, say, dodging, right? The bot moves away from threats. Fine, so does a bacterium. But then there's aiming: the bot shoots straight – ideally, with the best weapon it's got available. Maybe it even leads targets, on a good day.'

Alfred, and then Helen, and then me, took an acute left. Our new path led down toward the water. Helen still seemed to be listening, so I blathered on.

'A good bot acquires resources. That is, it runs around picking up weapons, ammunition and health. Maybe if it's clever, it knows how to hide. Things start to get a bit interesting with that.' I watched my feet, picking out steps on the steep path. I also wore pointy-toed boots, though black. 'But choosing a place to hide requires a little folk-psychology. It presupposes knowledge of your opponent's mind – knowing where he's likely to not look for you.'

Emerging onto level sand below me, Helen said: 'So this is where you need a doctorate from Berkeley?'

I'd never yet told her I went to Berkeley. But she can follow a bit trail too.

The Alsatian, having hit the beach ages ago, circled back around to us, tongue flapping with abandon. I leaned down to give his face a vigorous double-sided rub. I said: 'No, not yet. But move on to communication, and you're getting closer.' Alfred turned and ran off, spraying wet sand on me with his back paws. I flapped my shirt out.

'What's a bot going to have to say to his bot buddies?' Helen asked.

'Fair question,' I said. 'Right-o.'

(A quick note about my occasional Anglicisms, by the way. Very often they're the kinds of things I would never say back home. But Americans react with such delight to a well-turned 'cheerio' or 'blimey' that you sort of get trained to be all English here. And I'm not too proud to do tricks for tummy rubs.)

'For starters,' I said, 'they might want to coordinate. Say, tag-teaming on their opponents, or parcelling out fields of fire. Cover and advance, fire and movement. Good infantry tactics. I mean, yes, it's stuff any enlisted kid out of basic training can do. But it does require a little more adaptability of behaviour.'

Alfred stood now, noble-seeming, on a huge pile of rocks above us. The rocks jutted out over the water. Helen started to climb up after him. I hesitated before following. I said: 'Or how about playing possum. Acting wounded and retreating – leading an opponent into an ambush.'

'Okay,' she said. 'I could see where that would take some strong AI.'

'Just a tad,' I said, a little embarrassed that Helen and the dog both climbed a lot more gracefully than I did. 'Pretty much every game developer with bots has worked out the bits I've mentioned so far. But I'm looking at significantly higher-order awareness and processing.'

'For instance . . .?'

I jammed my fingers into a damp crevice, to lever myself up. 'For instance, mercy. When might a bot have a clear shot at you – but opt to give you a break? When it's just not fair to gun you down like a dog?' Alfred looked down over a ledge at me. 'No offence,' I said to him. I clambered up onto the flat spot where Helen now stood. Waves broke against the front of our rock, flipping fingers of spray at us. 'Where would a bot get a sense of fairness?' I said, then paused to catch my breath.

'Where would a human?' countered Helen.

'Where indeed. And when and why might a bot sacrifice himself for a mate?'

'When and why might a human?'

'And how can a bot come up with, oh, a flourish? Say, a spinning pirouette off a ledge while firing a fade-away rocket shot – and

24

hitting nothing but head? How,' I intoned, 'do you make a bot with a sense of style? How do you make a Magic Johnson?'

'Only God can make a Magic Johnson,' she said.

'So it is said,' I said. 'So it is said.'

Alfred jumped down to us and we all sat. The sun began its nightly plunge into the Pacific. The wind picked up. We sat listening as it whistled amongst the dunes.

'Aren't you going to ask me what I do at work?' Helen said.

'No. I don't expect you'll tell me much.'

'Why do you say that?' She almost sounded surprised.

I sighed out loud, relishing this a little. 'First, because what your company does is recounted in great detail online. Second, you know I'll already know what a behavioural geneticist does, which is what you are listed as on the website. And, finally, because I don't get the impression you're one of those people who talks about her job.'

We got up in the last light and started the walk back to the vehicles.

Here's what Helen Dolan does for a living, for the biotechnology company GenenW: She hunts the genes that make human minds go *kertwang*.

In general, the job of a behavioural geneticist is to try and determine which bits of the genome are responsible for which bits of behaviour. On one level, that's bunk, of course. Notwithstanding the media's regular ejaculations that 'scientists have discovered the gene for such'n'thus!' there generally aren't genes for things. Of the tens of thousands of active genes in the human genome, probably not one of them is a gene *for* something. What they usually mean is that scientists (like Helen) have found a gene that *breaks* something. Isolating a gene shared by a lot of people who can't talk and calling it 'the gene for language' is like clipping a car's alternator wire and announcing you've 'found the bit that makes the car go'. There are quite a lot of ways to break something as complex as a human mind.

But figuring out what breaks it is often enough. The more genes Helen can find that break things (Alzheimer's, mood disorders), the better GenenW can develop psychotropic drugs – and, one day, gene therapies – to make them work again.

Yeah, sure, okay, ending disease and misery's all well enough. But what's your health worth if you don't have a really good video game to while away the hours?

Let's just say Helen and I both deal with how minds work, and leave it at that.

'Okay,' Helen said, wheeling Alfred around toward the Miata. 'This dog is walked.' After boosting him in one side and climbing in the other, she burbled the toy engine up and motored off. I watched the 'Darwin Found God' bumper sticker recede into illegibility, while recalling her *Only God can make a Magic Johnson* line.

I then walked back to my bike in the deserted dusk. But instead of driving home I sat sidesaddle on the tilted machine and watched the last of the sunset glow around the dune edges, while the wind bansheed around and nipped at my exposed bits.

When the sun drops, I've found, the sand chills quickly.

Eight

I don't recommend drinking alone to anybody. But then again, I've begun to think hypocrisy is a pretty small-potatoes vice. It's certainly better at least to have decent principles, even if you don't quite live up to them yourself.

So I went ahead and cracked a couple of expensive cold ones when I got home.

And it was the universe that made me do it, anyway. Always the universe.

Puttering to a halt in my dollhouse off-street parking lot, I swung my leg over the top of the bike. I did the normal remove-the-helmet-without-taking-half-my-hair-with-it routine. I took two steps toward my door – and then the universe flagged me down.

The darkness had gotten good and worked up. I had the lot to myself. No windows betrayed the scenes behind them, though some glowed. The universe had me to its lonesome. The universe had my number.

Throat bared and stretching, I pointed my face skyward. I immediately caught sight of Orion. I used to think of Orion as my special, personal heavenly steward – until someone pointed out to me that he's (arguably) the most recognizable and (quantifiably) the brightest constellation in the night sky.

Much more disturbingly, I now knew: he doesn't exist.

He holds no club. He has no shield raised against the snorting charge of nearby Taurus. There's no sword. And no belt for it to hang from. There aren't four limbs.

There's not even an H shape.

So, what is there? Well, for starters, there's alpha Ori (also known as Betelgeuse) – a variable red giant about six hundred times the size of our sun, floating about four hundred light years away (that's two and a half quadrillion-ish miles).

And then there's Rigel – a blue-white giant and the sixth-brightest object in the whole sky. There's delta Ori, and Struve 747, and also NGC 1981 – actually a group of ten stars clustered too tightly to resolve, individually, without a telescope.

My neck began to hurt. I rubbed it.

All there is up there, all one cranes at, is a number of enormous fusioning balls of hydrogen, most of them millions of miles around, all of them at least trillions of miles away from us – and from one another – and tossing off photons which we sometimes manage to catch on the back of our eyes and then mentally represent as little electro-chemical pulses.

But I can assure you there's no H.

And definitely no unstoppable mythic hunter.

These are all just patterns we teach ourselves to see. Stories we tell ourselves.

And they say people are too literal in our thinking.

That's when I went inside and cracked that first cold one.

But first I said hello to the little guy, who sat moping in his room. Then I swung by the fridge. And then I sat down and logged in. And finally I composed some mail to the Retard, relating my thoughts on the indisputable non-existence of constellations. On the difficulty of even wrapping a human mind around the notion of them.

I cc'd Thad, as I always do on technosophical wank of this sort.

RTR wrote back, within about two hundred seconds, from some time zone where it appeared to be four o'clock in the morning.

From: user <user@ciber.biz>
To: keq@ctake.com
Cc: thad@ctake.com
Subject: Re: Stars

It is a little daunting, trying to wrap the mind around such things. The last time I looked, there were about 80 billion galaxies. Each has, oh, roughly 400 billion stars per. What does that total? 32,000 quintillion?

Let us take just one star. Let us take ours, for

28

convenience's sake. (It is a little smaller than average, but no matter.) It is about two and a half million miles around, at the waist. Volume-wise, it goes about 50 octillion cubic feet.

The distance amongst stars in a given galaxy tends to run to a few parsecs. (1 parsec = ~19 billion miles). The separation between galaxies typically goes a few megaparsecs (ignoring clustering).

So let us put the universe together then, in terms we can really get our heads around. In a nutshell, it consists of objects hundreds of billions of times larger than anything in our direct experience; in quantities hundreds of millions of times greater than any we can reasonably imagine; strung out at distances from each other trillions of times longer than the furthest distance we can perceive.

Sleep tight!

I knew it was lovely out, but I didn't think I could look that sky directly in the face again. Erasmus appeared to have called it a night. I turned off my monitor and went to stand at the window. I pressed my fingers through the blinds and stood there bathed in parallel lines of soft-blue star leavings. Just me and the stars. Just us lonely cosmos dwellers, home on a Friday night.

I wondered what Thad was looking at tonight. The cascade of his wife's pretty hair off the pillow? His son's cherubic smile from the bottom of the crib? Dear Thad – the man who wants to know if he's alone in the universe. Fair enough. But, hey – I know I'm alone in the universe. I know it. Here's how I know:

Think about your loved ones. The ones that make you not alone. Your immediate family. Your childhood best friend. Your godmother. You know where they all are right now? Give or take? Right, then.

Now picture them all wrapped up in a single person. That's what I had. I had a cherubic smile, once, a smile to smile up at me; I had pretty hair to smooth.

But that was just for a start.

Also picture hope for the future, picture faith in humanity, picture solace.

Picture strength in a handy external human charger-module.

Picture the ideal person you could almost be, right in the next person over. A human placeholder for your ideal place in the universe.

Picture this all in one person. That was Trevor. That was my big brother. He was my loved ones. The tendrils of his influence into the soil of my life went all the way to the bottom. He could do no wrong, and he'd been doing it by my side as far back as memory went. He was my not alone.

Maybe I was guilty of keeping too many emotional eggs in one fragile basket. But I was just a one-man kind of girl, I guess. For me, the one man was my brother.

Now picture the mid-nineties. Picture the tail end of the Troubles. Picture a train station in central London of a pretty Saturday in April.

Picture a one-ton IRA fertilizer bomb going off in a lorry in the street out front.

And finally picture your personal universe, your not alone, reuniting with the larger universe, on a particle-by-particle basis.

My brother's death was absurd. Trevor had never been to Northern Ireland; he could scarcely be said to have a politics. He hardly ever went into the City; and he was always careful. I was just a girl then. I didn't understand. I still don't understand. But now I know that no one understood.

So you see I'm not just alone in this country. I would be alone anywhere.

But, on the other hand, that was a long time ago; and a very long way away.

Tonight I bid the sea of stars goodnight and went to bed. Knowing full well my brother would still be gone in the morning. And that I'd get up in the morning and carry on living all the same.

It's pretty amazing what you can learn to live with.

Nine

Have you ever seen a chimpanzee on the back of a motorcycle? Actually, you may have and not realized it. (Bikers being such an odd, and frequently hairy, lot.) My chimp has got his own little helmet, glossy black like mine, only smaller. The helmet's got 'Primate Speed Freak' paint-stencilled on the back. Unlike human passengers, Erasmus has got a full four appendages for wrapping around my torso – and thus he's always got one or two free to point at objects of interest, on the roadside, or in the next vehicle over. You'd simply be amazed what you miss without a monkey on board.

So the next morning, Saturday, and call me touched, but I drove the two of us up half the length of the Peninsula, through most of San Francisco, and right over the Golden Gate Bridge – all in time to see the sun come up.

Just across that iconic, primer-coloured span lies Marin Headlands – a series of pebbly promontories that look back at the city, typically through a sound-suppressing fog cheesecloth. We sat up high, on a decommissioned artillery piece (there was a time when you couldn't tell when the Japanese navy might sail into the Bay), watching for the first sunlight through the morning fog, while San Francisco stirred to life below.

You couldn't hear a thing but the wind sweeping the rocks.

Erasmus and I have turned this into a bit of a ritual. The only thing that comes between us and it – and it does so often – is the overindulgent and immoderately late clubbing expeditions the night before. But, despite the couple of solitary beers, I'd had a relatively early Friday for once. This morning was our reward.

We stared out over the water, the mists and the diorama stillness, sitting side by side. I put my arm around the little guy's shoulder. I stopped to wonder if he enjoyed this for any of the same reasons I did. I like to think that Erasmus and I accept each other completely. I don't, in honesty, even really think that one of us is cleverer than

31

the other. But I have this fear, still, of some gap unbridgeable between us. In that moment on the cliffside, all that separated us were six inches and six million years.

I thought back, for reasons that might be guessed, to the walk where I explained, to Thad, Important Thing #2.

Flash Back To Let's Call It A Slightly Subsequent Walk

'And so how is the void treating you, then?' I asked, after we'd gotten clear of potential eavesdropping HR staff or suchlike.

Thad, though hardly without a sense of humour, has this admirable trait of taking everything you say very seriously. I guess this isn't that surprising for a guy living life as a character in a Sartre play.

'Pretty good,' he said in measured tones. 'I've been thinking about my protein computer. And I've decided I'm honestly unsurprised that the Church is so ignorant of, or in denial about, basic facts about human beings. About the way a mind really works.'

'Then you really won't be surprised by the other bit,' I said.

'The second thing,' he said. 'That I'm the output of an equation?'

'Yes. That you're the output of an equation.' I cleared my throat in preparation for the big evolution spiel. I adjusted my spectacularly dark wraparound shades on my face. I brushed a haystack-on-fire lock of hair behind my ear.

'The evolutionary scientist Richard Dawkins once said that we animals are the most complicated things in the known universe – and that our existence used to represent the greatest mystery of all time. But now the mystery has been solved.'

'Darwin solved it,' Thad guessed.

'Yes, precisely. Darwin – and his insufficiently heralded understudy Alfred Wallace. All with this little evolution-through-natural-selection business. Which, it has been suggested, is *the single greatest idea anybody has ever had.*' I looked around for squirrels, who might show up to throw little rodent spanners into my works.

'You and I,' I said, going, in honesty, for a kind of stentorian ring, which I do surprisingly well for a girl, 'are not little mini-replicas of God our Father in Heaven. The difference between you, the cow, the roach and the bacterium is one of complexity and not much more. You are made up of the same basic amino acids. You are what you are because of the slaughter of trillions of living things before you in a contest to see which version happens to be better at reproducing in a particular environment. We are all a test to see if we will work well and if we don't we're tossed aside like the piles of worthless chemicals we are.' I cast around breezily, pausing for effect.

'The only difference with humans is that we know this and it sucks.'

Thad whistled. 'No wonder the Church is a little cool on that one.'

Within a few minutes, as the early fog burned off, the surface of the Pacific started reflecting uncountable armies of hypnotic little sword-flashes at us, up on our perch. When the sun came out, it came out blazing. I seated my shades on my face. I wondered what to do with the rest of the weekend, which I had the whole thing stacked up in front of me.

I grabbed some four-fingered hand and the two of us waddled back to the bike.

When we got home, I left E in front of the telly and darted out for a quick thrash at the gym. I still go to one of the Stanford gyms I used to frequent in undergrad – the old one, with the Taco Bell mission architecture and where they never check IDs. I mean, sure, I could afford a real gym, one for grownups. But adults who use real gyms are usually a lot sweatier, flabbier, and generally less pleasant to regard than college students. Plus, you know, comforts of home, creatures of habit, and all that.

I slipped inside, bared my midriff, stretched out, and got into some bench work with dumbbells. The fact is, I probably work out a little obsessively. I'm possibly also a bit too attached to diet and exercise supplements. But, you know, if you don't control the shape of your own body, you don't control much.

The drugs may come back to haunt me. I may grow new, unheralded appendages when I hit menopause. It's funny how what you don't know can come around to get you. It's been suggested that the Roman Empire fell because of what surely seemed, at the time, like a very natural decision to make about plumbing. They just had no way of knowing that lead poisoning makes you both lazy and stupid.

Thad works out a bit too, at the adult gym up the avenue. But it's more of a holding action. He's gotten cushiony around the middle. But, then, what does he care? He's got a spouse, and adoring tykes. He doesn't have to impress anybody.

One day, after our first few walks, when we had covered some ground, so to speak, Thad came into my cube and he asked me, 'What do you think it means that you got hired here . . . and assigned to sit in the cube next to mine . . . just when you did?'

'I don't know,' I said. 'What does it mean to you?'

'That's not what I mean. I mean, what do you think the universe means by it?'

I refrained, just for that moment, from quizzing him about his position on whether the universe is in the business of meaning things.

I finished up, fairly well flailed from free weights and the Never-Cresting Stairwell To Nowhere, showered, and rode home. I took Erasmus out to grab some takeout and a movie. He picks out videos pretty much like the rest of us do – by looking at the picture on the box. They know us at the video store. This one counter girl always squeals when she sees him come in.

Ten

Holden is Thad's younger one, just turned three. He has that soft blond hair only cherubim get, baby fat, and a smile with no off button. Sometimes Thad, or his wife Leslie, brings him by the office; which, like, Thad should get to draw that month's salary just for the organization-wide morale boost. All Holden does is clomp around, and delightedly regard everything, and hug people. Everyone he meets.

It's as if, to him, it's so blinkeringly obvious that everything's just entirely okay, everywhere and for ever. With him, it's like – Oh, wow, I get to hang around in *the world*? All day? In Holden Gottlieb's universe, earthly paradise is old news.

Do you remember the first time you got email from someone in the same room?

From: thad@ctake.com
To: keq@ctake.com
Subject: meaning
Date: Mon, 12 Dec 2005 13:53:22 -0800

Okay, okay, I get your point. The universe may DO things, but it can't possibly MEAN anything by what it does. I understand that there IS meaning in the universe – but that it is a purely human-generated phenomenon. But, really, what's so wrong with amusing ourselves by *imagining* we see patterns in the universe? What's the harm in indulging in a little mystical thinking?

Thad

From: keq@ctake.com
To: thad@ctake.com
Subject: Re: meaning
Date: Mon, 12 Dec 2005 13:57:02 -0800

Only this: One day, the clouds stop looking like bunny rabbits. And then what have you got?

Eleven

Monday morning, 7 am-ish, and I threaded up the 101 on the keening Ducati. I'm entitled to use the carpool lane and sometimes do; but it's not as efficient as weaving through and around the traffic in any lane I like.

A motorcycle eliminates the three most annoying things about driving: You never have to wait in traffic (unless you really want to). You can park wherever the feeling takes you (anywhere with ten square feet to spare – and, even in a really obnoxious ten-square feet, a bike's a nightmare to tow). And it costs in the low one figure to fuel it up (which you have to do maybe a couple of times a month).

I accelerated to pass between a white Bronco and an adjacent gold Lexus – watching out for, you know, arms gesturing out of windows, unbidden swerving . . . untimely decisions to open a door and launch me (however fleetingly) into open air.

The driver of the SUV flicked cigarette ashes out the window; but I was passing on his passenger side. Smoking! God. In the history of bad cost/benefit calculations . . . Then again, people who ride motorcycles don't really inhabit the kind of risk/reward houses that bear much stone-throwing.

I wouldn't go so far as to call motorcycle riding a distinctly American vice. God knows you can find a few Brits roaring down the M4 on their BMWs and Triumphs. But the New World does just seem to have a taste for the big gamble. So, I took advantage of my expatriation to drop some old bad habits; and to pick up one or two new ones.

Do you know that they've identified a genetic predisposition to risk-taking? And do you know they've found it has a distinct geographical dispersion pattern?

It works like this: The further away you get from the birthplace of genus Homo, the more of it you find. Africa? Mesopotamia? Vanishingly rare. Europe, Central Asia? A tad. Southeast Asia,

Australasia? Getting warmer; getting a little fast and loose. North America? Warm to hot; careless to daft. Follow the trail all the way down to the southern tip of South America – the last stop on the humanity commuter train? Well, those guys down there are just nutters. I mean, it's a trauma-ward contest down there.

Hang on, though. Speaking of hospitals, I had to pull a quick multi-lane switcheroo, to avoid heading to one this morning myself. Would it really tax people to indicate before changing lanes? Sorry, I get tetchy when people other than me play silly buggers with my life.

So, anyway, how to explain all the predisposition to risk out at the edges of civilization? Easy. The humans who, in the main, survived long enough to reproduce were the ones who stayed home. Hanging around the cave may be dull but it does keep off many of the uncountable hazards of what is, let's face it, a pretty harsh biosphere.

The imprudent guys who wandered off? Sabretooth chow, most of them.

But not all. Of those who took off in search of a better bit of rock, a few found it. And they not only survived, but thrived. And who are those guys? Depends on where you live, but for most of us they're our ancestors. The ones who populated the globe. Those very special bad-asses who gambled big – and won. My brother used to say he'd rather be lucky than good any day. Most of us are descended from people who were both. And the further afield, the more of both you had to be to survive.

I put the nose of the bike down sharply, to the right, my knee out, to take the sloping offramp to San Mateo. At speed.

When I rolled into our building, the only cube with anyone in it was Thad's. He and I are routinely the early birds. For my part, I claim it's because I'm still on GMT. I don't know what Thad's excuse is. (Oh, wait, I do – small children.)

Did I tell you about the time I caught Thad with his gun out? He'd just pulled it out of the front of his waistband, and hadn't yet

38

tucked it away, when I padded around the corner of his cube. It was a dusky black SIG-Sauer P228 (I soon learned), which he sheepishly tried to slip into his bottom desk drawer – too late.

The gun wasn't in evidence this particular morning (though I knew right where I could find it, should, you know, God forbid or something). Thad was barely in evidence himself, hunched dramatically over his machine, fingers typing cracklingly, nodding and *hmm*'ing in approval at the race of characters across his screen.

Morning was his productive time.

'Morning, Yank,' I said to his sloping back.

'Morning, Limey,' he said, throwing a smile over his shoulder.

I let him be and plugged myself in next door. I had a quick look through mail – and then got moving on a problem that had actually been bugging me over the weekend.

I make my living as a manipulator of such ridiculously abstract symbols that most of my real work gets done at odd hours – whenever my brain is left running, really. I untangle conceptual and coding conundrums in the shower, on the bike, during exceptionally bad sex, etc. Though, it's not me doing the untangling, at least not the me I'm conscious of. Heck, all *I* am is a caretaker for a painstakingly nurtured and highly over-educated bio-information processing device.

Which is more or less appropriate, given that what I use it for is to try to build convincing computer simulations of actual human minds.

Today I was going to use it to, once and for all, write an equation to describe a certain very anomalous human behaviour: loyalty. I have to say, if we had any good idea where humans got such a trait, it would be easier to give it to bots. But, nonetheless, I had some manageable variables for my equation: How long must a bot have been playing with a human – or with another bot – to develop a sense of loyalty, an enduring bond? How wounded must a bot be, or how hopeless must he perceive a situation to be, before he abandons a buddy? How thick is blood?

It's been suggested that, in trying to architect mathematical functions to represent higher-order consciousness, maybe I'm at risk of starting to see things the way God does. Perhaps. But it's Helen's God I'm playing at.

Darwin's God.

And not just metaphorically. Somewhat more than half the time, the best way to develop these equations, these behaviours, is not to program them myself . . . it's to *evolve* them. This technique is called evolutionary computation, or genetic algorithms.

Basically, it works like this: you write some rough code, you start it churning, and you examine the output. Then you run it again. But with each iteration, you introduce a random mutation into the code. If the output's closer to what you want, you keep the mutation. Otherwise you ditch it. Go through the routine a few thousand or million times (and computers are nothing if not tireless) and you just might find yourself with a piece of software that does exactly what you want – but with *no real idea how you got it to do so.*

In my case, what this usually consists of is dumping a few bots into one of our levels, and letting them fight each other a few thousand or million times.

And, after a few hours of coding, right through lunch, in fact – I can stay awfully interested when I'm actually interested in something – just as I was undertaking to do the thousand-battles trick to try out my alpha code . . . that was when the building air-raid siren went off. A wailing klaxon, it beat the air up and down the halls, rippling the atmosphere in open cubes, and bringing all work to a halt.

Test Carnage time.

Twelve

Unlike the department directors, I get to stay safely in my cube during Test Carnage. Those guys – those higher-ups, those cattle-drivers – when the klaxon goes off, they all herd into a central room with a half-dozen plasma monitors wired to the central test bed server. This way they can watch the action from various scenic vantage points, or from the viewpoint of any player they care to flip to – even that of the bots.

Actually, the bots often prove to be the best test players. They don't have bosses they feel they need to let beat them.

So, now, when the klaxon goes off, when Test Carnage starts up . . . and the directors go running for their bunker . . . and all the other drones on the payroll frantically knock off whatever they were doing, fire up the game client, and get ready to rumble . . . well, I just send a whole bunch of my proxies on in to do my fighting for me.

My kids. My babies. My synthetic progeny – the bots.

Today, I pushed back in my comfy, ergonomic, rolling chair, piped some throbbing techno through my headphones, and picked out a starting lineup for my team. I decided to go with Enormo, Queen Sheba and NutLicker. These were the main guys I'd been working with lately. (Those are just my names for them, by the way. Someone more creative than me, allegedly, or whose job anyway it is to do such things, will re-christen them later.)

The music pulsed up. The game level resolved on my screen. My team dropped in – right into an instant balls-out firefight.

I immediately saw Enormo trading two-handed pistol fire with, it looked like, Sergey from engineering. Sergey was a solid player. Sergey had chops. But I'd recently taught Enormo a few tricks. He fired both his pistols dry – and then charged. He wasn't doing anything more dangerous than reloading while he ran forward; but Sergey got unnerved with my guy heading right up in his face, and retreated. By the time they'd both circled around and re-engaged,

Enormo'd had time to reload – and to start methodically lighting up the hapless Russian. Sergey went down in an ungainly pile.

'Yes!' I shouted, punching air.

I tabbed my perspective to Queen Sheba. She had picked up a grenade gun and a rack of proximity grenades, and was liberally distributing them near a doorway at the edge of the main arena. This was a portal a lot of guys were going to be coming through. And she had placed the grenades, I could see, to the sides of the doorway – out of sight, but just within range of their proximity fuses. After emptying the rack, she bailed.

Very nice. She'd probably score at least one or two kills in the next thirty seconds – by which time she'd be a thousand yards away. My girl!

I switched to NutLicker. Lamentably, I found him in mid-flight – about twenty feet off the floor and moving fast. It looked like, maybe, a well-placed rocket to the tootsies. He would not be alive when he hit the ground. I didn't stick around to watch.

It hurts to see them go down.

So, Test Carnage happens maybe once or twice a week. Usually it means a new level's gotten designed or, occasionally, a new weapon added. Once in a blue moon there will be a tweak to the core game engine – something that impacts the physics of the environment, or what the characters can do in it. Engine tweaks are a big deal. That's when you'd really better not disappear for a smoke break at the sound of the klaxon.

At C&TAKE, *everyone* fights. And I mean everyone – from the CEO on down to the secretary pool. And, let me tell you: after a few months or a couple of years of this stuff – much of it against hard-core geeks who've been playing first-person shooters since pre-school – you get pretty good. There are, for real, secretaries here who would kick your ass. Pretty much everyone in this building would kick your ass.

*

The personal pain I experience at the death of one of my bots is actually a professional pitfall. If I wanted, if I let myself, I could make them all but invincible.

I mean, consider: I, as a programmer – and thus they, as my programs – have real-time access to the location, trajectory, and velocity of everything and everyone on the board. I also know – or, to be accurate, functions I can easily access know – exactly how the weapons shoot. Point being, if I wanted it that way, my guys would virtually never miss. They'd also dodge a bit more presciently than anyone outside of a Matrix film. (It's pretty amazing how different things are when you're the one building the world.)

But having them always hit – and never be hit themselves – would miss the point.

I don't want to make them unbeatable.

I want to make them maddening.

I want them to be the guys you love to hate. The guys who kick your ass and make you like it. The guys you shout out loud when you get the better of them – then offer them a hand back up.

I flipped back to Enormo. I was only on him for a second when he warped to the centre of the arena – along with a half-dozen other players. This is another thing the test bed engineers do: they rig up these pre-scripted scenarios that they want to see played out. And then they very peremptorily drop people into them. It's a little disconcerting. Not to mention undignified. Like being one of God's toy soldiers, shoved into position with a fat irresistible finger.

Anyway, after the set-up, Enormo reacted a little quicker than the human players around him. But, unfortunately, he'd gotten warped right to the centre of this set piece – and quickly started taking heavy fire. He spun and focused in on one assailant – who turned out to be Sergey again. Enormo's combo rifle went dry straight away, and so he tried his blustery little charging-while-reloading manoeuvre from earlier.

Trouble was, this time, he'd already been shot up pretty good. And Sergey didn't fall for it. Because of RealPain™.

One bit of long-running beef our programmers have always had with other shooters was the way damage you take has absolutely no effect – until it kills you. The first problem with this is realism. Why would a guy down to 10 per cent health be able to run, shoot, and generally operate as effectively as a guy with 90 per cent health? But the other problem is that guys at these divergent levels of health also *look* the same. So you often end up with guys at close quarters, blazing away at each other, too close to miss – each betting that he can take one iota more damage than the other guy. Whoever goes into it slightly less hurt wins.

This is no way to run a gunfight.

Enter RealPain™. (We trademarked the name.) Our game engine pays attention not only to how much you've been shot – but where. Plinked in the leg? Welcome to Limpsville, baby. (Population: you.) Take a fatty plasma blast in the left arm? Good luck reloading that weapon next time you go dry! (Try sitting down and putting it in your lap.) Basically, damage you take has a functional effect.

But it also has a *visual* effect: a guy who's taken 90 per cent damage *looks* like a suppurating, shambling, mostly dead wreck. A guy walking himself down to the morgue. He looks like somebody you can polish off (and thus notch a kill for yourself) with, maybe, a well-spat watermelon seed.

Which was what Enormo looked like to Sergey during that charge. This time, Sergey stood his ground and sent him off to the Great Bot Beyond.

But, on the upside, I might pause to point out, Enormo actually still looks pretty damned cool even when he's all shot up. As far as the bots go, I'm the mum, you know – and I like to dress them up properly. Terrifying outfits. Big, clunky, ass-kicking boots. Extravagant sunglasses. Hair. I work with the designers to get the styles I want; but they tell me I take too much of an interest. Visual design is a whole separate department. They remind me my job's to make them smart, not pretty. But it's hard to let go.

I let go a little after six, a couple of hours after nearly a full afternoon of this. I leaned into Thad's cube to say goodnight: 'A'ight,' I

44

said. 'I'm out this bitch.' Thad always loses it when I say this in my west London accent. Every time.

Going home, I stayed off 101. Maybe I'd gotten my adrenalin jolt for the day.

I should probably explain why Thad has a gun (a real one). God knows he had to explain it to me – the morning I caught him with it. That briefly turned into a bit of a tense tableau, I can tell you. Britain doesn't really have guns. At least not ones that nice public school girls like me are allowed to see (much less touch). But I've always been a bit adventurous, open to anything, I suppose. And it was only a few minutes before Thad was breaking down the elegant little device for me, showing me how to put it back together – and, mainly, giving me the ten-minute version of the gun safety lesson.

He helped me remember that ignorance never kept anybody safe from anything.

And one evening the very next week I made him take me to the range. We shot for an hour, putting out several hundred rounds between us. And who would have guessed? I'm a pretty good shot! Was it all the time spent firing virtual guns inside of GibletWorld? Or just a natural talent? Either way, it turned out I can shoot a little.

So what was Thaddeus doing with a gun in the first place? And at work? It's not that he used to be in the military. (About which service he, again, maintains a resilient silence.) It's not that he has a home and a family, over which he feels acutely protective. It's this: He's a sworn-in reserve officer with the Palo Alto Police Department.

'Kind of a crap job, really,' he admitted to me. 'Mostly you get called up for crowd control and traffic duty at Stanford football games.' But I managed to drag out of him the reasons why he does it: One, he genuinely feels like giving something back to his community. And, presumably, his military training is a thing which he has to give back. And, two, he doesn't mind the second paycheck. (A family of four, in the Bay Area, pretty quickly gobbles up even a fat computer professional salary).

Thad continued to fascinate.

Thirteen

Conquering Erasmus, warlord monkey king, riding into battle on his heaving steed . . . shrieking out his joy and bloodlust . . . sending panicked pigeons skyward and terrified toddlers into their even more terrified mothers' skirts.

Have you ever seen a chimpanzee riding an Irish wolfhound? Perhaps you have and didn't realize it. Because, really, what are the odds such an image would even register? Nero, the Irish wolfhound in question – and Helen's largest regular doggie date – stands nearly three feet tall (yes, that's down on all four legs) and weighs north of ten stone. This is about the kind of bulk you're looking for to support an eighty-pound chimp. Nero is also quite a shaggy bugger – with plenty of natural rein for a simian jockey to grab onto.

It was hardly any time at all before these two together, this half-scale centaur, had caused such havoc that we had the Golden Gate Park Police hot on our heels.

The two animals hit it off so well basically because Erasmus pets like a world champion. A great little mimic, he's seen plenty of human-perpetrated dog caressing and scruff mussing. But the main thing, I believe, is that it takes someone with fur of his own to really master the art. (Much like men – notwithstanding all the patient instruction you give them – will never really know how to go down on a woman.)

Anyway, dogs generally just go limp for Erasmus. Limp.

So it turned out there was a way to get Helen to talk about her work. Basically, I had to hit her up for an intellectual deep-water rescue. But I only stumbled onto this after it proved even more difficult to get her to talk about her personal life.

We passed the incongruous Dutch windmill on the west side of Golden Gate Park. We'd come in on the Pacific side. She had her overgrown dog on a leash. I held my miniature person by the hand. We were all ostensibly looking at the tulips.

I didn't figure Helen for the type to reward subject dancing. So, I just said:

'What is it you're looking for?'

'You've decided I'm looking for something,' she said.

'Seems to me.'

'Maybe you're right. But, at this point, all you're very likely to get from me are artful dodges on that one. And I don't really care to insult you.'

'Thanks for that,' I said. Erasmus stopped to smell a flower. I stopped with him. 'It's not a big deal. But I don't know a thing about you. Except what's on the web.'

She took a breath before reciting: 'I'm 25–40 these days, not 18–25. I leave it blank, unless I can't, and then I check African-American. Over $100,000. I do not lie, cheat, or steal – my dignity threshold is too high. I prefer Braque to Picasso, and Sartre to Camus. I think Twain had it right when he said: "It is easier to stay out than to get out". I think love gets a lot of good lip-service. I play the three-spot – strong forward. And I secretly lust after Thom York of Radiohead.'

Erasmus turned and gave her a look. Then he continued, pulling me along.

Following, Helen said: 'How long will that keep you?'

Quite a lot of silence interceded before I hit on my second strategy. I waited until we emerged into a sunny clearing. I cleared my throat. I said:

'So, you won't believe this, but it turns out I'm actually frightfully in need of a good behavioural geneticist.' I tossed her a smile – which landed pretty harmlessly in the no man's land between our sunglasses.

'Your lucky day,' she said.

I looked around. Erasmus seemed to be eyeing Nero strangely. (Helen had let him off his leash.) I soldiered on.

47

'So the problem I have is to do with the human brain.' I took an indulgent breath; the air smelled of tulips. 'And the way the brain has managed to produce these really unlikely things like culture and literature and art. And consciousness. Things with, pretty palpably, no survival or reproduction value. But which for some reason evolved anyway. As products of the brain. I'm guessing you know something about how the human genome makes a human brain.'

'A bit,' she said, with no evident irony.

I hesitated. She didn't seem inclined to elaborate. I tried poking her. Literally.

She sighed mournfully. She leaned over and sadly caressed a tulip. 'Well, the first thing to know is that the structure of the human brain appears to be prescribed by at least three thousand distinctive genes. Which is fifty per cent more than for any other organ or tissue.' We started walking again. 'Basically, the human brain is the most complex object in the known universe.'

'Yes,' I said, nodding vigorously. I knew all this. But I'd got her talking! 'And so right there's my problem – *when* it got to be that way.'

'Well,' she said, 'according to the standard timetable in palaeo-anthropology, the human brain evolved to its modern form in the period between the appearance of *Homo habilis*, about two million years ago, and the advent of so-called anatomically modern humans, which was at least 100,000 years ago – probably more like 200,000. Over that period, the human brain increased in volume about four-fold.'

'Gotcha,' I said. I actually knew all this, too.

That was when Erasmus mounted up Nero – and the two of them cantered off. They sort of veered toward a group of picnickers a ways off, which seemed harmless enough. They weren't going that fast.

'But here's the thing,' I ventured. 'From 200,000 years ago until a mere *10,000* years ago, *all humans did with those huge brains was bang on rocks*. We've never found anything but a handful of stone and bone tools from that whole period. And then, 10,000 years ago

– so suddenly you'd hesitate to call it even a geologic eye blink – we came up with agriculture . . . and cities . . . and art . . . and elaborate tools . . . and elaborate political structures . . . and, finally, unspeakably complex technology. For instance, there are now five million patents in the US alone.'

'I actually hold three of them,' Helen said.

I've got two myself. But I didn't want to get distracted.

'All of this . . . this spectacular complexity, it happened almost literally overnight! And since culture, language, technology and art are all indisputably products of the human brain . . . presumably something in the brain explains it all. But, as you said, *the brain hasn't changed in 200,000 years. While culture exploded exponentially – much, much later.* What the hell happened all of a sudden 10,000 years ago?'

Helen laughed. 'Yeah, it's a problem,' she said.

But that was when we heard the first frightened shouts. Humans, of various sizes, seemed to be scattering across the clearing. I saw a woman holding a toddler, hiding behind a tree – and dialling her phone. Erasmus and Nero crested a hill, coming back into hailing range. Both had their tongues hanging out. Erasmus was pumping a fist in the air.

Helen and I turned and looked for the most direct path back out of the park.

After actually opening the passenger-side door for Nero (you don't want anything that big clambering over your paint job, I guess), Helen jumped in the other side. She then lifted herself back out of her seat, and shouted back at me.

'Hey. Why don't you come by our Thursday beer bash. I've got this colleague I think you'd like to meet. Vis-à-vis your problem.'

We'd never gotten back on topic.

'Hmm,' I hmm'd. 'What sort of colleague?'

'His name's A'hib. And he's sort of a . . . codebreaker. Party starts at five.'

She then sat down and peeled the Miata out of the parking lot –

we were still technically fleeing from justice – which caused Nero almost to fall out. Erasmus pointed and laughed; he jumped up and down in high amusement.

I told him to shut up and get on the bike before we got arrested.

Fourteen

So another reason I prefer not to sit around the house for any length of time is that I sort of mindlessly put things in my mouth. Mindless being precisely the right word for it. Spectacularly ironically, the obsessive exercise and the eating are really kind of the same drug: anaesthetic for thought and feeling.

Virtually any human activity, it appears, can be abused. That is to say: done to the point of crowding out consciousness. That much-heralded, higher, subjective, human consciousness. That intractable mental faculty that floats above all the other ones – and never lets us forget that we're here, that we exist, that we should probably be *doing* something. And that elevates us above all of our fellow planetoid riders.

I told Thad there's no perceptible survival value to subjective consciousness. Lately I've begun to think it's got *negative* survival value. You don't see the 'lower' animals turning to suicide . . . or falling into wasting addictions . . . or simply losing the ability to cope. Sometimes it seems like we spend half our lives being chased around the kitchen table by our own heads. Won't someone rescue me from my head?

As I sat in the courtyard on the bike, watching the sun pull its nightly disappearing manoeuvre, I thought of Trevor again.

So Trevor had this protective streak a hundred and forty miles wide. Being a big brother was such a major hunk of his identity. He was six years older than me. So for as long as I could remember, he seemed huge, reassuring – nearly grown up. It was always a bit as if I were his special charge, ever since we were small, really. When I got old enough to go out, at night, in London, with friends, without him, he'd get this same look. This look of pain at not being there to protect me. He couldn't bear the thought of it.

Though, I never worried about him going out without me.

Which tells you a little something about life and our imaginings of it.

So, when he was killed, it was a fortnight before I was to take my A-levels.

And, you know what, I scored better than I would have. I had kind of shut down. All that remained was a central nervous system – and a very, very smart brain. But totally unanimated. I mean, I guess I looked like a person. I moved. I was convincing.

Like a really good bot.

I claimed I came here for the universities. I said I stayed for the weather. But I could have gone to Oxford. And I never minded the English weather.

I really came here because it was as far away as I could get on the same planet, and I've stayed for the same reason.

Everything at home reminded me of him. My parents almost never talked about him, afterwards. Maybe I couldn't bear all the not talking about Trevor. All the horrified silence. I couldn't bear his absent face reflecting back at me from every surface in the house. I couldn't bear watching my parents not crying all the time.

People go away, I guess. But I didn't have to hang around and endure it – you know, as a puff of sad vapour in the empty sky he left, just hurting. Going away is a multi-player game, I guess. Any number can play.

On the other hand, if I'm going to hell, it will be because our parents have, to a certain extent, lost both their children. I can tell you I spend a colossal amount of energy avoiding thinking about that one. Though, of course, I write to Mum and Dad a great deal. I check email an awful lot.

I went in and checked email.

From: thad@ctake.com
To: rtr@anon.978.org
Cc: keq@ctake.com
Subject: What the universe wants

Okay, so I think I understand the 'naturalistic fallacy' –

52

the problem of mistaking what's natural for what's good or moral. That the existence of something in nature has no bearing one way or another on its morality. (The classic example being rape: The fact that, in all probability, rape IS an evolved trait. For males without resources or status – and thus no sexual access to women – taking sex by force is a last-ditch strategy that natural selection would endorse. But no one's allowed to say this because people think that if it's evolved it must be natural, and if it's natural it must be okay. And it CAN'T be okay.)

But, still. Isn't there *something* to be said for nature? For trying to accord ourselves with the way things are? To have some sensitivity to the way the universe seems to be ordered?

Thad

From: retard@anon.978.org
To: thad@ctake.com
Cc: keq@ctake.com
Subject: Re: what the universe wants

After the Exxon Valdez oil spill, a wildlife protection group rescued two seals that had been caught in the slick. Painstakingly, at the cost of hundreds of thousands of dollars, they nursed and rehabilitated the seals. Finally, they took them out to release them back into the Alaskan waters. Hundreds of people gathered to watch. Television news crews were onhand. A short dedication was made. They released the seals, who made it a hundred yards out before a killer whale surfaced and, in seconds, in view of everyone, ate them both.

Forget what the universe did, or wants. The universe created spiders that lay their eggs on moths, who then hatch and feed on the living flesh. The universe gave us cuddly kitties that 'play' with mice before devouring them. Frankly, fuck the universe.

Regards,
RTR

From: thad@ctake.com
To: rtr@anon.978.org
Cc: keq@ctake.com
Subject: Re: what the universe wants

Okay, okay, I get it. Morality – along with meaning – is a completely human-generated phenomenon. Still, I'm afraid you guys are going to turn me into an utterly cynical and secular bastard before you're done with me. ;-)

Thad

From: rtr@anon.978.org
To: thad@ctake.com
Cc: keq@ctake.com
Subject: Re: what the universe wants

Hang around a barbershop long enough and you just might get a haircut.

Fifteen

'. . . probably packing wood when you walked into her office . . .'

'. . . couldn't download it. I was at my parents', sucking the 56K ass-wagon . . .'

'. . . NEVER wear any makeup. Then one time I put on some lipstick and you're all calling me a slut!' 'It's that colour. It's like the precise colour of the ring that gets left on you after a blowjob. It's like – Maybelline Cock-Ring Red . . .'

Crowds, particularly crowds of strangers, particularly chattering ones, always make me dizzy. Put me off my balance. It's like social spaces have their own literal geometry, such like, or their own physics. A disorientating one.

'. . . Well, Bill, I don't know what to tell you. No, wait, I do: Fuck off . . .'

'. . . so you take the sabbatical, and maybe you miss the IPO. But you've definitely got an unforgettable experience under your belt.' 'I've got your unforgettable experience under my belt right here . . .'

And, then again, also, I say this: Yeah, okay, Helen's company, GenenW, happens to be in the business of conquering disease – of ending millennia of human suffering. Stipulated, sure. Their line is, you know, ushering in a golden era of bio-engineered health and planetary well-being, as it were. Banishing the ills to which the flesh has always been heir.

'. . . They're going to find a boat full of Russian sailors, dead, with huge smiles on their faces. And Carrie's suddenly going to know how to make stroganoff . . .'

'. . . no clue. We're absolutely shooting from the seat of our pants on this one . . .'

'. . . horse walks into the bar and the bartender says: "Why the long face?" . . .'

But they're still a Silicon Valley startup. At their weekly beer bashes, this sort of stable of well-groomed geek savants – indispensable outcasts, masters of a certain hidden universe – still have the same conversations they did last decade at their Internet startups; and the decade before that in aerospace.

They hold their weekly beer bash on Thursdays, I well knew, so they could pretend they have real-life friends and real-life lives to rush back to at the weekend.

Helen met me at the front desk to check me in.

Swiping her badge periodically, and pointing at my temporary one, she led us through a series of white and chrome hallways. Nice. Rubber plants not made of plastic. Soft lighting you don't notice where it's coming from.

The halls opened up onto some connected common areas – a kitchen, a TV lounge. An undifferentiated open space. We threaded through several mini-knots of consumption and conversation, before taking up a defensive perimeter in the particular corner where Helen wanted us.

'. . . I'm worried because the lyrics to Cibo Matto's "SciFi Wasabi" are starting to make sense to me . . .'

'. . . was the only guy who had negotiated an accelerated vesting deal for himself. And so within seconds of the opening bell, he's running up and down the halls with his hands in the air screaming, "BAAAANNKK!!! I MAAADE BAAANNNKKK!!!" . . .'

Helen fetched me a beer – an entirely decent one. With an arm sweep, she offered me food from the buffet table, which snaked out of sight. She recommended the fondue.

'Maybe not that,' I said. 'I seem to be turning vegan.'

'That doesn't surprise me,' she said.

This was the not the first time I'd ever seen her without her sunglasses. (The night we met was, at the club.) But this was the first time I saw her with eyeglasses. Dark-brown plastic frames, turned up at the corners. Hair pushed back, and up, and out, with a wide headband. I realized her sunglasses must be prescription, like mine.

'I never had been,' I said. 'But when you live with a vegan, it's hard to avoid.'

I stepped around a couple of Indian guys in shirtsleeves, stolidly guarding the table. I scored some garnishes.

'. . . *This? You call this hot? At my fraternity house we used to keep rolls of toilet paper in the freezer for after we ate curry. You'd hear some guy in a stall shouting: "Pledge! Bring me the good stuff!"* . . .'

After I'd slipped back into our cocoon in the corner, I couldn't resist asking Helen whether she liked the people she worked with.

She looked at me coolly, behind the glare on her glasses. She said: 'I try to limit my judgements about other people to just one: whether I want to be around them or not.'

I nodded, sipping from my brown bottle. 'With coworkers, though . . . I'm afraid that's pretty much the one judgement you never really get to make.'

She nodded. I took this to mean, *That leaves zero judgements.*

I hadn't eaten that day and the beer hit me straight away. Possibly relatedly, I found I didn't feel like deploying my defences with Helen. I felt like swamping hers.

'I think maybe I don't really understand people,' I said. 'Beginning with, emphatically, you.'

'Is it important for you to understand me?'

I shifted in place. It would be overstating the case to call it a squirm. 'I guess my evolving position is that a successful life is going to require some kind of meaningful – and, more to the point, coherent – interaction with other people.'

'And you don't feel like you're getting it done?' she said.

'Which? Coherent interaction?'

'Life,' she said.

I laughed despite myself. I killed my beer. 'Yeah, sure. I'm a touch worried about what I'm doing with my life.'

'For most people,' she said, 'it's more what their life is doing with them.'

I fancied this amounted to a peek over her fence. But then she went off to find A'hib for me. I ventured out of our corner for another beer.

'. . . *decided to get off my mood-stabilizers, while staying on my antidepressants. Sure, there's a certain risk of finding myself driving a rented Porsche off a bridge with a hooker in the trunk, but goddamn if I don't type fast . . .'*

'. . . Beginning of story: He's doing great work. End of story . . .'

'. . . asked them to please pass the clue bong to the left . . .'

She returned a few minutes later with a boy, a very pretty one. He had nearly the same shade of skin as Helen and, intriguingly, almost precisely the same bouncing scalp parade of black, tightly coiled ringlets. As they walked up side-by-side, I couldn't tell how I knew their ethnicity to be utterly different. But I did.

Helen introduced us unfussily. A'hib smiled untightly. For some reason, I offered to get him a beer.

'Thanks,' he said. 'But Allah forbids it.'

'You're Muslim,' I said carefully.

'No,' he said, still smiling. 'But that doesn't mean Allah's wrong.'

Very cute, I thought. I straightened my posture, regrouped, and hauled out the hated old standard. 'And so then what do you do for GenenW, A'hib?'

Helen answered before he could. 'A'hib here is meant to be writing code to drive our gene sequencers. But I'm afraid he's usually too busy mucking around with his quixotic side projects.' She looked across at him. Her look looked to me not unlike a look of affection. Which I'd never seen on her. She added, 'And he's never here, anyway.'

I began to wonder if she would let him speak. 'Where is he, then?'

'Your old horse pasture,' she said. 'Stanford.'

'I'm finishing a masters degree,' he managed to get in.

'In what field?'

'Genetics, naturally.' Helen again. '*But*, in undergrad, he was a code monkey. Just like you were. Computer science.'

I looked at A'hib anew, to see if he looked familiar. He might have been at Stanford around the same time as I was, but probably not quite the same time. I figured him to be three or four years my junior.

I polished off my second beer. It tasted oddly great. Principally to my brain.

Helen said: 'It was at Stanford that he made a name for himself. Not to mention his nickname: "Ahab". Which is also why he's basically got carte blanche to chase his white whales around here.'

I didn't understand. 'I don't understand,' I said.

'I'll get you another beer,' Helen said. As if this would help? 'He'll explain.'

I regarded A'hib as Helen strode crisply off. He had his hands in the pockets of baggy khakis, which cascaded over manifestly comfortable shoes. He wore an untucked button-down. He said: 'She's recounting minor past glories of mine. I used to be interested in cryptography. I and a few other guys managed to crack a certain encryption algorithm that no one else yet had.'

'Which one?' I asked.

'DES,' he said.

'Bloody hell,' I said. 'You cracked 56-bit DES? With that distributed brute-force attack? What was that called?'

'DESCHALL,' he said. 'I was only one of a number of people involved.'

But there could have been a hundred people on the core team, and I still would have been enormously impressed. It was a totally brilliant idea.

DES (Data Encryption Standard) was the first official US government encryption system intended for commercial use. A private-key cipher, with a 56-bit key, it was thought to be extremely secure – so much so that it would take decades, or longer, for even an insanely powerful computer to brute-force it. (Which is to say, to try each of the seventy-two quadrillion possible keys in order to determine the right one.)

What the government didn't reckon on was the Internet – which allowed a few smart kids to organize something in excess of 70,000 relatively puny computers into a deputized posse – each one trying keys, in parallel, and reporting back over the Net. Their loosely linked cluster of PCs, their rabble in arms, taken together, was trying something on the order of seven billion keys per second at one point.

About three months later – well inside of the 'decades' predicted – they'd cracked the code. And this one episode pretty much compelled the entire computer industry to rethink how it kept its secrets secret.

I was intrigued. I said: 'And your DESCHALL buddies called you "Ahab"?'

'I might have gotten a little single-minded about the cracking DES thing.'

I bit my lower lip. 'And the "white whale" you're chasing these days? Here?'

'Junk DNA,' Helen said, handing me a new beer. I hadn't seen her walk up. 'A'hib has this really unhealthy fascination with junk DNA.'

The term referred, I knew, to the 97 per cent of the human genome that is said to be 'unexpressed' – that is, thought to have no effect on how a human develops.

'He spends weeks on end,' Helen went on, 'and thus rafts of our money, digging around in it. In the no man's land of the human genetic code.'

'What are you looking for?' I asked him.

He paused and looked up at the corners of his own eyes. 'I don't know,' he said quietly. He wrinkled his nose. 'Patterns, maybe. Codes. Artefacts. I don't know.'

'Fascinating,' I said a bit breathily. 'Still. As I understand it, none of the DNA in there makes any proteins. That is to say, it doesn't *do* anything.'

'Maybe,' he said, not looking like he was admitting anything. 'That's definitely why nobody else is doing any work on it. Why they're all ignoring it.'

'They all who?'

'The other biotechs,' he said. 'As well as HGP. And Venter's group.'

I paused to access the right memory locations. He was referring to the government-sponsored Human Genome Project – and the private concern, run by Craig Venter, that had raced them to complete a rough draft of the genome. It occurred to me for the first time that if those groups had thought they'd needed to map the whole thing (and not just the active 3 per cent) it would have taken a lot longer than the decade or so it did.

'And so you,' I ventured, 'think there's something in there? In the junk DNA?'

'It's not so much that I think there's something in there.' He paused again. He exhaled. 'It's that we have no idea.' He checked out his shoes, then a wall. He said: 'Do you know NovaGene?' I did not know NovaGene. 'It's a biotech in Houston. Since 1986 they've had this practice of, every time they crank out a new genetically modified product, usually a bio-food or something, they DNA-brand it. That is, they actually *write the company's name* into the junk DNA. Or, well, the nearest codon rendering of it, with abbreviations for amino-acid specifiers.'

'Which are . . .?'

'Um – asparagine, glutamine, valine, alanine, glycine, and glutamic acid. They end up with NQVAGENE. But the point is, it's inscribed in every cell they grow, and every cell that grows from that cell.'

I tried to formulate my next question, which sounded silly in my head. But he went ahead and answered it for me.

'I'm not precisely looking for a trademark notice in the human genome, no,' he said. 'Really, the NovaGene thing just got me thinking. That, you know, you could write anything in there.'

'You mean that *we* could write anything in there.'

'Yeah. But also that, you know, anyone could have written anything in there. At pretty much any point. And it would never get erased. It would just keep getting propagated with the species. It would basically be immortal.'

This comment occasioned the completion of my third beer. I assumed that was the cause of my spinning head.

'So what kind of techniques do you use,' I asked, 'to look for patterns in there?'

'Funny you should mention that,' he said. 'Because Helen said you know something about writing genetic algorithms.'

A little later, as Helen walked me out, I prodded my brain into trying to remember whether the idea had been that I needed to meet A'hib – or that he needed to meet me. It all seemed a little fuzzy now.

And I could hardly think anyway, with multifold beer bash voices in my head, echoing through the glinting halls, through the corridors of my brain . . .

'. . . *first time I ever saw someone being carried INTO a party . . .*'

'. . . *suggested that orange peppers are so spectacularly good they make red and yellow peppers taste like green peppers . . .*'

'. . . *wasn't fucking ironic.*' '*It was ironic in an Alanis Morissette kind of way. You know, like when it's pouring raining out, and you can't get a cab to save your life . . .*' '*You mean it sucked.*' '*Right . . .*'

Sixteen

Friday morning, and Thad and I got out the door for our walk before many people initially got in it. The mist – I guess it was mist, I'd figured out only recently that fog is really just low-lying clouds – still lay upon the hills. Mountains completely ring the Bay on its south side – as if they could keep the outside world from our fantasyland here, could keep the forces of quotidian reality at bay. Or at very least keep the southern Californians out.

This is another long mental slog for people back home – the fact that southern and northern California are really more like separate countries, than the same state. The People's Republic of Northern California, they call it. I meet a lot of other transplants here – many from the east coast of the US, others from around the globe. We have a kind of a bond. As if we've figured out a really simple yet powerful secret – that living other places is crap and, ultimately, rather pointless.

'I'm *never* going back,' we say. (Back to wherever.)

Of course, if you're not lucky enough to be born in this country, getting through the door in the first place is the trick. Generally, if you're not being persecuted to the point that all your relations have already been gunned down, you have to demonstrate some godlike skills to offer the all-powerful US economy. But a lot of people, from a lot of places, manage it.

So – despite being completely homogeneous in the sense that everyone here seems to work in the same field, namely technology – the Bay Area is quite culturally and ethnically diverse. (One thing I really like is how good you get at catching dauntingly foreign names: 'Come on in! Grab a beer! And meet Omprakash, Xin Qian and Jedrzej!' 'Omprakash . . . Xin Qian . . . Jedrzej . . . pleased to meet you.')

As for the US East Coast émigrés – who merely had to pack up and drive three days to get here, no visa required – they *really* don't understand the decision to live outside the Bay Area. They all have friends and relations 'Back East' with these very sound-seeming-to-them reasons for continuing to live on what is palpably the wrong edge of the continent. But we all just smile, because we know that if the east coasters worked things out properly, they'd all rush out here and make the housing market even more of a cocksuck than it already is.

Thad is actually a northern California native, born and bred. He loves it here. Loves it. He has this quite serious-sounding plan to have the California state flag (which consists of, mainly, a bear) tattooed on his upper arm. The project awaits only approval from his wife. Which he's waiting for the right moment to seek.

That's another thing I like about the Bay Area: everyone is not merely allowed, but actually encouraged, to do whatever they want. (Barring spousal veto.)

'So what is your interest, really, in Helen?' Thad asked. 'If I can ask.'

'Well, not romantic, I don't think,' I said. 'For starters.' I'd already told him about the introductory hook-up.

'Do you normally date women?' he asked. Funny, we'd never discussed it. But another in a long list of California rules is: you never, ever, make assumptions about a person's sexuality. This is the region that spawned the expression 'member of the appropriate sex'; and which has made use of gender-non-specific pronouns a minor art form.

'Not really,' I said. 'Then again, I haven't dated anyone, of either gender, in a bit longer than I can recall.' Women, I think, have more room to manoeuvre with their sexual orientation than men do. Thad probably already knew this.

'I guess, with Helen, it would just be quite nice to have a woman friend. In the same country.' I didn't raise the issue of woman friends in any other country.

'Well that's great, then,' he said, sounding genuinely happy for me.

'Thanks,' I said. 'We'll see. She keeps inviting me round. But I'm

64

sure not drowning in affection from her. I confess I'm afraid she might, ultimately, end up being just another reminder to me of how alone we really are.'

'Do you really think we're alone?' he asked.

I didn't answer. It didn't seem a good idea to put my thoughts on record just then. Instead, I gave some consideration to doing a little weeping, the basic, you know, emotional overload sort of weeping, a little later in the day. When I was out of sight.

I have an H1-B work permit for this country. I've got the northern Californian shibboleths well memorized. Maybe even internalized. But where the rubber really meets the road, I'm still all English. Emotional displays aren't for public consumption.

I Took Another Dog+Monkey Walk With Helen, At Lunch Time This Time, Even Though I Didn't Really Know Where Any Of This Was Going

Can you bear a great many more bludgeoningly cutesy stories about Erasmus? I sometimes fancy myself like a mother of a too-precious newborn. That is to say, insufferable.

'I'm glad to see you got home okay,' Helen said.

Had she worried about me? 'Well, if you're going to risk your neck, completely needlessly, on a motorcycle . . . you might as well do so with a couple of beers in you.'

'I know all these former motorcycle riders,' she said. 'They all have friends or cousins or brothers-in-law who lost a leg, or a head, or the use of their lower body, in a bike accident. And then they, and everyone they know, all went out and sold their bikes, spontaneously, in like a three-day period.'

'Yes. I hear those stories myself.'

This was Bayside Park, on the Peninsula (where we both work). Helen had taken her new charge to the office with her. This was easy to do. No one minded. No one saw. Babs, a Yorkshire terrier, weighed maybe seven pounds – after a really heavy meal. You could keep Babs in a drawer. Which I gather Helen did, when she left her desk for coffee.

I'd had to swing by home to pick up Erasmus.

I kept trying to figure out what Erasmus thought of Helen. But he was mute on the subject. And he hardly seemed aware she was even with us today.

'Do you have a brother-in-law?' I asked. 'Or cousins?' This was leading. For all I knew, to date, Helen had been hatched.

'Would you want to meet them if I had?' she asked.

Jesus Christ, I thought.

I whistled to Erasmus that we should start circling back. He, and Babs, turned round to face us. The former still cradled the latter in his too-long arms. Which he had been doing since within five minutes of us all meeting up. He had carried that tiny dog through the entire park. Standing there now, he protectively brushed Babs's bangs out of her eyes. Babs sneezed. Erasmus rocked her from side to side.

The two of them passed by me and Helen, heading back toward the parking lot.

'The little bitch never let *me* hold her that long,' Helen said.

As we walked back, I already wasn't looking forward to prising the two animals apart. I also felt wounded that E seemed to be issuing oblique commentary on my emotional distance of late. I wondered if I, and my chimp, and my friend had become some sort of psychic triple-star system, with odd and unpredictable gravitational effects.

Later, Back At My Desk, I Swapped Some Mail With A'hib (He'd Given Me A Business Card), Just, You Know, For Grins

From: keq@ctake.com
To: ahib@genenw.com
Subject: junk DNA
Date: Mon, 03 Apr 2006 20:30:12 (PST)

A'hib,

So, realistically – how much data do you actually need to slog through? To cast your torch across the 'no man's land of DNA' (as Helen put it)?

And what does the data actually look like?

Cheers.

From: ahib@genenw.com
To: keq@ctake.com
Subject: Re: junk DNA
Date: Mon, 03 Apr 2006 15:31:32 (PST)

Hey. I'm glad you wrote.

So, all the human DNA is only about 3 gigabytes of data. (Albeit it cost over $3 billion to map – the active part!) So, I'm looking at about 97% of about 3 gig. But of course I've only got a fraction of it mapped. Basically I'm sampling.

What that data looks like is also pretty straightforward. The basic unit of DNA is the 'codon'. Each codon is a triplet of letters, and each letter in the triplet is one of 4 choices. The 4 choices are (good ole) A, C, G, and T. So a codon looks like 'ACG' or 'GTA' or 'CCT'. Obviously, that makes for 64 (4x4x4) possible codons.

String 3 billion of these together (each of which is, conveniently, 8 bits – or 1 byte), and you've got the human genetic code.

From: keq@ctake.com
To: ahib@genenw.com
Subject: Re: junk DNA
Date: Fri, 31 Mar 2006 15:50:00 (PST)

Thanks for the explanation. So, then – what sort of analyses are you doing on these strings? Strictly mathematical? Regressive? Pattern-matching? Or something in the vocabulary of genetics which will shoot right over my head?

And, of course, the question of the hour is: Whatever kind of data-crunching you're doing – why don't you just farm it out to 70,000+ machines (like you did last time) and knock it out in short order?

From: ahib@genenw.com
To: keq@ctake.com
Subject: Re: junk DNA
Date: Fri, 31 Mar 2006 15:59:59 (PST)

I'm doing pretty much every kind of analysis I can think of. (I guess you would characterize most of it as mathematical, and pattern-matching.) But I can imagine where someone with a different background than me might have different ideas about how to do it.

Most importantly, I'm guessing that a search technique that was *grown* or *evolved* by genetic programming techniques . . . rather than one I wrote . . . would develop the best ideas of all, ones we'd never have thought of. It would develop whatever tools it needed to find whatever kind of pattern might be in there.

In answer to your second question: I'm not farming the work out to 78,000 machines because most of those machines would have human beings attached to them. And whatever I discover in this project will not, I think, be the kind of thing I'd be inclined to share with 78,000 other people.

Seventeen

Much like my bots, I don't really report to anybody. And, much more critically, no one reports to me. I'm not even really a bare branch off the org tree. I'm sort of a little island in the upper-left corner. My job title? 'Principal scientist.' That's a fairly bloody cool thing to be, wouldn't you agree? That's what you get when you're the wizard. When you've taken five years out to get the doctorate.

Though, of course, you've got to spend your youth on something.

None of this means I don't have my travails at work. One of them walked into my cube, on Saturday morning, when I'd dropped by, you know, mainly just to drop by. At a tech company, even one that's not quite a startup any more, working on weekends is still the done thing. You've got to show your face now and again.

'Well, good morning!' said my travail, one Mark Kelly, our VP for marketing. It hadn't been my intention to show it (my face) to *him*.

While I'm thinking about it – whence this schism between marketing people and technical people? It's certainly been around longer than I have. Marketing people seem to have some vague sense that technical people lack business sense, fashion sense, and most of the important social skills. They think the work that engineers do is just bit-twiddling.

The techies, for our part, are not prepared to admit that the marketing people do any sort of work at all. What do marketing departments ever build? Great pyramids of bullshit. I think engineers really believe that the dollars we earn are qualitatively different from the dollars earned by the marketing people. And don't even get us started on the management people.

And so there was Mark Kelly, our vice president for marketing, with his elbow on my cube wall – all hair cream and cuff-links and teeth.

'Good morning, Mark,' I managed, not too tightly I hoped.

'So tell me about Version 6.0,' he said.

'Next rev of our product,' I recited. 'To follow Version 5 and presumably precede Version 7. Due out this year.' I just couldn't be arsed to play along.

'Ha, ha,' he chuckled humourlessly. 'What I actually want is to get your sense of whether we're going to hit June 1 for release.'

'Well, Mark,' I said, swivelling to face him, 'here's the thing. If the marketing department waited to announce release dates until after we had written, oh, at least a line or two of code . . . then there would tend to be a much greater correspondence between announced and actual release dates.'

He paused to swallow this and – I could tell from his facial manoeuvrings – to imagine he was out-thinking me. He smiled premeditatedly and said: 'Oh, you know better than that. Release schedules have always been done this way.'

I invited him to find a new and better way.

He ignored this and lamented, 'If you guys could only finish up development two weeks inside of schedule, we'd have the game on shelves when school lets out. Isn't there any way to make that happen?' Why was he hitting me with this? Because I was there.

I squinted at him and nodded thoughtfully. 'Well, let me think. Actually, yes, as a matter of fact, I think I *could* see a way of making that happen.'

'Really?' he brightened.

'It'll be a little tricky. We'll need to get everyone in the engineering section all together. Then we'll need procurement to buy us some dilithium crystals.'

'Dilithium?'

'Yes. Then we'll simply *realign the main deflector dish*' – and at this point I started gesturing kind of wildly, while he'd begun looking at me uneasily – 'and then we'll shoot out a stream of *anti-protons* into space, thus creating a *rift* in the space-time continuum, and taking us all *back in time* two weeks . . .'

'Thanks for that,' he said, walking off. I was seized with a spasm of relief.

I was spasming in altogether different ways, I can tell you, when I dragged myself off the dance floor at Chemical Mass in Noe Valley, late that night. A coworker who lives nearby, in the Castro, once gave me a tour, reciting, lilting, 'Now this is Noe Valley . . . dominant themes are sunlight and lesbians with children . . .' But neither of those was in evidence when I had rolled through the neighbourhood at around 10 pm.

I weaved around some tables, back to where Erasmus was supposed to be saving my place – he wasn't, he'd decamped to the bathroom again, but left our helmets on our seats. Helen had said she might be by, but I hadn't seen her yet. It had gotten past midnight, and I figured I'd hang around long enough for my body temperature to get back in a normal range. I sat and recalled the earlier part of the evening: dinner at Thad's.

Episodes like the morning's run-in with that executive marketron really just scream for guilty pleasuring – in this case, clubbing. And it had been a couple of weeks since my last such adventure. Moreover, I was already slated for dinner in San Francisco with Thad and his family. The kids always bed down at nine – leaving me perfectly positioned, spatially and temporally, for some cathartic whirling and perspiring.

Visits to the Gottlieb household are really more play dates than anything else. We grownups – me, Thad, and his wife Leslie – try to get in some quality conversation while the little ones – Kennedy, Holden and Erasmus – yuck it up. I like to think I'd receive invitations anyway, but I know I can always count on the kids to clamour for our presence at regular intervals. Face it, having a monkey makes you popular.

Leslie had greeted me at the door.

'Welcome back!' she sang, hugging me and petting E. I was wearing my club clobber, but under a more sedate cover-up. She took our jackets and helmets. We went in.

'Hey, old man,' I tried to say to Thad, who was emerging from the bedrooms – but Kennedy and Holden were already on us. Within seconds, they were rolling on the hardwood floor with Erasmus, all of them spinning inside a wild nimbus of blonde and black hair. Thad had to admonish them to say hello to me too.

We went to the kitchen, where things were smelling good. Cooking vegan for the two of us is never a problem for Leslie – because Kennedy (age seven) is vegan. She made the decision at age five. No one quite knows how she got the idea into her head.

'Did you go to work today?' Thad asked.

'For a bit. I evacuated shortly after Kelly invaded my cube.'

'That's the clueless VP you both hate?' Leslie asked.

'Yep,' Thad said. 'That guy has to drop trou in order to count to twenty-one.'

'Thad!' she admonished. But the kids were well out of earshot.

Leslie was also Catholic – they had met at Notre Dame, proper college sweethearts – and remained fairly devout. Of course, she knew about Thad's loss of faith, and his subsequent struggle to find new ideo-spiritual ground to stand on. But, apart from taking the kids to church by herself, it didn't really affect her that much. Thad still worked hard to provide for them. He was still loving and very present. He was just confused, and in pain.

Leslie was not well equipped to help him through this trial (in any concrete way). She made polite noises of concern, she was patient. But she had, inevitably, the air of a woman whose husband had the flu. She was just waiting for him to recover and get out of bed. But Thad's malaise wasn't simply going to run its course.

I remember we'd discussed just that, also on an early walk.

Flash Back To The 'Existential Flu' Walk

'I really appreciate everything you've been trying to teach me,' Thad said, walking a little more forcefully than normal. 'But it just kind of takes the legs out. I mean – my unique spark of beautiful, singu-

72

lar, sentient existence is due entirely to a blind, stupid, bludgeoning, algorithmic process? I'm the output of an equation?'

Gently (I hoped), I said: 'I wouldn't have put it to you that way if I didn't think you were ready to hear it. But, anyway, you must have already had a sense of it yourself, having gotten to where you are.'

'Some,' he said. 'But I'm starting to want to go back!'

'I hear you,' I said. 'Do you know the one about the turtles all the way down?'

'No.'

'Bertrand Russell reportedly once gave a public lecture on astronomy. He described how the earth orbits around the sun and how the sun, in turn, orbits around the centre of the galaxy. At the end of the lecture, a little old lady at the back of the room got up and said: "What you've told us is rubbish. I know the world actually rests on the back of a giant tortoise." Russell gave a superior smile before replying: "But upon what is the tortoise standing, Madame?" "Very clever, young man,' she said, 'but I've still got you. It's turtles all the way down!"'

We both laughed.

'The point being: if you've found something that works – a belief system that gets you through the day – then more power to you. I mean, really, far be it from me. Heck, the first time I came down with a really bad case of existential flu, I suddenly realized why people do have religious faith, why they believe: not because any of it's the least bit believable. But just because it's a hell of a lot more pleasant. Maybe even necessary.'

'Existential flu?'

'Sure. Lots of very smart people turn up with it. Effectively, it's a mind virus – a meme that invades your thinking, infects your soul. It can really floor you.'

'What are the symptoms?' Thad asked, interested.

'Mainly, the extremely forceful realization that *there's palpably no point to this*. Any of it. Life, existence. You just get hit right in the head with the facts that we haven't been put here for any purpose

73

whatsoever, and absolutely nothing is expected of us. Then, option-ally, you find yourself reaching the conclusion that continuing to get up every day and go through the motions is either an exercise in blind Darwinian survival instinct or, at best, a matter of amusing ourselves while we run the clock out.'

'Ow. What's the prescription for this flu?'

'Well, when the universe doesn't provide any meaning . . . then you have to generate your own somehow.'

'How do you generate meaning?'

'Lots of ways. Love. Family. Charity. Career. Learning. Explor-ation. But – and trust me here – it's best to start small. When you're down with the flu, you don't get healthy by stepping right out and running a marathon.'

'What *do* you do?'

'Well, first you stay in bed for a while. Just don't make things worse. Make sure you don't hurt yourself. Weeping bitterly seems to be a major theme.'

'I think I've gotten past that part.'

'Okay. After you're all wrung out, you wait until you're not actu-ally under attack by the viral meme. Until it's exhausted itself.'

'Does that always happen?'

'If you manage to keep taking one breath after another, it seems to. And when you start getting a little strength back, you want to try some convalescent activities.'

'Like what?'

'Well, there's some controversy about this . . . but some things seem to be better than others. For example, walking is very good.'

'Just taking a walk?'

'Yes. Pretty much anywhere. In general, anything that gets you out of the house. Talking's quite good, too. Eating: not so good. Movies . . . kinda depends on the film. TV's a non-starter.'

'Gotcha.'

'Exercise: no.'

'No?'

'No. But, sport: yes. Exercise is solitary, and solitary is bad.

Similarly, web-surfing: no. But email: yes. Especially with people who care about you. Going away: bad. Going home: good. Motoring: country, good; city, bad. Listening to music: totally depends.'

'. . . Nine Inch Nails out? Sarah McLachlan in?'

'You're getting it! Doing anything that helps other people: excellent. Anything that gets you out of your own head. Having coffee: good. Having drinks: less good. Video games, bad; board games, not so bad. Reading's inherently neutral – but it can be judged relatively, if necessary. Is the alternative TV? Or a hug?'

'I think this is going to be a long road.'

And we were only just getting into his first question – about finding meaning, post-God. I didn't tell him things would get much stickier when we tackled morality.

Helen finally showed up at Chemical Mass, looking all slutty. She had A'hib with her. Boy, did he look out of place. Erasmus grinned at him.

'Hey!'

'Hey. Hey, A'hib – you're a surprise!'

We were, naturally, having to shout.

'Yeah,' he said, leaning in close. 'Helen told me you'd be here. Did you happen to get my mail?'

'From how recently?'

'From tonight.'

'No.'

'I took the liberty of forwarding you some DNA sequences to play around with.'

'Junk?' I asked.

'Yes, naturally.'

'Whose?'

'Oh . . . yours.'

'*What?*'

'I hung on to your empty beer bottle on Thursday night, after you left. Then I shotgunned a few sequences from, you know, a few stray skin cells in your saliva.'

'Fuck's sake!' I felt violated. A'hib grinned maddeningly.

'Just kidding,' he said. 'It's from one of the eight guys in the human genome project. They all volunteered to be sequenced.'

I unbunched my shoulders a bit. This guy's a real character.

I hit the dance floor with Helen for a while, before calling it a night. Erasmus came with us this time – and A'hib guarded the seats.

Eighteen

There didn't seem any way to avoid the fact – nor acute conscious-ness thereof – that what I was doing was completely ridiculous.

I mean – have you ever actually performed prone leg curls? Personally? What's required is to lie face down upon a sticky vinyl pad (usually sticky with someone else's recent exertions), bum pointed at the sky, ankles hooked under a padded bar. Then, while you clutch at little handles alongside (I'm surprised they don't give you a leather strap to bite down on), you curl your legs, at the knees, up over yourself.

Dignified this is not.

Then again, it did occur to me that every single person in this room was doing something ridiculous. I mean . . . can we really even get into the business of assigning relative degrees of dignity to different flavours of weightlifting?

Everyone in this room is doing something ridiculous . . . hmm, there's probably a good allegory in there somewhere. Earth as giant weight-room – sprawling, spasming temple of pointless and arbi-trary and Sisyphean activity. And no room to judge.

But I guess you take your motivation where you find it. And all I know is those high-octane fruity club drinks have a ton of calories in them. And if you're going to be stuck in the world inside of a dying hunk of meat . . . it'd be nice for the meat to at least look like you fancy it looking.

I spent most of the remainder of Sunday plugged in at the office – doing some preparatory fiddling around with A'hib's strings of genetic data. (That's the thing about showing your face at the office – no one can see behind it to what you're actually doing with your brain.) Mainly, I was just getting a feel for the texture of the data – and doing a little pseudo-coding of an initial genetic algorithm to start sifting through it.

So here's the really funny – and compelling – thing about evolution through natural selection: it's an entirely *substrate-neutral process*. That is to say, its essence is algorithmic, mathematical. It's like a waveform function that can travel through air, or through water, or even through rock. The process needs a medium to express itself, but the medium's not really the thing at all.

Most people think evolution is something that only happens with species, through their genes. But, prior to Mendel – and Crick and Watson – no one had ever heard of genes. Darwin wouldn't have recognized a gene if it had crawled up his trouser leg and gnawed his privates off. He only knew *how* the process had to work – even if he had no knowledge of the medium in which it did so.

So, if you don't need genes exactly, what do you need? Three things: replication, mutation, and differential survival. You've got to have something that makes copies of itself (replication); the copies have to occasionally be not quite exact (mutation); and a given copy has to survive more or less well, in its given environment, depending on how it mutates (differential survival). If those three things go on, what you'll see is the best mutations spreading and dominating – because they are the best at surviving and copying themselves in that environment. And with each generation (or, well, few hundred or thousand generations), the bar gets raised higher. *That's* evolution through natural selection. That's survival of the fittest. And that's the breaks if you don't make the cut.

What are some examples of viable substrates for this process, other than genes? Well, memes, for an obvious one. This was another idea put forth by Richard Dawkins: the notion that ideas have lives of their own, and interests apart from the people who've got them in their heads. They spread from mind to mind, occasionally mutating – and those with a knack for surviving and getting passed on come to predominate. (What's scary about that one is that *good* ideas, i.e. ideas that are good for us, don't predominate; ideas that are good at spreading themselves, and sticking in our heads, do.) Another one, possibly, is universes. The cosmologist Lee Smolin has posited that our rules of physics are calibrated to such suspiciously tight tolerances because of a Darwinian competition of universes, which are constantly being spawned by black holes.

And a third example is: a properly wound-up piece of computer code.

In this instance, my particular objective was to write a self-replicating, occasionally mutating piece of software – the job of which was to sift through sprawling strings of DNA, looking for patterns. The beauty of this was, I didn't have to teach the program a thing (or know a thing myself) about pattern-matching, or regression analysis, or substitution, or statistical distribution, or variable variables, or scaling theory, or any of that bunk.

The program would, if set up properly, develop all of those techniques itself – from scratch. It would, in theory, develop any technique that successfully found patterns in the data. Because only those mutations, and those versions of the program, that moved toward finding patterns would survive and replicate.

I told you evolution through natural selection was probably the single best idea anybody ever had.

Nineteen

Do you remember the first time you got mail on the crapper? But perhaps you're not yet part of the wireless broadband revolution. I'll say this for WiFi: it cuts down on brightly coloured wiring for your live-in monkey to discover and chew through. Also, of course, multi-tasking is critical these days.

I shifted the laptop on the tops of my bare thighs and checked mail.

From: thad@ctake.com
To: keq@ctake.com
Subject: meaning
Date: Sun, 02 Apr 2006 08:01:43 (PST)

Hey, man, thanks a lot for coming to dinner last night. Leslie and the kids sure love having you both over. Come back soon.

I was thinking: Maybe next week we could try tackling the whole ethics/morality thing? I kind of get the sense you've been dodging it. But it's like I said. I still *think* I'm a good person. But I don't know how to tell any more. I don't know who decides. I don't know where the rules are written.

And I feel, honestly . . . scared. Like I said, I still think I can tell right from wrong. But without God to make it official, I can't help but see right and wrong as arbitrary, made up. Even worse, since I'm starting to think the rules are imagined . . . and since I'm pretty damned sure no one up above is going to hold me to them anyway . . . I have this terrible fear that I might just chuck the whole thing. Take up evil, try out villainy.

It's like that feeling you get on the edge of a cliff – where you can suddenly see throwing yourself over. You don't

80

want to. You don't think you're going to. But, somehow, the idea takes on a force.

Thad

From: keq@ctake.com
To: thad@ctake.com
Subject: Re: meaning
Date: Sun, 02 Apr 2006 10:21:56 (PST)

Thad — Hey, many many thanks for having us over. As always, both the company and the meal were first-rate. We'll be back soon.

As for your request/suggestion. <sigh> I hadn't forgotten. I mean, I knew this was inevitable. But you know what? I'm going to kick this can down the road. That is to say, I've just forwarded your mail to the Retard. Don't let it be said I don't know when I'm out of my depth. And a good referral is every bit as good as direct assistance . . .

See you tomorrow, mate.

As I fired this off, the door erupted in knocking. Evidently, Erasmus needed to take a slash. Hell. No privacy in this house. I do understand, though. When you pretty much eat fresh fruit non-stop all day, you do a lot of urinating.

''old your 'orses,' I snapped, reaching over to grab my mobile.

I'd brought this second consumer electronic device into the bathroom with me because it had been audibly beeping since I turned off the bike engine yesterday. As an interim solution, I'd jammed it under a couch cushion for the night.

I hit the voicemail button. After welcoming me in treacly yet soulless tones, it played a message from Thom – Thom being the development manager I interface with most closely, as far as the coding team goes. Thom's an all right fellow – but he hasn't yet figured out that I don't really want phone calls at the weekend. If he put it in email, which is much less intrusive, I'd probably deal with it. As it was, I queued the message for Monday.

There was a second message. I started to play it – but succumbed

81

to immediate confusion. Was this the message? Or the voicemail menu? The voice was the same. I must have missed something. It had gone by quickly. I played it again. It said,

'*Be careful whose ideas you run with. Pioneers get arrows in their backs.*'

What the fuck?! I sat up straight and regarded the phone in my hand.

'*Press seven to delete. Press four to save. Press star for more options.*'

I played it a third time. I didn't feel any better about it.

I mean, I'm as good-natured as the next person when it comes to practical joke butt-duty. But this was fucking spooky. Menacing threats in the voicemail voice?

Erasmus knocked again – and whined. Had I yelled out loud? I wasn't sure.

My laptop screen grabbed my eye – new mail flitting in.

From: Espresso Obsesso
<cmptr12@ntsvr.espressoobsesso.na>
To: keq@ctake.com
Cc: thad@ctake.com
Subject: Re: Morality Morass
Date: Sun, 02 Apr 2006 17:29:03 (GMT +1)

Whoa ho! Definitely best to bring in the SWAT team for this one; Retard to the rescue. You are sitting on something with a chair back, Thad? Right, then.

Humans have been trying out answers to the question 'How must we behave toward one another?' since the first man clubbed someone over the head for his pelt.

The winning entry amongst solutions to the problem of morality contest comes courtesy of religion. As religion has it, God – all-knowing, all-powerful, and definitionally authoritative on matters moral – has decreed our proper behaviour (what is proscribed, what is permitted, and what is compulsory) in a Big Book. All you have to do is read the Book; it is the beginning and the end of the story. Religion is also an enforcement mechanism:

Deviate from the rulebook, burn in Hell. Could not be simpler.

What is the problem with this solution? Nothing – if you can buy into it. So, that is the first horn of the bull. Which I gather, Thad, you have dodged. Or, rather, it has dodged you.

But, absent the assistance of the Almighty, the bull is also standing on a high-wire suspended over the Chasm of Moral Relativism – and, sooner or later, you are both going to fall in. I am sorry. You can argue moral precepts until the cows come home, but Hitler can stay up just as late as you can. And if mortals are allowed to say what is right and what is wrong, then, on some level, everyone's opinion carries equal weight.

I think you'll agree that both horns are unsatisfactory: God Almighty – or nihilism; the Divine Book – or all rules off.

I think there is yet some meta-ethical gymnastics to be done upon the bull's forehead. David Hume put it best: he said that while there is probably no moral shape to the universe – no absolute 'right' or 'wrong' – it is still important that we argue about morality AS IF THERE WERE. And it is through such arguments that we construct our own moral reality.

Under this view, while there is no absolute morality, there *can* be some moral structure – it just has to be *culturally negotiated*. We each query our own feelings about what is right and wrong, and we argue our case. And, with luck, at the end of the day we emerge with a rough consensus on what the rules are. And, ultimately, to the extent that we are all going to live together, we *must* manage to negotiate some norms we can all live with.

Yes, it is a hack, and lacks consistency. But, you know what, we have bigger problems than absolute intellectual rigour. We have 6.5 billion people stuck sharing the same planet, trying to avoid new genocides, trying to keep passenger planes from crashing into office buildings, et

83

cetera. So, really, whatever gets you through the week alive.

Regards,
RTR

I flushed, re-pantsed myself, and gathered up electronic equipment. I opened the door. Erasmus gazed up at me. He didn't look impatient. He didn't look as if he'd been holding it. He looked concerned.

'I'm okay, guy,' I said. He hugged my leg. 'Thanks for that,' I said. He let go of me and closed the door behind him.

Twenty

Do you ever get that Sunday Night Anxiety? That quiet assault on your end-of-weekend peace of mind? That chilling frisson, like a noise in the night, that grabs you, you know, maybe around 6 pm, and explains to you not only that Monday morning is coming – but that Tuesday through Friday are right behind it? And that they've got reinforcements? When you're a working stiff, these weeks of days are like bad guys in a climactic John Woo shootout, like orcs in the first version of *Doom*.

Eat all you want. We'll make more. Mondays uncountable, time out of mind.

Maybe you, like me, have a job you don't even mind so much. Maybe you're socking it away a bit, and maybe it's hardly painful at all being in the office minute-to-minute, most minutes. Maybe you even chose to be there, wherever it is you are.

But, you know what, decades of years of weeks of days will do it to anyone.

That's when a video and some takeout – and a sixer – are really the way forward. You'll see me and my roomie, through our big picture window, sitting in the blue glow, shoving and pouring things in our mouths. Which really works pretty well, as far as not thinking about Mondays – and the legions of Mondays behind them – goes. Simple, cheap, readily available tools for crowding out consciousness. You gotta love 'em.

Erasmus doesn't like the new week much better than I do. I'm okay at dragging myself down to the cubicle farm and plugging into my machine for the day. And he's not bad about amusing himself at home, on his own. But neither of us would quite write the radio plays of our lives with this much dead air.

'The Retard wrote me,' Thad said.
'I saw,' I said.

'No. After that. The Retard wrote me again – without cc'ing you.'

'Hmm. Going behind my back, are you? Friend stealer.' That made Thad smile. 'Well, what did the Retard have to say to you, in private?'

'It was an addendum to his message about morality. The Retard meant to say something reassuring to me at the end, but forgot.'

'What was it?'

'I remember it very clearly. It was: "Try not to worry too much, Thad. You can only walk so far into the wilderness before you're walking out again."'

This was our Monday morning walk. A lovely, misty morning. A little chilly. I'd left my mobile in my cube. I rubbed Thad's arm. Suddenly, I remembered walking with Trevor – in St James's Park, in central London, in the spring, by the water.

'That's nice,' I said. 'Did it make you feel better?'

'Yes. But I'd feel better if we knew where our moral sense came from. I guess there's no chance Evo-Psycho explains the moral sense?'

Flash Back To The Original Evo-Psycho Walk

'Repeat after me,' I said. 'Virtually all important human behaviours are evolved adaptations, selected for their survival and reproduction value.'

'All human behaviours are evolved for their survival and reproduction value.'

'The mind evolved just like the body.'

'The mind evolved just like the body.'

'Psychology makes no more sense outside of the light of evolution than biology does. Without that evolution bit, the only thing that could make something as complex as a human mind is God. And, needless to point out, we're cool on God.'

'So that,' Thad said, 'is evolutionary psychology? In a nutshell?'

'Basically,' I said. 'But this too has been a tough nut for a lot of people. For decades, the dominant paradigm in psychology was behaviourism – as well as something called the Standard Social Science Model. These notions, which all right-thinking people held, were basically that the human mind is a blank slate at birth – and it gets filled up entirely by the ideas and values of the culture into which one happens to be born. And also that cultures can differ arbitrarily widely – and, thus, so can human behaviour.'

'But that's not right?'

'No, it's wrong. It turns out most important human behaviour is not best explained by a few years of Pavlovian stimulus-response training, and some acculturation in the schoolyard – but rather by millions of years of selection pressures. It's evolution that shaped our behaviour – into distinct mental modules used to perform certain tasks, and that are already fully formed and in place when we shoot out of the womb. And every culture we've ever studied shows these same baseline behaviours.'

'What kinds of behaviours?'

'Everything from mating choices and sexual jealousy, to family loyalty and friendship, to competition and altruism and social and political hierarchies—'

'It might help,' Thad said, 'if you gave some concrete examples.'

'Okay,' I said. 'Pick a behaviour and I'll explain how it might have evolved.'

Thad paused and looked thoughtful. 'Well, I seem to be afraid a lot. Fear?'

'Okay. While linguaphiles collect a lot of colourful Latin terms for "fear of circus midgets wielding spatulas" or "fear of bearded men standing on their heads" or such muck, in reality almost all human fears fall into just a few categories.'

'Which are?'

'Um, I always forget one or two, but . . . fear of the dark, fear of enclosed places, fear of social opprobrium, fear of leaving home, fear of heights, fear of blood, fear of deep water, fear of large predators . . . that's most of them, I think. Can you see what they all have in common?'

'They were all the major threats to survival in the ancestral environment?'

'Very good! Oh – I forgot: snakes and spiders. Snakes and spiders are always scary. Erasmus, for instance, freaks out at coiled garden hoses sometimes. And, as far as I know, he's never in his life seen an actual snake.'

'Because snakes and spiders were almost always venomous in Africa?'

'Right again! There are maybe two varieties of venomous spider in all of North America, but it doesn't make any difference. We've been hard-wired to steer clear of them. These days, we should really be afraid of electrical appliances by bathtubs, driving without a seatbelt, fried foods . . . but it'll be millions of years before those fears evolve. If ever. Meanwhile, we're pre-programmed. Mis-programmed.'

'That's pretty amazing,' Thad said. 'What about a harder one? What about . . . happiness?' I didn't figure he had picked that at random.

'Well,' I said, stretching my wrists out, 'we tend to be happy when we're safe, warm, dry, well fed, healthy, prosperous, loved by our family, respected by our peers, and non-celibate.'

Thad arched an eyebrow. 'All the keys to Darwinian fitness?'

'Spot on! You hardly need me at all any more. So, yeah, happiness can be assumed to be a kick in the pants to make us get up and go seek out the keys to Darwinian fitness when we don't have them – and to protect them when we do.'

'So why does happiness always seem so fleeting? So elusive?'

'I regret that there may be a good answer to that question.'

'Go ahead. Hit me.'

'Well, there are a couple of problems with happiness. One is, how much fitness is enough? That is to say, if a caveman spent all his energy trying to build a hunting rifle and pining for a Coleman stove, instead of sharpening his spear a bit better and collecting warmer pelts, he wouldn't do very well. So – how do you tell how good you can reasonably expect things to get?'

'I'll bite.'

'The first clue is what the next guy has. If he managed it, odds are you can, too.'

'So our happiness tends to be relative to what other people have?'

'Yep – keeping up with the Joneses. The second clue is what you have already. That's by definition achievable – and the odds are you can do just a little bit better.'

'So we're always going to want a little more than whatever we've got?'

'Yes. Worse, we're going to be very vulnerable to the illusion that getting that next little bit will finally make us really, enduringly, happy. All of which should clue you in to the wretched fact: Evolution doesn't care if we're happy. Evolution only wants us out chasing that next sliver of Darwinian fitness. As long as we survive long enough to reproduce, evolution won't be bothered if our lives are black, living hells.'

'Man. That sucks.'

'Pretty much. And the tragedy of happiness has a third act: It turns out there are simply twice as many negative human emotions as positive ones.'

'You're kidding. Why?'

'Well, in the ancestral environment, more stuff was good, but only up to a point. Another pound of meat was good, but another hundred pounds wasn't a hundred times as good – especially without refrigerators. There were diminishing returns. But while there were not too many ways to become infinitely better off, there were quite a lot of ways to become infinitely worse off. You could fall off a cliff, get eaten by a bear, stabbed in the back by a rival, cuckolded by your wife, die of an illness . . . If you let a threat get by you, unlike an opportunity, you could be taken out of the game entirely.'

'So we're programmed to pay more attention to bad things than good things?'

'Yes. Statistically, it just pays better returns to, erm, accentuate the negative.'

'Man. That's depressing. But still totally amazing. Hey – before, we were talking about humanity's, um, special, higher-order processing. Consciousness. And culture, and language, and art. All the stuff the squirrel, and the other non-human species, somehow get by without. You put me off at the time. Did you mean that evolution, or rather evolutionary psychology, couldn't explain those kinds of things?'

'Well,' I said, choosing my words carefully. 'People who work in the field have certainly tried. They've floated ideas about consciousness as an override module for flexibility in our pre-programmed behaviours. They've tried explaining music in terms of the pleasure our brains get from hearing overtones and undertones, which tell us when things are near or far. Or explaining visual art in terms of little serotonin kicks we get from matching colours and patterns. Or viewing landscape paintings of suitable habitats for ourselves.'

'Sounds a little weak.'

'It is. It's awfully weak. As good as evolution is at explaining stuff like sexual jealousy, and fears, and happiness – all of those primal, lizard-brain, sub-cortical things that go on – it just seems like a real stretch to try to get rococo architecture and modern dance and new wave punk and abstract expressionism and French spring fashion collections and existentialist philosophy and E.E. Cummings and cosmology and particle physics and Rodin – out of survival and reproduction pressures in Africa. If you can explain how these things might have evolved . . . and how they did so *in the last 10,000 years*, which is all the time they've been around . . . well, you'll really have something.'

'What do you think will ultimately explain these things?'

'It'd be pretty damned interesting to find out.'

I spent the rest of the morning, and most of the afternoon, doing some brain-dead code cleanup for v6. When a release date starts getting this close, pretty much anybody who can tell a debugging tool from his own arse gets roped into this kind of work. Even if I, for one, am paid way too much to do it. However, unsurprisingly, I got distracted quickly. My fingers were typing one thing, but my brain had ducked out, running off after A'hib Khouri's white whale – his junk DNA pattern-matching project.

I stuck my frizzy head out into the hall – a pointless checking-if-the-coast-was-clear gesture – and then dug out the gene-traversing genetic algorithm I'd begun fleshing out on Sunday. After a couple hours' mashing, I'd banged out some alpha code that, well, compiled. I set it running – and mutating – overnight, and ducked out for the day.

I actually used the front entrance, figuring it would be safe by this point. To my surprise, and other mixed emotions, our front-desk secretary – excuse me, our 'admin', I never get that one right – was still at her station. She gave me a bit of a look, which I leaned away from. But as I passed, she said:

'Goodnight. Getting a little restless, are we?'

Normally, people can hurl staplers at my head in the halls, and it won't get me to stop (and get roped into conversation). But this grabbed me. I tried smiling. I said:

'Sorry. How do you mean?'

'Don't worry,' she said. 'It's just between you and me and HR. Won't go any further.' I tried levering my eyes wider, going for that look of perfect blankness. 'Oh,' she said, seeing me not catching on. 'We got an employment check for you today.'

'From whom?'

'You don't know?'

'I'm afraid I don't.'

'Oh. Well, they didn't say.'

'What did you tell them?'

'Just the usual name, rank and serial number routine – date of hire, job title and salary. Don't worry. Lots of people are looking around these days.'

'Right.' I passed on the opportunity to convince her I wasn't one of them.

*

When I got home, waiting for me were a lonely chimp and a piece of paper mail from Fargo, North Dakota. The mail was to inform me that someone – unidentified – had requested a copy of my credit history.

I turned off my phone and crawled into bed.

Twenty-one

It's not inconceivable that the apparently endless march of work weeks is abetted by, oh, some of the choices I make. For instance, I keep waiting, ripostes queued, for someone at work to ask me if I ever change clothing. (Riposte #1: 'Absolutely – every night, and every morning.') I mean, there's the fact that I do the same thing every day. If my outfit was suitable for Monday's activities, it'll be suitable for Tuesday's through Friday's. And it's not like I dig ditches for a living. The clothes don't get dirty. Not for days and days.

I guess I don't have any interest in fashion, in the sense of something that changes. That goes in and out. Which is not quite to say that I don't have sartorial preferences. It's just that jeans, a black T-shirt, and the ole pointy black boots (with optional black biker jacket) worked for me last year, and they work for me this year. I don't anticipate any shakeups next year.

But, then again, maybe I'm playing to my own fears. I claim to be horrified by the sameness of the days, this endless march – the one which we all know where it inevitably ends. And yet I dress like a good little soldier in the parade, indistinguishable from one day to the next. A Silicon Valley writer once said: 'You want to know where your fears are hiding? Tell me what you know about yourself. Tell me what you can't live without.'

After twenty-seven years, most of it unrelentingly introspective, I like to think I know myself pretty well. But where has it got me, really? Just look at me: educated to the highest level at the world's greatest universities . . . plugged in at high speed, all day every day, to the first-ever shared global repository of all human knowledge . . . officially designated as an expert on how human thought and emotion actually work . . . all told, I probably have more and better information about how and why we're on this planet, and how things on it work (including how we work), than anyone who's ever drawn breath.

Yet somehow I'm still not floating around on clouds of bliss. More like free-falling.

What, then, to arrest the fall? Or . . . *who*?

From: thad@ctake.com
To: keq@ctake.com
Subject: Rocococococococo?
Date: Tue, 04 Apr 2006 07:30:12 (PST)

I've got to be totally honest – I'd give myself zero chance of recognizing rococo architecture if it fell on my head in the street. And I'm not much for Paris fashions, either. But that said: Isn't the list of things you said that evolutionary psychology (and, thus, I'm presuming, science in general) can't explain . . . things like art and music and love and meaningful interaction between people – maybe even meaning, itself . . . aren't those, basically, the kinds of things that make life worth living in the first place?

If science can't explain them, what does it tell us about science? What does it tell us about us? Do we NEED these things explained? Broken down into pieces for us?

I'm not suggesting any answers to these questions. Far from it. All I know is it is a blast hanging out with you. That, and I feel almost maybe like I'm making progress. Like my legs aren't quite so out from under me. And I know who I have to thank.

Your friend,
Thad

Here, By the Way, Is How Good A Friend Thad Is (Or Maybe Just How Uncrowded A Field He's Competing In)

We had known each other exactly a month when I told him about Trevor.

It just came up. He asked if I missed my family back in the UK. And I told him.

He just listened. Listened to all of it, silently and solemnly.

Though, what I didn't tell him then, and still haven't told him yet, was the part about me running away. And that it was not only a place I was running away from.

I'm only just barely getting around telling myself about that.

From: ahib@genenw.com
To: keq@ctake.com
Subject: Saturday / sequencing
Date: Wed, 05 Apr 2006 12:03:21 (PST)

Greetings. I was glad to see you on Saturday night. I especially enjoyed the event as I managed to avoid embarrassing myself on the dance floor. (And I assure you it would have been embarrassment without precedent in the experience of anyone present.)

Have you, by any chance, had a chance to look at the sequence I sent over? If so, do you have any questions I can answer?

Cheers,
A'hib

From: keq@ctake.com
To: ahib@genenw.com
Subject: Re: Saturday / sequencing
Date: Thu, 6 Apr 2006 18:23:43 (PST)

Hello, A'hib. Yes, Saturday was fun. I'm pleased to have gotten my second lesson on how your sense of humour works. But I expect there will be more.

And yes, I have taken a peek at the sequence you forwarded. I've even gone so far as to start 'growing' some code to play with it (as per your suggestion). I've got a handful of different strains mutating along, each based on different parameters. As you intuited, it's not really necessary to program a lot of detail about regression analysis or other forms of pattern matching – merely to let them evolve those techniques on their own. The only rub, I've found, is in not begging the question of what, exactly, constitutes a 'pattern'. In a nutshell, that's really why the multiple strains – they get rewarded for slightly different results.

So, to cut to the chase – no, I haven't found much of anything. Just noise, really. Randomness. I mean, there have been a few repeating, or meta-repeating (or meta-meta-etc.-repeating) patterns – but only very short ones. (And, as you know, randomness inevitably produces short stretches of seeming non-randomness – five heads in a row on coin tosses, etc.)

It would help a bit if I had a better picture of the pattern I was looking for, or at least the likely length of such a pattern. I'm guessing something longer than a couple of repetitions?

Cheers yourself. (Where ARE you from, by the way.)

ke

From: ahib@genenw.com
To: keq@ctake.com
Subject: Re: Saturday / sequencing
Date: Thu, 5 Apr 2006 19:00:00 (PST)

Yes, longer than a couple repetitions. Something long enough to – how to put it? – convey something.

You probably noted that the sequence I sent you is a tiny fraction of the full junk sequence. Basically, I'm doing shotgun sequencing of junk overnight, when I can steal cycles on the big machines here. It's dribs and drabs. I'm sending some more on now. Try feeding it to your pattern-matching yeast. ;-)

I'm Pakistani. (Yet another ex-subject of the British Empire . . .)

A-

From: keq@ctake.com
To: ahib@genenw.com
Subject: Re: Saturday / sequencing
Date: Thu, 5 Apr 2006 18:23:43 (PST)

Convey something? Convey to WHOM? And FROM whom? Surely you don't really expect to find something written there? Like God left . . . some kind of README file, buried in our DNA?

Nonetheless, I've got your new sequences. I'll get back to you.

ke

And thusly did the new week pass, in jeans, black T-shirts, boots, v6 code cleanup – and riding herd on evolving swarms of DNA-bothering bots. And, hey, really, who could have predicted any of this last week? Much less a hundred years ago.

I'm convinced that certain aspects of the human experience are absolutely enduring and eternal. They put us through exactly the same wringers and spike pits that Shakespeare's players negotiated. You know the ones: love, betrayal, filial piety, rivalry, revenge, coming of age, leaving home – finding some kind of meaning in sublunary existence. Thad knows the ones.

And but then certain insights into the human experience are about five seconds old. Think evolution – knowing, for the first time, where we came from. How huge is that? But it's not even a hundred and fifty years old. Think evolutionary psychology – having a plausible theory for why we feel and act the ways we do, understanding how we got this way. That one's about twenty years old. Having the complete recipe for building a human being (the human genome map) – they're just finishing that one up right now.

When the timeless issues get re-examined in the light of these very timely new discoveries, then maybe we'll have something. Or, who knows, maybe it'll just be on to the next set of mysteries.

Twenty-two

Introducing people to one another is quite nice, I think. Geometric expansion of social networks, and suchlike. Not that I've been great about this kind of thing to date. But I thought I might give it a try. Just the three of us, my two friends and me, Friday evening drinks, al fresco, in downtown Palo Alto. Low-key. No dogs. No monkeys. Just pleasant, casual, human conversation.

I was never going to pull that one off, I realize now. I mean, hey, I'm wrapped up in weird side-projects, wrestling with elusive demons, and slightly spooked by the universe. Thad's in complete existential meltdown. And Helen . . . well, we all know Helen. Or, rather, we don't know her. We don't know her at all.

So, naturally, the casual conversation bit at our get-together went on about five seconds past the introductions – at which point Helen busted out with, 'So. Thad. I hear you've renounced your God.'

That's what I get for having provided advance intelligence briefings. But Thad takes everything in stride. The two of them were soon off to the races, theology-wise, while I sat uneasily sipping Cabernet. Running fingers stiffly through my hair.

'Thirty-eight years it took you to lose your religion?' Helen said. 'I'm always astounded that the majority of people on the planet manage to keep a straight face while espousing beliefs that are obviously, palpably, not true. Tell me. As a recent believer. Why do you think it is people do that?'

Thad smiled tentatively and leaned forward. Naturally, he was taking this as a question, rather than a provocation. 'Well, I guess when a person is raised in faith, they're surrounded by a certain world view that . . . fits together, more or less.'

'I see,' Helen said, holding his gaze in that cool way of hers. 'I'm told you're married. But your wife's still religious.'

'That's true.'

'And religion's not an issue between the two of you?'

'There are always issues in a marriage. You're single, right? Even after you tie the knot, there's still all the Venus and Mars business going on. Believe me.'

'No,' said Helen, drawing out the word, 'men are not from Mars, nor are women from Venus. Men and women are from Africa – the cradle of hominid evolution.' Thad laughed at this. But he wasn't allowed to laugh long. 'Despite that fact,' Helen said, 'you've still got these hicks driving around in Ford F-350s with "There are no apes in my family tree" bumper stickers on the back. What exactly does their world view fit with?'

This was where I should have interrupted. I could have said something breezy about how you could go back a mere six million years and everyone at the family reunion would look just like Erasmus. But so much for hindsight. As it was, I pondered Helen's fixation with teleological bumper stickers.

'I mean,' Helen carried on, 'I'm sorry, but science has just taken the legs out from under religion. There's no father in his heaven up above. We've looked – practically to the edges of the universe. We even sent guys up there. Nobody. And there's no hell below us. We dug, and it's dirt and rock all the way down.'

'Church doctrine,' ventured Thad, 'is that the Earth is 10,000 years old.'

I perked up slightly at that 10,000 years figure, squinting at empty space . . .

Helen didn't notice. She said: 'I can reassure the Church that God didn't create the planet 10,000 years ago. Solar debris created it 4.5 billion years ago. And God sure didn't create any of us. If he did, he's got a dark sense of humour.'

'How do you mean?' Thad said.

'I mean all the people who are born, or become, irretrievably broken. Have you ever spent any time around a medical center? If you do, you'll discover a whole underclass of people who spend all their days dealing with their chronic health problems. Ones that we can't, as things stand, do a damned thing to fix.' Helen scanned the street. 'You know what would really wake up the religious people? A good global apocalypse.'

Jesus Christ! What was all this? Had Helen been pining for a punching bag? Or did she just take an instant dislike to Thad? I had trouble seeing how anyone could dislike Thad. Maybe she had issues with white men. But of course I don't pretend to understand how race works in America.

'Did you know,' Helen said, touching her glass, 'that until very recently, there were more people working in the average McDonald's than there were out watching for killer asteroids? Go look at the Gulf of Mexico. That's an asteroid crater. Probably the one that got the dinosaurs, sixty-five million years ago. Think you're smarter than they were? In fact, you have a better statistical chance of being killed by an asteroid than dying in a plane crash. Why? Because an asteroid gets everybody. You think our presence is divine? If it wasn't for the presence of Jupiter in our solar system, we wouldn't be here now. Jupiter's gravity well has probably caught ten thousand asteroids that would have wiped all life off of this rock. But one's going to get through eventually. Yep, a new life form has got about seventy million years to evolve to the point where it can figure out how to knock out killer asteroids. Any slower off the mark than that, and you're outta there!'

The waitress came by and agreed to bring us another round of drinks. The sun was sinking. Lights were coming on up and down the street. There was kind of a weird, giddy vibe floating over the table. And Helen Dolan was just getting warmed up.

'And who do we employ to protect us from these things? The President of this country, with his outspoken, born-again religious faith. And under him, the nation's highest legislative body – where fewer than five per cent of the members hold any kind of degree in the sciences, much less an advanced one. These men, and they are practically all white men, enjoy virtually complete ignorance of the developments in science and technology, particularly in the bio-sciences, over the past twenty years. How can they conceivably make policy decisions? It's no wonder we have no national health care system. But we've got a military that dwarfs the world's next fifteen biggest combined.'

Thad perked up at this. He was getting into his second beer, which I had never seen him have two. 'Enjoy your freedom to knock the military,' he said. 'You live in the most free, most prosperous, and most secure nation in human history.'

'How do you reckon that?' Helen said.

'Free: You get up virtually every day and do whatever you want to do. When was the last time, other than tax day, the government came around to bother you? Prosperous: Our wealth is obscene, compared to the rest of the world – never mind to people through-out history. Three billion people still live on less than two dollars a day. You can't get coffee for two bucks in this valley. Secure: You go to bed every night knowing, *knowing*, that the Huns are not going to come over the hill, sack your village, rape your women, and slaughter your children. How many people have ever enjoyed perfect security?' Thad eyed his beer. 'Thank a veteran. A surviving one.'

I realized my lips were still parted. I also realized Helen and Thad were, quite unexpectedly, showing me all-new Helens and Thads.

All-new Helen replied, 'Well, this country's a hell of a lot more free and secure and prosperous for non-minorities, ones with no chronic health problems, and who make six-figure salaries in Silicon Valley.'

Just when I was sure this was all going completely and irretrievably south, Helen killed her drink – then reached across the table and put her hand on Thad's. 'You know what I've always wanted to see in a video game? A *second*-person shooter. Could you guys make one of those?'

Thad and I laughed violently. I spewed a little Cab. 'What the hell would that be?'

'You know,' she said, leaning back again. 'The perspective, on the screen, would be from the point of view of your opponent. You'd actually see yourself through his eyes – shooting at yourself. You'd have to manoeuvre based on seeing only the other guy's point of view.' Her smile faded a bit. 'I think that would be instructive.'

I shook my head. My God, what was all of this? Just when I thought I didn't know Helen, it turned out I really didn't know Helen.

I looked around me. Early Friday evening sidewalk strollers, smiling, lost in conversation, passed without care, a few feet from our table. White lights in the hardwoods made the leaves glow green. Cars glinted by. I looked over as a black sedan pulled up to the kerb just beside us. It had the darkest tints I'd ever seen. As the car sat idling, I peered at my own expression in the reflective glass, watching myself grow puzzled, then alarmed.

The car's engine revved up. It pulled out and drove off.

My phone rang.

Twenty-three

I had a bit of a lie-in Saturday morning. Don't be offended, but . . . you know what's so great about masturbation? The sparkling innocence of it. I mean, they could teleport in, say, the check-out boy you last had at the grocery store, right into your bedroom. And you could just finish up and smile, if you let yourself. There just can't be any shame in it – not when everyone, just everyone does it. It's *wholesome*.

I didn't even think about anyone in particular. Just a vague, strong, beautiful, protective, possibly even androgynous, bed-mate. Emphasis on protective, I think. Reality: overrated!

As I lay recovering, I remembered a dream I'd had. In it, I was groping through an abstract, mathematical space. I couldn't recall the shapes, or the math. But now I wondered if they had been double helixes? Great chains of As, Cs, Gs and Ts? Of course, the very fact of it occurring to me to wonder was a strong indicator that they had been. In this space, I'd been trying to make sense of the lines and vertices – but not just to understand them. With a view toward finding my way out.

I got up. It was sunny out, but it's always sunny out. Here's an adjustment you really have to make when you move to the Bay Area: Getting over the compulsion to go out and do something just because the day is beautiful. You'd die of exhaustion from the endless hiking, picnicking, and playing footie on the grass.

Of course, this is more of an adjustment for some than for others – Brits for instance. But, hey, sign me up. Oh, wait, I am signed up. I signed up a long time ago.

I got up and called Mum and Dad – separately, as they're separated. (The marriage only survived a couple of years longer than Trevor did. I'm told that's common; that when children die they often take their parents' marriages down with them.) It was early evening in the UK. I got them each at home and we had nice chats.

I talked about the tumult at work with the upcoming release. I mentioned Helen. No, I still wasn't seeing anyone. (I didn't mention the sleeping with Helen bit. Mum and Dad are really lovely. But they're, you know, conservative.) Mum talked about her garden, which is what she had been working in when I called. She's been tending that garden for decades.

After hanging up, I went out behind the building and turned some soil for an hour. There's a tiny patch of grass I'd been eyeing, thinking of putting in some tomatoes. The season for that was coming up. And, of course, digging in the dirt is good for the soul.

I went into the office in the afternoon, half out of interest in seeing what the genetic algorithms had done overnight; and half out of having no competing offers. I took Erasmus with me. He knows it's Saturday. He gets miffed, and I don't blame him, if left alone while I go back to work over the weekend.

I have to confess. Sometimes I'll be on 101, weaving in and out of the eighteen-wheelers, dicing with death. And suddenly I'll be horror-struck at what a terrible idea motorcycle riding really is. I mean, you know, in honest moments. Here's the basic idea: Let's take a car engine – and put a seat on the top of it. Then people can sit on top and just ride the engine down the street. Right in the midst of all the monster-car-crushing SUVs and cement trucks. Give 'em a helmet. They'll be fine.

Erasmus doesn't let it bother him. He loves the wind. He pounds me on the back with endorsement whenever I do something daring. I guess he has the same evolutionary hardwiring to deal with this that I do, which is to say none.

We pulled off the highway, slanting toward work. If we'd stayed on 101, we'd have ultimately zigzagged through San Francisco, then crossed the Golden Gate Bridge. (I was afraid Erasmus had gotten his hopes up that's where we were going.)

Did you know, as I didn't until recently, that of the hundreds of people who've leapt to their deaths off the Golden Gate Bridge, all but one or two have done so from the same side? Virtually always from the side facing back in toward the city. When I learned this, I spent quite a while trying to puzzle out why. I concluded it must be something to do with recrimination.

An American motif I've learned about is that of 'going west'. The basic idea is that if your life wasn't working out where you were . . . if you were a business failure, or if your marriage fell apart . . . you could always pull up stakes and go west. Try again. Start over. And if things didn't go any better than before, you could move further west. But, eventually, you hit the other ocean. California – land of hopes and dreams! But if things didn't work out for you there, they probably weren't going to work out for you anywhere. And there was nowhere left to go – except off the bridge.

So I figured suicides wanted to look back upon the city that had betrayed their last hopes. Maybe San Francisco would regret it when they were gone.

But then not too long after that, I happened to cross the bridge on foot myself. And I discovered that foot traffic is only allowed on the east side of the bridge – the side facing the city. So if somebody wanted to jump off the Pacific side, they'd have to walk all the way over, cross the highway, then sneak halfway back on the other side.

We pulled into the office parking lot. It was not nearly full. Nonetheless, I parked on the sidewalk, by the door. You have to do something to make yourself smile.

I put E in the big-screen TV lounge, set up on PS2. He likes the driving games. He'd also get a fair bit of company there, as people wandered by and stopped to play with him. There'd be a good flow. (Like I said, release day was less than two months out.)

I got to my cube, and Thad's. He wasn't there; never is on weekends. He was too old, and had too many children, to give a damn about office politics or perceptions. He worked hard all week, and then he went home.

I pulled my phone off my belt and put it on my desk. I sat. I looked, very ruefully, at the phone.

When it had rung last night, on the patio, out with Thad and

Helen, I'd excused myself to answer it. That's something I virtually never do – take calls when I'm with people. Maybe I'd wanted to step outside of the odd psychodynamic landscape of that table for a minute. Maybe the ring sounded strange to me. I don't know. Something.

Stepping around the corner, I flipped it open. I said: 'Yes, hallo,' in that bright way in which I'd been trained, and have never managed to shake.

It greeted me. By name. That voice again.

I found I didn't have anything to say (to the voicemail voice).

It, or she I guess, said, 'I'm calling to tell you something. To let it go.'

Finally, I managed a wildly original, 'Who is this?'

'It's your phone,' she said.

I was glad I had two glasses of wine in me. 'My phone's calling me?'

'Trust me, I'm your phone. Who knows you better? I hear your most intimate conversations. I live on your hip, pressed against your flesh. I've got all your numbers. And I'm here to tell you. I'm telling you to let this one go.'

I felt my lips hovering apart again.

Someone touched my shoulder. I spun wildly. It was Helen. She and Thad were up and ready to go. One of them had paid the bill. I slammed the phone shut.

'I didn't mean to bust in,' Helen said. 'Were you done?'

'Yes.' The two of them were staring at me. 'Right,' I said, 'we're off then.'

Monday Morning

'Aren't you going to ask me what I thought of Helen?' This was Thad coming into my cube, after I'd slunk in without saying good morning.

'Why? Do I have a "Please Bitch-Slap Me" note pinned to my back?'

Thad grinned, which he has this talent for doing with his whole matt of facial hair – curly, thick, red-shot, and now elliptical. He was relishing my reaction in advance.

'I liked her,' he said. 'She's obviously very, very smart. Almost as smart as you, maybe.' He crossed his thick arms over his thick chest. 'I mean, it seems to me she's got some issues. But she definitely got me thinking.'

'I should have remembered you don't mind being prodded. That you don't do being provoked.'

'Ah, well . . .' He shrugged. 'You should see me when Kennedy tries to renegotiate bedtime. How was the rest of your weekend, by the way?'

I nodded once and checked out his belt buckle. I said: 'Mustn't grumble, as my people say.'

Thad smiled again. '*Your people.* What's the saying? Two cultures separated by a common language? Actually, I had a soft spot for the Brits even before I met you. I never told you that. But right after 9/11, when Tony Blair came over and sat in the Capitol for the full session of Congress, that really got to me. That, and when they played our national anthem outside Buckingham Palace.'

'Here's to the special relationship,' I said.

'Plus, when I was in the military, my unit did some training with the British army. Really nice guys.' Looking as if he might have said slightly too much, he ducked back around our shared cube wall.

I checked in on my DNA-parsing brew. (A'hib's reference to it as 'yeast' seemed suddenly apt.) There hadn't been any results when I came in on Saturday, none to speak of. And I didn't see any now. It was starting to look as if the junk DNA was just that. Aptly named. Only noise.

Prior to Saturday afternoon, though, I didn't have any very good way to be sure whether patterns weren't there, or patterns just weren't being found. So I'd put my yeast to work on some strings of data in which I knew there to be patterns: an English dictionary, a few thousand lines of game code, cubes of 7 to a million digits, pi

107

(also to a million digits – though, this was a control, as pi has no pattern to it). A gigabyte of random alpha-numeric characters, except with a periodic checksum – every 256th character summing the ASCII values of the prior 255. A great heap of linear and multiple regressions. A binary representation of some architectural schematics; a binary representation of a picture of a flower.

Looking now, I saw that my genetic algorithms had found it all, or what seemed like it all. All the patterns I knew were there to start with. Plus a bunch I hadn't noticed. Even a few that, if they were patterns, were too complex or subtle for me to grasp.

But they still hadn't found anything in A'hib's sequences. At least, not the ones he'd sent me so far.

I'd not gotten bored with all this yet – tweaking the evolution-ary parameters for the algorithms, watching them grow. Plus I always like to be helpful (or so I tell myself). But, beyond that, I think mainly I was just hooked. Hooked on A'hib's . . . vision? Technically, I still didn't know what that vision was, at least not what it was to him.

But here's how it had coalesced for me, after a few days of work-ing on it (and now, it appears, dreaming about it). Simply put, there are things in our makeup, things about human nature – as Thad put it, maybe the really important things – that don't make any sense. Not in evolutionary terms, not in other terms. That I'm pretty sure have never been adequately explained by anybody.

The scientists have mostly punted on these matters. I don't blame them – the subjects are too soft for their tastes. How do you quantify love? Where's the data on art? How do you test theories about the nature of consciousness – when you can never have a plat-form, other than consciousness itself, from which to test it? The philosophers have left a lot of commentary, but of course it's mostly circular wank – and, of course, bereft of even an interest in data or empirically testable theories. The religionists have a clear answer – that we get our divine nature from God – but it happens not to be one that I can buy into. Not for a minute. Of course, it may be true. But there's no reason whatever to think so.

108

So on the one hand, this major chunk – maybe the critical chunk – of human nature is unaccounted for. It seems it couldn't have evolved, both because there's no reason for it to have and because it hasn't had time; we've only had culture, art, language, technology, morality, all that really good stuff, for a few thousand years.

And, on the other hand, 97 per cent of the blueprint for making a human being remains unexplored. And, apparently, uncared about. Unloved.

. . . Coincidence?

I hadn't actually spent much time talking with A'hib, certainly not at this level of abstraction. But I couldn't help feeling that I sensed what he was on about.

Of course, we were both almost certainly tilting at windmills.

But you've got to do something while you're waiting around doing nothing.

I wrote A'hib and asked him to send some more junk on, when he had it ready.

Twenty-four

Here's a striking fact you might not have at your disposal. Humanity went through a 'genetic bottleneck' – a very, very recent one. We now know that all living men are descended from this one single African bloke who lived about sixty thousand years ago. We can tell this for certain because men pass along their Y chromosomes intact to their sons. It only ever changes through mutation, which occurs at a basically constant rate. This makes the Y chromosome a sort of molecular clock.

We're also pretty sure that this common male forebear of ours – the universal grandpappy – was one of a new breed of hominid. These were guys who had tremendously big brains; and when they hit the scene, they promptly put the smack down on all the Neanderthals, as well as on *Homo erectus*. They really just put the Charles Barkley on those guys.

Which might tell you something about the propensity of our species – or, I should probably say, the males of our species – for spectacular, systematic violence. We didn't interbreed (that is, team up) with the other hominid species, as was imagined for a while. No, we wiped them out – either in the normal straightforward way, or else by dominating resources and driving them to extinction.

Not for nothing are other people scary. And strange men triply so.

'I put my guns down a long time ago,' Thad said.

'What about the SIG-Sauer?'

'Oh, that's not a gun. That's a . . . pea flicker.'

Thad, I imagined, knew something about the realistic propensity for violence by strange men. I could just never get him to talk about it. On Wednesday's walk, I was trying to work him around to the subject – without saying anything about why. This was already making me feel guilty.

'And anyway,' Thad said, 'my gunfighting record in civilian life is a perfect zero for zero. I intend to keep it intact.' He took a pretty expressionless look around at our immediate surroundings. It was sunny, breezy, and 68.4, as always. The breeze made little sparkly ripples on the lake. The leaves on the trees went at it. 'Of course, if anyone, God forbid, ever threatened Leslie, or the kids, or you . . .'

That did it. I started crying, in full view of another person – when he included me on his list of protectees. I suddenly realized Leslie was the sister-in-law I was never going to have; and that Kennedy and Holden were the niece and nephew who should have been mine. I cried with a frantic joy that I had the blessing of these surrogates in my life; but I also cried with a sprawling, black, vertiginous sorrow that I needed surrogates.

Suddenly, we had both stopped walking, and Thad was looking at me with terrific concern.

'Hey. *Hey*,' he said. 'What's going on?'

I'd seen that black sedan again, the one with the tinted windows – sitting right at the end of my block. And of course there was the employment check. And the credit check. Never mind the 'phone calls'.

But I don't think any of that was really why I was crying.

Still, as I regained the power of speech, I told Thad about A'hib, about the project he had me working on – and about the multifold spookiness that seemed to have infiltrated my life over approximately the same time period.

When we got back to our desks, the day was almost done. I had mail from A'hib – with a new sequence, the longest yet. A'hib had explained to me that, with limited resources, he tried to make informed decisions about which bits of the junk to sequence. You know, wherever it looked like the action was. But he didn't have a lot to go on. In this case, on a lark, he'd taken the opposite tack – doing some sequencing out in the real backwaters, a million miles from protein-making, codons that didn't look like they even had any ancillary influence on gene-flipping.

And so I gamely let loose my new minions on it – those self-evolving pattern-sniffers that had already locked in a number of effective mutations, while eating my test strings from Saturday (the cubes, regressions, flowers, etc.). Just before flipping the switch on that, I saw, from my next email, that Mark Kelly had roped me into a 4 pm meeting, on about thirty minutes' notice. A marketing meeting. Which started in three minutes.

This guy was killing me.

Though, that's another telling turn of phrase, isn't it? Whenever you say 'I'm dying of this or that' or 'such'n'thus is just killing me' . . . it may not literally be true. It may not be this or that actually doing the killing. But there's very little question that you're dying. It's the one truly universal human pastime.

So I figured I might as well amuse myself while running out the clock.

I started my programs.

Then I checked mail again, closed my mailer, and dug out a notepad and pen from amongst the desk clutter (useful props for feigning attention at meetings). I stood up and took a fortifying breath. I glanced back at my screen, where the algorithms ran.

I said, out loud, 'Fuck me' – and nearly fell over reaching for my mouse.

At which point, my desk phone rang. I diverted my arm to grab it. It was our front desk admin. She said I had a visitor.

In a complete daze, I walked out to the reception area. Standing alone on the carpet was a middle-aged man, unsmiling and official, in a grey suit. He had dark hair and eyes. He brandished a thin wallet with an ID badge in it and said: 'I'm federal agent Doyle. I'm going to need a few minutes of your time and cooperation.'

Thad insisted on coming by my place after work to talk. Also, unquestionably, to check up on me. Mainly, he wanted a full recounting of my run-in with the authorities. When he'd come by my cube to check on me before going home, he immediately knew that something had happened. But I hadn't wanted to discuss it in the office.

And that was what had really gotten to me about the episode, I think – that it had happened at the office. That this man had come by my workplace, where I'm (at least for the moment) a respected professional. He had come and found me right where I live. And I got the feeling that was his point.

'So he came to your cube?' Thad asked. The two of us, plus Erasmus, were sitting on plastic furniture on my patio. Erasmus was hogging the snacks I'd put out.

'Erasmus *D*!' I scolded. He replaced half of his overflowing handful of sugar-dusted strawberries. He looked more resentful than chastened.

'No,' I said, turning back to Thad. 'I got a call from the front desk that I had a visitor. I went out. And there was this guy in a suit. I took him to a conference room.'

'When he showed you his ID, how carefully did you look at it?'

'I don't know,' I admitted. 'Not very, I suppose. I didn't know the US Food and Drug Administration had enforcement agents. I barely knew the US had an FDA. I certainly didn't know they oversee biotechnology.'

Thad nodded seriously and reached for a strawberry. 'Federal agencies oversee everything in this country. What did he say his name was?'

'Doyle. No first name.'

'And how long did you two talk?'

'It couldn't have been more than ten minutes.'

'Can you remember exactly what he said?'

'Probably not. But I'm pretty sure I got the gist of it. He said he knew I had been "recruited" by employees of the biotechnology company GenenW. He asked me if I knew that research in genomics is subject to federal statutes. Then he asked me if I knew the penalties for violating those statutes.'

'I'm guessing,' said Thad, 'that he told you the penalties.'

'Not precisely. I think "severe" was the most specific term he used. But, mainly, and this was the totally chilling bit, he unsubtly hinted that I could be deported. He said that, after 9/11, revoking a visa is easier than issuing a parking ticket.'

'That is scary.'

'Yes. Though, I was less scared when I realized he wanted something from me.'

'What?'

'He said his people were investigating GenenW. And that if I were to tell him everything I knew, and might subsequently learn, about what GenenW was working on, he would make sure I didn't have any trouble. Immigration-wise.'

'Jeesh.' Thad shook his head – then looked puzzled. 'The prospect of being a federal informant made you less scared?'

'No. The realization that I had some leverage.'

'Ah. I see. So what did you tell him?'

'That I'd do what I could to help. That I didn't know very much about GenenW, but that I'd look at my files, and give him whatever I found.'

'Is that what you're going to do?'

'Oh, no. Not that.'

Thad smiled. 'Smart girl,' he said. He paused and rubbed his chin. 'You said you've felt as if you've been watched all week. Do you think it could have been him?'

'It would certainly make sense,' I said. 'I'm sure the government has got the resources to know where I am, to tap my phone. And probably lots worse.'

'If it was the government.'

'What do you mean?'

He didn't answer that. He got up. 'Hey, come inside with me for a minute.'

We went in and Thad sat down at my home machine. He pulled up www.fda.gov. He navigated to their Office of Enforcement area, then poked around until he found a phone number. He picked up my desk phone and dialled it.

I saw him punch a couple of voicemail buttons. Then he spoke briefly to somebody, waited on hold, then spoke to somebody else.

'This is Sergeant Gottlieb of the Palo Alto, California PD,' he said into the mouthpiece, in a surprisingly businesslike tone. After a pause, he read out a badge number. 'We have a citizen here,' he continued, identifying me by full name, 'who was approached yesterday by a man identifying himself as an Agent Doyle with FDA Enforcement. Can you please verify for me that you have an agent by that name working in our jurisdiction? Yes. Thank you.'

He looked back up at me, but didn't speak. I stood. We waited.

'Yes. Yes, Sergeant Gottlieb. How do you do. Yesterday, in Palo Alto, California. Doyle. D-O-Y-L-E. You're sure. Right. No, that does it for me. I appreciate it. Goodbye.'

Thad replaced the receiver.

'No FDA Agent Doyle,' he said. 'No FDA investigation in Palo Alto.'

Erasmus walked in the open front door, looking at us like *What?*

Twenty-five

Thad went back to his family. But not before arranging hourly cruiser drive-bys for the night, courtesy of his law-enforcement colleagues. He also asked me if I kept any weapons in the apartment. No, I didn't keep any weapons in the apartment. He made me wait while he went out to his truck. He came back with an outsize canister of pepper spray. He spent five minutes instructing me in its use.

Even before he left, I felt like crying again. Being cared about is heady stuff. Everyone should have a big brother. They should issue them at birth.

E and I sat around playing checkers. He's not very good. But we're both too smart for noughts and crosses (excuse me, 'tic-tac-toe') and both too stupid for chess. He didn't even put up his normal spirited defence tonight. He sensed my disquiet, and shared it, as he always does, on both counts.

But the game kept us moving toward bedtime. Eventually, there'd be the solace and the safety (real or merely felt) of sleep.

Surrogate big brother or no; guarantor of my personal safety or no; there was one thing I didn't confess to Thad. Something I didn't dare confess, or yet know how to. And this was: the matter of what had drawn my nose magnetically back to my screen the day before, that had sent me fumbling for my mouse, that had me cursing aloud in shocked disbelief (just before I was accosted by non-FDA agent Doyle).

This was: the matter of what my pattern-searching algorithms had found.

The trouble is: I don't *know* what they found. Not yet.

Though I'll be fucked if they didn't find something. I mean, I would have just fainted dead away, or perhaps danced a jig down the halls, if my mysterious visitor hadn't turned up right that second to

116

distract me. I mean: *it found something*. A pattern. *In* the DNA sequence.

But here's the thing you've got to understand: one problem with a computer program that's evolved rather than designed is that – while it might get very good indeed at achieving the desired results – it will always be worthless at explaining *how* it got those results. Put another way: the program pretty quickly evolves to a level of complexity that's beyond the ability of a human programmer to read or understand. It becomes a black box – input one end, output the other, and voodoo magic in the middle.

So, as of this moment, all I know is that one of the algorithm's little *Eureka* 'I've found something, madam!' flashing lights had gone off. And also that it seemed to be highlighting every 128th character within a short stretch of the new sequence – just a few kilobytes, right at the end. But what did that set of characters have in common? What *was* the pattern – if it was a pattern? Okay, it pretty much had to be some kind of pattern. There's just no law that it be one recognizable, or even comprehensible, to *me*.

The good news is: each algorithm writes out a log file, describing in mathematical terms what it attempted, pattern matching-wise, with each iteration of parsing the sequence. Of course, with thousands or millions of iterations, the log file would soon swamp my disk – so I have it set to overwrite itself every hundred iterations.

But it's also set to save out a copy of the log if and when it finds a pattern.

So that means I had a record of activity that, theoretically, if interpreted correctly, would tell me just what tricks the algorithm had used to find this pattern. And if I could come to understand the tricks, it was only another hop or two down the path to figuring out the nature of the pattern itself.

For reasons that might be guessed, I hadn't had either the time or inclination to pore over the data at the end of the day it appeared. But that log file would still be there tomorrow.

I don't know. Maybe you'd say it's daft of me to continue messing about with this genomic Easter egg hunt – at the same time that

117

strange men, identities unknown, falsely claiming to be federal agents, have come round looking for me.

Maybe you'd say I shouldn't be carrying on in this vein while anonymous inquiries are being made about my life, and cars with dark tints are cruising my neighbourhood. And when my own phone is calling me up and haranguing me.

Maybe you can't dodge the feeling that I'm not being very sensible, or showing due concern for self-preservation.

Maybe you're right.

Twenty-six

Morning, very early, and I locked up the apartment – more conscientiously, it seemed to me, than on previous mornings – hopped on the Ducati, and blasted off north. Today I had a real spring in my step; or, to put it in motorcycle terms, a twist in my wrist. What was it that had woken me up, and launched me up the road? Fear? Or hope?

Lao Tzu said that both fear and hope are phantoms that arise from thinking of the self as self. He sure must have had that one right. Because I wasn't thinking about a damned thing except for the essential nature of the self. (Though, perhaps not in terms he would have recognized in 400 BC . . .)

I braked to a halt in the lot, leaving a little rubber on the ground; swung my bent knee over the seat – a trick I learned from watching reruns of *Maverick*, with that implausibly dreamy Lorenzo Lamas; and quick-marched through the front door of the building. I didn't even have my helmet off until I hit the stairwell.

I grabbed coffee on my way to my desk, logged in, and looked at mail for five seconds. Then I ducked into some headphones, swivelled my monitor down a bit – and pulled up the last log file from yesterday.

It was some crazy-looking shite.

I figured I was actually going to have to write a whole bunch of new code just to parse the logs and figure out what the old code had done.

So I got to work.

Just past noon, Mark Kelly came by to give me shit about missing his meeting.

'I'm afraid now's not an ideal time for it, Mark,' I tried.

He took a big, sonorous VP breath. He said: 'Is that so? Well, I

119

think we need to discuss it now. Discuss if you have some kind of a personal issue with me, that is.'

I felt some part of my always-tentative professionalism skidding around sideways. My perspective had shifted dramatically in the last two days, almost without me noticing. 'Well, Mark, if that invitation is sincere, I confess I'm enormously tempted to comment in detail about a wide variety of your personal traits . . . but it's going to have to suffice to say you're not someone with whom I care to be interacting just this minute.'

The pitiable fellow couldn't figure out whether to puff up further or deflate entirely. But, already on his way back out of my area, he managed, 'I'm only going to tell you one more time to come to meetings I schedule you for . . .'

So I said: 'And I'm only going to tell *you* one more time: you're a wanker.' Though he might have been out of earshot by then.

I shook my head. I was now distracted and pissed off, but I'd made good progress; so it seemed a good time for a break. I looked over the cube wall, but Thad had already gone to lunch. (I'm not big on lunch, and Thad is religious on it, so we rarely try to coordinate.) I grabbed my phone (old habits) and slipped out the back door.

I didn't go far, taking up a position holding up one of the building's external walls. I thought about my work on analysing the pattern in the genetic sequence, about telling off Kelly, about continuing with this project in the face of current events, and finally about the pattern again. Decisions I seemed to be making.

Here's a really frightening thing about human cognition. There's a huge amount of evidence that the better part of our seemingly rational decision-making is all so much shameless self-justification – usually, justification of decisions that our subcortical (i.e. subconscious) areas have already made for us. Typically, we rewrite history so that the reasons seems to precede the decisions. But it usually isn't so.

You can see this in a cognition lab. Take a guy who's had a commissurotomy – that is, had the major connections between the two halves of his brain severed – so the two sides of his brain no longer talk to each other much. Then show something to just one side of this guy's brain, the side that's not responsible for language. (You do this by showing it to the eye on the opposite side of his head – or playing it to the opposite ear, or letting him touch it with the opposite hand.) Then ask him ('him' being the side that deals with language) what you just showed him. He'll say he doesn't know. But then ask him to guess. Most of the time he'll guess right.

But then ask him how he was able to guess correctly. He'll still insist that he never saw the thing in question. But, usually, he'll think about it and then tell you a really lovely just-so story: 'Oh, I knew it had to be a wheelbarrow because wheelbarrows are used to carry bricks, and bricks are red and laid in stacks, and your tie has red horizontal stripes.' And you can bet he believes his own story. He *believes* it.

Read a few case studies like this and you start to get a sense that most of our decisions, even the big ones, maybe *especially* the big ones, really get made under the hood – well away from our consciousness of them. All our so-called reasoning is just fanciful stories we tell ourselves. The philosopher of mind Daniel Dennett has gone so far as to define the self as the 'centre of narrative gravity'. We just want the stories of our lives to make sense.

My phone rang.

I didn't want to answer it. I did so anyway, hand trembling. It was her. *It.*

She said: 'What are you doing?' I winced. 'Who do you think you're kidding?' Somehow, I knew where this was going. I pulled the phone slightly away from my ear, sensing the coming diatribe. 'C'mon! You don't need to be looking into your genes. Much less some other guy's. You need to be looking into your own heart!' Here it came now. And I was really starting to hate this bitch. 'You need to resolve your own issues about the loss of your brother!'

'Fuck right off!' I barked back. 'What do you even know about it? You . . . fucking phone!'

I punched at the device's power button with a palsied finger, stormed back inside, plugged myself in, and didn't get up again for ten hours.

Ten hours later, I had it.

Riding carefully home (once again, I probably didn't enjoy that razor edge of focus that's so salutary when one is riding an engine down the street), I reviewed my results mentally.

Okay, so what the pattern was, or what it looked like at any rate, was in fact another checksum – similar to the one in the test data I'd thrown together over the weekend. That's why the bot found it within a few seconds – it had already learned how to recognize checksums.

This one wasn't of ASCII values, and it wasn't even precisely a checksum – both of which facts made it harder to find. Though, kind of eerily, the marker, the checksum, appeared every 128 characters – half of the one in my test string. (Then again, 128 is a power of two, two to the seventh, so not the most surprising periodicity to find in nature.)

At any rate, to cut to the chase . . . essentially, to see this sequence, if it is one, you have to jump through three hoops. First, assign a numerical value to each codon. As A'hib had explained it, a codon is a triplet made from three of the four characters A, C, G and T. And so there are 64 possible codons. (Power of two again.) Okay. So we simply view AAA as having a numerical value of 1, AAC as 2, AAG as 3 . . . all the way up through TTT, with a value of 64. So that's the first trick.

Second is to make every 128th character a checksum of the prior 127.

But third is to recognize that the checksum isn't precisely a checksum. It's a *mod* of a checksum. Since the theoretical values for codons only go to 64, it would be impossible for one codon to represent a sum of the values of the prior 127 (which would be a lot bigger than 64). Instead, the 128th character is had by taking the sum of the prior 127 and *moding* it by 64. Mod – if you're a ways off from sixth-form math – divides one number by another and returns the remainder. So if a sequence of 127 codons sums to 8,405 , then the 128th character would be the remainder of 8,405 divided by 64, or 21.

Or so it freaking well appeared to me. I mean, it took me a while to get to that. I had to work backwards from each step the algorithm performed, reverse-engineering the calculations it had used to get each result. When I'd worked out the threefold method, I went into the DNA sequence and double-checked the algorithm's results by hand. Twice. And right after that, when it started to look like maybe I wasn't hallucinating all this, I went online – nih.gov, a genetics primer, some hot search-engine action – to see if this sort of checksum was, like, some entirely well-known fact about the genome of which I just happened to be magnificently ignorant. But if it was, I remained in ignorance.

And yet again, I only found a half-dozen repetitions of the pattern, a half-dozen checksums, in the sequence A'hib sent. They were right at the tail end. Did they continue, in further sections of the DNA I didn't have? Still, with only a few occurrences, it could have been coincidence.

Well, no, okay, it couldn't have been coincidence. There's no way 127 codons would just happen to sum and mod to the value of the 128th. *Six times in a row.*

Oh, and one last thing. If you're also not real familiar with encoding and compression terminology . . . the reason they call it a 'checksum' is that it allows for error checking. Typically, you create a checksum of a bunch of data before you encrypt it and/or send it over a network. At the other end of the wire, if it turns out the numbers in the sequence do not sum to what's listed as the checksum, then you know the data got corrupted somewhere along the line.

Of those six repetitions of the pattern I found? Just one of the checksums was very slightly off. It was as if . . . and, you know, I'm probably overreaching here . . . as if there had been a slight corruption of the data – a *mutation* – somewhere between my reading of the pattern and . . . somebody else's writing of it.

*

Telephony's a justly obsolescent technology, invasive and imprecise. You can't deal with a phone call ten minutes from now. You can't review the contents of a phone call, file it, search it, copy and paste a section into another phone call, nor forward it to someone else for action. Phone calls put people on the spot. I never call anybody whose email address I've got. Which is everyone I know.

But the second I was pretty sure about what I was looking at, pattern-wise, I picked up the phone and dialled the main number at GenenW. I navigated the voicemail company directory to A'hib Khouri. When I got him on the line, I asked him how quickly he could sequence and forward the next five megabytes or so immediately following the sequence he'd just sent me.

That certainly got his attention.

He said it was going to be an overnight job at best (assuming he could swipe time on one of their high-speed sequencers). He said he'd get back to me, which assurance I had no reason to doubt, and then he hung up on a dime.

I rode home, locked the door, and huddled up with my chimp and my pepper spray, waiting for the morrow. And for the five meg of new data.

Twenty-seven

In the morning it had rained. And was carrying on raining.

You'll recall from my earlier explication of the rules of Bay Area weather that this is not really allowed – rain outside of the rainy season, that is. Still, it happens. Like solar eclipses. And the rain, with its attendant morning mist, created a not dissimilar atmosphere of unreality and ominousness.

I ran through all the required motions of shower, toilette, dressing.

As I sat on the edge of the bed, leaning over to lace up my boots, a scurrying on the floor caught my eye – something locomoting quickly and purposefully toward me. Bent at the waist, I squinted at its approach – and finally made it out as a large pollen spore. So it wasn't alive, nor locomoting toward me, after all. Or was it? It had a stem and several intricate, wing-like branches. It had been designed by evolution to do just this – to scoot around. It just ran on wind power, rather than on biomass. It was doing what the universe wanted it to do, no less than if it had been a bug, or a bloke, or something more 'alive'.

I sat down for my customary breakfast with Erasmus, fresh fruit and juice. I've mentioned that bonobos are largely vegan – fruitarian, in fact. Funny thing about fruit: it's the only food that 'wants' you to eat it, in an evolutionary sense – which is to say it's happy to be devoured, knowing you'll later scatter its seeds about (ensconced in nice dollops of fertilizer).

Rain notwithstanding, I guessed the universe wanted me to go to work. Though, technically, it remained silent on the subject. I dug up my rain gear, suited up, and went.

From: real_name@mlhst.freenets.il
To: keq@ctake.com
Subject: ?
Date: Fri, 14 Apr 2006 19:00:12 (GMT +3)

Salaam, my friend. I had not heard from you in a while, and wondered if you are well. Also, I worried about Thad, naturally. I hope he was not too shaken by our course of cold comfort regarding morality, nihilism, sharing a crowded planet without killing one another, etc.

Also, admittedly, those subjects are on my mind. I happen to be sitting in a cafe in Jerusalem on a Friday night, half-curious to see if I explode out the front window before I get through my mail. The Middle East could certainly use a few more people as confused about morality, as enticed by nihilism, as your friend Thad.

Best,
RTR

From: keq@ctake.com
To: rtr@anon.978.org
Subject: Re: ?
Date: Fri, 14 Mar 2006 08:30:52 (PST)

Hello there, dear old RTR. Your thoughtful message was quite timely, and muchly appreciated. Thad's a tough trooper, more so than you know; he can take it. And I'm sure what he WANTS is the truth – whether he finds it to his liking or not.

As for me . . . eh. As usual, it's hard to complain. Life could certainly be a heck of a lot worse. But things are a little strange, in that I've gotten, um, involved in a bit of hoohah that's quite fascinating – but which might not prove salutary to my career, nor possibly to my health, etc.

Tell me: when you know you're really onto something . . . how do you know if it's something you really *should* be onto?

ke

From: ahib@genenw.com
To: keq@ctake.com
Subject: 5 meg mas
Date: Fri, 14 Mar 2006 08:42:02 (PST)

I had to lie, cheat, and steal to get the sequencing time I needed, but here it is. It's the marker you indicated +5 million codons. They're contiguous. Now will you tell me what it is you've found?

A'hib

As I swivelled in my seat, I happened to catch sight of my own face in my conical cubicle mirror (the kind geeks often stick on the edges of their monitors to keep from getting snuck up on). I was wearing some kind of rictus of unsinkable determination. I hadn't been aware of it.

I plugged A'hib's new data into the parsing algorithm.

The result came back in a little over a minute. The pseudo-check-sum pattern continued – for just over four million bytes, most of the new data. Then it stopped.

I chose a few segments at random and checked them by hand. Same deal. Exactly four megabytes of the repeating pattern.

I looked down at my hands. Was I looking at copies, in my flesh, of the pattern on my screen? Repeated in each of my cells, trillions of times in total? It seemed very hard to believe. I wasn't parsing my own DNA. Just some guy's. But the nucleic acid codes, even the junk, were supposed to be nearly identical across members of a species.

So, stipulating that this pattern was there, forming the larger pattern of a hand and tapping away in massed legions right on my dusty keyboard . . . what the hell did it mean? Whole new question, that.

From: real_name@mlhst.freenets.il
To: keq@ctake.com
Subject: Re: ?
Date: Fri, 14 Apr 2006 19:42:35 (GMT +3)

How to tell if something you are really onto is something you really should be onto: it is.

RTR

I took some deep breaths, slumping in my comfy, ergonomic, rolling chair. I wrinkled my nose and brushed away some wilful hair. I checked the clock, and considered the work, work-type work, I should probably be doing. The hell with it. I could certainly now count on Mark Kelly to leave me in peace for a bit. And, I remembered, I could count on the rest of the company doing as well, at least for a while – for the same reason I'd been able to tell Kelly where to stick it: I was basically unfireable.

I opened a new mail message to A'hib, cc'ing Helen. Then I hesitated. This wasn't a secure mailer. Probably Helen, and certainly A'hib, had public encryption keys – but I didn't know what they were. Barring public-key encryption, email is basically postcards. It can be read by anyone with access to any router (or, technically, any bit of pipe) between you and your recipient. I hated to be paranoid; but it's not paranoia if there really are black sedans following you around, fake federal agents questioning you, etc.

I scribbled down the GenenW number, palmed my mobile, exited, and stood in the shelter of an awning. Rain came to ground and splashed on the toes of my boots. I dialled and got A'hib straightaway. I asked if he could meet for coffee – quite soon. Like, now. He could. I suggested he should bring Helen. He agreed. So that was that.

I went back upstairs for my helmet and rain gear.

Going back out, the front door this time, I was swaddled in skintight Gore-Tex, with my helmet on. I could no more be touched by the rain than if I were in a vault. I got on the bike, which I'd actually parked in a space, and cranked it.

As I reached to flip my visor down, a car pulled in front of me – perpendicular to the space, and the bike. A dark sedan, in my path. Albeit with normal, clear windows.

Throwing droplets, the front passenger door opened and an umbrella emerged, with a man behind, then under, it. He wore a suit, gold-rimmed glasses, and neat hair. He trotted the few steps to where I stood over the bike, hailing me by name. It was a question. I didn't respond. He flipped out a wallet with an ID in it.

He said: 'I'm sorry to catch you on your way out. My colleague and I need to ask you a few questions. We're with the USFDA.'

I wound up the engine, popped the clutch, squealed the tyres, ran over the man's foot, curled around the back of their car, and blasted out of the parking lot.

Another nice thing about a motorcycle (even if it doesn't come up very often): you absolutely, positively, cannot catch one with a car.

Twenty-eight

And yet another thing that almost never happens is traffic cops pulling over motorcycles for speeding. The attitude of the law enforcement establishment seems to be, Hey, it's your neck. The worst a gal on a bike is liable to do is maybe dent somebody's side panel as she crushes her own thorax against it. So, have at it – and good luck.

I got to the café in eight minutes.

I'd suggested one in Redwood City, which was still close to all of us. Palo Alto seemed too familiar, too central. It had me spooked. (As did everything, admittedly.)

I parked behind a dumpster in an adjacent alley, went back round the corner, entered, removed my helmet, and took up a position in the back. I was first to arrive. After sitting and dripping on the tile floor for five minutes, I got up and ordered coffee. As I paid, I was startled to notice Helen and A'hib standing under the awning outside. Standing with two uniformed police officers.

Shit.

Or was I overreacting? I had no yardsticks for reasonable reaction in my current situation. I froze, watching the group of four through the glass. They talked back and forth – with, it seemed to me, increasing animation. One of the cops stuck his finger up to A'hib's chest. That tore it. I pushed my way out the door.

One of the officers, the one with the finger, was saying to A'hib: '. . . just calm down, buddy, and take two steps backward.'

Helen, shaking her head, leaned in toward him to read his name tag. She said: 'Excuse me. Pardon me, Officer . . . Frumley. This man's last name is Khouri. How about addressing him as Mr Khouri?'

'Are you kidding?' Officer Frumley seemed untaken with this suggestion.

No one had yet acknowledged my entrance on the scene. I

130

belatedly registered that both officers were white. Something about Helen's posture made me think of it.

'No,' Helen said flatly, 'I'm not kidding. Why do you assume this man is not worthy of your respect? For all you can possibly know, this man is the best playwright the Bay Area will ever produce. Or best shooting guard. Or computational geneticist. What do you know about him?'

'Look,' said the cop, with one word betraying that the balance of power had shifted, 'we're just here to protect people. We got a report of suspicious activity.'

'By a Middle Eastern-looking guy,' Helen said.

The cop moved a jaw muscle. 'They outlawed racial profiling.'

'Nice answer,' Helen said. 'Look, if you want to see identification, we'll be happy to oblige. If you want to take it further, we can get lawyers involved. Otherwise, we're going in for coffee.'

The officer hesitated. 'Enjoy your coffee,' he said.

When we had gotten seated in the back, I said: 'Helen, I admire your civil libertarianism. I really do. One of the reasons I love this country is you've got a bill of rights, which Britain hasn't. But now's a poor time for me, personally, I think, to be having dramatic anti-authoritarian clashes.'

'Why's now worse than any other time?'

I realized I had a lot of explaining to do.

After breezing through an account of the multifarious inquiries into my employment and credit histories . . . of the ubiquitous, dark-tinted, driveby-shooting-mobiles . . . and of the legions of insatiably inquisitive faux-FDA enforcement agents . . . (I decided I couldn't bear to mention the phone calls, i.e. the calls from my phone) . . . I tried to move us right into the interesting bit: the repeating pattern in the genetic sequence.

But while Helen played to type by refusing to be flapped, poor A'hib seemed quite unnerved by my various little contretemps.

'But we're not doing anything wrong,' he protested. 'And GenenW's not under investigation for anything!'

'Would we know if it were?' Helen said from under a single arched brow.

'Anyway,' I said, hands cradling a coffee bowl, 'I told you. They weren't really federal agents.'

'Then who were they?' A'hib was on edge. 'And how do they even know what you and I are doing?'

'Look,' Helen suggested, 'it's just as you said. You're not doing cloning, splicing, or anything that could remotely be construed as illegal. All you're doing is poking around in the genome – which has been, *de facto* and *de jure*, in the public domain, since HGP finished the rough draft of the map.'

A'hib stared at the tabletop. He didn't appear to have been listening. 'They must be reading our mail. Every message we've sent back and forth has been in cleartext.' Belatedly, he looked up. 'Sorry, what did you say?'

'I said the genome's in the public domain. Your project is harmless.'

'No,' said A'hib, suddenly seeming very clear on this. 'No, it's obviously extremely dangerous shit – in a vat so deep we're stirring it with an oar.'

'Just looking around in the junk DNA?'

'No.' A'hib shook his head, seeming calmer now. 'Not just looking.' He tapped his fingers on the Formica tabletop. 'Finding. We've found something.'

'But what?' Helen asked. 'What exactly have you found?'

They both turned to me. I gave them the scoop on the pattern – from numeralization of the triplets to mod'ing of the checksum. From soup to nuts.

The first, the really big, thing was to have them reassure me that this was in fact a new finding. That there wasn't any known predisposition in the human genome, or any sequenced genome, to tabulate checksums on itself. This really was a discovery – a puzzling, anomalous, inexplicable one. Completely freaky, really.

I was very pleased to have two genetics professionals attest to this. I mean, yeah, I'd done some cursory research, but what do I know? This is always a danger when working outside your field – discovering fire, or inventing a wheel, or some such.

But that didn't mean they could tell me what it was. Or what it meant.

'So what the hell is it?' I asked anyway. 'What does it mean?'

Helen exhaled audibly. 'It's not necessarily that weird. I mean, the nucleic acid codes have all kinds of error correction. A checksum's a kind of error correction.'

'A man-made kind,' A'hib said. 'Not something we've ever seen in nature.'

'It's just math,' Helen said. 'An algorithm. It could easily have evolved.'

'It could evolve number assignments to each triplet?'

'It could be . . .' Helen took off her glasses and wiped away some condensation. 'It could be just one of those things. Natural mathematical elegance. Like the golden mean. Like fractals.'

If she was convincing anyone, that person wasn't A'hib.

'It's a message,' he said, with finality.

'From who? To who? How can you know?'

'I just know,' he said. 'It's what I've been looking for. I had a dream.'

'You had a dream,' she said incredulously. 'That God left you a DNA note?'

'I didn't say God,' he said.

I had been silent. 'I had a dream, too,' I said.

'Goddamn,' Helen said. 'Am I the only person of science here? In your dream was there a Post-it note stuck on a double helix?'

I hesitated. She had a point, ridiculing us. 'No,' I said. 'There was a set of directions. Directions out.'

'Look,' Helen said, throwing us a last friendly life-preserver of rationality. 'I know you both know dreams don't mean anything. You can dream there's an elephant in your glove box, but that doesn't mean you'll find one there when you open it in the morning.'

133

'You're right,' A'hib said. He looked at me. 'She's absolutely right. It doesn't mean that.' He looked back to Helen, locking eyes with her. 'But the fact is: it's morning, we've opened the glove box – and there's some species of pachyderm in there.'

Helen let her head fall forward floppily. 'You don't know if it's an elephant. You don't know what it is.' She rolled her head back again. 'Okay. Okay. Just supposing it is a message. How do we read it? How is it encoded?'

I piped up tentatively. 'Well, the pattern presupposes sixty-four values for the triplets. Effectively, that could be a sixty-four character alphabet. If so, we've got just over four million characters of message, using that alphabet.'

'But how do we translate this supposed alphabet?' Helen said.

No one answered. Finally I suggested: 'Well, we could probably all stand to get smarter on linguistics. I knew a guy in the field at Berkeley. I could ring him up. Though, it also strikes me that this problem isn't unrelated to cryptography, A'hib. And, meanwhile, there's certainly a lot of other analysis we could do on the data.'

A'hib looked conflicted. 'But should we?' he asked. 'Keep working on it? With everything that's been going on, I mean.'

'I don't know,' I admitted. 'This is your white whale. Is it worth it to you to keep hunting it?'

He stared out past me and Helen. He said: 'You're on a work visa, right?'

'Yes, I am.'

'Me, too. Though I'm up for citizenship this year.' He paused to exhale heavily. 'I guess we may as well keep chucking harpoons until somebody deports us. Or kidnaps or kills us . . .'

'That's the spirit,' I said. I think perhaps I hadn't wanted to be the first to admit that I was married to this project. To following this trail, if a trail it was . . .

'Plus,' he added, 'how can we fail, with a Brit on the team?'

I smiled gratefully. 'How do you mean?'

'Well, they never would have cracked the German Enigma codes in World War Two, if the Brits hadn't provided that lovely Bletchley

Park in the countryside for all the American codebreakers and computer scientists to work at . . .'

'Cheeky bastard! And the Yanks built a nice facility in New Mexico for Einstein and Bohr to invent the atom bomb!'

Helen, the only American at the table, laughed. 'If you're going to pursue this, one thing you might want to do is start encrypting your mail about it. In fact . . . if you've had guys come by your office looking for you – twice – you really might want to get all the project data off of your work machine. Before someone waltzes in and swipes it.'

'Oh, hell,' I said. 'It's true. Though, I don't know if I dare go back there today. The spooky men from earlier might still be about. I'll go in tomorrow morning and clean up. Management has called a proper holiday – no one should be there over the weekend.'

It was only after we had parted that I remembered the incident with the police outside the café. I hadn't seen any other dark-skinned men around, before or after Helen and A'hib showed up. And the police had seemed to arrive virtually as they did. Which prompted the question: Who had made the call about suspicious activity?

And to whom was our activity suspicious? Not nobody, I was beginning to think.

Twenty-nine

Back in my own bedroom, that evening, I proceeded to get slinky. Very slinky indeed. Fake-leather trousers – with not a square inch of fake leather to spare. Midriff halter top. The usual boots. Then I packed a tiny overnight bag. It was just a couple of essential bits. But I didn't figure to be staying here tonight.

I could have gone to Thad's. But I wasn't going to. Sure, I was interested in my own safety and comfort; but I've got higher values. Strange men were out there looking for me – and I'd much sooner have them find me, than risk leading them to Kennedy and Holden's bedroom.

So instead I was going clubbing. It would be a fine way to get lost for the evening. And, if it didn't take care of the entire night, it could easily take care of the best part of it. And, anyway, it was Friday. Life goes on.

I decided to leave behind Erasmus D, faithful chimpanzee side-kick. While he's unimpeachably loyal and a fine bodyguard (bonobos are peaceable – but not harmless!), still it makes one kind of conspicuous going around with an eighty-pound gorilla. I tried to explain the situation to him, and he tried to understand. I left the computer on so he could surf the web. (More porn, usually, I'm afraid.)

By the time I was ready to go, the rain had stopped, so I ditched the Gore-Tex and wore my usual zipper-festooned biker jacket, over the rave getup. By the time I hit the highway, the sun had poked through the clouds – just in time to set. But the pavement was still slick. I drove accordingly. Like the mortal being in mortal danger I emphatically was.

It was still well pre-clubbing hour when I hit the city. So I angled onto the surface streets, parked, and lingered over a forearm-sized veggie burrito at a hole-in-the-border taqueria in the Mission

District. As I sat and chewed, I checked my phone. No voicemail. Then I checked email, also on the phone. Nothing of note.

Having gotten through as much of the burrito as prudent (for a woman whose top doesn't cover her stomach), I ordered a cerveza, and sat sipping for a while longer. My thoughts were, alack, poor company. Finally, when the hour had crept up into an acceptable range, I headed out.

I'd intentionally picked a club I'd never been to (but had heard mentioned often). Consequently, I had trouble finding it. But, needless to say, no trouble parking when I did. I also got admitted without issue or delay – once I revealed what I had on offer beneath the jacket and the helmet.

I got another drink (a rather fruitier, pricier one) found a seat in the back, and scanned the room. I saw one or two familiar faces (and outfits). But no one I would say I knew. Or who knew me. Much to my frustration, I also discovered I didn't feel hugely like dancing. This was ironic. (*In an Alanis Morissette kind of way*, I mentally added.) Another drink helped. After that, I braved the dance floor.

And then came the advances. Wave upon wave.

Ultimately, I hooked up with the fourth boy who hit on me. I figured anyone with an agenda, anyone who had been following me with this purpose in mind, would have to be either very lucky or very good to come out on top in this particular game. I mean, pardon the immodesty, but on a night like this, in an outfit like this, there is no lack of boys buying tickets for the Me Sweepstakes. (And usually a few girls.)

The pretty, witty boy I did pick, I did so mostly on the strength of the latter trait. I mean, it was clear he wasn't exactly the brightest tool in the happy meal. But he made me laugh. And I hold that a sense of humour is the lens through which you're most likely to get an undistorted glimpse of another person's soul – at least, within the constraints of thirty minutes of shouted pseudo-conversation at a club.

His place was a short cab ride away. He was polite and kind, to my great relief. He was even soft-spoken, outside of the noise tunnel

137

of the club. There was also no sex, just snogging. And, okay, a little manual stimulation. No point in getting all worked up – and staying that way. But, shagging strangers is just too dangerous in San Francisco.

As I said, the club would have killed most of the night. (They go to five or six, I forget which.) But it was a public place. Plus I would have had to stay upright. You're not buying that, are you? Right, then. Fair enough. Was I also lonely? Yes. I was. Also not a little scared. And the prospect of a little human contact, a few hours of physical comfort, is an awfully compelling thing to dangle in front of the lonely and scared. Which is, I'm afraid, what most people are most of the time.

I lay in the bed in the dark, under a thick duvet, close to the floor, listening to the pleasant breathing of this nice stranger a foot away. With him asleep, my thoughts had come skulking back, looking to buttonhole me. Asking awkward questions.

Why, oh why, they asked, was I carrying on with this – when I didn't even feel safe in my own home? Rather than going back to work today, I should probably have gone to the police. Thad could hook me up. I could even take a little time off; I had holiday accumulated. And it wasn't like I was doing my job lately, anyway.

So, why? Why, Santy Claus, why?

All right, thoughts, I thought. You want answers? You want the truth? Fine. The truth was, I believed maybe we really were onto something with this mysterious sequence. With this unheralded pattern in the genetic soup. This suspiciously well-ordered tattoo upon the soul. Maybe what we found would even, in the end, somehow go toward making sense of things. Of life. Of death.

Maybe even of *my* life.

Maybe, having evaded me elsewhere, meaning would turn up here.

Because you've got to believe something will make sense of things, right? I mean, I probably don't, not really, not deep down.

But, nonetheless, you've got to.

When the fluorescent clock ticked over to 6 am, I rose carefully, dressed quietly, walked the twelve blocks to my bike, and drove straight to the office.

For once, the lot was almost completely empty. Like I said, management – sensing imminent stress flame-out – had mandated a proper full weekend for all staff. Plus, it wasn't even eight in the morning. But, even given all that, there were still a couple of vehicles in the lot. One was Thad's truck. Another was a white van. I'd never seen it before. Cleaning crew?

It was rather like Thad to come in on the one weekend he wasn't supposed to. In his way, he's as much a rebel as I am. When I got upstairs, he wasn't in his cube, though his coat was. He'd probably hiked downstairs to the server room. Occasionally, he has to do things sitting at the consoles of the database servers.

I sat and logged in. First thing I did was take all the data from the genome project, zip it up, and encrypt it all with my private key. Then I transferred it over the wire to a server at Berkeley where I still had an account. Now I could get to it from anywhere. But, hopefully, no one else could. Then I deleted the local version of the data, the whole folder – and defragged my hard drive, to erase its ghost. (I hoped.)

Then I checked mail. And another man had high-tailed it out of my life.

From: A'hib Khouri <ahib@genenw.com>
To: keq@ctake.com
Cc: Helen Dolan <helen@genenw.com>
Subject: change of plans
Date: Sat, 15 Apr 2006 03:38:42 (PST)

Listen. What we agreed on. It's all changed now. Those men, the same men you described, they're on to me now. I saw the same black sedan. And when I went home last night, one was sitting in my living room – I saw him through the window. I ran for it, and went back to the office.

I'm starting to believe the sequence, the pattern we've found, is a HUGE deal. That it really means something. And that these people want it from us. Look, I'm attaching a zip file, ok? It's got the HGP identifier of the specific genome we used, details on the sequencing method, and, mainly, the exact location of the sequence on the genome. I've DES encrypted the whole thing using the first 128 bits in the pattern (triplet values) as a key. You should easily be able to decrypt it – but whoever's been snooping our mail won't. DON'T LET ANYTHING HAPPEN TO THIS.

I'm going to get out of the country, at least for a while, back home. If you don't hear from me . . . actually, I have no idea what to tell you to do with this. But I for one am going to keep trying to decode it. Just somewhere safer.

-A'hib

I pulled off A'hib's encrypted file and sent it up to Berkeley behind the earlier one. Then I deleted the mail. And I knew just what I needed right about then: Thad. I was going to find him, I was going to tell him everything. And he was going to make everything okay. Everybody else had let me down or gone away – but Thad never would. Thad never would.

I took the stairs, two at a time, down to the server room. Reaching the outer door, I realized I'd left my security badge. Stupid. I knocked on the steel door. No one opened it. Thad might be wearing his headphones. I went back up the stairs, two at a time. As I reached for the handle on the inside of the stairwell door, my phone rang, from its clip on my belt. I stopped dead. I considered. I had a feeling.

I answered it.

'Don't go out there,' it said, the phone that is, naturally, betraying a sense of alarm that ill-comported with the serene voicemail voice.

'Oh?' I said. 'Why not? Afraid I'm getting close to the secret?'

'No,' she said. 'You're getting close to danger. Crack the door. Just a crack. And peek down the hall.'

I snorted sceptically. But I did as instructed. After cracking the door gingerly, I stuck some curls out, and a forehead, then an eye. The way the door opened, I could see straight down the wide hallway, which was lined with cubicles on both sides – ending with Thad's, and then mine. Two men were standing in my cube. They were wearing black suit jackets – and hats. I pulled the door shut.

I pressed my back against the cold concrete of the wall, and put the phone back to my ear. I said: 'Right. Who the hell is that, then?'

'I've got to go,' the phone said. Where does a phone have to go? 'Just wait until they leave, then you can go back for your things. Good luck.'

'Hey. Hey!' But I was talking into a dead line. I snapped the phone shut.

I had to admit that sounded like good advice. The men out there couldn't get the sequence, as it wasn't there any more. I cracked the door again. And I saw they were now exiting my cube – carrying my desktop machine! Feckers!

Now I was brassed off. You can't bloody well just come into my place of business and make off with my computer. It's a violation.

I looked again. The two of them, each holding one end of the CPU tower, were walking away, towards the stairwell at the other end of the hall. Away from me, from my cube – and from Thad's.

I squeezed out the door and fast-walked down the carpeted hallway, staring fearfully at the backs of the men. When I reached Thad's cube, I ducked into it. Crouching low, I opened the top desk drawer, reached over its lip, and felt around. When my hand appeared again, it had a matt black SIG-Sauer P228 in it.

I slipped it out of its nylon holster. I wrapped my fingers around its moulded rubber grips, feeling the weight. I flicked the safety off with my thumb. I looked down at myself: I was tarted up in skin-tight, faux-leather trousers and a midriff halter top. I was holding a huge gun. And how could any of that be wrong? I stepped out into the hallway.

The two men, juggling my machine, had just reached the other stairwell door. I raised the gun at their backs. I shouted: 'Oi! You two! Don't drop that!'

After startling and stopping dead, the two turned to face me. They gently lowered the machine to the floor. And they straightened up. My eyes went wide.

They were Hasidic Jews.

The hats I had glimpsed were stovepipe-style, with flat, circular brims – and they had curly sidelocks of hair hanging out of them. Under the black suits, they wore white shirts and black ties. One of them had Coke-bottle glasses.

I almost laughed out loud. I quickly lowered my gun, embarrassed.

But before I knew what was what, the two of them had raised guns back at me. Pointed at me! And mine was still pointing at the floor, in which attitude it appeared it would stay. The two Jews, covering me unflinchingly, walked smoothly forward.

They were walking me down.

Dammit.

As they drew within ten feet, one of them, the one with the glasses, shifted his gun to his left hand. With his right, he reached into his jacket pocket and produced a rag and a small bottle. I imagined I could see where this was going.

I screamed. I made it a good, ripping one.

With that, the two pounced on me. In a heartbeat, they'd dis-armed me, clutched my body, and pressed a very medicinal-smelling cloth over my mouth and nose. I had the presence of mind not to breathe, which I figured I could carry on not doing for about a minute. I couldn't decide whether to struggle against their grip on me. It would use air.

As I pondered, facing back down the hall, I saw the first stairwell door – the one I'd come out of – swing open. A figure stepped briskly into the middle of the hall.

That figure was Thaddeus Gottlieb.

Thirty

Only one of the two men held me now. But he held me well. The other had taken a step to the side. With that much delay, and no more, they raised their arms – and began firing their guns. The atmosphere around us thickened and overloaded with expanding gas and splattering reports. The air rippled. My eyes slammed shut like books.

When I opened them a second later, when the reports had taken pause, and their terrible echoes faded, Thad was gone. He no longer stood at the end of the hall. Nor was he lying in it. He just wasn't there. He'd completely vanished.

The man holding me did so with one arm, locked around my head, the crook of his elbow pressing the damp rag against my face. For some reason, then, he spun me around behind him, away from where Thad had been, as if he were . . . shielding me with his body? I found myself facing the opposite way, back up the wide hallway.

With that, I realized I'd resumed breathing – resulting in a *massive* head rush. Just as it occurred to me to try and break free, I found I had little strength to do it with.

And then the gunshots started up again – as good and loud as the first volley. Then, as suddenly as before, they stopped. Then began again – and as the man behind me fired, I could feel his body pivoting from left to right.

Then silence.

Then firing again – while pivoting from right to left.

I couldn't see anything. I couldn't think. I hadn't any idea what was going on.

Both guns carried on firing, for just another second; then only one gun; then a loud click of metal. And both guns had gone silent.

Vision sliding out of focus, body sagging into the arm that held me, I heard a crack, a yelp of pain – and then a thud. Then another crack, another shout – and the arm had let me loose. With nothing holding me up, I collapsed. Right into Thad's arms.

He looked down into my half-lidded eyes, wearing the exact same serious and respectful expression as ever. Oh, my God. I was swooning. The ceiling spun above us.

And then another gunshot rang out, just a single one, from further away. A mist of red puffed into my field of vision. I blinked from it, automatically, not understanding. When my eyes opened, Thad had gone again. And I felt the floor pressing heavily into the back of my head.

I managed to roll over onto my stomach. At which I discovered Thad lying just beside me, on his stomach, prone, arms outstretched – aiming a gun with both hands. It looked to be . . . his own gun, the SIG. I followed the ray of the gun barrel.

Forty feet further along, in front of the original stairwell door, there stood another man in black. A third man. I'd never seen him. He was pointing at us. As I tried to bring him into focus, more noise exploded beside me, rounds triggering off from Thad's gun, accelerating like a pull-started lawnmower.

I watched the third man leave his feet, recede down the hallway as if sucked through a hose, and then collapse in a black, angular pile of himself.

My cheek lay on my outstretched arm. I couldn't even swivel to look at Thad beside me. I succumbed to sleep like a woman tumbling off a pier.

I Woke Up In The Back Of A Moving Ambulance

A man sat beside me, wearing a suit, with the jacket off. He had a badge on one side of his belt and a holstered gun on the other. He said:

'Hey! How are you feeling there, ma'am?'

I realized I was strapped down to a gurney. I wiggled. The man hastily loosened my straps. He asked again, 'How are you doing?'

I pushed myself up on my elbows.

'Thad,' I said simply.

'Thad's good,' the man quickly answered. 'Thad's fine. Don't worry. He was shot. But the bullet just creased his leg. It sprayed a bit of blood around, but it was a lot less serious than it looked.' The man had a very solicitous and comforting manner. He looked Hispanic. He put his hand gently on my upper arm. 'We got him bandaged up, and he walked out of the building himself. Hardly even limped.'

I slumped back down again. My head felt clear; but my body seemed to be running on dead batteries.

The man beside me hesitated a few beats. Then he said: 'My name is Detective Robert Santillan. I'm with the Palo Alto police department.' He paused again, holding my gaze. 'Can you tell me who the men were who attacked you?'

I exhaled heavily. 'What he did back there . . . I just can't believe it.'

The detective raised his eyebrows. 'Thad? It looks like he saved your life, yes. Or at least saved you from abduction. Also . . . I can tell you he really read us the riot act about taking care of you. And you had better believe nobody wants to have to answer to Gottlieb. Not on this one.'

I was still trying to get my mind around what I'd seen – or, really not quite seen – Thad do in that hallway. Looking off into the distance, trying to recreate the scene, I muttered: 'I mean . . . I know he used to be in the military . . .'

The detective laughed gently. 'Is that what he told you? Yes, you could say he was in the military. He was a staff sergeant in the US Army's 1st Special Forces Operational Detachment – Delta.' The detective used a tone of careful understatement. 'Delta Force.'

'What is that?' I asked. 'Is that like commandos, or special forces . . .?'

The detective sighed. 'Special forces, yes. It's like . . . it's like being in the military, except at the level of the NFL. It's like being a professional athlete – except the sport is killing people.' He seemed to sense this was a little grim. 'Look, you know Thad is in our reserve

145

officer program, where he holds the rank of sergeant? We don't have any other reserve officers who are sergeants. When we saw his application – and checked that his background was what he said it was – we fell all over ourselves to get him in the door.'

I squinted and shook my head. 'He told me he does traffic duty . . .'

'Yes, sometimes. And sometimes he trains our SWAT team.'

They Made Me Stay In The Hospital For Twenty-Four Hours

I'm pretty sure this was more to have me where they could keep an eye on me, than from any legitimate medical need. There was already a uniformed officer in place outside the door of the room when they wheeled me in. The detective, Santillan, got me settled, then told me he'd be back to talk later, when I was feeling stronger.

The room was private, clean, and prettily white. Warm sunlight splashed onto my lap through the drapes. I power-tilted the bed up a bit and settled in. It occurred to me this was as good a place as any to spend a lazy Saturday. And lots safer than some.

Erasmus would be fine. And no one was expecting me anywhere.

I read *People* magazine, just for the camp value, until sleep took me again.

I couldn't believe how long I slept. It must have been some combination of the drugged cloth, the shock of the attack – and the minimal sleep the night before. When I woke it was dark out.

And I woke to the sound of struggle. Shouting.

By the time I got my bearings, the door had flown open and men were rushing the room. They were also dressed strangely. But differently so.

Some kind of robes this time.

Fuck this noise, I thought, as the men fell upon me. *Fuck this right in the ear.*

146

Thirty-one

So there's this notion of 'local fitness peaks' in the evolutionary landscape. The idea is that Darwinian fitness doesn't plot, on a multi-dimensional matrix, as a single towering mountain of best practices for survival and reproduction. Instead, there are lots of little peaks, groups of traits that work well together, niches of specialization. For instance, humans have done well by mastering a certain cognitive niche. We're slow, we're weak, we have dull teeth and no claws, and we can't smell worth a damn or even see in the dark. But we're very good at out-thinking the competition. It works for us.

But one problem with local fitness peaks is that they're peaks – you can go to the top of them and no higher. Once you've fully optimized all the traits that make up that niche, there's nothing to do but make a living and hang out. Which leads to the second problem: evolutionary landscapes change, often violently. That is to say, the hill of which you are currently the king is probably going to fall out from under you. Just for an example, there might be massive global climate change, or a killer bacterium, or any of a number of things that might make your set of specialized traits totally worthless.

Which leads to the third problem: organisms (and organizations, as well) spend quite a lot of time and energy fighting their way to the tops of fitness peaks – getting really good at whatever they've decided to be good at. But if the landscape is eventually going to change, and that peak is going to disappear, the only way to survive long-term is to pick a different fitness peak and fight your way anew to the top of that one. But – and you can probably see where this is going – to move to a new peak requires first descending *back down* the fitness landscape. It requires becoming intentionally, *by definition*, less fit, worse at what one does, in order to find that next new way to be good again.

And most of us are wildly averse to becoming less fit, much less doing so intentionally. In fact, evolution emphatically doesn't support this type of manoeuvre – only new traits which improve fitness straight away get selected for. Evolution can't think ten steps ahead, or see around bends in the road.

Which is probably why the vast majority of species eventually go extinct.

These new bad guys had shown the good grace to simply put a hood over my head and tie my hands behind my back, rather than drug me. They were even relatively gentle (this is relative to the earlier bad guys). Still, all in all, I felt like throwing up. I'm sure I couldn't have taken being knocked out again.

When the hood finally came off, the first thing I saw was more blackness. I heard footsteps and a door creak open and closed again. Then a dim bulb came on overhead. And the second thing I saw was Helen Dolan's lovely, cappuccino-toned face. Albeit, she was looking about as expressionless and sardonic as she always did. As if being kidnapped were just one more goddamned thing.

We were both tied to chairs, with our hands behind our backs. My bonds felt secure, but not painful. I smiled weakly.

'Fancy meeting you here,' I said to Helen.

'Hiya,' she said back.

And that seemed to be about all we had to say to each other just then. I nodded cordially and let my gaze wander off. I checked out the room. It was your basic fifteen-by-twenty prisoner's cell, with a bare bulb, water stains on the ceiling, and a single door. Well, okay, it looked more like somebody's basement washroom than the Count of Monte Cristo's dungeon abode. But I was using my imagination.

Finally it occurred to me to ask: 'How'd they get you?'

'Oh,' Helen said. 'I went home from work last night and they grabbed me when I walked in my door. I think I broke at least one nose before they wrestled me down. They didn't seem to be expecting rough stuff.'

'Well done.'

'Yeah, exciting, huh. How about you?'

I told her all about the shootout at the office. She didn't seem to react – except to the bit about the Hasidic outfits. Then her eyebrows knitted and she looked out past me for a moment. I didn't think anything of it. I felt the same way: deeply confused. I went on to detail the raid on my hospital room, about which there weren't many details.

'So Thad's okay?' she finally asked.

'Yes, thank God. I tell you, you think you know somebody . . .'

She snorted lightly and nodded. As if to say, *You have no idea . . .*

The door to the room opened.

Two men appeared. They both wore all black. However, what I had mistaken for robes in the chaos of the hospital room I saw now were very long shirts, knee-length, buttoned at the neck. Under this, they wore sheer, almost pyjama-like trousers. They both had black beards and somewhat wild, matted hair. Even more disturbingly, as they stepped in I saw they both had painted marks on the dark skin of their foreheads: a curved white line around a red blotch.

Any words I might have had stopped in my throat.

Without preamble, and with calm and workmanlike expressions, the men stepped over to Helen and began to untie her. As the ropes came free, one of the two held her by the arm – but almost respectfully, it seemed to me. He guided her to her feet and out the door, and the other one closed it behind them.

And so there I was left in the dim glare and silence, *sans* recourse, *sans* dignity – and *sans* Helen. I slumped in my chair, picked a focal point way out past the facing wall, and tried to think.

Clearly, the old fitness landscape had dropped completely out from under me. In this new environment, my education and skills were of no value. I couldn't code or hack or architect my way out of this one. My outsize value in the high-tech labour market afforded me precisely no leverage, and exactly zero options. Even my looks were probably more of a liability than anything – as I was at the mercy of men who could rape me at whim. All of my painstakingly developed traits summed to . . . precisely dick.

Yep, this was surely a landscape all-new, and entirely unfamiliar.

149

I didn't even know which way was up – i.e. what would get me killed versus what would help me to survive. I mean, seriously, I had been doing things like conducting possibly illegal genetics research, running away from putative federal agents, and confronting computer-pilfering killer Hasids with borrowed firearms.

I was pretty sure I'd just navigated myself straight into a fitness sewer.

An hour had passed, at a guess, when I heard the first muted sounds of gunfire. That was also about when I'd decided to get out of my own head and start worrying, instead, and in earnest, about Helen. It turned out I didn't even have enough savvy to know whether the gunfire should make me worry more or less.

There were multiple flavours. Single pops, then long rolling bursts. More single pops. Though these all came through the walls and ceiling muted, more like thumps than pops. Were the police rescuing us? Or were the kidnappers executing Helen, with excessive élan? Were they all firing guns in the air like a crazed militia?

Fuck fuck fuck.

Oh, the hell with it. For all I knew, it was probably a third set of malefactors, coming to spirit me away to some all-new place of helpless confinement. Lacking any conceivable alternative course of action, I settled in and waited to see what happened.

A minute or two later the door opened.

Behind it stood Helen. She presented as untied, and unheld. She looked alert, but sanguine. She came over and began to free me. As she stepped out of the doorway, another figure came into view behind her.

This second figure wore close-fitting, full-body, tan fatigues and lightweight hiking boots, and was sighting intently down a menacing, stubby, high-tech-looking assault rifle – holding it at the shoulder and covering the outside hallway to the right. As Helen took the last strand from my wrists, and I stood up, the figure pivoted smoothly to cover the hallway in the other direction – and, in the process, swung a dark-brown, neatly braided ponytail over one shoulder.

150

I stopped and stared. I could now see the newcomer had an attractive oval face with fine features, no makeup, and an expression of perfect, focused calm. She stood in profile, one eye half-closed, squinting levelly through her glowing gunsight, her shooting posture perfect, cool as a marble statue in deep shade.

In an unwavering, indeterminately accented voice, she said: 'Time to go.'

And that was my initial, and enduring, impression of Basha Levy. Holding a huge gun and leading us out of the desert.

Thirty-two

I suppose I forgot to mention I was wearing, all this time, a hospital nightie and booties. There seems to be a firm rule against hospital admission for persons wearing any outfit less monumentally ridiculous than this one. Notwithstanding the ever-present danger of my bottom hanging out the back of the gown, I ran with unselfconscious vigour out of our place of confinement. I did so on the heels of the woman with the rifle, hastily covering the length of wallpapered hallway outside, then leaping up a carpeted flight of stairs. Helen brought up the rear.

On what I took for the ground floor, the woman gestured through an open doorway and said: 'Your effects are there. You may want to retrieve them.' I hesitated before darting into a large but spare room, ringed with stacks of cardboard boxes and . . . were those spears propped against the wall? Mercifully, I did not confront any visual evidence – other than some bullet holes in the decor – of the recent gunplay.

Laid out on a folding table I quickly found my trousers, top, boots, jacket and dainties. And overnight pack. And phone! I realized at least two groups of strangers must have gathered up and transported these things for me to be reunited with them now. But I didn't ponder this long. I scooped them up in an armload and hustled back to the others.

With that, we exited the building (a two-storey residential house, perched on an isolated hill), piled into what smelled like a rental car, and headed for the horizon.

The stranger drove. Helen rode shotgun. And I lay in the back seat and dressed.

'My name is Basha,' she said, still wearing her jumpsuit, but stripped now of webbing, pouches – and assault rifle. 'For now, let us stipulate that I work for a friendly, though non-Western, government.'

I could not place her accent – which might have told me some of what she would not. It sounded sort of Slavic, but sort of not. Then again, I hadn't heard more than a dozen words of her speech prior to this – including over the course of a two-hour drive. She had put off all of our questions but two. ('Where are we going?' I'd asked. 'Into the Santa Cruz mountains.' 'Um . . . where did we start?' 'Freemont.')

Now, the three of us were tucked away in a small cottage, part of a redwoods-nestled lodge complex in the hamlet of Boulder Creek – as warranted, smack in the Santa Cruz mountains. This structure consisted of a single main room with adjacent bathroom and kitchen area. The decor could be called rustic. The setting was private. And it would no doubt feel quite peaceful – to anyone capable of such a feeling.

'Forgive me,' I said. 'Because I really do, I'm sure we both do, appreciate you having rescued us. Thank you very much for that. But . . . why exactly are we being subject to the attentions of a "non-Western government"? And do we have a choice in the matter?'

She regarded me for a second – knowingly, it seemed. Or perhaps indulgently. 'You already have the attention of the US government,' she said. 'But I do not think it could be described as entirely favourable to you.'

'Why is that?'

'For one thing, the man from your parking lot is, I believe, still icing his foot.'

'Oh, dear,' I said. 'That was a real federal agent?'

'Surely,' she said. 'But not FDA. From the Department of Homeland Security. Science and Technology Directorate.'

'How do you know all this?' I asked. 'How can you know I ran over his foot?'

'I read his email,' she said flatly. 'At any rate, my point is this: if I were the two of you, I would not necessarily be too well disposed toward players of one nationality versus another. Of course, the US government is not any worse than the next one over. But, still, their

153

intelligence agencies are as much a force for good as the wind is blowing.'

Helen hadn't spoken through all this. I don't think she'd said anything since the rescue. I had judged from her silence and cautious stare that she wasn't investing much trust in our bene- factor. However, upon hearing this last comment, her expression seemed to lighten – her eyes, perhaps, even smiled. She said:

'Hey, good, bad, you're the one with the gun. And I'm pretty sure there's something you want from us.' She tilted her head down and arched her eyebrows. 'Right?'

Basha looked away, a little breezily, and then back. She said: 'Per- haps I am merely a guardian angel. Perhaps your God has sent me to engineer your salvation.'

'Stranger things have happened,' Helen answered instantly.

'Stranger than all this?' Basha countered. 'No – actually, they have not. But, of course, this is not the hand of God. It never is. Though sometimes it may as well be . . .'

This last she seemed almost to say to herself. But then she came back to the room and looked each of us in the eye, in turn. 'Of course,' she said. 'You have no reason to trust me. But, still, you have questions you would like for me to answer. I invite you to ask them.' She stopped speaking and sat still, watching.

I cleared my throat meekly. I said: 'Who were the men who attacked us?'

'Which ones?'

'Right,' I said. 'Um, the first ones, who shot up my office. The Jewish ones.'

'They were radical Qabbalists.' With that she went silent again.

'Okay, I'll bite,' I said. 'Why did radical Qabbalists want my com- puter?'

'What was on that computer?' Basha replied, with just a trace of a grin. 'No, never mind. We both know what was on it – or what they thought would be.' She paused and smoothed her jumpsuit at the waist. 'But is it not obvious why they wanted it? Or perhaps you are not so conversant with Qabbalah?'

I nodded embarrassed assent. I saw that Helen sat stony and silent again.

Efficiently, and with regular intonation, Basha recited: 'It is a 2000-year-old system of Jewish mysticism and esoteric theosophy. It exists in many aspects – a cosmogony of emanation, methods for spiritual ascent, methods for controlling spirits and demons. But at its heart it is very much mathematical, or numerical. Qabbalah assigns numerical equivalents to the letters of the Hebrew alphabet. These values are used to study and decode the text of the Torah. So while that sacred text, in its literal interpretation, serves as a daily guide to proper conduct in life and religious observance . . . it also has a shadow level of deeper and concealed meaning. According to their arcane rules, and with years and decades of study and illumination . . . Qabbalists believe that the hidden word of God may be revealed and understood.'

She paused. After this impromptu discourse, the silence stood thick and palpable in the dim room. A bit of breeze swayed the redwood branches through the window beside the bed, on which I sat. Finally, Basha asked us:

'Does any of that sound familiar?' She looked particularly at Helen. 'God's literal expression of life in the world – also invested with a hidden, coded meaning?'

Helen said: 'So you're suggesting these Qabbalists are now genomicists?'

'Is this surprising? The Torah is an expression of God – but so is humanity. He inscribed both with His hand. If there are secret messages encoded in the one . . .'

'All right,' I said. 'That makes a creepy sort of sense. DNA's a kind of language, with an alphabet and a vocabulary and expressive of things. So if God wrote it, he could also have encoded secret messages in it. But none of that explains how these guys knew about what we were working on. Or why they came after us.'

'Their interest in these matters is not casual,' Basha said. 'They

155

have been monitoring, closely, with avid interest, the progress of the Human Genome Project, along with Celera Genomics.' Celera, I knew from A'hib, was Craig Venter's company, formed to race the Human Genome Project to a completed map of the genome. 'As well as other biotechnology concerns. They have been watching – from the shadows. And also from not so far in the shadows.'

'What, they have spies? Among us?'

Basha looked noncommittal. 'I do not have specific information. But there is a toolbox for such work. Embedded operatives might be in theirs. Surveillance, wire-tapping, and paid informants almost certainly are.'

'How about guns?' I asked, my voice cracking. 'Trying to kill my friend and colleague?' This seemed to be my first opportunity, in all the madness, to pause and be angry about what had happened to us. I guess I'd been too shocked to feel indignant.

'Try to understand,' she said. 'Qabbalah is practised widely – and for the most part harmlessly. But this particular group is brutal. They are known as the Cabal – the one word actually derives from the other. And you must abandon your image of gentle, slightly silly, sidelocked Hasids. These ones are different. For instance, they are at least loosely connected with the Kahanists.'

Either I or Helen must have drawn a visible blank, as she added: 'Meir Kahane was a radical Zionist, who wanted to transfer the Arab population of Israel and the territories to Arab, or at any rate other, lands. He was assassinated in 1990. It was a follower of Kahane who shot thirty-four Muslims in the al-Ibrahimi mosque in 1994. The point of this being: these are the sorts of people who do not necessarily mind leaving a lot of hats on the ground. They are zealots – nothing matters to them except what matters to them. And they believe that what is up for grabs now may be nothing less than a direct pipeline to God.'

Even with this chilling description, Helen looked more thoughtful than afraid; she looked very unlike I felt. My face frozen, I sat staring at the aged and slightly warped wood of the floor. Finally, voice unsteady, I asked: 'So what do they want from us?'

Basha reached over and put her hand gently on my knee. I looked up into her eyes, which glinted as she said: 'I was hoping we might take a look at just that.' She rose, walked to the corner, pulled a laptop from a duffel bag, and set it booting on the bed beside me. I managed a weary smile. Helen just shook her head.

Thirty-three

'I don't actually have it on me,' I quickly disclaimed.

'No, and good thing,' said Basha, speaking to me but looking at the screen of the laptop as she booted it up. 'You were wise to divest yourself of it. But I trust you left a copy where you can retrieve it.'

'If we can get online, yes.'

'Not a problem. We have wireless here.'

'But is that safe?' Helen interjected. 'Could we be traced back?'

'We could not,' said Basha, spinning the laptop on the bed toward me. 'I have a VPN in place from here to my server back home – strong crypto, a steel pipe. And even if our packets are sniffed and traced, they will not lead to this place.'

'Where will they lead?' asked Helen, a bit pointedly.

Basha didn't answer, but merely watched me and waited.

I logged into my Berkeley account. I downloaded the encrypted project file – which took only a few seconds, less time than I would have liked to think about the next step. I went ahead and grabbed my private key. It still required my password to unlock.

I paused. I looked over at Helen, who held my gaze.

Basha interpreted, correctly, this silent communication. She said: 'I cannot help you with matters of faith. You two should take a moment to discuss it – before making a decision about whether to trust me.' With that, she rose and left out the front door.

Helen's expression, as ever, was a cipher. Through the front window, I could see Basha walking away. And I had the confusing feeling of being now in *less* familiar company. Matters of faith, indeed . . . I looked back to Helen.

'What do you think?' I said.

'I have my doubts,' she said. 'We could just leave. The two of us.'

'And go where? Back to the police, in my case? Who's going to protect us, if not her?' I sighed and sank down. 'Oh, I don't know. Maybe you're right.'

My phone beeped once from my belt, the text message beep. I looked down, then back up at Helen. She didn't speak. I pulled the phone and read the screen. It said:

> Since u ignored my advice & got in2 all this, u'd better learn 2 trust ur instincts. But 4 now, I'll tell u this: B's here b/c she's ur friend. But H has an agenda! B careful what u let her talk u in2. L8r, P

For the love of God.

Helen gave me a *Well?* eyebrow arch.

'Text message,' I said tiredly, replacing the phone. 'Just spam.' Boy, I hate lying. But how do you explain to someone your phone's got it in for them? This was all getting way too complicated.

I shook my head, in part to clear it. I said: 'Well, I'll say this: Basha seems a damn sight friendlier than all the other people who've come after us lately. And if she meant us harm, she certainly could have done it already.'

'She hasn't gotten the sequence out of us yet,' Helen countered.

'And who's to say she shouldn't? We don't even know what it is we're guarding. Maybe she can tell us. Or help us figure it out.' With that, I got up – too quickly to entertain objections – and went out the door after Basha.

Leaning over the laptop, backs sloping, faces bathed in LCD glare, the three of us pored over the project data. I pointed out the location of the sequence on the genome (which Helen was able to put in context for us), as well as some sample screens of the code itself. Then I ran the pattern matcher, showed how it went off, stepped through the log file – then demonstrated a few iterations of the pattern (or, rather, the math behind it).

'Oh my,' said Basha. 'This pattern is truly in everyone? In all human DNA?'

'With minor variations,' Helen said.

Helen, as the domain expert, drove the laptop now. She tabbed through some screens of data; then ran the pattern matcher again. Brow deeply furrowed, dark-brown eyes glinting in the pixel-light, she scrolled intently through the results screens.

'You missed something,' she said finally. 'There's a second-order pattern.'

Basha and I leaned in. 'How do you mean?' I asked.

'You didn't look all the way to the 128th iteration of the pattern. The last codon in the 128th set . . . here, look . . . every . . . 16,384th codon. It doesn't mod as a checksum of the prior 127. It's a mod of the checksum of the *prior 127 checksums*. It's not just groups of 128 codons. It's groups of 128 groups of 128 codons.'

'You're right,' I said. 'I didn't see that.'

'But your algorithm did,' Helen said. 'It's all in the output. But I can understand how you might miss it. Particularly if you were in a hurry.'

I looked at Basha now. She too was squinting, and looking off through the wall.

'So you can tell us what this means?' I asked her bluntly.

'What?' Basha had to refocus as she looked back to me. 'No, I do not know if I can tell you what it means.' She went and sat at the desk again. 'But I have a few ideas. Mostly not my own. But ideas.'

'Whose then?' Helen asked, pushing the computer away from her.

Basha didn't answer directly. She looked at the floor as she said: 'You know . . . we even had a pet name for this, should it turn out to exist. It was entirely hypothetical, of course. We did not think the Qabbalists, or the other groups . . . or the genomicists and biotechs they were tracking . . . we did not think they would ever turn up any such thing.'

I was beginning to feel frustration. 'What sort of thing?'

'We called it the Pandora sequence. Just to have a name. For a hypothetical message in the DNA. The object of the Qabbalists' search, that is. Hypothetical or no.'

'So you're saying we've opened a Pandora's Box?' I asked.

Basha exhaled thoughtfully, then looked me in the eye. 'Not

quite. Most people know only that part of the story – with the box. But there is more to the Pandora myth.'

She rose and went to the kitchen alcove, opened the refrigerator, and removed a bottle of water. She gestured, offering same to me and Helen. We both assented and she brought three back to our circle. She sat and continued.

'Yes, the gods gave Pandora a box, warning her never to open it. And, overcome by her curiosity, she did so anyway – and out flew "plagues for the body and sorrows for the mind". So, Pandora gets a bad rap for that. But it is usually forgotten that Pandora, in the Greek mythos, was also the first woman on Earth.'

Basha sipped her water. Condensation dripped across the smooth olive skin on the top of her hand. She went on, reciting again in her flat narrative tone.

'Before the earth and sea were formed, the universe was in a state of chaos. God reached into this chaos and helped form the realms of the planet: earth, sky, sea and air. Then Zeus gave to the Titans the job of creating living things for the new planet. The Titan Epimetheus made man out of mud, helping him to stand upright – so that he would be the only animal on earth to gaze upward towards heaven.' Basha paused and seemed to give me a bit of a look.

'And then Epimetheus bestowed gifts upon all of earth's other creatures, giving wings to some, cunning or strength to others. By the time he came to man he was out of gifts. He went to his brother Prometheus for help. So Prometheus rode in Athena's chariot up to the sun, where he lit his torch and brought fire down to earth as a gift for mankind. But Zeus was displeased – fire was meant only for heaven. To repay them for their presumption, and also to serve as a counterbalance to the power of the fire, Zeus devised an elaborate punishment for Prometheus and his brother. Namely, women.

'And so Pandora, the first woman, was made in heaven – with every god contributing something to perfect her. Aphrodite gave her beauty, Hermes persuasion, Apollo music . . .' Basha looked from the laptop, to Helen, to me, in turn. 'Even her name, Pandora, means "all-gifted". The gift that Zeus himself gave to her? Curiosity.'

161

There was a silence. Then Helen said, a little archly: 'Well, that's quite a legacy we girls share, then, isn't it?'

Basha seemed to ignore her. Instead, looking at me, she said: 'A legacy whose origins some have been searching for.'

'How do you know that?' I asked. She did not answer. So, instead, I asked: 'Is this what we've found, then? The source of our . . . gifts? Our powers of rational persuasion, of appreciating beauty? Our music, our curiosity? Our singular stance of gazing up at the heavens?'

'Christ,' sighed Helen. 'This is like the coffee shop again.'

'Who can say?' answered Basha. 'We know so little. But perhaps our sidelocked friends are correct. Perhaps it is a message you have found.'

'That's just what A'hib was going on about,' Helen said, obviously exasperated. 'Am I the only non-crack-smoking individual involved in this caper?'

'If it is a message,' I asked Basha, '. . . can we decode it?' I seemed to be joining in this sport of ignoring Helen. (O ye faithless!)

'It seems very unlikely,' Basha answered. 'If it is some kind of coded message, a linguistic one, then it is written in what we would call a "language of closed semantics". Even ignoring the deep cultural dependencies of any language . . . if one does not have a translating dictionary – or, at the least, a sample piece of translated text – one cannot decipher a totally unknown language. It is a sad fact of linguistics.'

I must have looked a little sceptical, as she added: 'Not for no reason was it necessary to have the Rosetta Stone to decode the Egyptian hieroglyphs. When you need a Rosetta Stone, simply, nothing else will do. Silent languages do not otherwise speak.'

'So that's it, then?' I asked glumly.

Instead of answering, Basha turned back to Helen. 'This new finding of yours – you say that the pattern in the sequence is not a linear series of characters . . . but rather a matrix? A series of series of characters?'

'Yes, it could be read as a matrix,' Helen said. 'A three-dimensional matrix . . .'

'Rows and columns,' I suggested. 'But also divided into *pages* of rows and columns. Are you going somewhere with this?'

'Yes,' said Basha, closing up the laptop. 'I am going down to the bar. With your permission, I would like to take a little time alone to play with the data. All right?'

Helen opened her mouth. I said: 'Yes. Yes, of course.'

Basha stood. She paused, with the laptop under her arm. She went to the corner and dug into the same bag from which she'd produced the computer. When she turned around, she held a stubby black handgun – butt forward. She proffered it to me.

'I gather you know how to use one,' she said. 'And the safety rules.'

'Jesus,' I let slip. 'How do you know so much about me?'

She ignored the question (she seemed to have a real talent). 'This one is a little different from Thad's. It is a Glock and so has no external hammer – and no manual safety. There is a round in the chamber now. If you pull the trigger, it will go bang.'

'Oh, hell,' I exclaimed. 'Thad! He's going to be worried sick about me.'

'I will send him a note to tell him you live,' Basha said. 'But do not call him on the phone. Unless you are anxious for the Nagas to find you again.'

'The who?'

'Your recent kidnappers,' Basha said. 'I will tell you about them when I get back. But I do not care to fight them off again, so please stay off the phone.'

I realized Basha still held the gun out towards me. I hesitated, then took it.

'Oh, and—' Basha thought to add, 'it is a Glock 30, chambered in .45 ACP. So it will go bang very loudly. Ten times. Be careful.'

And with that she was out the door again.

Thirty-four

Only a minute or two after Basha left, Helen also rose and excused herself.

'I need air,' she said. 'And a few minutes in my own company.'

I saw her palm her phone as she rose. I hesitated. When she reached the door, I managed: '. . . You won't go far, will you?'

'No,' she said, not turning. She pulled the door closed behind her.

I was left alone with my thoughts, with a few dust motes floating in the slanting sunlight – and with an assault rifle propped in the corner. It occurred to me that if it was rash or imprudent of me to be so trusting of this strange woman, within a few hours of meeting her . . . well, she was showing at least as much trust towards me. I mean – leaving me alone here with all these guns?

I looked down at the Glock, still in my hand. I found the push-button release and dropped the magazine out the bottom. The bullets inside were quite large. And they had deep, hollow tips. I knew this made them more deadly. I replaced the magazine.

Then again, I thought, Basha seems to know a heck of a lot more about me than I know about her. But, perhaps if you're a secret agent, it's your business to know things about people. And, anyway, trust is a funny old thing. I couldn't shake the good feeling I had about her. And good feelings had been a little thin on the ground for me lately.

I also knew that instincts and gut feelings have a basis in neuro-anatomy. The amygdala is another subcortical area – that inner part of the brain so much more ancient and primal than the outer cortex where our so-called 'executive' functions happen. The amygdala has a habit of noticing very fine details in our environment that our conscious minds miss – particularly as they relate to matters of our survival. It then feeds them back to us when they might be life-savingly relevant – usually as a hunch or 'a bad feeling about this' – and always much faster than rational thought happens. Thus the gut reaction is a very real phenomenon – we've just got it in the wrong part of the body.

Speaking of the body, mine soon fell back and melted into the bed. I must have still been exhausted. The stillness and peaceful sunlight took me back to dreamland.

I awoke – no idea how long after, but still alone – to my ringing phone.

Did Basha say I couldn't take any calls – or just not make any? Best not to take any chances, I reckoned. I let it ring on, pushing myself up on my elbows and looking around. The phone kept at it – long after voicemail should have picked up.

I guess I knew what that meant.

'Yeah,' I said tiredly – belatedly developing a gruff phone manner.

'I'm glad you've finally started listening to me,' she said. 'The last time you blithely ignored my advice it nearly got you killed.'

'What is your interest in my welfare, anyway?'

'Let's just say conscience sometimes needs an outside consultant.'

'So now you're my voice of conscience?'

'Look, I didn't call to argue abstractions with you. Hold please.'

'What? Hold—' but the voicemail voice had been replaced with piped-in Muzak. It was 'Girl from Ipanema'. I looked balefully down at the Glock in my other hand.

Too many seconds later, the voice came back: '. . . yes, I have her here. I'm connecting you now.' Another voice said hesitantly: 'Um, thank you . . .'

'Thad?' I said.

'Yeah. Hey! Is that you?'

'Yes, yes, it's me!'

'Are you okay? I just got some strange anonymous email about you . . .'

'It's true,' I said. 'I'm fine. I don't know what the hell's going on, but I'm fine.'

'Um – who was that just now?'

165

'That electronic-y voice?'

'Yeah.'

'Um . . . oh, shit. I forgot I'm not supposed to be talking to you. I've got to go. But, listen, really, I'm okay. And I'll be in touch soon. Okay?'

'Wait! Don't hang up . . .'

But I had, with sadness, pressed the End button. The screen showed a call length of a minute and half. And I had a feeling I'd just gotten myself in trouble with Basha.

And with that thought, she came back in the door.

'Where is Helen?' she asked. She put down two paper sacks in the kitchen and then the laptop on the desk.

'She stepped out. For air, she said.'

Basha smiled, but it seemed a little forced. 'I brought food. Help yourself.' From her corner of belongings, she retrieved another handgun, and what looked like a phone of her own. Holding them in either hand, she exited again.

But she returned before I'd finished rifling the sacks. Helen walked in less than a minute later. Shortly, we were all settled around the room with boxed salads, sandwiches (tomato, avocado and sprouts – very California), fresh fruit and fresh bottles of water.

'So—' I said, sprouts clinging to life at the corners of my mouth, 'you were going to tell us who the other villains were? The kidnappers? In the long shirts?'

'Those long shirts are called *kurtas*,' Basha said, between measured mouthfuls. I guessed, with envy, that here was a person who had perfect self-discipline in her eating.

'But first . . . just for the record,' she said, turning to Helen, 'can you tell me exactly what you told these ones? In the upstairs room?' Although we hadn't really discussed it, I was coming to understand that Helen had been under interrogation by the men who took her out of the basement room we'd shared.

'Let me try to recall,' Helen said, wiping her mouth efficiently. 'I believe I had just finished suggesting some anatomically unlikely sexual pursuits they might profitably pursue. And I was then con-

166

sidering inviting them, singly or as a group, to bite my ass. But I didn't get a chance because that was when you showed up.'

I suddenly remembered why I did like Helen: she just didn't give a fuck.

Even Basha couldn't resist a smile. And she seemed satisfied. She put her food on the desk beside her. 'Okay, this other group. The ones who abducted you. They are Nagas, of the Dadu Panthi sect. You know your Hindu denominations?'

Helen and I must have looked blank again. 'They really spare you scientists the humanities education, do they not? Okay, there are a billion Hindus on Earth – but it is a very splintered faith. The three major classes are Vaishnavas, Saivas, and Saktas. But beneath these are dozens of sects and cults. Some you have heard of: the Sikhs, the Jains, the Hare Krishnas. Most you have not – Choliyas, Gurukkals, Saiva Brahmins.'

She paused to nudge her handgun (which seemed to be a twin of the one she'd given me) and her phone, both of which lay on the desk beside her. 'The first class, the Vaishnavas, have a southern school and a northern school. The southern school holds that self-surrender is the only way to salvation. But the northerners, called the Vadagalai, believe that it is only one of the ways. They believe the seeker must be like the child of a monkey – which has to exert itself and cling tenaciously to its mother. They call this Markata-Nyaya – Monkey Theory.' There came that look aimed at me again.

'These Dadu Panthis are one of the Vaishnava cults, of the northern school. Their founder, Dadu Dayal, lived in the second half of the sixteenth century in Rajasthan – which is the northwest province of India, adjacent to what is now Pakistan. He gathered his followers around him and the group became known as the Dadu-panth. They have remained in Rajasthan until the present day. The Dadu Panthi themselves are divided into classes. There is a mendicant class who shave their heads and carry only a single cloth and a water pot. And a class of ordinary householders and tradesmen.

'And then there are the Nagas – the warrior ascetics. This soldier

167

class was widespread in northern India in the eighteenth century – much less so today. They fused the roles of renouncer and warrior, and were vowed to celibacy and to arms. They can be recognized by the marks on their foreheads – and their beards and long, matted hair. In the past, they sometimes smeared their bodies with ashes – or even went naked. They favour spears, intricately carved, in combat. Or, at any rate, they did in the eighteenth century. Little is known about them today.'

We paused to absorb all this. Though not for long. Helen broke the silence: 'And now you're going to tell us about their interest in genomic science? Or perhaps these guys are more interested in proteomics. Or glycomics.' I couldn't tell why she adopted this tone. It seemed to me that if there was one person on the planet less likely to respond to her provocations than Thad, it was probably Basha.

But, in fact, Basha pinned Helen with her gaze and said: 'Unless you would like a second chance to figure out one single thing on your own.' So, obviously, what I know about people and their responses to other people wouldn't fill a boot. 'Come on – you must know at least one thing about the beliefs of Hinduism.'

'Reincarnation?' I ventured. Helen showed no inclination to play this game.

'Good,' Basha said. 'And what does reincarnation have in common with genetics?'

I scratched my puzzler. 'They both pass information about the makeup of people across generations?'

'*Very* good!' said Basha, seemingly genuinely proud of me. 'You get a cookie. Or, no, I see we have no cookies. You get . . . a spare magazine for your Glock.' She produced one and handed it to me.

'Thanks!' I said. I realized I hadn't any pockets to put it in.

'I do not mean to be exclusionary,' Basha said, turning to Helen. 'But I am assuming you have no interest in, nor knowledge of, firearms?'

'Yes,' said Helen. 'I'll pass on your gang initiation rites. But I am interested in what you're suggesting – that these Hindus are imagining DNA as some kind of conduit for reincarnated souls?'

Basha took a breath. She said: 'Think of this in larger terms. The extremely fast and forceful march of science – especially neuro-science, evolution, cosmology – has taken much of the foundation out from under religion.' I saw Helen light up in response to this; and I remembered her strikingly similar comments from that patio in Palo Alto.

'These people, the devoutly religious, they principally endeavour to stick their heads further into the sand – but can only burrow so deeply before they are coming out the other side of the Earth.' I wrinkled my nose. Where I had heard a comment like that before? 'They can either watch their beliefs crushed by science, one by one. Or perhaps they can try to co-opt it. And, the fact is, there is more than enough data storage in the strings of so-called junk DNA to transmit the basic psychological makeup of a person – a soul, if you will – across a generation. Or across many generations.'

Helen looked interested but sceptical. 'You understand that would require Lamarckian evolution? It would require mental changes over a person's lifetime to somehow be written into their DNA . . .'

'And you surely understand,' Basha gently countered, 'that until the full expanse of human DNA is mapped and experimented upon and genuinely understood . . . there is no way to prove definitively that the Lamarckian theory of evolution is false.'

'Yes, you've got me there,' Helen admitted instantly. (She's stubborn – but very, very quick.) 'So . . . you're saying these Nagas think they are going to find the non-mystical transmission of reincarnated souls – in what appears as unexpressed DNA?'

'Just so. But not necessarily the Nagas,' Basha answered. 'The Nagas are muscle. Most likely someone is behind them – probably the Dadu Panthis. Though, perhaps someone further up the chain of Hindu sects.'

'For mercenaries,' I ventured, 'they actually seemed quite gentle. Particularly as compared to the Qabbalists – who shot first and never did ask any questions.'

Basha paused and exhaled. 'Yes, it is a funny thing. On the one hand, the Nagas are not bad sorts – honourable, with a warrior code. Also, their tribes in the south were said to retain matriarchal customs, to practise matrilineal inheritance, and to put no sexual or marital restrictions on women.'

'. . . So they're feminists?'

'Basically. For all these reasons, when I retrieved you, I was glad I was able to drive them off without bloodshed. Still, of course, I was prepared to take their lives – or have them take mine. Which brings me to my "on the other hand" . . .'

'Uh, oh.'

'They are, on the other hand, very fierce warriors. If you have something their faith requires . . . if you stand in their way . . . they will fall on you like darkness.'

Helen broke in on these atmospherics: 'And you're saying that, as were the Qabbalists, the Nagas were spying on GenenW? And on HGP? And on other biotechs?'

'It seems that they were. And when the original genome map of active genes was completed, the Hindus got especially interested in the unexpressed DNA.'

'If they were so interested,' Helen said, 'why didn't they just sequence it themselves? It's not like DNA samples are hard to come by. Everybody's got some.'

'They do not have access to the kind of gene sequencing horse-power one needs for a project of that scale. They had to wait and see what the serious players produced.'

'Speaking of the serious players,' I said, 'do you know if A'hib Khouri is okay? If he made it safely back to Pakistan?'

'I do not know for sure,' Basha answered. 'But it does not look good. If he got out of the US, by air at any rate, he did not do so under his own name. Still, one never knows. If I learn more, of course—'

But with that there was an extraordinarily unexpected knock at the door. I looked around and saw that Basha's gun had leapt to her hand, before I'd thought of mine. She held it forward one-handed, walked to the door in a slight crouch, and touched the knob.

By this time, I had my gun up as well. Helen crouched behind the far bed. Basha exchanged serious looks with each of us. Then she pulled the door roughly open.

And behind it stood Thaddeus Gottlieb. He wore jeans, a short-sleeve button-down, and his shaded eyeglasses. He put his hands up slowly, palms facing toward us.

Thirty-five

Thad and I sat together on two adjacent bar stools. I'd gotten Basha's permission for the two of us to speak alone, down at the bar – the bar of an entirely different lodge, two or three towns over (and even deeper into the Santa Cruz mountains).

'You used the phone,' Basha had declared, without particular rancour, after closing the door behind Thad. She still had her gun out, but trained just off him, and her trigger finger straight out along the barrel.

'Sort of,' I sort of admitted.

'Can you turn it off now, please?' she said, turning the locks on the door.

'I'm not sure it will help.'

Basha squinted briefly with curiosity, but let that pass. Turning to Thad, she asked: 'Are you armed?'

'No,' Thad answered evenly. 'I do have a handgun out in my vehicle.'

'Well . . .' said Basha, putting her sentence on hold for what looked like a second and a half of dedicated processing time, '. . . keep it handy as you follow us out. And please obey all traffic laws.'

With that, she began slipping guns, electronics and sundries into her two zip-up bags. Helen and I didn't need any prompting to follow suit. In four minutes we were out the door – and the cottage lay completely bare. We even took the trash out with us.

In the car, Basha tersely explained that if Thad could find us – however he did so – others could as well. I looked over the back headrest at Thad following in his truck a steady six car lengths behind. Basha drove directly and unerringly to the town of Felton, fifteen minutes south. Twenty-five minutes after Thad's knock at the door, we were checked in to a functionally identical cottage in another, similarly rustic, lodge.

'No WiFi here,' Basha lamented, pulling her rifle out of her bag

172

and propping it in, relatively, the same corner. Going back for the laptop, she added: 'I have a Bluetooth connection to my satellite phone. But it only goes 60kbps.'

As Basha set up the new room, the rest of us stood idle. That was when I requested my time alone with Thad.

'Go ahead,' she said, fiddling with her phone to get it talking to her computer. 'There is a bar in the main lodge, which should not be crowded. Take your Glock,' she added, before turning from the laptop to Helen. 'Perhaps Ms Dolan and I can use this time to work together on the Pandora sequence. Put our heads together on it?' This seemed a genuine and friendly overture. To my surprise, Helen took it.

'Yeah, okay,' she said. 'Maybe we'll make some progress – toward falsifying your secret message hypothesis.' She followed us with her gaze as Thad and I exited.

It was only after we had walked to the large central building that I realized Basha hadn't asked a single question – other than in regard to the gun issue – about Thad or his presence here. And he had repaid this courtesy (or snub), until now.

'Well, it's a little hard to say who she is,' I admitted. Thad and I both drank tea. I'd considered something stronger. But there are a couple of ways of calming the nerves – and with all the guns, and Naga caste warriors, and whatnot about, it seemed best not to dull my wits. 'But she seems to be very much on our side.'

That seemed to be good enough for Thad, at least for the moment. I asked him how he'd found us.

'The department,' he said, meaning the police. 'We've got real-time access to call data from telecom providers. The logs show which cell tower a given call comes in on. There are only a couple of towers in the Santa Cruz mountains. And only a few places to rent a room in Boulder Creek.'

'I guess that badge is quite a handy thing to flash around,' I said.

'I try not to go crazy with it,' he said.

Thad seemed slightly affectless. Respectful, as always – but moving and speaking a little more deliberately. As if he were taking care not to rush to judgement about anything. As if he were only here in case he could be of help. Which I felt certain was precisely the case.

Despite Thad's lack of prompting, I realized I should fill him in on all that had happened since my abduction from the hospital. I also told him as much about Basha as she had told me. Finally, I really tested myself by trying to deliver the Qabbalist/Naga lecture – who they were, what they were on about . . . how dangerous they might be.

'So, basically,' I concluded, 'you've got one major faith group who want the sequence because they think it contains a secret message from God. And guys from a totally different religion who want it because they think it's a medium for transmission of reincarnated souls. And they're all armed and dangerous.' I snorted with mordant humour. 'And they seem to be awfully fond of me.'

Thad absorbed all of this in silence. When he spoke, I realized his mind was still a few topics back.

'Listen, I really feel like crap about what happened. I'm just really sorry.'

'About which,' I asked. 'The bit where you saved my life at the office? Oh, hell – how is your leg?' I leaned under the bar, pulling at his trouser leg, mortified that I'd forgotten he'd recently been shot.

'It's totally fine. Forget it, really.' He sort of pulled me back above the bar. 'I meant what happened at the hospital. I mean, we had two officers outside your door . . .'

'Oh hell, again! Are those guys okay?' Can't believe I forgot about them.

'They're fine, too. Just knocks to the head.' He sighed. 'But what I'm trying to say is that I feel awful. It was my responsibility.' His face really clouded now and he stared at the bar top. 'The thought of those people having you tied up in a basement, where they could have done anything . . . it just makes me really . . . ragged.'

'Ragged?'

He sighed again. '. . . Terrified, furious, and a little crazy. All at once.'

174

Uh, oh – here came that troublesome lachrymosity again. I had heard sentiments like this before; I'd had someone feel this protective of me. Just not for ten years. I hugged him, wrapping my bare arms around his broad, sloping shoulders.

'It's fine, Thad. Really. I'm completely okay. And you're here now. I know you'd never let anything happen to me. And it's all working out fine, okay?'

He took a slow breath, which seemed to clear his head. 'Is it? Do you know what you're going to do now? You still have something these people want. And I can't promise we can protect you from them – not with a straight face. So what now?'

I de-hugged myself from him and arched my brows. 'You know, I hadn't really thought of it. It's pretty much been moment to moment, up until now. And never a dull one.' I finished my tea. 'Tell you what. Let's go back and see if we can't start up a discussion about what to do next. You know, I can't pin down just why, but I really rather like this Basha person. I feel like I've known her longer than, um, looks like about eight hours now . . .'

I went to pay – carefully pulling bills out while keeping the gun in.

We walked back to the cottage in silence. When we got to the door, for some reason I peeked in the front window before opening the door.

'Have a look at this,' I whispered to Thad.

He leaned around beside me. Through the glass, we could see Helen and Basha sitting Indian-style on the far bed. Their backs were to us – and both sloping over the laptop which sat open before them. Their sides were pressed together. Even from behind, we could see their animation – first one would gesture with her hands, then type at the keyboard; then the other would take over.

Quietly, I said: 'Perhaps we should give them a bit longer. Walkage, old man?'

'Yeah,' Thad answered, straightening up. 'A walk with you, and I'll be a new man. Or, at least, the same old man.'

*

'Bob Santillan told you all that, did he?'

So I'd gone ahead and broached the big mystery topic with Thad: the exact nature of his military background and service. I hoped he would see no point in being coy now. The two of us walked side by side on a red-clay-and-tree-root footpath, a network of which paths appeared to spiderweb the hills around the lodge.

'Yes. He seemed in awe of you,' I said. 'Did you have a very dangerous job? In Delta Force?'

Thad paused, shoved his hands into his jeans pockets, and sighed aloud – seeming to resign himself. 'Not really. I had the same generic job most guys in the unit had. I was what they called a door-kicker.' He took his dark lenses out of his shirt pocket and attached them.

'I guess I'm not sure what that means,' I said.

'Delta was originally conceived of as a hostage rescue team, in the context of counter-terrorism. The idea was that if some terrorists – and this was the late seventies, so we're talking Baader-Meinhof Gang, Palestinian Fatah groups, etc. – if some terrorists took American hostages, we were a fast-response group. Our job was to take down the building with the hostages and the hostage-takers in it. We'd kill the lights, drop in some flash-bang grenades, some guys might fast-rope in from the roof. But most of us would kick in the doors, storm in and flexicuff everyone in the building – optionally shooting anyone who seemed to be armed. Afterwards, somebody else would sort out the terrorists from the hostages, from all the flexicuffed people.'

'Sorry – flexicuffs?'

'Yeah, it's, uh . . . you know those plastic bands that we use to bundle up network cables? The ones that only tighten but don't loosen? Pretty much like that. Anyway, Delta had started doing a lot more stuff by the time I joined the unit: diplomatic protection, training foreign special forces, Scud-hunting in Iraq. But everyone who wasn't specially trained as a sniper, or a medic, or communications guy, was still a door-kicker.'

It was strange and thrilling to hear Thad – quiet, unassuming

176

Thad – talk in these terms. He still sounded like him. But I guess a dangerous past spices anyone up.

We crested a hill, shed the canopy of trees, and the sky opened overhead. The sun landed on us. I stepped into the open and formulated my next question. 'May I ask why you never talk about this? Is it just modesty? Or . . . perhaps something happened that you'd rather not recall.'

'Something happened, sure,' he answered with no hesitation. 'Heck, you already know about it, really. What I've been dealing with – the whole God thing, which led to the how-to-get-along-without-God thing. It started in the service. Years ago.'

'Is it something you care to talk about now?'

He exhaled and looked out over the mountains, which were splashed in sunlight. We could also see the cabins and the main lodge, below us amidst the towering redwoods. 'You probably already know that story, too, believe it or not.'

'How do you mean?'

He laughed. 'Sorry. Now that I've been all mysterious about it, I feel like I've built it up. Basically, I was with Task Force Ranger in Mogadishu, Somalia, in 1993. The one that got so famously shot up when two of our helicopters got knocked down.'

'That they made the book and the movie about?'

'Yeah. But it wasn't just that, the Battle of Mogadishu, that did it to me. That was just sort of the punctuation mark on the whole thing.' He took a seat on a large boulder. I joined him. 'I mean, there we were, halfway around the world, trying to help feed these hundreds of thousands of starving people. And trying to protect them from all these armed assholes, these just profoundly evil men, who were stealing the food shipments. Who were keeping these people starving basically for profit, and as a political tool.'

'That must have been awful to see.'

'Well, it was. But, on the other hand, after we got there, we pretty much squared away the situation. The food was coming in and getting distributed. The warlords were on the run. We had person-ally captured most of their top leadership. But, the point is: I figured

177

what we were doing over there was truly God's work. I mean, what could be more meaningful than feeding and protecting all these defenceless people? I had that whole, romantic, stupid, Christian soldier idea in my head.'

I wanted to tell him that there was nothing stupid about it.

'And then, you know, this one October afternoon, we went out to arrest another couple of these bad guys. It was a daylight raid, in a kind of dicey area. But, still, we were skilled professionals. And, mainly, we were out there doing good – trying to help. But things started to go wrong. And before we knew it, I swear to you, this whole teeming city just rose up against us. Before we could get out, I mean, it literally seemed like every man, woman, and boy over the age of five was shooting at us with AKs and RPGs. After a few hours of being cut off and mostly pinned down, it didn't feel like fighting opponents. It felt like fighting the city itself, some kind of organism. I saw footage from the command and control aircraft later, and that's exactly what it looked like. A living city surging at us. We'd keep beating it back, but another wave would roll in. It was like shovelling seaweed against the tide. Except not seaweed. People.'

'I'm so sorry,' I said. 'You guys really got pummelled, didn't you? Did you lose friends?'

'Yeah. Delta lost a few guys. They were my friends. But it's a wide-spread myth that we got pummelled. In fact, it was one of the most one-sided battles in history – in our favour. About a hundred guys, Delta and Army Rangers, fought off an entire city, thousands and thousands of militia members, for most of a day and night. Any less skilled force would have been overrun and wiped out. But we never were. And we only lost eighteen killed total. Though I think most of us were wounded one way or another before we got out.'

'Were you wounded?'

'No.' He paused and looked away. 'Not physically.' I could hear his breathing now. 'When I say it was one-sided. The estimates of enemy killed were anywhere between five hundred and a thousand Somalis. But . . .' He seemed almost to be hyperventilating now. 'They were just coming from everywhere. Windows, doorways,

178

alleyways, rooftops. They were mostly armed men – but also some women, and boys. And here was the insane thing: there were these huge crowds, these crowds of mostly unarmed people, who were spilling though the streets, interspersed with the militiamen. Like they were perversely drawn to right where they could most easily get killed.

'And so, for the first couple of hours, we were all pretty careful with our target selection. At first, we only fired on clear targets who had fired on us. And then, later, on any clearly armed targets, whether they were shooting at us right then or not. But, still, you'd have to, you know, snipe some guy with a rifle in the middle of a crowd, most of which was unarmed. But the firefight just went on and on, and they just kept coming, and we started taking casualties. It was getting really hairy. And after you saw a couple of buddies, not five feet from you, get hit – and some of them not get up again – you stopped erring so much on the side of caution.

'Maybe you'd throw a grenade over a wall, not really knowing what was on the other side. Or you'd shoot blind into a window you thought you were taking fire from. It was crazy. We were fighting for our lives. And a lot of bodies hit the ground. I still believe most of them were militia who were coming after us. But not all.'

I put my hand on his shoulder. 'You must have done the best you could.'

He shook his head sharply. 'That doesn't matter,' he said, voice choking with emotion. 'Because *we killed a thousand people* that day. I probably killed twenty of them myself.' I could see his jaw muscles twitching, in profile. 'We went there to help those people. And we ended up shooting into crowds. Killing ten-year-old boys.'

He took off his glasses and ran his forearm across his eyes. 'After that, I couldn't believe in anything. Definitely not in God. Not the one I'd been taught to believe in.'

I squeezed his shoulder. 'What did you do afterwards?'

'I rode out another year, the last one of my hitch. I was able to function. But I had turned really pensive. I had no faith in what we were doing any more, anything the unit was doing. I just went through the motions. When the year was up, I left the army.'

'And you've been dealing with the fallout all these years?'

'No. I didn't even really start dealing with it until a year or two ago. I just put it in a box. I kept going to church with Leslie and the kids. I kept taking communion, reciting the rosary. But, again, I was just going through the motions. Ultimately, I came to grips with the fact that I had to find something else. I had to find something.'

Then we sat in silence on our boulder and watched the sun set.

We walked back to the cottage in the purple half-light of the trail's dusk, the 500-year-old redwoods augustly ignoring our passage. And when we got back we found Basha and Helen in a state I would not have predicted in this lifetime (or any lifetime coming up soon): both smiling – smiling the full width of their faces – and with their arms around each other's waists.

'Oh,' said Basha to Thad and me, straightening, still smiling. 'We have something to show you.'

Thirty-six

'Saint Jude Thaddeus,' Basha intoned. 'Blood relative of Jesus Christ – and also reported to resemble him.' She brought her subtly wry look to bear on Thad. 'That is your namesake?'

We had all pulled up seats in front of the laptop. Basha seemed, to me, to be delaying for drama's sake.

'Yes, I was named for him,' Thad said. 'How'd you know that?'

Ah, Thad's first Basha-ignored question. 'Patron saint of lost, impossible, or forgotten causes – and of desperate situations.' Her trace of a smile dried up. 'But beaten to death with a club in first-century Persia – and then beheaded.'

'Someone's going to get beheaded,' Helen suggested, 'if you don't get on with the program.'

Basha turned to her. 'Should we explain first? Or let it speak unaided?'

'Let's see if they can guess what it is,' Helen said.

'Fine.' Basha scanned faces. 'Ready?' We were ready.

She pulled up a media window on her screen. And then she played a movie clip. It was digital video, postage-stamp size, and greyscale. It was grainy and jumpy. It lasted maybe thirty seconds. I wasn't sure what I'd seen. Something flying, a face, a shape. Then buildings. A pair of hands.

'Do you know what it is?' asked Helen, smooth skin glistening with excitement.

From beneath squinted eyes and furrowed brow, Thad ventured, 'Is it . . . the worst video game splash screen from 1988?'

'Watch again,' said Helen.

I leaned in and tried to pay closer attention. The window was so small! It opened on a sphere, then zoomed in. Upon it were figures, I think. It zoomed out again – and something flew into the frame. Something flying. A flying thing. It flew in toward the sphere and the figures, the 'camera' view following. I rubbed my eyes. When I

181

opened them, the flying thing was drawing something away from one of the figures. A shape. A geometric shape.

A fucking double helix.

That much was unmistakable – or else I was going barking mad, straight nutters, double helixes on my addled brain. I straightened up, stiff, wide-eyed, and pinned Helen and Basha with my eye. I missed the rest of the video.

'Where the hell did this come from?' I asked.

They both looked me in the face, seriously, in silence.

A little while later, when one or another, or probably several, actually, who knows, of the multifold groups of bad guys had tracked us down again, and everything turned to violence and chaos, and we had to shoot our way out of there, and flee for our lives, and whatnot . . . well, I tell you, I had the strangest experience.

It was the funniest thing, really. But as soon as the shooting started . . . it all suddenly seemed really, very much like being in a videogame – like being back in GibletWorld. I mean, I know I shouldn't have felt that way; not at all. What could a stupid first-person shooter video game have to do with real fighting, genuine mortal peril, bodies hitting the floor – and not getting back up again?

But all that notwithstanding, when the real shooting started, I found myself pulling out my bot tricks. All that stuff I taught my bots about dirty fighting? All that theoretical knowledge about infantry combat tactics? I mean, yeah, I had to use my arms and legs, rather than keyboard and mouse; but it was conceptually the same. Functionally, for my brain, it was somehow all the same.

And it also turned out that the past – in this case, my wild charge, with Thad's gun, against the Qabbalists, back at the office – really was prologue. It hadn't been an anomaly, or outlier, a confusion of my behaviour. It had merely been a warm-up.

Here's how we trick ourselves. Out in the real world, the so-called veridical world, we think we've got a good view on reality. But it's illusory. I mean, for starters, we see a fraction of the electromagnetic

182

spectrum. We hear in a tiny frequency range. Our senses don't even provide enough data to accurately resolve three-dimensional spaces. Left to solve equations in too many variables, our brains, their onboard perceptual software, takes shortcuts, makes assumptions about how the world is laid out.

Television, movies – 3D video games – all exploit these assumptions, they fool us into thinking we see things that are not there. First-person shooters use every trick in the book to make us see virtual spaces, virtual opponents, as real: perspective lines, differential lighting, angle and depth of shadows, motion, texture. And these tricks *work*. These spaces are real to our brains. So are the experiences we have there. And, after years of playing these games – but only after my first full-scale, veridical-space gunfight – I was suddenly deeply unsurprised that the military now uses these games to train soldiers.

'One difference,' Basha told me afterward, when she and I – numb, emotionally overloaded – were debriefing, 'is that you do not take incremental damage as you do in GibletWorld. Out here in WorldWorld, you cannot afford to be shot even once.'

Thad also told me a number of useful things, much later. 'In combat,' he said, 'confusion reigns over all. Almost always, people on the ground are simply struggling to do two things: One, to stay alive. And, two, to figure out what's going on – because knowing what's going on is almost always the best way to stay alive.'

He explained that soldiers often go through three psychological phases: 'The first is "I won't get hit" – a belief in your personal invulnerability. The second is "I can avoid getting hit" – you still believe in your ability to control what happens to you. You think: "How I take cover, how I expose myself, when I choose to fire my weapon – all these choices will affect whether I survive." But the third stage is "I'm going to get hit and there's nothing I can do about it." This usually comes after seeing a lot of buddies go down.'

All of this was later, of course. But, the thing was: by that stage of events, by the time of the shootout, I felt like I actually had a pretty good understanding of – *empathy* with, even – people

183

choosing to kidnap, or to kill, or even to die, for this thing. For this thing we'd found. I really thought I could understand what would drive them to the other side of the world, make them take up guns, and spears, and wireless scanners, and email packet sniffers. What would keep them going, drive them on. After this thing.

It was because: it was the truth. This thing. It was the truth.

What I still wouldn't come to understand for a bit longer was that certain people were equally motivated, had an equally compelling stake, in *suppressing* that truth – keeping it hidden from the rest of the world. Ensuring that it never got out.

But, you know what? Ultimately . . . I also learned that there was yet a third level of motivation. Some of the players in this game had come around the world not to acquire, nor to deny – but simply to protect. Not out of desire, not out of jealousy.

Just out of devotion.

And I knew that this devotion really *was* worth dying for. That the love of a single true friend was worth a thousand revealed truths. That it was worth everything.

But the force of revelation is a heady thing. You can't figure everything out all at once. Your brain would probably explode.

'It's an encoded video,' I said. I put my hand to my forehead. 'The Pandora sequence is a fucking animation, a movie. And I take it there are a hundred trillion copies of this movie – in each of six and a half billion human beings?'

'Kind of overkill, isn't it? Talk about spam.' That was Helen. I took it she'd had a real conversion on this issue. Give her credit as a scientist, I guess: show her the proof, and she's a believer. 'But we were only ever going to be able to see it when we got to the point of being able to read our own DNA.'

'Just like bloody NovaGene,' I muttered. 'We've been trade-marked. Branded. But in a live-action film.'

'But it is not a film,' said Basha quietly, from where she stood now by the window. 'Or not *the* film. It is only a preview, I think. A . . . theatrical trailer.'

184

'What? How?' I asked.

'You need to watch it again. You must watch more closely.'

'I'm not sure it'll help,' I said. 'But, first – tell me how you two figured this out. Tell me how you did this.' We all seemed nearly to be whispering now.

Basha and Helen exchanged looks. Basha shrugged her shoulders. 'God,' she said drolly, 'always traffics in visions. No?'

Helen laughed, scattering some of the tension. She said: 'Okay. Basically, we knew it couldn't be a text message. As Basha explained earlier, anything linguistic – in the absence of a Rosetta Stone – would have been closed to us, indecipherable. So, if there was no even theoretical way we could read a letter . . .'

Basha spoke up quietly. 'It was the second marker, the second-order pattern, the one that Helen found. That was the clue. That, and your description of it as not just a matrix of rows and columns – but *pages* of rows and columns. What has rows and columns of discrete information values?'

'A digital image,' I answered. 'Rows and columns of pixels, each one representing a colour value for each point in the image.'

'Or, in this case,' said Helen, 'a greyscale value: sixty-four shades of grey.'

'And what,' continued Basha, 'is a sequence of digital pictures?'

'Digital video,' I answered. 'I'm still having trouble with this . . .'

'Okay, from the top,' said Helen. I sat back down at the machine with her, as she called up the data of the pattern. She narrated as she pointed with the mouse:

'The sequence, the full length of the pattern you found, is exactly four megabytes. Okay? As you know, there aren't a million bytes in a megabyte – there are two to the twentieth power: 1,048,576. So, that's 4,194,304 total bytes – or, in this case, codons. Within the sequence, there's a marker, your pseudo-checksum, every 128 codons. This marker represents the end of a single line of bytes, or codons – or pixels. That is, a single row of 128 pixels.'

This I followed. But I also really needed the opportunity to look at the data again – in all of this spooky new light – to really get my head around it.

'So. There's a second-level marker,' Helen continued, 'every 128 times 128 – that is, every 128 rows. This marks the last row in a "frame". With a resolution of 128 pixels by 128 pixels in each frame, there are exactly 256 frames in the whole sequence.'

'And what's the frame rate?' This was Thad. He had been standing in the corner for the last minute or two – maintaining a pensive silence. Basha rose and stood near him.

'We had to play with it,' Helen answered. 'We tried 32 frames per second, like a motion picture. But it blasted by, we couldn't make anything out. At 8 frames per second, it seems to resolve. And, at that rate, 256 frames give us a 32-second running time.'

'Play it again,' I said. But I went ahead and reached across Helen to start it myself. After it ran, I said: 'How did you derive the greyscale values for the pixels?'

'Just based on your 64-value system for the codons. One end is white, the other is black. Everything in between is an evenly spaced shade of grey.'

I tapped my fingers on the laptop housing.

I said: 'Ascending? Starting with white?' Helen looked at Basha, who nodded in assent. I pulled the laptop toward me and began typing, blazingly.

'I knew it looked like a bloody photo negative.'

Thirty-seven

Here's what we decided we saw.

Here's where we came to, as a group. (If that's what we were.)

Without the greyscale values inverted, mind you, in their proper order and not looking like a negative, it was a heck of a lot easier to make out. Though, I don't want to overstate the case. It was still a tiny, 128x128-pixel thumbnail video, with a low frame rate and no colour. The four of us watched it about a hundred times in a row; we paused it; rewound it; slowed it down and sped it up; we advanced through it frame by frame.

Later, even after we reached our rough consensus, Thad still sat alone, playing it over and again. (Or doing something with it; he'd retreated to the bathroom. I for one thought this was kind of strange, but nobody said anything.)

But this was our consensus. This was the putative story-line of our 32-second feature. This was the narrative structure of the film, as interpreted by four viewers . . . four critics . . . four not entirely disinterested parties . . . sitting in the dark.

The opening shot, that sphere, was a planet. We stipulated that it was our planet.

We were willing to stipulate this, because, on zooming in, the shapes of land masses seemed to appear. In particular . . . a conspicuously Africa-shaped land mass.

As the shot closed in tighter on the planet, things moving around on its surface resolved. Creatures. Bipeds. Hominids. The first few seemed to have long-ish arms, so we guessed they were us but not us – our forebears. But these multiplied, before the camera as it were, as if time were speeded up radically. And they seemed to change in shape as they multiplied. By the beginning of the second scene, they were proportioned about like us in the room. There were more of them; but still all in Africa.

The second scene was . . . and, believe me, we all had to check our heads before signing off on this one . . . the, um, flying saucer scene. No, it didn't quite look like something from *War of the Worlds*. It was too small to have much of a shape at all. It was a dot. A flying blob.

And it flew down to Earth (if Earth that was).

It descended toward the Africa shape – our virtual perspective following. It approached the hominids. It approached a single hominid in particular. And with this, everything else in the scene sort of fell away, leaving just the hominid on the left and the flying thing on the right.

At this point, it became clear that we were looking at more of an instructional video like, than, say, a realistic video narrative. An info-graphic, as it were.

And then this led into the double-helix scene. There was no mistaking it. The flying thing exerted some kind of force on the hominid – drawing from it the unmistakable molecular shape. It then seemed to perform an . . . operation . . . on the double helix. The shape shifted, spun, and buckled. It then merged *back* into the human figure. And, as the flying thing flew into the air again, the human now merged back into his mob of bipeds, back into Africa.

And, with this, the mob began to multiply – and spread. Soon it had spilled out across the globe. But not just the figures. Structures, also – and groups of structures, possibly elaborate ones. We tentatively agreed they were cities.

Within them, things were . . . happening.

This was terribly hard to make out; and our consensus fractured somewhat. I was pretty sure I saw two figures dancing. Basha just thought they were talking, animatedly. Another figure . . . seemed to *make* something. Thad swore up and down it was a book; he saw characters upon it. Helen felt sure it was a mechanical device. A machine.

Suffice it to say, there was a lot of rapid, complex activity. And/or production.

And, mind you, this was all wide open to interpretation. But that was ours.

Okay. So far, so strange.

But the last act was where we had real trouble. I mean, we could pretty clearly make out what happened then. The details, the shapes, the action. But we failed to understand what it meant. We could make no sense of it.

First, the view zoomed back from the cities out again to the flying thing. From the flying thing came . . . two hands. Two completely disembodied human hands. The hands floated for a second; then pressed together. When they touched, something came out of them – it looked like a conical beam, maybe a projector beam. At the end of a beam was . . . something. Something kinetic. It might have been images of something; but as a portion of an already-tiny frame, it was impossible to make out.

Then the hands pulled apart, the beam disappeared – and the hands plunged to Earth. They flew toward another land mass, different, but also recognizable. One starkly boot-shaped. It landed on the left edge, a bit further than halfway down its length.

And that was it. The end.

'My head's going to explode.' I pressed it, my head that is, against the inside of the front door. As I did so, I heard Thad come out of the bathroom. I looked over the crook of my elbow: he didn't have the laptop. I looked back into the darkness of my arm.

No one spoke. I heard Thad take a couple of steps across the wooden floor.

In an admiring tone – but that of a non sequitur – he said: 'This yours?'

'Yes.' That was Basha.

'Bull-pup configuration,' Thad said. He must have been looking at her rifle. I knew this term because we had a gun like that in the game. It means the magazine comes out behind the grip and trigger. Which makes the rifle short while the barrel stays long.

Thad continued: 'Polymer housing . . . red-dot reflex sight . . . 5.56 millimetre. Beautiful weapon.' He paused; Basha didn't answer. He then asked: 'TAR-21, right? Replacement for the Galil and M16?'

'TAR-21C,' said Basha absently. 'Compact version. It replaces the M4 carbine.'

I looked up then – in time to see Thad give Basha a short but appraising look across the small room. He gently put the rifle back in the corner. Then, wordlessly, he returned to the bathroom. No one said anything.

I repeated: 'My head's going to explode.' Then I said: 'I think I need some air.'

'Take your Glock,' Basha repeated, as if playing a recording from earlier.

I stepped out into the cool night. I was alone. It was very dark.

Right, then. Who *were* these people, anyway? I asked myself as I pressed the heavy door closed. A true friend? A new friend? And a faux friend? How was one to know? And what was this . . . *thing*? This thing we'd found? And, much more to the point: what in hell were we doing?

Of course, that's always the big one, right? What are we doing?

I picked my way gingerly out along the path Thad and I had taken before. After my eyes adjusted, I found there was a haze of moonlight. I followed the trail into the woods, back out of the woods, and up the sloping hill. I managed to find our boulder from before. I sat.

It was brighter up on the hilltop. The universe gazed down on me – again. That nonexistent Orion guy carried on all that funky twinkling. But I knew he was a fake.

Were these other characters any more real? Was their twinkling at me just so much fusing hydrogen? Pleasing patterns I'd invented, stories I told myself?

Oh, yeah – and what in hell were we doing?

Alone again, I felt I could pose these larger, thornier questions. I mean, I'd been in pretty close quarters with these people for quite some time now. (Not to mention with a few other people, even stranger ones, along the way.) And I'm pretty accustomed to having time to myself. I'm not sure my mind quite works without interference in the presence of others. It's like some kind of field effect.

Speaking of which. Speaking of minds. Speaking of strange effects.

All right, then, the hell with it. I had to make a decision as to whether I was off my rocker, whether we all were. Here it was: Space aliens came to Earth some thousands of years ago and (presumably for good reasons of their own) monkeyed around with the DNA of one of the resident hominid species – which then proceeded to take over the entire planet and basically go apeshit with culture, commerce, art, language, and a whole bunch of other really complex behaviours never before even hinted at in four billion years of evolution.

And, oh yeah – the aliens didn't just perform these software upgrades on us.

They left a fucking README file.

Which no one had ever read. Until tonight. *This* night.

'Fuck's sake!' I shouted out loud – up at the universe. I found I had jumped to my feet. Suddenly, articulating all this, I didn't just feel flummoxed. I didn't just feel like I might be off my rocker. I felt excited and energized out of my mind. My whole body surged with enthusiasm, wonder, and awe. I mean, yeah, *of course* all of this was completely, unutterably, argument-endingly impossible.

. . .

But what if it was TRUE?

I sat on that boulder, in the cooling air, for the better part of an hour, watching Orion and the rest of the oblivious cosmos do wide, lazy circles around me.

Thirty-eight

That was when Thad found me.

After I almost shot him (he'd come up quite stealthily), he took his previous seat beside me on the (now rather chillier) boulder.

'So what do you think?' he asked, earnest as always.

'It's all completely mad, of course.'

I saw his square head nod slowly in the sweet light.

'On the other hand,' I hastened to add, 'as Basha pointed out earlier: we don't have any good way to prove it's wrong. I mean – it *could* have happened. Right?'

In measured tones, Thad said: 'I've been trying to think of reasons why it's not possible. I don't think my view is worth very much. I don't know anything about genetics. Or about palaeo-anthropology, or evolutionary psychology . . .'

'Not true,' I said. 'As usual, you don't give yourself enough credit. You're new to it – but you probably know a lot more than almost everyone on this rock tonight.'

'What? More than the two of us?'

I laughed. 'No. I meant the bigger rock.'

'I know,' he said. 'Just giving you a hard time.'

I squeezed his shoulder. 'So did you think of any? Reasons why it's impossible?'

'Not one.'

'Me neither. Also – we're probably obliged to admit it's at least as plausible as any of the other explanations that have been put forth. Put forth for . . . *this*.' I gestured expansively in the dark.

At this point, I began talking to myself, as much as to Thad – to sort my own thoughts. 'I mean . . . we have the facts that human culture, in all its multifaceted glory, only sprouted up ten thousand years ago. Yet *Homo sapiens*, and the neuroanatomy of our brains, evolved to modern form probably two hundred thousand years ago.' Thad dutifully absorbed my monologue in silence.

'Then we have the near impossibility of accounting for these complex features of humanity – art, culture, science, philosophy – in terms of *any* conceivable selection pressures in our ancestral environment. So there's no way to make sense of it in the light of evolution – which is the *opposite* of the case with almost every other aspect of life on the planet. Evolution explains just about every other known fact of biology.'

I pressed two fingers to my temple. 'So if human higher functions didn't come with our big brains . . . and if they didn't evolve . . . then what does that leave?'

'Little green men,' Thad answered gamely.

'Fuck's sake,' I said, shaking my head. 'The theory's been put forth before that life itself didn't originate on Earth. That some kind of bacterial spores either landed here on meteorites – or else that beings from elsewhere seeded Earth with such spores. It's called, oh, bugger . . . my head's swimming. Panspermia. That's it.' I gripped the smooth, cool sides of our seat with both hands. 'But I've never heard it suggested that, while life originated locally, the higher life of our minds was bequeathed from above.'

'The Pandora myth,' Thad said. 'All of our gifts – bequeathed by the gods.'

I snorted out loud. 'The religionists! They were right all along.'

'In a certain sense,' Thad said. 'God-granted souls . . .'

'Or, if not the religionists, at least the creators of our myths. It's said that myths are fanciful stories we tell to help us understand real things about the experience of being human. The Pandora myth,' I repeated. 'A story about gods descending and granting us our special gifts . . . It seems as if Baṣha knew this, somehow – or at least suspected. God, I just wish I knew where the hell *she* came from.'

'Oh. That I can tell you,' Thad said. 'She came from Israel.'

'What?! How do you know that?'

'Her rifle. It's manufactured by Israel Military Industries – specially for IDF, the Israel Defence Forces.'

I paused to swallow this. 'And no one else could have one?'

'Maybe. They're brand new, so I wouldn't think they'd have

193

gotten around. But she gave herself away when she said it was to replace the M4 – which is the cut-down US M16. Only the IDF is going from one to the other – which is why they designed it.'

'Sly boy,' I said.

'Yeah. I sort of tricked her. Anyway, she's almost certainly IDF – or possibly Mossad, or Shin Bet. Some Israeli security service.' He shrugged. 'I could be wrong.'

'I don't think so. I couldn't place her accent before, but now you mention it . . .'

Good old Thad.

When we got back to the cottage, we found Helen and Basha having the same conversation. Of course, I'd had this one with Helen before – the where-the-hell-could-our-unspeakably-complex-human-nature-have-conceivably-come-from discussion – but Basha seemed by no means unfamiliar with it.

'And not merely writing sonnets and piano concertos, building factories and cathedrals,' she was saying. 'Yes, the Cologne cathedral, which took six hundred and fifty years to construct, is a striking work of architecture. But it is also a work of faith.'

'You mean religion,' Helen said, removing her glasses. 'You're saying the faculty of religion could also have been implanted in us by these . . . tinkerers.'

'How else? Have you another way to account for ninety-five per cent of the human population holding beliefs that are almost certainly untrue? Under evolution, it seems clear that the holding of false beliefs about the world – that propitiating the gods, for instance, can make the crops grow or heal the sick – would be selected against. Misunderstanding the world never helped anyone to survive or reproduce.'

I chuckled and – remembering Helen's diatribe against Thad's late religion – advised Basha that she was probably preaching to the vicar.

Helen smiled. 'Yes. And yet the belief in the supernatural, an afterlife, the succour of a creator figure, received rules of proper

194

conduct – in short, revealed religion – is perniciously, almost universally popular. Something's got to explain it. This?'

Thad spoke up from the corner (which he seemed to have claimed as his official spot). 'But why? Why would they saddle us with something like that?'

'Perhaps,' said Basha, 'their thinking was that only with faith would we be able to endure the exquisite torment of sentience, self-awareness, consciousness.'

'Then how did all of us, everyone in this room, miss out on that?'

'We have learned too much, I think,' Basha said. 'Perhaps faith was only meant to get us by until we worked things out properly.'

'Have we?' persisted Thad.

'I think we are probably in transition.'

But from here we transitioned ourselves to an animated, albeit highly speculative, discussion about the possible meaning of the final reel of the movie. This was the (even odder) scene of the two hands – pressing together, then falling to Earth. Thad participated for a minute or two longer, then disappeared back into the bathroom with the laptop. (We didn't need it – after a hundred-plus viewings we had every frame burnt into our brains.)

'Okay,' Helen said. 'We're pretty sure they are not human hands.'

'Why not?' I asked, scooting closer.

'Because they're not attached to a human. Or to anything. And their shape's off.'

'Right. The fingers are too long and thin.'

'So we are assuming,' added Basha, 'they are artificial, some kind of artefact.'

Helen hurried on. 'And it looks to us like when they're pressed together, they show something. Project something.'

'Another video,' I suggested. 'Except . . . something longer, more complete.'

'Our feature presentation,' Helen said, with a trace of a smile.

'Yes,' I said. 'If it were some kind of electronic device, used to convey additional visual information—'

'—and was dropped off, for us to dig up one day,' Helen interjected.

'Yes,' I said, nodding. 'And if it were a device, self-contained, self-powered – rather than a compressed, four-megabyte movie that had to be slipped cleverly into nucleotide sequences – then it could be of any length. And of much higher resolution.'

'And in colour.'

'That would be nice,' I agreed. We were all smiling with the energy of these ideas. I believe we were bouncing on the bed very slightly. 'But here's the real question: *what would it show?*'

Thad peeked out of the bathroom just then.

'Hey,' he said, 'sorry to interrupt.' He turned to Basha. 'Can I borrow that sat-phone from you – so I can get online?'

'Yes,' Basha said, rising and handing it to him. He took it and closed the door.

I hardly registered this; I was off in my own head. But I spoke aloud: 'For starters, it could explain, in great detail, how exactly they modified our genetic code.'

'And how we can hack it,' added Helen. 'Now that we know how to do so.'

'Perhaps you overesteem your field,' said Basha. 'Genomicists had dismissed unexpressed DNA almost out of hand. Now it seems they were over-hasty.'

Helen looked slightly defensive. 'Hey. There have been some developments in that area. We'd been figuring out that those genes, while they didn't produce any proteins, weren't completely idle. They at least did some flipping of expressive genes.'

'Sure,' said Basha, grinning at Helen mockingly. 'Sell that one to the natives.'

'It's true,' I couldn't help but agree. 'You guys mapped all the so-called expressive genes, then dismissed the rest as junk! It's starting to look as if that's where all the action is. It just flew under your radar. Well, everyone's but A'hib's . . .'

'Jesus, A'hib . . .' Helen breathed. 'If only he could see this.'

'Perhaps he has,' said Basha. 'If he lives, he has the same data we do.'

'Let's not talk about that,' I said. 'What else? I mean, it's wide open. If these hands, this Artefact, plays another movie, if it's a complete set of documentation . . . God, the questions it could answer. About our makeup. About our history. Hey, it could have – I don't know, some kind of contact information? How to ring our benefactors up – once we'd worked out genomics?'

'Now you're getting a little Carl Sagan on us,' Helen said.

I saw Basha had returned to her serious self. 'Whatever information the Artefact might relate,' she said, 'it will relate nothing to us if we cannot find it.'

'Which seems all too likely,' Helen added. She turned to me. 'That was Italy, where they fell, right? You agree that was Italy.'

'Yeah,' I said. 'That seemed to be Italy. But if they intended us to find this thing, why didn't they place it somewhere a little more specific?'

'It is not clear,' said Basha, 'how they felt about us finding this, or when. Perhaps it was assumed that by the time we developed genomic science, we would also have developed some kind of technology for scanning the surface of the planet.'

'Or maybe,' said Helen, 'it's made out of some very funky material. It could even be radioactive.'

'That would definitely help,' I agreed. 'If we knew for sure that it was. And if we had rather more resources for searching for it than we do. And if we could even be sure they exist, that we're interpreting any of this at all correctly . . .' I sighed.

'Even then,' said Helen mournfully, 'what do we do? Go rummaging around the coast of Italy, looking for a pair of disembodied hands? *Scusi signori. Avete visto mani?*'

We were all laughing at this – a little longer than one might expect, probably due to the late hour and surreal situation – so we didn't hear Thad open the bathroom door.

'You won't have to rummage,' he said. 'I can tell you right where they are.'

Thirty-nine

'You're joking, right?' I said, finally, into the sudden void of laughter.

'No,' Thad said, holding his position in the doorway. 'Even from the first time you played it, I couldn't shake the feeling that I'd seen those hands before. But I figured, given everything, it was a safe bet I was just losing my mind.' He let slip a trace of a smile, and his eyes twinkled as they often do. 'Still, it was torturing me. I kept looking at the video – and finally, it hit me. But I had to go online and look to be sure. Hang on.'

He turned around, then came back with the laptop, placing it on the bed. He called up the media window, frozen on the pair of hands, probably the first frame of them. Then he called up a browser window. It was open to www.vatican.va.

'Uh, oh,' Helen said. I think she had some idea where this was going.

Thad clicked through to the page for the Vatican museum, then the Gregorian Etruscan section – from the link colours, he'd already followed them, but was just leading us through the same path. He clicked the first link there: Room I, Early History.

'*Bloody hell . . .*' I breathed. 'Pair of Hands, Seventh Century BC . . .'

Thad began reading aloud: 'Decorated with small golden studs and very long fingers, they are made from a single bronze sheet, closed at the wrist and slightly folded at the edges. Possible comparisons indicate Vulci as their place of origin and production.'

'Where's Vulci?' I whispered.

Thad already had a map. He pulled up the window. It was on the Italian west coast, about halfway between Florence and Rome.

'The hands, back to the hands,' I urged.

We stared at the two images side by side. The first, from the Trailer (as we were coming to think of it), was of course very coarse. And the second, on the Vatican website, showed damage: both

198

thumbs were missing, and the right hand had lost a fingertip and a bit of wrist. But there was no denying it. The inhumanly long and slim fingers were the same shape. But the patterns of the golden studs on the palms sealed it. We'd taken this for speckling, or just noise, on the hands in the Trailer. But – aside from a couple of dots missing in the photographed version – the dot patterns on both hands were identical.

'It figures,' said Thad, seeming mordantly amused.

'What?' I asked.

'That the Church is involved. There's just no escaping . . .'

'Oh, Thad,' I said.

'I am afraid he may be right,' said Basha. A trace of dark cloud lay on her fine, normally dispassionate features.

'How do you mean,' I asked.

'In addition to the Qabbalists and the Nagas, there is another group I did not mention. A group of . . . Papists. Possibly associated with Opus Dei.'

'Oh, jeesh,' muttered Thad. 'And how are Opus Dei involved?'

'I have a poor understanding of that,' she admitted. 'Which is one reason I did not bring it up. But I have some intel that this group has had involvement.'

'What sort of involvement?' I asked.

Basha raised her eyes to me. 'For a start, we think it was they who were shadowing you these last few days.'

'I thought you said that was the Feds?'

'Yes, well. Not only the Feds.'

'Do you know why the Catholic Church would be watching me?'

'No. But we have surely developed some grounds for speculation. It is possible they intended to scare you off the project – off your work searching the genome.'

'Why scare me off?'

'Perhaps to protect something.'

'Protect what?'

Basha didn't answer. But after a few seconds of heavy silence, Thad did.

'Are you kidding?' he said. 'Do you have any idea what kind of an operation the Roman Catholic Church runs?'

'Do you think,' I asked, 'they understand what they've got in their museum? With the Artefact? And do you think they know what we've got? With the Pandora sequence?'

'Imagine if they had even an inkling,' Thad said. 'Think about what they would do to protect this secret. If it got out, it would bring down an empire.'

'C'mon,' said Helen, looking dismissive. 'It's just another Church.'

'No, you're wrong,' said Thad. 'No other Church exists as its own sovereign nation-state. No other Church has a billion members pledged to follow the decrees of an infallible leader, God's living representative on Earth. But it's not even that. It's the money I'm thinking of. The Vatican as corporation.'

'I'm sure there's a lot of money involved,' Helen said. 'There always is.'

'Not on this scale,' Thad said. 'Look, I don't know how much of the history you know. But the Roman Catholic Church basically dates from the fourth century, when Constantine made it the state Church of Rome. Even back then, through the Middle Ages, money was key. Rich families could buy positions for their sons within the Church; peasants had to pay to have their children christened – and non-baptized children could not go to heaven. You had to pay to get married, you had to pay to be buried in holy ground. There were collections, Church tithings, sales of relics and indulgences.'

He sat down on the edge of the bed before continuing.

'Since then, it's gotten worse, not better. In 1929, I think, Pope Pius XI signed the Lateran Treaty with Mussolini – exchanging recognition and support for the fascist government for ninety million dollars in cash and the establishment of the Vatican as a sovereign state – tax-sheltered. The Vatican Bank has used that status to invest in real estate holdings, stocks, off-shore trusts. Today, no one really knows the net worth of the Vatican. Most estimates are over fifty billion dollars – in securities, gold reserves that exceed those of some industrialized nations, real-estate holdings also larger than many countries, and any number of palaces filled with art and treasures.'

'Could they really think all that's at risk?' Helen asked. 'From the four of us?'

'I'm not thinking so much of the holdings,' said Thad. 'More about the income. There are something like 2,500 dioceses worldwide – all of which send a portion of their donations to the Holy See. I don't know how much that is. But just the two hundred or so US dioceses take in like two hundred and fifty million dollars a week. The amount they send to Rome is undisclosed. But it's all tax-free, in both the US and Italy.'

Thad took his own glasses off now and tiredly rubbed the bridge of his nose. 'Okay. Now, can you imagine? If it turned out that the human soul doesn't come from God – from the Holy Father who sent Jesus Christ his only begotten son to the world to die for our sins?' He put his glasses back on. 'But from *little green men*?'

'I guess that might cut into the collection plate,' Helen said archly.

We all sat in silence – until Helen spoke up again. But her tone had changed.

'Let's go get it,' she said.

'Get what?' I asked.

'The Artefact,' she said. 'Those hands. That movie. These answers.'

'What? From the Vatican?' I asked, mouth not closing. 'Are you daft?'

'They don't have any right,' Helen said calmly. 'To keep this from us. I mean, from the world.' She squared her shoulders. 'I don't know about the rest of you. But I for one don't intend to let the goddamned Church have a monopoly on the truth.'

I realized she was totally serious. I looked to Basha. I gave her my best does-that-make-the-least-bit-of-sense? look.

Basha demurred. Lowering her gaze, she said: 'Look. It is very late. And the last day has been very taxing, to say the least. We should all sleep for ten hours, and then carry on this discussion.' She turned to Thad. 'Will you stay here?'

'I can't,' Thad said. 'I've got to go home.'

'Very well. But you may not return.'

'I see,' Thad said quietly.

Basha reached out and touched his elbow. 'It is nothing against you. Just that you could be followed back here. And I have no more backup hideouts.'

Thad squinted very deeply. 'All right. I'll stay then. I need to call my wife.'

'Use my phone,' Basha said. 'It cannot be traced.'

Thad took the phone and stepped to the front door. He turned back to face us. 'Hey,' he said. 'How did you know I was named for a saint?'

'Just a guess,' Basha said mildly. 'In a Catholic family, the odds are good.'

Thad nodded and paused. 'What does your name mean? Basha.'

She smiled. 'It is Hebrew. It has two meanings. One is "stranger".'

'And the other?'

Basha turned her back, reaching into her bag. '"Daughter of God",' she said.

While Thad was outside, we girls undressed for bed. It looked like I'd be sharing one with Helen (not for the first time).

Before getting under the covers, I took a last look at the laptop – at the Vatican's web page for Pair of Hands. 'Humph,' I said under my breath. 'Rather earlier than seventh century BC, I'll warrant. And *definitely* not Etruscan . . .'

Forty

When I woke, I didn't know where I was – nor what had woken me. The cool air smelled oddly clean (free of chimp), and the touch of the sheets unfamiliar on my skin. It was extremely dark in every direction and I was terrifically confused by dreams, caught halfway between that world and . . . I didn't even know where.

I tried to lie still and get my breathing under control.

I realized there was a very faint light coming in through some drapes – but only when a shadow passed by them. It seemed a human figure, walking slowly and smoothly. In a second, it had gone.

And then everything came back to me in a single surreal rush. Oh my God. Was this my life?

As my eyes adjusted, I found I could make out two lumps in the next bed over – one large, one small. And then I realized I was the only lump in mine. Helen had gone.

Not pausing to ask myself whether I should (or why), I rose and dressed silently. I felt around for my eyeglasses and my bag (which held both the emasculating phone and the reassuring pistol), then padded to the door. I opened it a quarter-inch at a time, but it did not squeak.

Outside, the air was chill. The celestial light illuminated the external scene much better than inside. But I found I had no idea which direction to go – which way Helen might have gone. My first thought was the main area, the lodge. But of course it wouldn't be open now. That pretty much left wandering the trails. I set out, walking slowly and quietly – and listening carefully. As if walking through a dream.

I didn't consciously head toward the bare round hilltop – which I thought of as mine (or, at any rate, mine and Thad's). I took a totally other trail. But perhaps they all led to the heights. As I approached an opening in the tree-line, seeing star-cluttered sky before me, I heard a faint voice. I froze where I was and struggled to hear.

Crouched there in moonlight shadows and crisp air, boots sinking into the soft peat, I wondered again: was I really still in my dream? How long might it have been going on? The last day? A week? Dreams are real while they last, it has been said. Can we say more of life? I wondered how much longer all of *this*, whatever it was, might go on.

Pushing away my reverie, I tried to focus on the voice. It was whispered, it was sporadic. It was unintelligible. I would not be able to make it out from where I stood.

Crouching lower still, I took several painstaking steps forward. The round hilltop came into view, over and around a last bit of foliage, which kept me concealed. And right there on my very own boulder, surprisingly clear and bright in the moonlight, sat Helen. Nodding, and then speaking, into her mobile.

But the wind was rising and falling over the exposed pinnacle. It only brought me a word here and another there.

'. . . know yet. Anything, for all I . . .' said Helen.

'. . . say for sure,' she continued. '—orrow's possible.'

Belatedly, it occurred to me that Helen might simply be calling a friend, a relative, a lover I didn't know about. Explaining her absence, indicating that she was okay. I started to feel guilty – hiding in the bushes, spying on her – if her mission, however clandestine, was innocent.

I'd begun straightening up to withdraw, when she moved, bringing my eye back. She held something in her lap, and now tilted it up toward her face.

Still remonstrating with the wind, she said: '—portant right now. Ready?' The wind took issue. Helen countered: '. . . locus fifteen queue twenty-two dot three.'

I thought my neck muscles might snap from trying to push my ears toward her.

'. . . four mega-codons,' she said, then, '—scribe the encoding scheme.'

Bitch. So much for innocence. Suddenly I didn't know what to do or how to feel. So I just crouched there with my head hanging.

Quickly enough, though, I decided I wanted to avoid getting caught rather more than I wanted to any hear more of this. Maintaining my crouch, I backed slowly away from the clearing. When Helen was safely out of sight, I rotated in place.

And found Basha crouching a foot behind me. She held one finger to her lips.

I fell straight on my arse; but did at least manage to avoid crying out.

'Come on,' Basha whispered, nearly inaudibly. She reached out her hand to me.

'Okay. Who is she, then?' I asked dully. Basha and I now sat in the near-dark at a picnic table, in a small field behind the lodge.

'Is she not your friend?' Basha countered.

'Evidently not.' I ran my fingers, albeit with difficulty, through my hair. 'Actually, I never did feel like I knew her. Now I know I didn't.' I sighed heavily.

Basha put her hand on mine. 'Look. Judging people is a tricky business. What do you really know? That Helen is working for somebody, and that she is interested in the Pandora sequence. But all the rest of us, we also work for somebody. And we are also interested. It does not necessarily make us villains.'

'Who is she working for, then?'

'Not only GenenW, I can tell you that.'

'Very funny. You've known about Helen all along, haven't you.'

'I have suspected. But I know very little. When I say I can only tell you she works for someone in addition to GenenW, I mean it. The rest yet eludes me.'

'I was beginning to think you knew everything.'

'Pity the person who does,' she said. 'Questions are more useful than answers.'

I looked up at her and squeezed her hand. 'I think you must be right, there,' I said. 'And I have to say – I feel that the longer I spend with you, the more prone I am to a healthy scepticism about things. About everything, really. You're having your effect.'

'Yes, well,' Basha said, sighing. 'Hang around a barbershop long enough and you just might get a haircut.'

I froze dead, with her hand still in mine.

'Oh my God.' I peered at the black ovals of her eyes, shadowed in the pretty moon-cast oval of her face. I swallowed dryly. 'You're the Rootin' Tootin' Retard.'

'*Oy veh*,' she said. 'I mean, oops. Yes. That is me.'

'Oh, God,' I muttered, pulling my hand back and burying my face in it. 'Life's just too hard . . .'

'Life is certainly hard if you think it is,' Basha/RTR said.

Forty-one

After my complete and total debilitating shock, I think I was able to perceive, in myself, a subsequent warm rush of relief.

'I knew it,' I said finally. 'I knew you were no stranger – the Hebrew meaning of your name notwithstanding.'

'No,' she said gently. 'No stranger to you.'

'But who *are* you? Really? Thad said you're Israeli. A soldier, or security agent.'

'Ah,' she sighed. 'It appears the cat is truly out of the bag. I should have known Thad's interest in armaments was not idle.'

Her reference to Thad reminded me of the cottage, which reminded me that Helen would be returning to it. 'Shouldn't we get back?' I asked. 'Before Helen does?'

'Not necessarily,' Basha answered. 'It will not hurt to give Helen a little something to wonder about herself.'

I smiled at that. 'But . . . if we don't know where Helen's real loyalties lie . . . how can we be sure we're safe with her here? Why would we keep her around?'

Basha paused before answering. 'For one thing – it is an old principle of counter-intelligence that a double agent you have unearthed is almost always more valuable kept around than tossed out. Or turned off.'

'So – we keep our friends close and our enemies closer?'

'Something like that. And for another thing – as a genomicist, she is quite useful to have around, given our circumstances. No? For instance, I am not sure we would have decoded the sequence without her.'

'What is *your* background?' I asked.

'My studies were in philosophy and theology. At Tel Aviv University.'

'No great surprise there,' I said. 'I wonder, actually, if the three of us don't complement one another nicely. Though – that qualifies you to be a secret agent?'

She laughed. 'You might be surprised. Look, you have learned quite a lot on your own. And, in point of fact, you and I are already friends, after a fashion. You have had to get to know me; but I have felt I knew you from the start.'

'I do admit,' I said, 'you seem a bit less philosophical in person.'

'Yes, well. Right now we have issues on the ground that must be dealt with. Philosophy is for idler times – sitting back at our desks, in air-conditioned offices . . . But my point is that I see no reason not to confide in you.' She paused before going on.

'My name is Basha Levy. I am twenty-five years old, and a *sabra* – meaning I was born in Israel, on a kibbutz in the Upper Galilee. When I was eighteen, I began my mandatory service with the Israel Defence Force. However, I was nominated for the special forces – and, ultimately, passed selection for a group called Unit YAMAG. This is a part of the Israel Border Guard, but charged with counter-terrorism, hostage rescue, tactical assistance to police units – and also intelligence-gathering and infiltration of domestic terror and criminal groups. Can you see where this goes?'

I considered. 'You've been watching the Qabbalists. The Kahanists. The extremists.'

'Not just watching. For all purposes, I work for the Cabal. I have been fully infiltrated with this group, for nearly a year.'

I nodded. 'So then, I suppose I can see where you have some sympathy for Helen – with her multiple employers.'

'Yes. For all I really know, Helen also works for IDF. Or another of our two dozen security agencies. Who knows? So often, there are levels and levels. And then more levels below.'

'Still,' I said. 'Infiltration, counter-terrorism, hostage rescue . . . they let women do that kind of thing?'

'Oh, I'm Israeli,' she chided. 'We need, and use, everyone. The rag-tag force that fought off five invading Arab armies and won the War of Independence in 1948 included many hundreds of women.

208

Many of them died. Today, admittedly, some of the special forces groups exclude women. But some do not.'

I shook my head to try and clear it. 'Right, then. That much makes sense to me. If you were watching the Qabbalists, and the Qabbalists were watching GenenW, looking for their . . . coded message, their pipeline to God . . . then I can see how you knew about Helen. As well about A'hib, and what he was working on. But – you and I have been corresponding for much longer than I've known either of them? How?'

Basha paused. She seemed to assess me in the dark.

'Let us table that for tonight,' she said. 'Suffice it to say, as you have guessed, we did not meet by accident. Nor did you and Helen meet by accident. You have my word that I will elaborate. But now I want to sleep. And I also want you to sleep.'

'Fair enough,' I agreed, as we both rose. 'I thought I trusted you – and I was right about that. I do. Also,' I added as we began the walk back, 'I'm very glad to make your acquaintance. Properly, in the flesh.'

'Likewise,' Basha said, warmly.

When we got back to the cottage, Helen was back in our bed – pretending to be asleep, I think. In the morning, we'd all probably have to pretend we didn't know what we all obviously, necessarily, knew. That we'd all been out sneaking around.

And, to my surprise, I found this intrigue more amusing than anything else.

Slipping under the covers, then lying giddily beneath them, I tried to imagine what tomorrow would bring. For some time now, each new day had proved more spectacularly unlikely than the last. And, to my scarcely controllable delight, I realized that the seemingly endless march of indistinguishable days had been . . . pre-empted.

Forty-two

When morning found us, it spilled its slanting early light on four substantially dazed and ill-at-ease people. If a white male ex-military American database administrator and father of two, an African American scientist, a British expat computer programmer, and an Israeli special forces soldier have ever before woken up in the same small bedroom . . . well, someone surely would have made a joke about it by now.

Which notwithstanding, the first thing we all did (after fumbling through morning greetings, ablutions, and dressing) was all walk together into the bar – gunning for breakfast and, mainly, coffee. We picked up a little of the former and quite a lot of the latter and took it back to the cottage with us.

We'd just begun nibbling, and intently caffeinating, when Helen moved to reintroduce, still with an entirely straight face, her suggestion that we invade the Vatican museum and liberate the alien Artefact.

'It's just a bag job,' she said, a little too coolly. 'We break in, we steal it. I mean, four people as smart as us? Please. We can figure out a way.'

I'd begun reciting my catalogue of objections to this, and had gotten to number six or so – on the sheer implausibility of robbing one of the world's top museums – when Thad interrupted.

'You'll probably be surprised to hear this,' he said, 'but Vatican security's not actually all that tight. Definitely not as daunting as you'd imagine.'

'How do you know?' I asked.

'For the same reason that I recognized the hands in the first place. I mean, almost every Catholic who can afford the plane ticket has been to visit the Vatican. But I actually spent a semester working there, when I was in college.' This seemed to call for some elaboration. 'I went to school at Notre Dame – a Catholic university.

And I also happened to play football there. Because of this, as a junket, a perk, really, I got set up with a winter term abroad, in Rome. I took a couple of classes at Notre Dame's extension there. But I also had an internship, just a part-time job really, at St Peter's.'

'I never knew that,' I said.

Thad looked a little chagrined. 'It was just more big-time college football excess, really. But I guess I didn't mind taking advantage at the time.'

'More power to you,' said Helen. 'So how much do you know about the museum? The security setup, the layout, and whatnot?'

Thad took a swallow of coffee and bit off half a croissant. He stood off in his corner again. It was like some spatial manifestation of the gender divide. 'The bad news is I didn't work in the museum. The good news is I actually worked, basically, security detail. Most of the time, my job was in the basilica itself. Keeping an eye on the crowd, keeping an eye on the relics and artwork.'

'Does the crowd there get rowdy?' Helen asked. 'Mosh pits and crowd surfing?'

Thad grinned. 'You joke. But fifteen or so years ago, some crazy guy took a hammer to Michelangelo's Pietà – the famous statue of Virgin and Christ. He knocked poor Mary's nose off before they stopped him.'

'So after that they brought in the Fighting Irish?'

Thad laughed aloud at that. 'Yes, and put the Pietà under bullet-proof glass.'

'But surely they have other security than college interns – even football players.'

'Yes, they do,' said Thad. 'The Swiss Guard.' These three words he intoned seriously. 'For five hundred years, they have been the personal bodyguards of Popes. There are one hundred of them, they wear funny striped suits, and they carry state-of-the-art weaponry – from the sixteenth century. Swords and halberds.'

Helen seemed cheered. 'No problem, then. Right?'

'Yes and no,' Thad said. 'First of all, there's also a Vatican police force – though they tend not to be in the basilica, or the other inner areas. But, also, as for the Guards – they're both ceremonial and they're not. First off, to join, you have to be Swiss, Catholic, male, at least five foot eight – and already fully trained by the Swiss military. Second, they've got the monkey suits and the pole arms. But when the Pope goes out, they put on plain clothes. And even when they're carrying the ceremonial weapons, they do have firearms in locked boxes nearby.'

'Do you know where they keep them?'

'No. But I do know a couple of things. For one, there has been some unflattering talk about them in recent years. That they've been getting slack, that there's dissension in the ranks. A number of years back, there was a big scandal – the captain of the Guard was found murdered, along with his wife. Their killer was also found dead – one of the Guards, who they said committed suicide. It was all very dodgy-looking. The Church did its own investigation and there was suspicion of a cover-up.'

'Did they seem incompetent when you were there?' Helen had a lot of questions.

'No,' Thad said. 'They seemed like okay guys. They were serious. But there weren't that many of them. For instance, we would sweep the Basilica at closing time – and it was typically one person to sweep each transept, the nave, and behind the altar. Basically four guys for this huge cathedral.'

'Did you ever have anyone hide in there? After closing?'

'Not that I'm aware of.'

Helen bit her lip. 'Wouldn't help us anyway. It's the museum we need to get to.'

'That's the other thing, though,' said Thad. 'There's actually a passageway. From one to the other. I wouldn't quite call it a secret door. But it's only opened up to let tour groups, usually VIP tour groups, slip through. It leads directly from the basilica into the Sistine Chapel.'

'You're kidding.'

'Nope. And the Sistine Chapel is the last stop on the museum tour. It leads directly to the rest of the museum.'

I spoke up after holding my tongue as long as I could. 'That's all very interesting. But I still can't quite believe we're having this conversation. I mean, even with Thad's inside knowledge, what you propose can't be possible. Besides, he only knows the basilica. Who knows what security's like in the museum? It's one of the world's most famous. It would be like robbing the Louvre. You wouldn't suggest that, would you?'

'It would depend on why I wanted to,' Helen countered. 'I've read that there's generally understood to be no way to sell anything you steal from someplace like that. There's no market. If something gets lifted from the Louvre, when it eventually turns up, everyone knows exactly where it came from. So, to an extent, they're counting on catching you when you try to actually profit from the theft.'

I shook my head. 'Okay, never mind the odds. What about the stakes? Have you considered what you'd be risking?'

Helen pinned me with her eye, head tilted down and to the side. 'And what about you?' she said. 'What are you willing to risk? To find out the truth. With a capital T.'

She had me there. I might risk quite a lot.

'Okay,' Basha finally said, a little tiredly. 'Enough for now. This is all quite hypothetical. But I will do some research. Let me contact my people – and see what they know. I can very likely get floor plans and such. And probably a survey of the security. Perhaps even an overall assessment of whether this idea is possible to pursue.'

'More than fair,' Helen said.

I didn't comment, but only pointed my gaze out the window, where the sun now flashed wildly. But then I turned to Thad, a familiar question on my lips.

'Yeah, definitely,' he answered, before I could ask it.

Out in all the light, I switched my glasses, he darkened his, and we headed out.

'Mate,' I said, when we'd gotten a few yards down the trail, 'you really are one lapsed Catholic.'

'Why do you say that?'

'Well, it was bad enough last night. When you demonstrated enough knowledge about the Church's financial dealings to file a racketeering suit.'

He nodded. 'Yeah. Actually, my lapse of faith was both cause and effect of that. Have you ever been to St Pete's? I mean, it's a pretty damned lavish place. That got me thinking, so I did a little research on the church's finances. That seemed to solidify my idea that I was in the wrong place.'

'The wrong place – for what exactly?'

'For meaning,' he said. 'And solace. But meaning, mainly.'

I let a bit of trail go by under us in silence. 'What about now?' I asked. 'After what we've found. The sequence.'

He didn't answer for some time. 'I don't know,' he said finally, sounding troubled. 'Does this mean it's all fake? I mean, if everything we've ever accomplished as a species . . . was made possible by some guys just tinkering with our DNA?'

I answered cautiously. 'I don't think so. I mean, first off: why would our higher natures be more real if they were a product of Darwin's algorithm – interacting with a bunch of arbitrary environmental selection pressures? Versus, as it seems may be the case, the work of a group of intelligent designers? Secondly: I don't think anyone, no one in the Church certainly, ever suggested that our makeup was fake when they thought it was all produced by a *supernatural* intelligent designer. Little green men are more like God than evolution is. They had a purpose in mind.'

'Good point,' said Thad. 'And what's God, anyway – but a really powerful unearthly visitor? And what was Clarke's Third Law? Any sufficiently advanced technology is indistinguishable from magic?'

'Precisely,' I said. 'But there's an even more fundamental point, I think, and it's this: really, the most our genetic makeup can do is give us a *propensity*, or maybe a capacity, for art and culture. It can't give us art or culture itself – or music or literature or philosophy or love or deeper meaning. It can't give us the reality of these things in all

214

their particular glory. Genes can't build a Cologne cathedral. Only we can.'

'Yeah . . . but does that make the Cologne cathedral any different than, say, a beaver's dam? A product of pure, hard-wired instinct?'

'All I can say to that, Thad, is: go look at it for yourself.'

Thad laughed. 'Actually, I have. I was stationed in Germany for a while.' He looked around at the beautiful scene as we came out onto the hilltop. 'And you're right. That building is completely amazing.'

When we got back, about an hour later, we found Basha and Helen poring over the laptop again. They both looked up when we entered. Helen smiled and said:

'Hey. Check it out. Basha got us floor plans, schematics, patrol and maintenance schedules – all kinds of dirt. You wouldn't believe some of this shit. She's awesome.'

Didn't I know it. I looked at her admiringly.

But Basha was looking at Thad. She said:

'You were right about the door between the basilica and the Sistine Chapel.'

We spent the rest of the day, nearly eight uninterrupted hours, in a flurry of fantastical and skin-tingling tag-team pursuits, including: brainstorming; hypothesizing; sketching; introductory infiltration lectures; contingency planning; picking Thad's brain; writing Basha's home office for more intel; making lists of needed gear; and, ultimately, kind of dumbfoundingly . . . booking flights.

When we had finished . . . when it seemed to us that we had made every preparation that we might reasonably make (in the service of such a completely unreasonable undertaking) . . . Basha put the laptop to sleep, and we all sat around enjoying a minute's silence.

Taking it all in.

Feeling, I imagine, a bit like a team.

Finally, I put my hand on Basha's arm. I said: 'Well? What do you think?'

215

'I think,' she said, shaking her head slowly, 'that we are digging a deeper ditch for ourselves and handing up the shovel.'

I looked around at the others. Thad was chuckling silently; Helen serious as ever.

Forty-three

Of course, Thad couldn't go with us. We knew that all along.

When he emerged from the cabin, for the final time, he found me sitting on the stoop, with the laptop in my lap. Ostensibly, I was reviewing video archive footage of the target building; but really I think I was just outside sulking. In denial.

He sat down gently beside me. 'Whatcha got there?' When I didn't answer, he leaned in carefully. 'Looks like . . . Papal inauguration ceremony?'

'Yes,' I managed, without much enthusiasm. 'I grabbed it from the BBC. I'm supposed to be looking for things in the basilica that aren't in the floorplans. But they just keep showing some guy in a red beanie on his knees kissing the Pope's ring. Who the hell *is* this guy?'

Thad leaned in closer, squinting. 'Umm, guys in red are usually cardinals. If he's putting the signet ring on the Pope's finger, that's probably actually Cardinal N'Dasoo.'

'Someone we should be worried about?'

'Definitely. He's head of the College of Cardinals – the body that *elects* Popes. So he may actually be the one running things, behind the scenes. He's also Secretary of State.'

'Of what? Italy?'

'No. The Holy See. I told you – the Church is its own sovereign nation. And . . . if I remember correctly, in the seventies N'Dasoo was also nuncio to Chile – where he was known to be very chummy with Pinochet.'

'Great. Powerful *and* sinister.'

I still hadn't met Thad's gaze. 'I have to go now,' he said.

'I know.' I finally looked up at him.

'Don't get me wrong,' he said, standing and reaching out a hand to help me up. 'No one wants to know the truth about things more

217

than me. And, frankly, hate to admit it . . . but the whole Caper looks like way too much fun.'

We'd found ourselves borrowing Helen's term – and mentally capitalizing it.

'Aside from the huge likelihood of getting arrested or killed,' I amended.

'Aside from that.'

'And it would not do to have Kennedy and Holden's daddy arrested or killed.'

'Or Leslie's husband,' he added. 'She'd kill me a second time. Anyway, I just can't. I couldn't take off like that. I couldn't take a risk like that.'

'I know. Say no more, old man,' I said. 'But you'll be missed.'

'Just come back,' he said sternly. 'Okay? Come back.'

'I will,' I promised. 'And you know I mean it when I say I'll miss you. You're' – oh, shit, crying again – 'you're my big brother. You're the big brother I've still got . . .'

We hugged for a long time. Thad cried, too. Big galoot.

He was in his truck and pulling away before I remembered, running after and banging on the window. 'Wait! Hell, I can't believe I nearly forgot . . . can you take Erasmus for me?'

'Sure. He's at your place?'

'Yes. Just swing by and identify yourself. He'll open up once he knows it's you.'

'No problem. He can stay as long as he wants. Kids'll be thrilled.'

And with that, Thad pulled away for good, as the sun touched the treetops.

One of the last special services Thad had performed, in our planning, was to point out that today was actually . . . Easter Sunday. No one had noticed. But, of course, if we attempted our stunt straight away, it would be during Easter week celebrations in Rome.

This actually turned out to be a good thing – the visiting hours of both the basilica and the museum were modified during this week. To our benefit.

'So then the stars really are being aligned for us,' I said.

'No,' said Basha. 'No one aligns the stars for us. But sometimes they do happen to line up. At those times, it is up to us to move.' Epigrams like this sounded, to my ear, an awful lot like the RTR. I was beginning to merge the two identities in my mind.

And as I stood and ruminated on that, still watching the dust settle from the rumbling departure of Thad's truck, Basha/RTR emerged from the cottage.

'How are you feeling?' she asked. 'With Thad gone.'

'Okay,' I said. 'I just hope I have the strength for all this.'

'You're strong enough if you are,' she said.

I cocked my head. 'You mean – I'm strong enough if I think I am. Right?'

'No,' she said, with the wry smile. 'It is not actually that complicated.'

I nodded in respectful, if bemused, silence.

She said: 'Do you ever take walks with people not Thad?'

'Is that a proposition?' I asked. 'You're on.'

Once we'd gotten out on the trails, Basha said: 'Despite my brave words for you – in fact, what we are attempting is likely to be a close thing. We all must pay close attention. And it is important that we keep things from going south at the outset.'

'Why?'

'Because we all know which way the road south goes.'

'Which way?' I asked.

She looked at me sidelong. '. . . South.'

I found I could formulate no argument against that.

Motioning me in front of her as the trail narrowed, she added: 'We are also going to need to keep an eye on Helen. If and when things get hairy . . . what is the expression? When the cat is amongst the canaries? Well, we may be bringing our own cat with us.'

'When the wheels are off the wagon,' I mused idly. 'When the water is out of the pool . . .' I pulled myself from this reverie and asked: 'But surely you can call for some sort of backup from your people? If we get into trouble?'

She didn't answer until after we'd emerged onto the ever-useful hilltop. I didn't even have to prompt her to take a seat on the ole boulder. I sat facing away from her; and soon we had our backs pressed together, resting each upon the other.

She still didn't answer, by the way. (No surprise there.) I tried another question:

'Right, then. Now. How did you and I meet?'

'Online,' she said.

'Yes, well aware. I mean, specifically. I've long forgotten. But I doubt you have. Since it was not happenstance.'

'No,' she said. 'In a word, I left breadcrumbs for you. I posted something in which I knew you would be interested – in a place I knew you would find it.'

'So I'd think it was my idea to contact you. Clever. But why?'

'I have told you I was working with the Cabal – but I mean that literally. My job was never to keep them from finding a Pandora sequence. Merely to keep an eye on them – and, if necessary, to keep them from using the knowledge for ill.'

'What sort of ill?'

'Specifically, who knows? But more generally – either in opposition to the Israeli government, with whose policies they tend to disagree. Or, more directly against our Arab neighbours.'

'Israel pays you to protect your sworn enemies?'

'What can I say? Morality is not relative to what the other guy does. But, not to be so lofty . . . they could also get us in trouble with world opinion.'

'Gotcha. But, you said you were working with them. How exactly?'

'Just simple surveillance, at first. Helping them to spy on the Human Genome Project, and on the biotechs they saw as most promising. But, quickly enough, I developed my own interest. In the project.'

'Knowing you, I don't doubt it.'

'Of course, the Qabbalists felt the biotechs were moving too slowly. For my part, after learning as much as I could, I grew to feel that they were also moving in the wrong directions. They all ignored the unexpressed DNA, the so-called junk. HGP and Celera's completion of the genome map indicated that the human genome consists of only 33,800 genes – expressed ones, ones that create proteins – many fewer than the 100,000 that were expected. There was some surprise over this. But, it seemed obvious to me, and I would have expected it to seem obvious to them as well, that so few base pairs could never design something as wildly complex and diverse as human nature.'

'So, what then? Did you try to impact their research, channel it in some way?'

'No. I was unqualified. As much of an interest as I had taken, and as privy as I was to their research data, it was not my field. But, at the same time, I began to feel that . . . how to put it? That genomics was too important to leave to the genomicists.'

'Who then?'

'I decided what they most needed was a good cognitive scientist. Someone who had a sense of the real processing requirements of human cognition – of something on that order of complexity. And who could convince them that 33,800 genes was an inadequate amount of programming, simply on the face of it. I looked, but to my surprise, the biotechs employed not a single expert in cognitive science. So I undertook to dig one up on their behalf.'

'Enter me,' I said. 'How'd you find me?'

'Berkeley has one of the top programs. And you were one of their top people.'

'Thanks. But I still feel used. That you rang me up just for this purpose.'

'I had not rung you up yet. I merely bookmarked you. Around that time, I also learned of what A'hib Khouri was doing. Inside of GenenW – but on his own.'

'How did you learn that?'

'Reading his email.'

'I'd think someone as savvy about crypto as A'hib would be more careful.'

'Almost no one is, whether savvy or not. Generally, why bother? At any rate. I saw that he was at least looking, to my mind, in the right places. But neither did he quite have the skills or background to make real headway. After more research, I decided what *he* needed was a good programmer of genetic algorithms. To search the gene-space.'

'Uh, oh,' I said.

'And who was doing the most interesting things with genetic algorithms? The AI community. But who was making the most substantive progress in AI?'

'The video game companies,' I answered for her.

'Yes. They had the most money to play with. And, usually, the most incentive to get something actually working. In real applications.'

I figured I could finish this story on my own: 'So you went looking for genetic coders. And imagine your surprise and delight when my name came up a second time.'

'What can I say?' Basha said. 'You are literally one in a million. One in a billion, I should say. We would be lucky to find six people on the planet with your combination of background, education, and skills. And broadness of perspective.'

'Forgive me if I still feel a little hurt. That I was just a skill-set to you.'

'You were that, at first. I began our correspondence hoping to get a sense of your skills and temperament. But I very quickly found our interaction to be its own reward. I hope you can believe this. You might consider that I spent much more time trading mail with you than either the Cabal, or IDF, would willingly have paid me for.'

I paused to get over my pique; to get over myself. 'I do believe you.' I tried to think through all this. 'But wait. You say you picked me out for this project. But I'm belatedly remembering how I actually got involved. I met Helen – at a club. Randomly, I thought, at the time. And she introduced me to A'hib. So what the hell?'

'What the hell, indeed. As I said, I had my own ideas about what the biotechs, GenenW and Khouri in particular, needed to be doing.

222

And what sort of help they required. But I could only safely do so much on my own. I was only meant to be monitoring email, peeking at files. I was not physically there – nor was I in touch with any agents on the ground.'

'The Qabbalists actually had agents inside?'

'Who knows?'

'Speaking of which,' I added, 'weren't you in great danger? Of the Qabbalists discovering you're an IDF agent?'

'Oh, they knew I was IDF. But they believed they had turned me, as a double agent for them. Against the government.'

'Christ. Which made you a triple agent?'

'Technically, I suppose.'

'Wasn't that very difficult – and dicey? Convincing them you'd switched sides?'

'Not really. These are people who believe that they are God's Chosen. They are zealots. They think everyone should see things their way – so it was not so hard to convince them that I did.' She shrugged. 'At any rate, as for GenenW, I did not know if the Cabal had agents there. But I knew I did not. So I did what I felt I could: I told the Qabbalists my ideas – and I also told them about you. That you could help.'

'Ouch,' I said. 'I don't suppose I can thank you for that.'

She paused briefly. 'No. But perhaps you can forgive me. There is no question that I got you involved in all of this. But you should also know . . . I came here, to the US, on my own volition. Not with IDF. Technically, I am on holiday.'

I startled at this. 'Why did you come, then?'

'I do not suppose I ever expected you to find anything. But when you did, it soon became apparent that the Qabbalists had designs on you beyond simply monitoring your work. As did the Nagas . . . and the Feds . . . and, apparently, the Papists.' She sighed. 'Suddenly, you became a nexus of attention. And, suffice it to say, there was no telling what might happen to you then. And whatever did – it would be my fault.'

And with that she ended her speech. Her breathing, as measured by the rising and falling of her back against mine, remained slow and regular. But I guessed she had a lot more control over her physical reactions than did I. Or Thad. Or anyone I knew.

'So you just . . . booked a flight? And came in blazing to rescue me?' I felt her shrug against my back.

By this time, the sun had gotten serious about setting orangely upon our rock, once again. I sat in the richly tinted glare, and ran all this around in my mind. Finally, I realized there was still one glaring anomaly.

'Wait a minute,' I whispered. 'If you pointed the Qabbalists toward me . . . and then Helen came and found me . . . acting as if we met by chance . . . doesn't that tell us who Helen's actually working for?'

'The facts are certainly suggestive. But you already know about conclusions . . .'

'. . . They are not to be jumped to.'

'Yes. With this many wires crossing in the junction box . . . who knows how someone finds a thing out? Or from whom? And there are other facts. For instance, when I stormed that safe-house, I found Helen sitting in a circle with those Nagas. And she did not give outward signs of being under duress. I could be wrong.'

'Jesus.' I tilted my head forward – and realized that some of my ten thousand fine kinks had insinuated themselves into Basha's braided ponytail. 'You know, she is a very cool customer. Maybe she just doesn't show duress. Then again . . . she might have tied herself up in that basement. As a human prop, for my benefit.'

Basha only sighed in response. By now, this was the only reminder I needed from her to reserve my judgement.

But I figured I did have an answer to my question about whether we could expect Basha's friends to come bail us out, if and when our escapade in Rome went south . . . She had gone off the reservation. And us right with her.

Forty-four

'Even at a time like this, huh?' Helen asked, ribbing.

I lay sprawled and contorted on a small patch of clear floor – running through a baroque stretching routine. My cheek and my leg were at that moment in contact.

'Always,' I answered, in a tone I imagined would disinvite further inquiry.

'And may one ask why?' she persisted.

'Because,' I said, swivelling smoothly into a groin stretch, 'I am irretrievably trapped, each moment of my existence, inside a bag of dying meat. I at least want the bag shaped like I want it.' I rose and began scouting for something to jam my feet under for sit-ups. The desk looked good, but Basha was sitting at it, working on the laptop.

'Yes,' Basha muttered, 'but all things being equal, we would prefer for the dying to happen later rather than sooner. And there are a few things here we might go over again . . .'

As I bent my knees before the bed frame, head on the floor, I ignored Basha's call to seriousness. Instead, I lamented: 'You would think the LGMs might have modified our troublesome eating behaviours, while they were in there fiddling around . . .'

'LGMs . . . ?' Helen asked. 'Jesus – little green men?'

'Sorry,' I said, between breaths and sit-ups. 'Got that from Thad.'

Helen looked at me over the edge of the bed, upon which she lay – and over the tops of her glasses. She said: 'Maybe the meat dies . . . and yet you live on.'

'A little late in the day to be getting religion, isn't it?' I was mainly focusing on keeping my back straight.

'What I mean is, maybe the Nagas are right. About genetic reincarnation.'

I finished my set and grabbed my knees. 'Well, anything's possible.'

'You and I don't happen to believe in reincarnation,' said Helen, leaning back against her propped pillows, 'but we're in the minority on this planet. Of course even genetic, scientific reincarnation would require procreating. Which, in my case at least, is one thing that's not possible.'

'Not ever?' I asked.

'Are you kidding? Even in a kennel, you get to play around with the dogs for a few minutes before taking one home for life.'

Basha swivelled on her chair to face us. 'Where I come from, having babies is a kind of duty.' She seemed to have given up on the work/seriousness idea.

'Duty to who?' Helen asked.

'God . . . our people . . . the land.'

'Helen's got issues with commitment,' I said, rising and wiping my face.

'Hah,' she responded. 'And you don't?'

I laughed. 'At least I let my pet stay overnight.'

Basha looked down at me. 'Is having Erasmus D not like keeping a child?'

I rose, crossed the room, and looked for my bag. It was probably time to commit that spare set of underwear I'd held in reserve. 'A little,' I said. 'But it's like having an extremely well-behaved permanent six-year-old – one who never goes through any difficult phases.'

As I grabbed my bag off of the dresser, it trembled in my hand. My phone's ringer, in vibrate mode. I'd turned the blighted thing off yesterday; much good that did me. It carried on buzzing in my hand.

'I'll be right back,' I said – casually enough, I hoped.

'Are you crazy? Do you want to get locked up in a dungeon underneath St Peter's Square? Or have some Swiss Guard with a pike get . . . medieval on your ass?'

I walked a number of steps further off into the darkness, phone pressed to ear. Then I pursed my lips and hardened my expression. 'Hey, listen,' I said. 'You. Is this the Catholic Church? Are you the Papists – trying to scare me off? Because it's not working.'

'Supposing I am,' the phone said. 'Then the jig's up, isn't it? Then you have to abandon this hare-brained idea.'

'Look,' I said, exhaling tiredly. 'If you've got something positive to contribute to my existence, I'm all ears. Otherwise, I'm sorry – the status quo just wasn't cutting it.'

She started to say something, but I interrupted. 'And anyway, everyone knows the genie doesn't go back in the bottle. Everything's different now. Everything's changed.'

'Oh, yeah? What's different? What's changed? Tell me.'

'Well . . . everything, that's what!'

She held her digital tongue for a few seconds – as if to let my rather weak last comment sit out in plain view, wilting. 'Oh, yeah,' she said, finally, dripping sarcasm. 'So you've discovered – maybe! – that galactic interlopers descended from the sky ten thousand years ago and injected your ancestors with a genetic predisposition to higher functioning. Now what? Hmm? You don't have to get out of bed tomorrow morning? You don't have to go to work and support yourself? Or feed your chimp? Or love your parents? Or figure out who you are? Who you *really* are, in your long-buried heart?'

I choked out an offended: 'Excuse me?'

'And you won't have to miss your brother any more?'

'I'm ringing off now. Thanks for calling.'

'You'll no longer have to find some kind of *meaning* for your life? Some kind of completely personal meaning? No matter whether your genes turn out to have been designed by God Almighty – or by . . . Bozo the Syphilitic Clown?'

Later, I'd come to realize the phone, abrasive as it was, had a point – several, in fact. But at the moment, its harangue only cemented my perverse resolve. Snapping the phone peremptorily shut, stalking back to the cottage, I focused fiercely on three facts: A) I couldn't go home again – not right at that moment, at any rate; B) this all had to get resolved one way or another; and C) yeah – I *did* have to know the truth of the matter. The Truth about things. Capital T.

*

When I got back inside, Helen and Basha were talking business again.

'So no word yet,' Helen said, 'on a source for the uniform?'

Basha, sitting now with the computer in her lap, appeared slightly put upon. She looked over her screen at Helen and said: 'As they say, I have my best people on it.'

Helen held her gaze. '*Get better people.*'

Uh, oh.

But Basha laughed this off, breaking the tension. She sighed. 'Burglary is not really my specialty. Then again, infiltration is. I suppose they are first cousins.'

I couldn't help taking Basha's part in this. I said to Helen: 'I don't expect you'd care to try any of this without her. And mouthing off won't help much, will it?'

Probably all to the good, Helen also chose to stand down, by laughing. 'Hey – at least I'm putting my ass where my mouth is. In Rome. In harm's way.'

'We all are,' I said. 'I know what. Why don't let's all go down the pub together and have a pint? We've worked hard today. We deserve to get out of this shack for a bit.'

'Going out, not to mention drinking,' Basha objected, 'might not be very clever.'

'We'll bring guns,' I said. 'It'll be fine. Let me just get a quick shower . . .'

The pub (which was also the restaurant) held one or two other lonely drinkers, as well as a family finishing dinner. We'd hardly seen anyone about the lodge so far; it was a little early in the season. We took the back booth, and I went for drinks.

When I returned, holding three glasses of beer in a precarious triangle, Helen was asking: 'So why in Italy, do you figure?' Basha only arched her brows.

Bringing the glasses to the rough wood surface of the table, intuiting her meaning, I said: 'Probably because it's just about the world's most recognizable land mass.'

'Or they could have left it in Florida.'

'Then let's say a little prayer of thanks that we're going to Rome – not Orlando.'

We all clinked glasses and drank. It was tasty – some Santa Cruz microbrew.

'Here's what I don't understand,' I said. 'If the Pope and his crew have got this alien artefact . . . which holds information that would discredit their whole theology . . . why do they keep it on display in their museum? Instead of locked up in the basement?'

'Vanity, maybe?' Helen suggested.

'Perhaps that,' Basha said, wiping foam from her lip. 'But, often, out in the open is the best hiding place. There are a number of ways to suppress information.'

Helen, having somehow already knocked back half of her drink, said: 'I've long speculated that there's a whole branch of the US government just for suppressing things.'

'What sorts of things?' I asked.

'Are you kidding? Name it. Virtually any major scientific or industrial breakthrough is all but guaranteed to have some constituency of people who'd be ruined by it. And who are probably paying off the government.'

'Like, for instance,' I said, '. . . the oil industry?'

'Yeah,' said Helen, nodding and sipping. 'You can't tell me they haven't already developed a cheap, renewable, non-polluting energy source at this point – or at the very least could have. But the US oil industry, even despite all the imports, is still worth billions. And you've got ex-oilmen in the White House, for Christ sake.'

'It's true,' I said, thinking about it. 'And, you know, they shut down the tokamak fusion reactor at Princeton a few years ago . . . just as it was getting close to producing a sustainable reaction.'

'Right!' Helen said. 'Fusion would solve most of our problems. Even an incremental step, like hydrogen fuel cells, would make a big difference . . .'

'Didn't the administration recently devote a bunch of money to fuel-cell research?' I asked.

'A dodge,' Helen said. 'It deflects criticism. They're not serious. It's like Basha said – there are a lot of ways to suppress things. By co-opting them, in this case.'

'I might have thought,' said Basha, who I noted was taking very small sips, 'that they would have worked out an implementation of quantum cryptography by now. This would provide unbreakable privacy for electronic communications.'

'And you think the NSA wants to let that happen?' Helen practically barked. She killed her beer. 'They probably hire anybody they find getting close to success with that. Or just pay them to stop doing research.'

'Like paying farmers not to grow food,' I said.

'Yes! Fucking farm subsidies! While African farmers are starving. Bastards.' Helen got up for another round. I was nearly ready for another; though Basha wasn't.

It all seemed clear to me, suddenly: it was alcohol that was the catalyst for Helen's Jekyll/Hyde routine. Of course, it was a little more complex than that. It seemed to me she had a lot of anger in her heart; most of it due to various social injustices, sins of the culture at large – and the men in charge of it. It was just that the exalted coolness of her carefully crafted persona did not permit the venting of anger, the presentation of resentment. Resentment is unattractive; and to vent anger is precisely to lose one's cool. It only took a drink or two, though, to swamp that seawall. Or, probably more likely: the drink gave her the permission she needed to tear it down herself.

Helen returned, sat, handed me my beer, and got into her own.

'Speaking of crops . . . what about crop circles?' I asked, swivelling to Basha, who sat beside me. 'Or UFOs? Could it simply be that too many cranks believe in it for anyone else to take it seriously?'

Basha nodded. 'The most obvious way to suppress information is to completely restrict access to it, to keep it from getting out at all. But there is an opposite strategy: to flood the zone with garbage

230

information, wild conspiracies – theories that are close to the truth, but off to one side and the other.'

'Interesting,' I said. 'That trick never occurred to me.'

'There are a variety of such tricks,' Basha said. 'For instance, sleight of hand – putting the information in terms that deceive. Lotteries, for an example. If those who ran lotteries asked their players to guess a number between one and sixteen billion, few would pay for the privilege. Instead, they have them pick six numbers between one and fifty. Which is the same odds.'

'State governments,' Helen added, 'would lose a fortune.'

'Doesn't that money go to education?' I asked.

'Don't even get me started on education reform. Why don't they base public education on modern, scientific, pedagogical principles? Because they don't want educated citizens, they want docile workers. The whole system dates from the industrial revolution, churning out good factory workers. I mean – *bells* between classes? Please.'

'You must really resent the taxes you pay,' I said. Getting to the bottom of my second beer, I started to get into the spirit. 'You know what I have my issues with? Hate to say it, but the British monarchy. They do very little but hold property, foment scandal, and piss away millions for their upkeep. And, I suppose, distract people from real issues.'

'Like who killed Kennedy,' Basha said – subtly poking fun at both of us.

Too subtly, as it turned out. Helen and I clinked glasses. 'Who *did* kill Kennedy?!' we shouted in unison. I saw Basha shaking her head.

Thusly did we close out the evening, weaving back to the cottage arm-in-arm, enjoying the pleasant glow of a beer buzz, and our warm camaraderie. I realized I was so happy to be there with friends – with *woman* friends. It was all hugely pleasant.

And it was even to last a few hours more. Nearly until dawn.

Forty-five

Only a few minutes before first light. That was when my phone rang again. Not in silent mode. Not even the quiet ring I normally keep it set at. Full volume. I leapt from bed, flailing around for the shrieking device.

'I thought I told you to keep that off,' Basha muttered, from the other bed.

'I do. It doesn't help!'

I finally got hold of it in the dark, flipped it open, and began to power it off. But I paused a half-second to consider whether that would even have an effect. In that instant's hesitation, the back-lit text on the screen caught my eye. It said:

'DANGER!!! OUTSIDE!'

Uh, oh.

I snapped the phone closed (at which it left off ringing) and sprang smartly to the front window. I pulled the corner of the drape. Behind it: dark figures running in both directions – circling around our lonely (now beleaguered) outpost.

I whirled around – but found Basha already crouched beside me. Behind her, I could see Helen sitting up in bed. Basha said, in a sharp but calm whisper:

'Pack; everything; now.'

And with that, the three of us began turning in all directions, bodies rubbing, shins bumping – trying to move a million miles an hour while making no sound.

Just as before, in about three minutes we'd completely packed – excepting only what the darkness might have swallowed, and which eluded our touch. I'd like to credit our growing experience with this manoeuvre; but it was more that we hardly had anything.

At Basha's prompting, we slung the assembled gear upon our bodies. I had my small pack strapped around my waist; and we slung Basha's two duffel bags, one each, across my back and Helen's (who

232

had no bag of her own). Finally, Basha cinched tight the last strap of gear-festooned webbing that she'd pulled out and climbed into; and hefted her rifle from its resting place in the corner.

I had the Glock she'd gifted me with in hand, the spare magazine in my pack.

Helen remained unarmed, but looked alert and ready to move.

We stood regarding one another in the near dark for two seconds.

At which time the doorknob rattled. It did so horrifically quietly. This sent the level of tension in the room up to commanding new heights – where it remained as if nailed to a mast.

Basha put her weapon to her shoulder and trained it at sternum height on the door.

None of us breathed so much as to fog a mirror.

The doorjamb fragmented violently – before the shock wave of a single gunshot.

I jumped a foot in the air. Helen staggered backward across the room. Basha stood like David in her oblique, wide-legged stance – and put one, two, three, four perfectly evenly spaced rifle shots, in the span of a single second, into two square inches of the chest of the man who rushed in behind the swinging door.

As this ill-starred invader hurtled straight back out the way he came in, Basha stepped forward, removed her left hand from the rifle stock, and pushed the door closed again. She then stepped smoothly back into her original spot.

I think all of that transpired before I even touched the floor again. But as I did, I heard the window behind me rattle. It did so very distinctly. I spun to face it. But that's all I managed to do – offer it a baleful gaze. True, what I'd just witnessed was not my first fatal shooting; but I'd been a lot more groggy the other time. Now, I had frozen.

Basha spoke my name – a call to duty. It brought me around.

I raised the Glock and mechanically fired three rounds, from left to right, across the square of the window. The .45, triggering off in my hand, felt powerful – yet winsomely smooth. Like riding a stallion; like winding up my Ducati. The pane shattered and vacated. The drape twisted in the newly admitted breeze. That was the only effect I could discern. But the window rattled no more.

The silence flooded straight back in.

All around us: the black and cool and supple living body of the night, its sublime and magisterial stillness . . . which we were murderously puncturing at distinct intervals with the percussive roar and lightning-strike flash of firearms in an enclosed space . . . it made me feel . . . it made me feel . . . more powerful than I ever had before in my life. As if the night were ours to control, to switch on or off. To marshal to our whims, whip into a deadly elemental fury, an animal familiar perched upon our shoulders, striking unerringly and irresistibly, on command. Calling down storms. Ruling the night.

A shudder ravished my shoulders. I pressed my teeth together to keep from laughing out loud. I vibrated, at a low frequency. I continued covering the window.

'Down,' Basha said.

Over my shoulder, I saw her upper body in the same gracefully static posture, but lower now, one knee to the floor. I followed suit.

Noise from the bathroom. I pivoted to cover it.

Basha hissed at me. 'How well do you know the trails?'

'Passingly well,' I said. I was amazed to hear my own voice, amazed to hear it betray not the least fear, nor uncertainty.

'If we climb to the hilltop, can you loop us back around here? Another way?'

I hesitated one beat. 'Yes.' I thought I could see what she had in mind: a mad chase over the hill – then, with enormous luck, back around again to our car. One chance to get away clean.

Sound of glass now, shattering in the bathroom.

Basha's face showed an instant's consideration. 'Cover the door,' she said.

With that, she stood, set her rifle against the wall, drew a hand-gun, opened the bathroom door, and stepped inside. Two shots

234

came back out, fuzzed by the porcelain echo chamber of the tiny room. More glass noise, crunching; then a heavy thump.

Basha reappeared – dragging a body.

It was a Hasid, black-clad and bearded, dead. Dead as Darwin.

And I immediately apprehended, somehow unmistakably, that she had *dragged* his body in through the bathroom window. It was not a big window.

'Almost time,' Basha said. 'I go out first. You run by me and lead the way up the trail. Then Helen. I bring the rear. Clear?' Helen and I nodded vigorously.

It actually wasn't at all clear to me how we were going to get out of the cottage, surrounded as we were – not without ending up as did Butch and Sundance. Basha cleared all that up in the next fifteen seconds.

She removed a cylindrical canister from her webbing, pulled its pin, cracked the front door, and tossed it out. Immediately, she activated another and tossed it through the window I'd shot out; and a third out the bathroom window. Hissing noises broke out from multiple directions – and thick white smoke climbed the black trellis of the night.

Basha leaned over the corpse on the floor and grasped it by its garments.

'A little help,' she said.

I rushed to heft the other side of the ex-Qabbalist. At her direction, we lifted and tossed him floppily out the window, the glassless one. Almost immediately, gunfire erupted outside. We leapt away. A few rounds chipped at the wood edge of the window; a few came right through it. But I sure wouldn't have wanted to be that dead guy on the other side. He was getting shot to ribbons.

Moving fast, Basha pitched a fourth canister out the front door. Rather than painting the night white, this one tore a hole in its heart, out of which flooded concussive noise and light. The instant it did so, Basha followed it straight out. I thought I'd stayed so close on her heels that I might trip on them; but by the time I'd fully emerged, she had already taken a knee and gone to work with the rifle – putting out rounds fast.

I put my head down, sprinted full-out for the trailhead, and didn't look up once.

White and amber muzzle flashes nonetheless flared in my peripheral vision – from a dozen points in an otherwise undifferentiated blackness. Killer fireflies.

The unappeasable night had regrouped – and switched sides.

Forty-six

Thank God for that three-walk-a-day habit, right? Running head-long up pitch-dark and root-strewn woodland trails, as a manoeuvre, was dicey enough. But it must have been dicier still for our pursuers, who'd never tried it before. And of course we had the rabbit's traditional advantage over the hound: as motivation, the prospect of dinner can never rival that of becoming dinner.

We burst onto the rounded hilltop in a blessedly tight knot. Pursuit seemed gathering, down the trail behind us – but not fatally imminent.

'Which way?' clipped Basha, dropping the magazine from her weapon and replacing it with one from a chest pouch.

I gazed out across the greyer blackness of the hilltop. At its far end, I thought I could make out the dark tunnel of a break in the trees – the other trailhead from which I'd spied on Helen. 'There,' I said, pointing.

Basha yanked on a rod, chambering her weapon. 'Go, one at a time – and fast,' she said. 'Meet me there.' With that, she picked out the thickest nearby tree, knelt behind it, braced her rifle, and started firing back down the trail.

I couldn't see any targets; and neither, I guessed, could she. She fired at regular intervals and in a regular spread, sweeping smoothly left to right.

'Go!' I shouted, giving Helen a shove. She took off, bag bouncing on her back.

I waited until I saw her cross the halfway point, the boulder. I spared a last look for Basha, who did not turn. Then I took off myself.

Exposed as I felt out in the open, I didn't sense any immediate danger. Basha's holding action seemed to be working. I spared one look over my shoulder: receding muzzle flashes in the darkness. The rearguard holding the line.

I passed the boulder. I found I could see now; the sky was paling with dawn.

And thus I could make out Helen's figure up ahead. I began to slow as I approached her back. She was standing motionless. And there was something else, something a few feet beyond her.

As I skidded to a halt, just behind and to her side, I saw what it was.

A single man in black – but not a suit. A long shirt, a *kurta*. Fuck! *Never Scylla without Charybdis.* The dark-skinned and shaggy Naga held a spear at waist-level – and, in his other hand, a tremendous silver revolver. But he held it pointing down, by his side. Not trained on Helen. He wore a curiously inquisitive expression, his lips parted, his eyes wide.

My lips, by way of contrast, I had pressed into a bloodless line. My eyes? Resolute slits. And, as I came round Helen, my gun was well up – parallel to the ground, unwavering, and trained dead on the man's chest.

'Don't even,' I warned him.

He didn't appear inclined to – until two seconds later, when his expression changed, inexplicably. A weird flash of alarm.

And, to my horror, he raised his gun.

There was nothing for it. I triggered off as fast as I could, three or five rounds, the impacts catching him on one side. He spun around and down, all twisted up with his spear.

Oh my, oh my, oh my. Oh dear.

Watching guys get shot was one thing entirely. Not this.

But I immediately knew I had botched the job, reacting too slowly. He'd already gotten a shot off, a single bludgeoning roar. It all sort of happened at the same time. My shots. His shot. His fall.

I flinched in terror, every inch of my flesh tightening in cellular panic, anticipating a catastrophic blow.

But it didn't come.

On a sudden intuition, a chill on my neck, I spun around, Glock trained at head height. There was nothing there – in fact, it was lower, at toe height. A body, in a black suit, Uzi still gripped in its white hand – and an enormous hole in its chest. A black hat lay on the ground nearby. How he'd snuck up behind us, I figured God alone knew – and alone had time to wonder about it.

I spun back around again, and found the man I'd shot twisting on the ground. And as my expression softened, peering over my gunsights, downward, at this thing I had done, this writhing object I had created, this story I had horrifically pre-empted . . .

. . . as I did so, the darkness came slowly alive in a wide arc behind it. What had just a moment before been black foliage, and black bark, and black air, turned into a black shirt beneath a black-ringed head – and another, and a third, perhaps more. And more spears and guns. It was like an undifferentiated darkness of shirts and hair, become animated. The night growing beards.

But the group pulled up short at the sight of their fellow on the ground.

And now I could make out faces – shocked and concerned. And frozen.

I grabbed Helen by the collar with my free hand. I growled an animal '*Come ON!*' With the same motion, I brought the Glock back up and fired it twice more, blindly, hitting I couldn't say what. My next shot clicked on empty. But I was already pulling me and Helen both into a frantic, turf-kicking, one-chance-and-one-chance-only, headlong – what's the expression? – advance toward the rear.

As we sprinted back up the hill, my red-tinted Rubicon receded into darkness behind us; and I had no more time to think then of what it meant to have crossed it.

We met Basha at the mid-point – smack-dab at our lonely boulder. She also appeared to be conducting an advance to the rear, a fighting retreat. But as we linked up, back to back, it became clear that we were all out of rear. There was nowhere else to retreat to.

We hunkered down – not behind, it had no behind – but around the rock.

I had just enough time to switch magazines.

*

239

'I thought they wanted to take us captive!' I yelped, as rounds began coming in good and thick – and from both sides.

'Even fanatics,' Basha shouted, whirling and firing, 'may not want to get killed taking prisoners.'

But then she stopped talking; and carried on doing what she was doing – doing the most amazing thing. She'd gone back into that one-kneed stance she seemed to favour, just off to the side of the boulder, while Helen and I cowered next to it. And she fired a dense series of rapid but aimed shots back toward our original pursuers at the trailhead. Then she wheeled around in place and did the same in the opposite direction, toward our new assailants.

And then she whirled again, firing back in the first direction. Over and again.

Every two or three spins, she changed magazines – mid-whirl.

She did all this with no cover, oblivious to safety. She seemed literally to be taking cover behind a wall of withering fire – two such walls.

Within a few seconds, my awe at her bravery gave way to alarm – at the thought of her back exposed on each turn. I sat up from behind the rock, assessed her attitude – and took aim in the opposite direction. Each time she whirled, I tried to do so as well. I couldn't see anything but distant muzzle flashes. I sniped at those.

When I went dry, I ducked back down. Having stopped firing, I could hear sharp cracks, angry hornets of collapsing air pockets. Rounds going by – just barely overhead.

Looking across, I saw the magazine drop from Basha's rifle. She pulled another from her webbing – but this one was for me. She tossed it over. It was two, in fact, in a pouch. I saved my thanks for later; in any case, she had already gone into her own reload. I got my new one in and released the slide. I heard a yelp of pain.

Oh, God.

I looked up and over – in time to see Basha fall.

Oh God, oh God . . .

Keeping my cheek to the ground, I speed-crawled to her.

'Do you intend to put out any more rounds?' she asked calmly

240

but instantly on my arrival. 'Or just nose around here in the dirt all morning?'

BLOODY hell . . .

'Maybe I was conserving ammo!' I said, wild-eyed and defensive. Really, I was furious at her for making me think she was dead.

'Keep shooting, please,' she said tiredly. 'The bullets are more useful outside the gun.'

Coming to understand that she was not badly hurt, I raised myself up over her prone form and resumed firing. As I went dry again, and began to reload, I ducked in automatic reaction to something dark and fast-moving – flying over my head. It disappeared into the gloom. It was a spear.

'Jesus Christ! Watch your head!'

But by now Basha had started firing again from her prone position and didn't hear me. When she went empty, she shouted up at me: 'This position will not do.'

There was an understatement.

'We have to break out,' she elaborated. 'Can you run?'

'Yeah, fine. But how about you?'

By this time, I'd developed a sense that the Nagas and Qabbalists were actually shooting more at each other – over the top of us, rather than at us. Not that this mattered in the least – the crossfire would kill us just as dead. More dead, if anything.

'Pick a flank,' Basha said, breathing hard. It looked like the two groups had fanned out to form a near-circle. But they were still strongest at the point we'd come in, and the one we'd tried to go out off. I pointed off to one side.

We'd either find a trail or make one. Anything was better than this.

Basha pulled another canister and yanked the pin. She hauled back to toss it; but stopped short, convulsing. And I saw where she'd been wounded, a dark and wet crease across her shoulder. I plucked the grenade from her hand. She looked up at me with shining eyes in the near-dark.

241

I looked back to Helen, where she clung to the rock. 'Follow me,' I said. 'And help her! Understand?' She nodded.

With that, I gave the canister my best hurl toward the tree line. I ducked down, covering Basha's body with mine. And I began to feel her up. I came away with her second Glock, in my left hand, just as the explosive went off.

From a literal sprinter's start, I took off at a dead run, arms held stiffly forward. I heard the germ of a protest from Basha behind me, but it faded fast.

I fired off one, two, three rounds at nothing. As I neared the trees, which curled with smoke from my grenade hit, I heard firing, close by – and saw a muzzle flash at my two o'clock, from the trees. Not pausing my sprint, I swivelled at the waist and shot with both hands, aiming just below the flash. It went out, and didn't come on again.

And then I was back in the woods. I whirled in all directions, then paced the tree line ten yards up and down. It seemed clear. I turned back to the others and waved.

But they were already up and moving, one's arm around the other's shoulder.

Facing the running pair, I spread my arms out wide. But not in greeting. Rather, with either gun aimed toward the two groups at either trail head, I started slowly firing – and soon attracted incoming fire. But if they were shooting at me, they weren't shooting at Basha and Helen, who were more exposed. I stood my ground.

My right-hand gun went dry.

The running pair were almost to me.

A black figure emerged from the tree line to my left, about twenty yards beyond my earlier sweep. He broke out and ran toward Basha and Helen – bringing a gun to bear.

I stepped into the open – but didn't have time to reload (no more ammo in any case), nor to switch the loaded gun to my right hand. I took aim with my left. I didn't even know how many rounds remained. I tracked his motion, leading by the smallest fraction. I fired. He tumbled and slid into the dirt, like a felled buffalo, nearly at their feet.

I tried to start breathing again.

Sounds of the unremitting gunfight fading behind us, we crashed headlong through the forest. But both the trees and the under-growth proved mercifully thin. Navigating by instinct, we soon emerged onto a narrow trail – which led us back to an unfamiliar edge of the lodge area. But familiar enough.

Hearing police sirens crescendoing in the distance, we crept up on the rental car – where we found a single Qabbalist sitting guard on it and scratching under his suit jacket. He froze mid-scratch when unexpectedly faced with three muzzles from the near-dark. Basha stepped forward slowly – then stabbed her rifle barrel toward his throat. He dropped his Uzi and went over clutching at his neck and gasping for breath.

Helen and I dumped the bags, weapons and wounded in the back. I indicated I'd drive. Helen climbed in the passenger side.

I took a last hasty look round. In addition to the live one hack-ing at my feet, the pale first light landed on the bodies of two or three dead Qabbalists, ones Basha must have tagged on our breakout, I guessed, lying in a semicircle around our late domicile.

'Right, then,' I said to no one, really. 'We're off.'

I climbed in and gunned it.

Forty-seven

'There is something very important that I must tell you.' Basha spoke over a cocktail – self-prescribed medication, an analgesic for the filleted and blackened flesh of her upper arm. 'Something which you should have known much earlier.'

'All right,' I said quietly. I too was nursing a cocktail – and now also anxiety at the prospect of troubling new revelations. Basha paused a few more solemn beats.

'It is all well and good for video games,' she said finally. 'But in real life . . . shooting two pistols, one with either hand, accurately . . . is simply not possible.'

'I see,' I replied, nodding gravely.

'No one is a good enough shot for that. You will only miss twice as fast.'

I stared at the seat back, taking this advice to heart.

We were at that moment going six hundred miles an hour; thirty thousand feet above the ocean.

'Are you listening?' she asked. 'These things are important. I am trying to help in your development. Do you want to be an avatar in a game for the rest of your life?'

But with this, she could no longer keep a straight face. We collapsed into giggles, and each other – and called for another round of drinks.

Helen, who doesn't care for silliness, sober or drunk, took her leave for the toilet. Basha and I immediately began another private conference; we'd begun developing this habit, taking opportunities to manage our group within the group.

'It was because of Helen that they found us, wasn't it?' I asked. 'If she didn't actually lead them to us, her late-night phone calls must have given us away.'

Basha didn't disagree. 'We may have erred on the side of the cavalier.'

'And what about now?' I found I had turned serious quickly. 'Can we even go through with the Caper now? With her?'

Basha sagged slightly. 'With the plan we have developed . . . we cannot go through it without her.' She sighed. 'Also, you will recall . . . Helen was very much in the line of fire with us. If she is working with either the Hindus or the Hasids, they showed a profound disregard for her well-being.'

'Which doesn't necessarily mean a thing.'

She smiled archly. 'Ah. It learns after all.'

I gave her a pout and a gentle shove – on her good shoulder. 'But it seems at least a little more likely that she led them there by accident. At least some of them. And what of the Naga? Who could have shot me, but instead shot the Qabbalist behind me?'

Basha kept her typically judicious, and sceptical, silence.

I could almost hear her answering, though, telepathically perhaps: *In this life, we cannot always shoot everyone; sometimes a choice is all that is left us.*

The Atlantic flashed by beneath.

Helen had never been to the Eternal City, and I had. For that reason alone, she got the nod to go out shopping with Basha. Some of what we needed couldn't be got in California; some couldn't conveniently or safely be transported by air. In any case, I was to stay and hold the fort – a large room we'd rented just off Piazza Venezia. This was the big one, where Mussolini used to whip the crowds into a frenzy.

Possibly at some risk, I ultimately decided to go out anyway, alone. I left a note; I took a gun. I just needed to walk. I had no one with whom to talk out my issues; but I had a lot of issues nonetheless. An internal dialogue would have to do.

I turned right out of the piazza, heading toward the river Tiber.

Rome's a funny old place. You'll be walking down what seems a perfectly modern city block and find a whole section of ancient ruins right in its middle. There's such a confluence of antiquity and modernity that sometimes the eye is fooled and you can't tell one from the other. Or which they're trying most to preserve.

Though my feet kept moving, soon enough I stopped noticing the colours and contradictions of what had been headquarters of human civilization for a thousand years. I'd got distracted by a more dazzling and puzzling tableau: I'd turned my vision inward.

Underneath all the levity Basha and I shared on the plane – a kind of bonding by making light of shared dangers, I reckon – a lot more was going on. Most of it complex, and much of it conflicting. Undeniably, I felt of many minds – and not a few hearts.

Just for starters, it was getting impossible to ignore the fact that people kept getting lightly wounded around me. And not just around me – but in the act of preserving my precious English arse. And not just any people – but ones I really, really liked and cared about. I decided I couldn't bear the thought, even fleeting, of one of them getting more seriously hurt. Or terminally hurt. Suddenly, I felt completely glad that Thad was eight thousand miles away, home with his family.

But beyond and beneath the concern for comrades, I also had to come to terms with the violence itself – specifically, the over-the-top (by anyone's standards, I guess) shootout at the lodge. As I said before: in some ways, it was no different than the game – no different at all. Point and shoot. Don't miss. Keep moving. Be better than your opponent. Prevail. It was, in truth, enlivening.

And never so enlivening as immediately afterwards – when we'd made it, when we were driving away. Just to still be breathing, when so many others weren't . . . I'd never felt my own life so keenly before. Every glint of sun on the blacktop, every roughness of the wheel in my hand – it was sheer joy to be alive to experience it. It had all become the most sublime gift. Every second. Every vista. Every heartbeat. Unexpected and rapturous.

But, then, of course, the fight itself had also been utterly terrifying, and absurd, and dreadful, and heartbreaking – and spectacularly surreal. Firearms discharging? With nothing but clear air between their sparking muzzles and human flesh? Gunplay? Lives wagered – and forfeited? Knowing you'll see another sunrise, or even the rest of this one, only if you're very lucky or very good?

246

The balance of a lifetime, all your remaining days, come down to a few mad minutes, the steadiness of your aim, lines of sight, cover and concealment, fields of fire.

And then the killing itself, when it inevitably came. I didn't know if I could even really begin to process that – or whether I wouldn't be dealing with it for the rest of my days (as I'd been lucky enough to emerge with some). That's what really lurked under all the levity: the face of the young man I had shot – wide-eyed, inquiring, standing ten feet from me. And as well the face of the other one, the runner, a mere silhouette, whose face I had never seen. But which I could somehow see perfectly, now.

And God only knows who else I might have hit. I was hardly being careful, or discriminating. And I finished the morning with an awful lot of bullets outside the gun.

Did it matter that I'd acted in self-defence? Did it matter that we've got 'God-given' mental modules for just this sort of behaviour? Before the last few days, I'd never seen this behaviour in myself, nor used those modules. Now, I felt sure I had run panicked through enough unfamiliar rooms of my mind, seen and felt and done enough that was all-new, to be more than a little frightened of myself.

With that, I looked up to find I'd reached the river. I stepped out onto the Ponte Palatino and walked halfway out. This was one of the more modern bridges, made of steel as well as stone. But the crumbling remains of the empire-era bridge it had replaced stood in the middle of the river, just beside. More currents of contrast and contradiction, swirling across oceans of time. I put my elbows on the rail and watched the waters flow.

I mentally took a step back – because of course there was the larger context for all this. Realistically, I probably faced a little more information than I could assimilate at once – assimilate into my world view, my self view. (It's been said that a religion is nothing more than a way of regarding oneself and the universe at the same time.)

On the one hand, it appeared that we had just discovered that

247

much of what I think of as myself, my higher self – morality, self-consciousness, my participation in the whole project of civilization – all of that probably came to me hard-wired, a designed package, bestowed by advanced otherworldly designers. And, on the other hand, I had just been exposed to a whole side of my makeup that almost certainly still came from the evolutionary crucible – those violent, defensive, selfish behavioural adaptations imprinted into my subcortical areas, into the old lizard brain.

Or, to jump metaphors: this was the killer ape, uncomplicatedly willing to do violence in the service of its interests, or those of its kin or clan, in the service of survival. Fight, flight, blind and fierce self-preservation . . . Not for no reason do we play these violent video games. Something deep in us must revel in the lethal, or at very least brutal, contest. It must be so – or our genetic germlines never would have made it this far.

And there I had been, for the first time, not in a game, but in a true simulacrum of the evolutionary crucible: It really had been me or the other hominid. And I not only chose without an instant's hesitation – I prevailed. I survived, and the other guy didn't.

So. Where did all this lead? Where did the designed higher self meet the evolved killer ape? Where did my personal rubber meet this slick, black road I found myself travelling? Despite what I told Thad – that it hardly mattered whether or which traits were truly adaptations and which were gifts from on high . . . still, I needed to know where the dividing line lay. I needed to understand the most fundamental landscape of my psyche. In the best tradition of my sentient phone, I needed to take a long clear gander into my own soul – and I needed to look all the way to the bottom.

What I needed was to get a look at that alien Artefact. Then perhaps I'd know.

Looking up over the ancient, crumbling bridge, I could see the dome of St Peter's glowering across the river.

I fingered the pistol in my pocket.

The Caper – and the Truth – awaited.

Forty-eight

The Setup

Here are some interesting facts you will probably learn about St. Peter's Cathedral should you ever do any serious planning to break into it.

The piazza and double arc of colonnades out front, which are topped by a hundred and forty marble statues of the saints, were designed by Bernini. Perhaps a little provocatively to the conspiracy-minded, in the middle of the piazza stands a 300-ton Egyptian obelisk. This originally lived in Alexandria, but was summarily relocated by Caligula about two thousand years ago. According to legend, he placed it in Nero's circus, where it witnessed the execution of innumerable Christians – including St Peter himself. (Another rumour had the remains of Caesar cached, for several hundred years, in a metal globe stuck on top.)

The church itself, a classic cruciform-design cathedral, was erected over the spot where St Peter was believed to have been buried after his martyrdom. It was completed in 1626 – after a hundred and seventy-six years and forty-eight million dollars of construction. The vestibule – which itself is much bigger than most churches you've been in – has five entrances and a roof decorated with exquisite stuccoes. When you step into the basilica proper, the vast scale and absurdly ornate decor compete for the privilege of knocking the wind out of you. The interior is 608 feet in length, 450 feet wide at the transept, and 54,393 square feet total. The dome goes 138 feet across and rises 452 feet above street level – about one football field, standing on end. It was designed by Michelangelo, specifically to dwarf the nearby dome of the Pantheon.

The interior is also by Bernini – including the hundred-foot-tall and unspeakably elaborate altar, known as the Baldacchino. Monumental statues, ornate alcoves and arcades, mosaics, gilding, life-size angels (whatever size that is), and grand balconies crowd all around – and a space this huge takes some serious crowding. But Bernini has help in filling the room: the legions of tourists, students of art and architecture, and religious pilgrims that throng the basilica for most of the hours they keep the doors open.

On this particular day, the doors would be open only a few minutes more – at which time I would be taking my personal religious pilgrim impersonation to great new histrionic heights. In the meantime, I merely wandered around, eyes lowered, attempting to look devout – and trying like hell to keep from scratching indecorously at my habit.

If you marry God, does he automatically dress you in scratchy and awkwardly cut wool? Or did Basha and Helen just grab the cheapest habit they could find? This question was not idle, as I fully intended to take out my discomfort either on God, or on my co-conspirators, when this was over. Depending, you know, on how it all turned out.

I'd probably have a better sense of that shortly – at closing time. Meanwhile, I carried on doing little circuits of the not-so-little room. Keeping an eye on the Swiss Guards. Trying to spot undercover Vatican police. And occasionally passing, eyes over-dramatically averted, Helen and Basha. The former wore a sleek jumpsuit underneath a long trench coat. The latter, merely street clothes – casual, looking every inch the university student on spring break. She even had the oversize backpack. But not one that held textbooks. Or a jumper, or a journal, or spare rolls of film. Not one thing like that.

And just so you don't think we were merely indulging our sense of drama, just looking for, you know, a really grand set piece, by going in via the basilica, as opposed to straight into the museum . . . well, that's one big difference between the entrances to one and to the other: metal detectors, a whole security station, front the museum. And you can bet your bottom shekel Basha's backpack wouldn't have passed muster there.

But the basilica you can just stroll into, unmolested. It's some-

250

thing to do with the tradition of sanctuary, I think. And we were hardly above taking advantage.

I checked my watch. Show time.

The Diversionary Tactic

The scratchiness, the stiffness, yeah, I had some beef with all that. The damned wimple. But I couldn't deny: the coif and headband kept my hair very handily under wraps. And that was key. The hair, in all its wild amber glory, that Celtic catastrophe of personal grooming, could have been a real telltale. It was hard to be sure I wouldn't be recognized, as it was. I mean, these guys knew who I was, or some of them surely did. But the acid test would be coming up now.

I stood directly before the tomb of St Peter himself, right in the centre of the whole joint, my hands clasped in prayer. I gave it a minute, just the standing in place bit. I stole a quick peek at my watch. I saw two of the Guards beginning to herd visitors toward the door. Nothing for it, now, I reckoned. No putting it off. No going back.

I began with a little low-key rocking; just a little swaying in place.

But I pretty quickly upped the ante with some solid moaning.

From behind half-lowered lids, I could see I'd begun attracting attention.

I went arms out, then – and palms turned up. I was feeling some anxiety about the speaking in tongues thing. I mean, I'd studied up, and rehearsed a bit. But still, I might give it a miss. Play that one by ear.

I figured Basha must have been in position by then. And I saw the first couple of striped suits angling briskly my way.

'Holy Mary – mother of God!'

That sure quiets down a crowd.

'Blessed virgin!' I yelped, not in the least discreetly. 'Sweet virgin!'

I mean, yeah, most people here were probably devout Catholics.

But nobody likes a Jesus freak. Off-putting. Frightens the little ones. People backed off smartly.

I was looking up now, head thrown back, beholding the Glory – the stained-glass centrepiece of Bernini's masterwork. My arms raised and wide.

Now. *Should . . . I . . . fall to my knees?* Nah, I decided that would only make me easier to subdue. Instead, I did three tight circles, running in place. Habit billowing.

'*Sorella . . . per favore . . . per favore . .*'

This was the first of the Swiss Guards to reach me. I couldn't see him. I had my eyes rolled back in my head.

'There! There!' I hollered. Did I mention I was doing my best Irish brogue? Oh yeah. 'Can't you see her? It's the Virgin!' I pointed upward, roughly at the Glory. That's when the first hand clamped on my arm. I pulled away, with authority. They didn't try to touch me again – until I started dancing around in earnest.

'Can't you see her?! Blessed virgin!'

At this point, the poor bastards must have just said the hell with it – and proceeded to put the smack down, at least two or three of them tag-teaming on me. I guess once you decide to get physical with a nun, you just want to get it over with. I arched my back and hollered as they carried me out, horizontal, arms and legs.

Flourish. Exeunt.

And, forgive the immodesty – but I was fucking smashing.

My only regret was that I never got to see Basha's acrobatics routine, when she catapulted herself, and her oversize bag, up and into the second-storey reliquary niche, into the dark recess behind the statue of St Longinus. (We picked his alcove mainly because he's the only saint holding a spear; this would soon come to amuse us rather less.) At any rate, the important thing was that no one else saw her do it, either. Touch wood.

The Nun Recovery Operation

Helen's initial gig was definitely the most dicey. But, simply, no one else could do it. She was the only one of the three of us tall enough to be a Swiss Guard.

It had been our ardent hope that the good Vatican authorities would detain me long enough for her to perform her quick-change act and get into position. We weren't disappointed.

I soon found myself detained in a back room, some kind of sacristy. I gave the shouting and writhing a miss, de-escalating to some light lolling and head rolling. Bit of panting. I was in that attitude when the Swiss Guards, with demonstrative relief, finally passed me off to a young Vatican official. From his outfit, he was a prefect, or a prelate, or something. Thad taught me but I forgot. Anyway. He tried Latin and Italian before interrogating me in English.

I played the recovering religious zealot: adamant that I'd had a vision, but penitent to have caused such a ruckus. I was of the Carmelite Sisters of Loughrea, here on a sponsored mission. No, I didn't have any identification on me; my passport was at the convent where I'd taken lodging. Yes, the guards had searched me. No, of course, I understood perfectly. Dreadfully sorry. But if the Virgin Mary appears to one, one can hardly control oneself, can one?

Having established my harmlessness, and that I'd acted alone, I soon had a Swiss Guard escort back out the front of the building. I couldn't tell if these were two of the ones who'd wrestled me down. God! they all looked the same. The important thing was that nearly an hour had passed since closing time. The crowds had long gone. Everything had been locked down. The lights burnt low.

And the last security sweep had gone through the basilica.

And Basha, moving through the shadows, would have already begun work defeating security measures – specifically, disabling the alarm contacts on our back door.

With my gallant escort, one on each arm, I reached the vestibule and the front entrance. One of these gentlemen released my elbow to work the lock. Having done that, he began to swing open the heavy door – with a view to tossing me out of it. But he paused mid-operation – at the sound of approaching footsteps. We all turned.

The vestibule was an especially dim area, far from the candles of the altar.

We could just make out another Swiss Guard, walking straight at us, head angled low. At ten paces, not slowing, the newcomer announced, in a gruff voice: '*Nuovo programma. Va alla carabinieri.*'

My two guys straightened up and cocked their heads; but an instant later fell into radical slouches – slouching all the way to the floor, in fact, as Helen, reaching us in her stripy medieval costume, applied 500 kilovolts to each of their chests, in quick sequence, via handheld stun-gun. I managed to catch both halberds, which kept them from clattering on the stone floor.

I darted back into the basilica to check if the coast was clear. Then, in a mad rush, we dragged the two unconscious figures back inside. We were meant to dump them in the Chapel of the Crucifix – a tiny, enclosed room near the entrance. We couldn't be entirely sure that no guards would go in there tonight. But we had to gamble they wouldn't do so in the next hour or two. We tucked the bodies as far out of sight as we could.

Then we hightailed it through the shadows of the right-side aisle – just another female African-American Swiss Guard, and English pagan nun, enjoying St Pete's wild after-hours scene. I felt completely adrenalized, as did Helen, I could tell. And we were well pleased with ourselves: our stunts had gone like clockwork – not a hitch.

It couldn't even quite be said that we 'only forgot one thing'. As that thing had never come up in our planning, we'd never had it in our heads to forget in the first place. It was only much later that I realized what it must have been: we never relocked the front door to the joint. And we certainly hadn't stopped to consider that the guard had swung it halfway open – a motion that must have been visible to, oh, anyone who might have been lurking around outside keeping an eye on things.

And I hardly need point out that we were not having the kind of adventure where you could assume you weren't being kept an eye on. That, or maybe it was just a bad neighbourhood. The kind of place where you can't leave your door unbolted. Or God only knows who might wander in.

The Insertion

But we weren't thinking of that then.

When Helen and I reached that door in the back of the basilica, the one that led to the Sistine Chapel, still undetected, smiling and breathless, Basha was nowhere to be seen – by design, no doubt. She quickly materialized out of the shadows – and reported that she'd already sprung the lock and disabled the security contacts.

She held the door for us as we slipped through, with nary a sound.

Well, almost without a sound. I couldn't resist saying it, if no one else was going to. I spoke covertly into my sleeve: 'We're in.'

Forty-nine

It had occurred to me to ask Basha, in the days just prior, during one of our private conferences: 'Hey . . . if you're on holiday – how were you able to get this wealth of information, about the Vatican, from your employers?'

'I may have gone rogue,' she answered, 'but I can still get intel support. Israelis do not cut one another off when they go on holiday. Nor ask too many questions when their help is needed.'

So, the good news was that we knew there were no motion sensors in the galleries. As long as we didn't muck about with anything along the way, we probably wouldn't set off any alarms. The bad news was that we had to traverse the entire length, virtually every inch, of the museum building – and also get up to the second floor. And there would be foot patrols of security guards. We knew the location of their stations, but their patrol routes were either not formalized, or just weren't a matter of any record.

First we had to cross the Sistine Chapel itself. This had been left pitch-black, so you couldn't see a thing. Michelangelo's immersive mural has been described as the single greatest work of art ever executed by a single person. But I'd seen it before and had felt a little let down: the ceiling's too far away to make out well, your neck hurts trying – and, frankly, it looks kind of fake since they cleaned it. But I did feel sorry for Helen not getting to see it. Another time, I guess.

At the far end of this long, airy room, Basha paused to pass out additional kit. LED flashlights for everyone. Changes of costume for me and Helen – black, lightweight jumpsuits, identical to the one Basha wore (she'd peeled off her student disguise earlier). And a familiar old friend for me: my Glock 30, now in a belt holster with two spare magazines. (Basha already had hers strapped on.)

With a few small tools, Basha did a similar electronic bypass number on this door as she'd done on the other.

Hand on the knob, she gave us last-minute instructions

(reminders, really): 'No noise. Stay low. Lights off unless I tell you otherwise. And look sharp for guards.' And with that, we began history's most rushed tour of the Vatican museums: The Borgia rooms, modern religious art, the Borgia courtyard. Wild dash across the agoraphobia-inducing Belvedere courtyard. Slink up the stairs of the Library courtyard. Straight shot down the Gallery of the Tapestries, the Gallery of Candelabra. Marvellous stuff, all of it. Even dark and blurry. Really awe-inspiring.

We, all three of us, knew the floor plan of the place like our childhood homes. Our routes in and out we had burnt into our brains. And it was gratifying when every corner appeared right where we expected it.

Twice we crossed paths with lone security patrols. Both times we spotted them well before they us; and a two-minute crouch in the shadows sufficed to let them go by.

Almost there now: Sarcophagi; Regolini-Galassi Tomb; Bronzes. Kick ass.

And then we were there: Room I of the Etruscan Museum.

And there they were, one foot away from us, inside a glass display case. The Artefact. Pair of Hands. Palms facing away from us, each hand on a little Perspex stand. We spent two seconds admiring them; then I took up position at one doorway, Helen at the other – and Basha began sawing open the foundation of the case, with a clever little circular saw that made absolutely no sound, to get at the alarm wiring.

I looked back and forth over my shoulder while she worked. Ahead of me lay Room II, twice as long, more glass cases. Dark. Silent – until it wasn't. I heard a brief and indistinct ruckus echoing from its opposite end. From round the corner, I thought.

I hesitated. I considered reporting in to Basha and getting orders. But she looked fully occupied, with her little voltmeter and bypass wires, a circuit board half in and out of the cabinet, alligator clips in her mouth. So I acted on my own initiative and padded to the end of the adjacent room, staying low, working around the rows of display cases.

At its end, another doorway, a bend of corridor – then a long straight stretch.

At the end of that: three men, shrunken by perspective, but clear.

The first of the men: recognizably one of the security guards.

The other two: wild hair and beards. No discernible clothing. Obscure dark markings upon slightly less dark skin.

This struck me as big news. Something worth interrupting Basha's work for. I scrambled back to do just that and arrived in time to see Basha produce a cute little steel hammer – and unceremoniously smash the glass of the display case. It chimed, tinkled, and fell away. And that was it. The loot was ours.

'Hate to break in,' I broke in, with an apologetic whisper.

'Yes?' she asked, turning from the case. I saw Helen watching us; but continuing to stand her post (unlike me).

'A pair of men, two rooms over, appear to have captured one of the security guards.'

Basha nodded in acknowledgement.

'I might not have brought it up. But I'm worried they may be Nagas.'

'What makes you think that?' she asked, the model of mature patience.

'Well, they're naked. And smeared with ashes, if I'm not mistaken.'

She nodded thoughtfully. 'Yep. Nagas, all right. We should go.'

She reached for the Hands, holding her bag in her other hand. As she began to tuck them away, I made so bold as to interrupt again.

'Sorry – shouldn't we, you know, just to be sure? Just so we know?'

Basha hesitated. 'How close are they?'

'Oh, a few hundred yards,' I replied. 'I think we have a moment.'

She nodded and handed me the Hands. I took one breath. With no other preamble, I pressed them straight together before me.

So, merely as an aside . . . it's occurred to me that you might think I've been acting a little jaunty through all of this bit. You know, for

258

a person committing multiple felonies in the *sanctum sanctorum* of one of the world's great faiths; and almost entirely surrounded by spear-, pole axe-, and gun-toting belligerents. You might accuse me, and the others too, maybe, of getting a little giddy, even. Light-headed.

Fair enough. As for causes, I can only really speak for me. Personally. Indeed, I was aware of the seriousness of everything we were doing, of all we'd gotten caught up in. The events we directed, those we managed to parry, others that might yet get the best of us. And I was, surely, on a certain level, afraid of what I knew could easily happen: death, injury, confinement in a foreign jail.

Yet I know my attitude belied this. Why? Part of me is tempted to try and claim that I had really only just found my groove. Hit my stride, yes? That I had been born to this. That I was cut out for this line of work, had found my calling. In a word, that I could be another Basha. This sounds nice. But, in truth, it was both more and less than that.

If I had honestly to put the back of my hand to my spiritual fore-head, what I would have found was this: My earlier fever – the one I'd felt driving away from the shootout, that keen sense of my own life as some unexpected gift, of every sensation of the world as rapturous – had never entirely gone. It had grown fainter, a glowing ember where there'd been a blaze. But it had not gone out. And now, back in harm's way, it had flared again. It was more than excitement, the effects of adrenalin, a physical reaction. More even than mental or spiritual. Ultimately it was . . . philosophical. It was existential. But I would only come to understand it fully at the end. After so much – after all this shit – had gone down.

And, as well, there was still the little matter of the alien Artefact.

She nodded and handed me the Hands. I took one breath. With no other preamble, I pressed them straight together before me.

Yep, these were them all right. This was what we had come for.

An oval of light, made solid, congealed, seemingly embodied somehow, materialized a foot in front of me. Floating . . .

259

luminous . . . a hung moon . . . but solid as stained glass. It glowed: not brightly, not faintly – enough to sparkle off the glass shards on the floor, to glint fetchingly off the lenses of Helen's glasses, as she padded over to us now, hypnotized. Its light turned the room an otherworldly aquamarine.

Arrayed in dense groups across the front of the floating oval: tiny moving pictures, animated windows, also oval in shape. Too much happening to take in. Like standing before a wall of television screens, a monstrous one, but from a half mile away; like Times Square, like Shinjuku. It was impossible to tell what we should make of it. The eye could not quite track.

Basha reached out her hand. She touched one of the oval windows. It was the one in the very upper right. It seemed to be an outer-space scene, the black cosmos, a single star, planets.

At her touch, it ballooned smoothly, springing up in front of the first oval, expanding hugely and lunging slightly, toward our faces. As it spun up, the view zoomed on a planet, clearly Earth, visibly orbiting the sun; and then back out again. The planet stopped its motion, reverse course, and reverse-orbited back the way it came. Then it accelerated, until it was completing a revolution a second, then more. At the same time, a counter appeared – some equivalent of chalk lines, in the upper corner. With each revolution a mark was added. When there were eight, they shrunk into a tight group. A new group of eight counted off, then shrunk down beside the first group. The first eight groups of eight shrunk again. And so on.

So now we knew someone counted in base eight – and that they wanted to tell us something about a large span of years gone by.

But then the video shrunk to postage-stamp size again. Behind it was revealed Helen – she had leaned in behind, where, evidently, the main display had remained. And she'd touched another oval – an obvious diagram of the molecular structure of DNA (or perhaps RNA). It expanded to replace the former window.

And now we also knew how the interface worked: a window of smaller windows, which could be enlarged. Basically, it was a

260

graphical user interface – a windowing GUI. And that wasn't the only familiar metaphor that presented itself.

'It's not a Film,' I breathed. 'It's a bloody multimedia DVD. Interactive . . .'

The whole spectacle evaporated before my slack face.

'Yes, it is,' Basha agreed. 'And there will be time to explore it later.' I looked down and saw she'd pulled the Hands gently apart, along with mine. 'Time to go.'

And for some reason I recalled that those were the first three words she ever spoke to me.

But then we heard clear footsteps, approaching rapidly from the next room, to our immediate right, the one I was meant to be watching. And also the one that led to our planned route of escape.

Exit Stage Left.

Fifty

This little change of plans, this admittedly peremptory rerouting of our withdrawal operation, did not initially present itself as a big problem. Not only did we know the whole place like natives; but we'd specifically formulated an alternate route out. A couple of variations, in fact.

When we did start worrying, I confess, was when we kept encountering tied-up security guys. Tied-up security guys in and of themselves were, in one way of course, simply a relief. One less thing, you know. The problem was that they also served as calling cards: 'Nagas about.'

We reversed course twice, circling back round, not keen to be sharing any part of this building with our Hindu competitors. At the third tied-up guard, Helen exclaimed in frustration: 'Fuck! It's like they're taking over the whole building.' But that, I suppose, was a strategy that gained viability with the advantage of numbers.

Much worse, the third tied-up guard turned out to augur actual, not notional, Nagas nearby. We spotted them sweeping the hall ahead – and so we beat another, hastier, retreat. But we were quickly running short of alternate exit routes.

Basha betrayed no sense of panic. I knew, of course, this meant nothing. Also, soon enough, I saw she had her gun out. I followed suit.

Crouching, padding, moving fast and breathing faster, we emerged from a hallway onto a long balcony, an overlook of the other big courtyard. It was completely crawling with Nagas – naked ones. (Though, several had satchels slung over their bare torsos – I guess even the nude can't do a big invasion without a few things.) And I found I was started to feel pretty annoyed with security around here. I mean – what were these muppets doing all this time? Wasn't anybody in charge?

We backed away from the edge, and I looked to Basha, eyes wide: *Well?*

She held my gaze, face still dead-pan. 'Trapped,' she said. 'Like rats.'

I gave her a second look. A rather sharper one.

We did enjoy one small break shortly after: looping back around, we found the northeast stairway clear. That at least allowed us to get back to the ground floor.

We darted into what I immediately recognized, for reasons that might be guessed, as the Octagonal Courtyard. This holds several of the world's most famous statues, including the Apollo Belvedere – and the Laocoön. Other than these silent stone people, the court-yard proved empty. And it stayed that way right until the moment we'd got halfway across it. At that point, four fierce-eyed spearchuckers spilled through the opposite doorway, right in our path. They were, needless to point out, starkers.

Seen up close, running, their ash-smeared members flopped wildly.

And then I noticed they also had handguns, along with the spears.

Basha drew a bead with her Glock; I followed suit.

But she didn't fire; I took her lead there again.

I guess I had, perhaps unconsciously, over the last few days, formed a mental picture of Basha's favoured tactics. For her, the main chance always seemed to involve the discharging of firearms – rapidly, accurately, and (most of all) immediately. Maximum violence, instantly. And just make sure you don't miss.

So I didn't initially understand her change of tactics here. The restraint, and getting drawn into a standoff. Later, she explained this to me: it wasn't so much that we were outgunned four to two. It was rather the matter of the close quarters – a little too close to miss – and the already raised guns all round. She probably could have shot these men, maybe even all four of them, before they shot us. But shooting them first would have been small comfort. Because shot guys, even skillfully shot ones, can usually still manage to get off a round or two. An old witticism has it that coming in second just means you're the first person to lose. Switch the positions and you get the idea here.

So, instead, we kept our guns on them, as they on us. They fanned out into the courtyard. We backed away across it. Very shortly, though, I found I'd backed into the business end of a spear. Which smarted. I whirled about, finding four more naturists, who'd waltzed in through the same doorway we'd come in.

Trapped like rats, indeed. Just as before, on that hilltop. Except with no boulder to crouch around.

Instead: a statue.

Laocoön was a priest of ancient Troy. When the Greeks rolled their famous gift up to the city gate (as the tale is told in Virgil's *Aeneid*), Laocoön alone warned his fellows against it – even going so far as to chuck a spear of his own into the flank of the wooden horse. Later, after the city fell, the goddess Athena – who must have had an agenda – set serpents on Laocoön and his two young sons, as punishment.

The statue, which depicts this attack, and which dates from the first century BC, is considered the greatest of all Hellenistic sculptures. Not just the agonized expressions of the man and the boys, but every tendon and line of their snake-encoiled bodies, speaks their doom. Conveys that there will be no escape, and that they know it.

The statue was lost for fifteen centuries. It was unearthed in 1506 in a field near the Colosseum in 1506, where it had probably been buried in Nero's house. It was immediately recognized as a lost masterwork and paraded through the streets of Rome, where it entranced the whole populace. Among the gawkers, reportedly, was a young Michelangelo. He is said to have been awed and inspired, and to have used the twisting, terrified bodies of the Laocoön family as a model for many of his works – including the Last Judgement on the wall of the Sistine Chapel.

*

So. Eight predators, two hunting groups of four, all unspeaking, manoeuvring in the dark, a distinct sinuousness of movement and of aspect. Pairs of fangs – one of steel, one of wood – menacing us. Originally, in Hindu mythology, the Nagas were Vedic serpent-people – children of the Goddess Kadru, guards of treasure palaces, keepers of the sources of mystic knowledge.

Retreating before them: three hairless hominids, beleaguered prey, outmatched, panning their own weapons rapidly – trying to cover too many attackers at once. Menaced, advanced upon, encircled.

Finally, in reality, what we had was three very capable and thoroughly modern women run to ground by naked men poking at them with sticks. And with their backs to a two-thousand-year-old scene of treachery, agony, and the impossibility of escape. And of more nakedness (the Laocoöns are also starkers).

Basha let her gun roll over her finger, on its trigger guard, and raised her other hand in the air. Helen followed suit, putting her empty hands up. I flirted, internally, with a couple of crazy ideas; but not for real long. In a moment, we'd been disarmed. One of the Nagas spoke into a small hand-held radio. Half a minute later, a new figure strode into the courtyard.

This one was a little shorter, a little slighter, than the others. And clothed – in the traditional black *kurta* and pantaloons. Like the rest of us, his face was obscured by shadow. It was only when the others parted, and he stepped in close, that we came in for the *big* surprise.

Helen said it first: 'You!'

As one gets older, one comes to learn, I think, through one's own experiences, that all the homilies and platitudes we've been force-fed are actually true; that clichés got to be clichés for a reason; and that even the most hackneyed phrases can still prove to be, on certain occasions, perfectly apt.

'You!' I echoed.

'*Le mani, per favore,*' said A'hib Khouri, holding his palm out to us.

265

'Ha fucking ha,' Helen replied – quite humourlessly, if that need be pointed out.

A'hib had let his beard grow out a bit; and had let his hair go entirely. And of course, there were the strange clothes. But, otherwise, he was just as we'd seen him last.

I was feeling a little humourless myself, and snorted sardonically. 'You've been working for them all along.'

'Not just working for them,' he answered. He showed a little of that cute smile of his, brilliant teeth in a fine dark face. 'I *am* one of them.'

'I know Stanford promotes diversity,' I said. 'But this is a multi-culturalism too far, don't you think?' He didn't answer, so I tried a more pointed question: 'Why?'

He shrugged, genially. 'It's my path. It always has been. It was the Dadu Panth who sent me to Stanford. And to preparatory school before that, in Jaipur. What I've learned I have done so on their behalf. For their purposes.'

'I thought you said you were Pakistani,' I said.

'I lied. I'm sorry.'

I shook my head and smiled. 'No, I'm the one who's sorry. I didn't know you very well – but well enough to see that there's more to you than a religious zealot, a plant, a guided missile. You're too clever to be brainwashed.'

He cocked his head and squinted slightly at me, considering. One could see a trace of amusement, a bit of light glinting on the whites of his eyes. He said: 'Maybe we'll get to discuss that one day. Right now, we've got to go. The Artefact. Please.'

But his request was superfluous. The others seized Basha, and her backpack. She didn't resist. In a moment, they had dug it out. They also took the opportunity to very quickly (but, as before, gently) bind all of our hands and feet with rope.

A'hib watched this. Taking hold of the Hands, he gave them a brief searching look. One of the others tried to take them from him. But instead, A'hib grabbed that man's satchel, put the Hands inside,

266

and slung it over his back. He made a circular motion with his finger and began to turn away. But then he hesitated.

'One thing,' he said. We were all ears. 'Yes, we deceived you – I did, most especially. But we never intended to hurt you, any of you. Even the business in the Santa Cruz mountains. Yes, our goal was to capture you, to learn what you had learnt. But we also went up there to preserve you – from those others. We knew what they were likely to do to you if they got to you first. And we intended to keep that from happening. I hope you can believe that.'

He adjusted the strap of his satchel. 'Goodbye. And best of luck in your escape.'

With that, he tossed something shiny at our feet, and the whole group drained out of the courtyard even more quickly than it had flowed in.

I leaned over and with bound hands retrieved the object.

'It's a fucking butter knife,' I said.

I think we were all pretty depressed at that point.

Fifty-one

'This has got to be the world's dullest fucking butter knife,' I muttered sullenly, sawing at Basha's bonds. 'As if they specially assigned someone to a whole weekend of buttering rocks.'

When I'd cut them loose, and they me, I said: 'Now what?'

Instantly, Helen answered: 'We go get it back.'

'Come again?'

I'd asked Helen once, earlier, during one of the rare moments we had alone without Basha, why she was so driven to recover the Artefact. 'It will probably vault genomic science ahead fifty years,' she answered. I'd assumed an unspoken addendum was that *she* would vault it ahead – if the Artefact was in her possession.

'I'm not leaving here without it,' she said now.

'You may well not,' said Basha, endorsing a sense of Helen's words I don't think she intended. 'We cannot expect this place to lay dormant through much more of this.' It was true. The absence of alarms, officials, or tumult was starting to seem creepy. 'Realistically, we must focus on getting ourselves out.'

Helen kicked the base of the Laocoön, but raised no other objection. As we began our exfiltration, a second stealthy crossing of the length of the museum, I could hear her cursing A'hib's name under her breath.

We encountered only incapacitated guards, and no Nagas of any sort, on our way out. The latter enjoyed a nearly ten-minute start on us, and appeared to have made good use of it. Also, our luck with security, alarms, Swiss Guards and whatnot, seemed to hold. Nothing stood in our way.

That is, all the way up until the moment we exited the Sistine Chapel, and re-entered the basilica. It was here that everything – and more – had been bulldozed into one huge pile to stand in our way. Right between us and the door.

It seemed likely, I would reflect later, that A'hib and his band of merry Nagas had made the same obvious mistake we had: that of leaving the front door ajar. Or, who knows, maybe the Qabbalists had emanated themselves or spiritually descended right down from the top of the dome. It hardly mattered.

What did matter was that they were beneath the dome now, directly in front of the towering and magnificent altar. They were at least twenty strong, armed to the yarmulkes, mostly with Uzis, most of them impressively scowling – and standing in a murderous circle around the group of Nagas. Of the latter, seeing them all crowded together for the first time, there were about a dozen. They still carried their weapons – though the Qabbalists shouted at them to drop them – and they were still on their feet, backs to one another. And, though completely surrounded, they looked less desperate than defiant.

A twenty-on-twelve Mexican standoff.

I figured A'hib & Co. must have walked into an ambush on their way out. Better them than us, I guess. And it was a grand place for an ambush: open central area, surrounded by four huge pillars, any number of smaller ones, and all the shadows you care to lurk in. The Qabbalists had obviously decided to hang out until somebody, it didn't matter who, emerged with the loot. Then they'd sprung their trap.

Also evidently at the mercy of the Cabal, in the back, just in front of St Peter's tomb, was a group of three Swiss Guards. These were kneeling, their bladed weapons on the floor ten feet from them, their hands behind their heads. I guessed they were the remainder of the night security crew for the basilica. The Qabbalists got the ones Helen and I had merely bypassed. Credit them with thoroughness.

Despite all these dubious developments, still one very beautiful thing had happened here. No one had seen or heard us come in. We three crouched in a darkened back corner, getting our bearings – and watching the Nagas and Qabbalists flailing on the cliff edge of what seemed likely, at any instant, to turn into an unmitigated bloodbath.

'For God's sake,' I hissed at my companions. 'The Nagas are completely surrounded. Why don't they surrender?'

Basha gave me a slightly sad *They're not the kind of people who surrender* look.

'So what's the plan?' asked Helen, a little testily.

Basha surveyed the scene. She said: 'We might be able to slip out down the aisle on this side. However, if we wait for their dispute to heat up, we almost certainly won't be spotted. Though we then run the hazard of stray bullets.'

'Fuck's sake,' I said, feeling sick at Basha's clinical treatment of the incipient slaughter. 'When this goes south, it's going to be nine-millimetre dodge ball. With A'hib and his men right in the middle. We can't just leave them.'

Basha's face told me she took my comments seriously. But she only said: 'These are people who know the risks they take. And, in any case, I do not see that there is anything we can do for them.'

I looked over at Helen. I could tell she wasn't anxious to leave either; though I guessed it was for her own reason – in case the Artefact should pop loose. I remembered her comment from the lodge: We were three very smart people. We'd figure something out. I racked my brain. I turned back to Basha.

'Do you have any more of those smoke canisters?'

'No. The Nagas have them now. Why? What did you have in mind?'

'Look,' I said, pointing. 'They're standing in a complete circle. If they can't see, I don't think they would dare shoot – they'd hit their own people on the other side. At the very least, it would mix things up. Maybe give the Nagas a chance. Plus, it would get us out of here unseen.' Damn!

Basha sighed. 'I do not have smoke. But I do happen to know . . . they have quite an impressive argon fire suppression system in here.'

'Can you set it off?'

She reprised her sigh. 'Yes.'

*

I'm not sure how I've gotten so good at interpreting Basha's looks – how we've achieved such an uncanny nonverbal rapport (in one direction, at least). Something to do with the still-water clarity of her face. And perhaps, as well, some connection that she and I shared. Her final look to me asked why I was so keen to risk my neck to help these fierce naked people.

Either because we hadn't the time . . . or because I wasn't entirely clear on it myself . . . or, you know, just conceivably, because I was embarrassed about it, I didn't pause to tell her then. But, in the privacy of my own heart, I was pretty sure it was mainly because I knew that one of A'hib's soldiers had saved me, saved me and Helen both, back on that hilltop. And that I had shot the poor guy, maybe fatally, for his trouble.

I owed for the flesh.

Yes, I hardly knew A'hib at all. But, then, Basha hardly knew me – and she'd come halfway around the world to single-handedly pull my tail out of the fire. And before Basha, it had been Thad – saving me at the office. By any accounting, it was surely my turn to pitch in.

And, no – I did not intend remaining an avatar in a game for the rest of my life.

'Look,' I said calmly, 'I want to take a shot at saving A'hib.'

'I want,' said Helen, 'to get my goddamned Artefact back.'

'And I,' sighed Basha, 'I think I want to get my head examined, at the earliest opportunity. Okay. Here is what we do . . .'

I don't know why I had my phone with me. It doesn't even work on European GSM networks. (Like that matters.) But, in fairness, when it wasn't giving me a hard time, it was usually bailing me out. It started up its buzzing as Helen and I circled the perimeter of the basilica, getting into position.

'Yeah,' I whispered, ducking through shadows.

'This is it,' she said. 'If, after all this, you get yourself killed trying to save those Nagas . . . or, worse, trying to get that unholy Artefact back . . . you and I are through.'

271

'Through. How do you mean through?'

We had to pass a line of sight to the standoff. It hadn't grown any less tense in the last three minutes. We raced by the gap, staying low.

'I mean through. Fini. You'll have no more help from me. I'm off the case!'

'Fine,' I said. 'You're a mixed blessing, anyway. Good riddance.'

'Good!' she said.

'Fine!'

But neither of us rang off. After another few seconds of sputtering silence, she broke down – and grudgingly gave me a tip. She told me that no matter what, when the lights went out, I should not go for a weapon. This was confusing at the time; but proved to be excellent advice, in good time.

And I was pleased that I seemed to be learning how to manage my phone.

We were almost in position.

And what was this plan of ours? Well, as we'd found ourselves unarmed, unequipped, and basically impotent, the best we could manage was this: Basha was going to make her way to an electrical closet on the opposite side of the room, short across a couple of wires, and set off the fire suppression system. Meanwhile, Helen and I would move down the aisle as far as we could – from where we'd have a straight shot to the front door, once our cloud cover came down. Basha would meet us there.

But if, by some chance, we first got a chance to help A'hib, we would do so. If we saw some possibility of grabbing the Artefact, we'd do that. Of course, there was also the very real possibility that everyone else involved might soon be dead. Which would leave the Artefact free for the taking.

But under no circumstances were we to hang around for more than sixty seconds after the shooting started. That was how long Basha figured we had to get out the front door with any prayer of evading the cordon that would come down around a . . . well, a large-scale gun battle inside the Vatican.

I don't know how much faith Basha held out that either Helen or I would follow these rules. I don't know which, if any of us, thought very much would come of our plan. And I have no idea why we thought the Qabbalists and Nagas would wait for us.

Counting the Swiss Guards out was also kind of short-sighted.

Fifty-two

'For the last time! Drop the weapons! And hand over the Hands!'

That was one shrill fucking Qabbalist. And from where I stood, the contrast between him and the Nagas couldn't have been more stark. From our hiding spot, I could actually make out A'hib himself – his face, his posture. For a twenty-something grad student, he was one cool cucumber. He was packing now, too. All the Nagas were.

Everyone was. Except us.

Two concentric circles, shifting and rotating unevenly in the flickering light of the hundred candles burning on the altar. Candlelight glinting off pivoting gun barrels. Bloodlessly gripped spears ready to go. Hairy naked bodies. Cheap black suit sheen. Set jaws all around, quick breaths, unblinking eyes betraying fearful whites. Nearly three dozen firearms – and probably not a single one with the safety engaged.

And all the saints and angels looking down serenely, and uselessly, upon it all.

It seemed nearly unavoidable that quite a lot of people here tonight were going to get to test their divergent theories about the afterlife. But I knew all we were going to learn was a horrific lesson about the spectacular fragility of the flesh-and-blood human body. Which we already well knew. What was the truth worth? Capital T?

Not this. Definitely not this.

The lead Hasid shouted his demand again.

I could see A'hib merely shake his head calmly. I think he'd had enough talk. He and his were ready to take their chances – and go on to the next life, if it came to that. It increasingly appeared that it would.

Even if the Hindus hadn't been outnumbered and fatally surrounded, they were also badly outgunned. Spears and .44 Magnums are not to be sniffed at; particularly in capable hands. (Both

Basha, and the game, had taught me that the main thing is not to have dangerous weapons; the main thing is to be a dangerous player.) Still, the Jews were fully automatic – Uzis, thirty-round magazines and 950 rounds per minute, cyclic. All I could hope was that they'd hesitate to use them – in the indoor fog bank we planned to create presently.

But Basha did not, it turned out, manage her next feat of electrical engineering before the first shot rang out. It wasn't from an Uzi. And it wasn't from a revolver.

It was from a SIG. I'd forgotten that SIG was a Swiss company.

In all the blustering, and threatening, and gun waving and what-not, everyone had kind of forgotten about the Swiss Guards kneeling behind them, and before the altar. I guess when it appeared that the end really was nigh, one of them had decided to try his luck. To use his holdout exploit. He turned, pressed on some kind of panel (presumably hidden, but I couldn't see it either way) right in the tomb of poor old St Pete – and he came back around strapped with a pistol. And firing.

He dropped two of the Qabbalists, ones in the rear of the outer circle, single shots to the back – before one of the Nagas, who'd been facing off against those same guys, fired one thundering round through the gap – dropping the Swiss Guard. (Sending him hurtling fifteen feet, actually.)

Three shots total. Then perfect silence again. Everyone leered in every direction. You could somehow feel the catches in three dozen throats.

Me being who I am, I couldn't help but entertain some loony idea that the two groups would make friends over this incident. Teamwork and all. Not bloody likely.

But then the fire suppression system spun up, a comprehensive overhead hissing. And the argon smoke came down – good and thick. Fast, too.

And then, for just one more still moment, all these strung-out guys seemed to have no idea how to react. And I, similarly, suddenly had no idea how we'd expected them to.

But then when visibility had dropped to under ten feet, the Nagas went and did what they'd probably been itching to do for quite some time. They sent up a mighty shout. And they went after those Qabbalists with their spears.

It quickly became apparent that the billowing fog really did make gunplay awkward. A few shots were certainly going off. The odd ripping peal of Uzi fire. The shudder-in-your-bowels thunder of the Magnums. But one had the sense, despite being less and less able to see a damned thing, that most of these rounds were going astray. Were even aimed at the ceiling, in many cases. It had turned into a mêlée, hand-to-hand.

Don't get me wrong. The whole thing was still complete bloody chaos, harrowing and nightmarish, a free-for-all. But at least it wasn't a point-blank wholesale massacre – a circular firing squad. At least we had given A'hib's team a fighting chance.

And now it was time to take ours.

I grabbed Helen's hand. I tugged. I used Basha's immortal line: 'Time to go!'

She relented. We ducked our heads, pointing our noses down what still seemed to be the aisle. And we began zooming through the low-lying clouds.

We'd made it ten steps before a bullet sliced in front of my nose. Yowzers! I could actually see it – the tunnel it tore in the argon. I tucked my head in even tighter, regrouped, and started to go headlong again. But the slack had gone out of Helen's arm.

Turning to get her moving, I quickly saw what she had – a Naga staggering toward us, backward out of the fog. He hit the deck ten feet away – either dead or knocked cold. He landed on his satchel – out of which popped a familiar shape. They'd been taped together now. But it was unmistakably them.

Helen tore loose from my grip. But no sooner had she wrenched free than a practically disembodied foot – like it was on a stick, wielded just for this purpose – came out of the fog and gave the

Artefact a mighty kick, back into the fog, back toward the centre of the tumult.

I could see now that it had been a Qabbalist, sprinting by, banging on a jammed weapon. He disappeared again just as quickly.

I looked to Helen, but she didn't spare the half-second to look back. She just squared her shoulders, put her own head down – and dived into the mists after the thing.

Fuck.

I stood there stupidly, in a slight, stupid, crouch.

'Kate!' a voice shouted, from somewhere behind me.

I turned. It was Basha, coming out of the fog from the other direction – the direction of the vestibule, the front doors. The direction of our escape. She cradled an Uzi. She must have liberated it somewhere along the way. No surprise there.

'Kate,' she said again, more quietly, closer. She held out her hand to me.

Oh, that's me, by the way. That's my name: Katherine Elizabeth Quinlan. But I've always gone by Kate.

Right, then. So there it was. On the one hand, the three of us waiting around in hiding, setting off some sprinklers, waiting another sixty seconds to cut and run . . . that was all one thing. But on the other hand: freely choosing to plunge, eyes open, straight into this manifested *Purgatorio*, this malevolent cumulus of death and hazard . . . that was quite another. This was where to stand upright and do my bit would entail hanging my ass out entirely in the wind.

To my right, Basha – armed, confident, calling me to safety.

To my left, a white swirl that used to be Helen, disappeared into the belly of the beast. Alone. If I left her that way.

And here's what I thought of, in that single instant I had to decide.

Suppose Thad was right. Suppose the existentialist fears that came from his loss of faith were valid. Suppose, at the end of all this, there's nothing at all – that I really do end up staring at the inside of a pine box. And suppose no one is watching what I do, judging from above – only empty cosmos, and silence. 'The universe we observe,' said Darwin, 'has precisely the properties we should expect if there is, at bottom, no design, no purpose, no good, no evil, nothing but blind pitiless indifference.' Suppose it's just so.

Nevertheless, I knew – not in that magnificent onboard protein computer of mine, but rather in my bones and in my flesh – that what I did in this moment still had meaning. Here. Now. To me. It had meaning to me.

Basha knew my decision before I did. The communication went both ways now, I guess. As I turned away, I saw her pull out the folding stock of her weapon, thumb the selective fire switch, and take off purposefully at ninety degrees.

I plunged into the fog.

Pairs of bodies rolling on the floor. Gun-hands clenched at the wrist. Grunts, bellows, gunshots – less frequent now, and the more terrifying for it. Slick, dark patches of stone. The whoosh of spears swinging, staff-like, through the cottony air.

And the claustrophobically close cloud walls – swirling around in an agoraphobically enormous space. Black hats everywhere – in the air, on the ground, rolling by. Beards, beards, beards. The odd penis.

Like a San Francisco fog bank, those irresistible mist armies rolling over the hills at water's edge – but in some horrible, twisted, weird, parallel-universe Bay Area. Hard weather in a Lovecraftian Hell.

And no Helen to be seen.

Head down, eyes darting wildly, I kept running in the direction I'd seen her go. I tried to ignore anything not poised to kill me. And still, in here, only the keen sense of being already dead somehow kept the fear shoved back down my throat.

Then, unexpectedly, the overhead argon blowers cut out – and the banks of chemical fog began to clear, surprisingly fast. Draining off, probably, into the extensive catacombs below. The good news was that I might now be able to find Helen. The bad news was that if I hoped to get us both out alive – much less back up her attempt at the Artefact – now was looking strikingly like the time to do it.

There! I saw her struggling with a Qabbalist, the Hands clutched between them. On the ground, a spear. I snatched it up on the run – and the energy of my hurtling body multiplied that of my mighty, wide-arc swing. I caught the man under the arm. Emitting a mighty whoof, he hurtled back into the mists. Helen retained the Artefact.

She looked up and smiled her thanks at me.

But then another black-suited body – or, hell, who knows, maybe the same one, tumbled back through the looking glass – hurtled into the frame, into solidity, from the opposite direction. He caught Helen around the waist and they both went down.

No one retained the Artefact this time. It had been launched sky-ward.

And the only way we can deal with the next six seconds is in movie slo-mo.

Helen falling to the stone, under the mighty bulk of the big Hasid.

The taped-together Hands accelerating, heading toward the dome in a high arc.

My head swivelling to Helen as she crunches to the stone floor, eyes wide.

And Helen, just before having the air crushed out of her, mouthing, soundlessly, the single word: 'Go . . . !' Her hand snakes around her tackler; pointing skyward.

Me bending at the knees and straining forward. Pushing off. Eyes tracking the flight path. Vectoring.

Little contrails curling around my calves, my acceleration. The last of the argon.

Immediately, a black-clad figure in my path. Swinging round to face me. Bringing his submachine gun to bear. No time to stop. I'll either knock him down or he'll knock me down. But instead a small dark hole opens in his shoulder; then another in his neck. The force of the bullets knocks him away, orthogonal to my path – and out of it.

I'm not slowing.

The Hands coming down now – dead before the altar. Me looking up – past the Glory, up towards the awesome concavity of the Dome. At its very top, God reclining in his heaven. A choir of angels below him. And, at bottom, inscribed around the drum, in Latin, the words: 'You are Peter, and upon this rock I will build my church; I will give you the keys to heaven.'

In position now, skidding to a stop, sliding on my knees. My hands reaching up.

In peripheral vision, to my left – a squad of Swiss Guards, really a whole squadron now, storming the basilica from the back corner. Fog almost gone now. To my right, another black-suited figure rushing at me. Running full-out.

I hold my ground. I'm not moving. Either he'll hit me first, or the Artefact will.

But another series of shots ring out.

The rushing figure goes face-first into the stone; sliding up next to me.

Is one of those angels in the choir above my guardian? Does its rifle cover my advance? Fire and movement? Good infantry tactics?

My eyes stay locked onto the heavens.

One more second.

Touchdown.

The Hands are now in my hands, clasped together, held before and above me.

As if in prayer.

I don't have a chance to smile before I feel . . . the press of cold steel on my neck.

Helen on her feet again, stepping forward with a found Magnum, held untremblingly. The resonant click as she pulls the heavy hammer back.

Cut. Fade.

Fifty-three

And so that's right about where we came in, I think.

The cognitive neuroscientist Steven Pinker has this really lovely trope about how the big human brain is like a personal digital assistant (PDA). He says that quite a lot of his colleagues have adopted these gadgets – but he prefers to stick with his good old-fashioned spiral notebook and pen. And the reasons why are some of the same reasons why having a huge, complicated, human brain is not quite the end-all-be-all we make it out to be.

A big brain requires an excessive amount of power to run – at 2 per cent of body mass, our brains use 20 per cent of the body's oxygen and 25 per cent of its glucose. It takes a lot of time and effort to learn to use one properly – we spend most of our lives either being, or raising, children. It makes easy tasks hard – with all the processing overhead, we do simple things like reacting to a loud noise many times slower than does, say, a lizard. It's big, bulky, and fragile – we are very prone to head injuries, not to mention broken necks from carrying around that thick, heavy, wobbly skull.

Pointing out the significant costs and downsides of a huge brain is Pinker's way of debunking a common confusion: that intelligence is the ultimate end of evolution. In fact, it's not – it's merely a neat trick. Like flight, or night vision, or an elephant's trunk.

Naturally, because we're clever, we think being clever is the 'goal' of evolution. That, given long enough, everyone would evolve this way. But evolution is not a ladder; it's a bush. There's no top, and if there were, it's not clear intelligence would sit there. Great white sharks have been kicking ass and taking names for millions of years. And high intelligence probably wouldn't help them do one whit better. Would it?

Well, who knows.

What I do know is that all our clever planning . . . all our complex higher functions – like loyalty to friends! . . . piled up on top of our millions of years of killer ape survival instincts and tactics . . . all of this had served to land us precisely . . .

In deep shit.

I mean, I had a halberd to my neck.

We were facing, before us now, the reconstituted ranks of Swiss Guards – what appeared to be a significant chunk of the remaining hundred of them. And they were not, alack, all armed with medieval weapons this time around.

Behind us, we still had a whole bunch of Nagas and Qabbalists, many of whom remained combat-effective, scattered about. With the clearing of the smoke and the invasion of the Papal Guard, they had broken off their mêlée, picked up dropped weapons, and backed warily off. Some had taken cover behind pillars; some behind bodies. Others stood in the open. All seemed to be on hair triggers.

So much for loyalty. So much for cleverness. So much for my turn saving the day.

But, then again, the day wasn't over yet.

Maybe there would be one more rescue in this story. Just one more.

For some reason, I remembered my phone's recent admonition. And I prayed for the lights to go out. Ideally, very soon.

Fifty-four

Instead, at the very peak, the seeming breaking point, of all this tension, silence, and coiled violence . . . instead, the front ranks of the Swiss Guards parted. From the breach, a figure walked briskly forward. He was elderly and bespectacled. He wore long robes, wrapped with a red sash - and a cute little circular red hat . . .

As he came closer, the light glinted on his austere glasses – and I decided they looked familiar. His face now looked familiar. The whole guy looked very familiar.

Him, I thought simply. The guy from the video. Cardinal Whotsit. The ring-bearer. The Vatican Secretary of State. The Pope Picker.

He had a factotum in tow, tripping in his robe swirl. I soon recognized him as the same young functionary who had interrogated me after my little . . . vision, my episode of the vapours.

As these two strode solemnly forward, the contingent of Swiss Guards fanned out before them – pivoting and pointing handguns and submachine guns. They may have bollocksed up securing the basilica, earlier. But they obviously took the physical protection of guys at the Cardinal level pretty seriously.

And as the pair drew up close, I saw the factotum's jaw go for the floor.

'You!' he said, ogling my familiar face in the candlelight.

Yeah, me, him, everybody. He'd best get over being surprised. The rest of us had.

Not one for chitchat, the Cardinal presumably being a busy guy, he got right into it. He spoke in English; accented, but clear – and forceful.

'So you would not be dissuaded,' he said. He was speaking, I realized, directly to me. Gulp. 'Your vanity bade you meddle with God's holy formula for life.' I gathered the Cardinal was cool on biotechnology.

His voice swelled now to be heard by those behind me.

'And you have come for the bronze Hands,' he cried, nodding at my package. 'Bringing this horde of ill-doers trailing with you. But the Hands are the work of the Devil! They may never be taken from this place. Leave now – and look to your souls.'

I had no idea how to respond to any of that.

But, let's see – who's never at a loss? Ah, yes.

'They belong to humankind,' Helen said, all business. She still held the monstrous revolver; though she'd lowered it from the head of the Guard beside me. 'You have no right to them – even if they don't jibe very well with your theology.'

Uh, oh. Was Helen going to say nay to a Vatican decree?

But before she could go on, that same shrill Qabbalist, I think, still alive and on his feet, unfortunately, put in his two cents from out on the floor.

'We are not leaving without them! We do not care if it means killing everyone here! Or dying ourselves – every one of us! This place is not holy to us! All that matters is the Truth! God's hidden word! We will have it!'

With this little peroration, the St Pete's Easter Week Celebration Gun Battle Tension-Meter ratcheted itself right back up again. As did quite a lot of gun barrels, spears, halberds, etc. – as everyone started anticipating the worst, and getting their game faces on. The Swiss Guards in particular didn't like the looks of this at all; they started edging out between the Cardinal and the invaders.

And here we were again. Another goddamned standoff. Replete with lots of grizzled veterans of the first one, a whole bunch of fresh reinforcements – and everyone still armed to the nines. I just couldn't believe it.

I mean, I was still alive – even after everything. Helen was on her feet. And Basha hadn't been hurt. Oh, I knew Basha hadn't been touched. She was out there somewhere, doing her thing. Waiting for her moment. Waiting for her look.

So we'd made it this far intact. But the odds of finishing up that way, as far as I could tell, hadn't improved one whit. And the odds

284

of getting out clean – free, unarrested, unmarked – had dropped, it seemed sadly self-evident, to zero. Or thereabouts.

I could hear hammers locking back. Somebody cleared a chamber, ejecting a single round tinnily onto the floor. The factotum covered up his head. And, worst of all, my halberd-guy pressed his blade just that much more insistently into the (not real fleshy) flesh of my neck.

And then . . . and then . . . the room went down.

The whole room.

At Instant Zero: the lights went out. And I mean – *out*. Not a glowing emergency exit sign; not a flickering votive candle. Trapped-behind-your-own-eyelids darkness. Which-way-is-up-again meaty black space.

At Instant One: The first explosion. That first flash, like God's own road flare, like a movie projector bulb exploding in your face, sealed my eyes tight. But there was little I could do to react to the accompanying percussive roar. My poorly adapted human ears stood exposed; and then shut down, deafened. Blind and deaf.

At Instants Two through Eight: Seven more explosions in rapid sequence – reprises of Instant One, minus some of the shock. But not minus much. Luckily, most of the blasts seemed to happen at some remove, around the perimeter of the room, behind me. Rather than point-blank. Still, they sucked the moisture right out of my mouth. This makes me think it was open (my mouth).

I couldn't feel the halberd blade. I considered that even a negative sensation must mean that it hadn't taken my head off. I pulled it (the head) down with me toward the floor. Muted, like typewriter key strikes, I heard brief flurries of gunfire around the room. Someone was shooting; presumably at someone else. Or maybe at nothing. I tried to not even think about going for a weapon. I just cowered.

And, by way of a confession: Yeah, okay, I also wondered if God was intervening. Or maybe the little green men. Who could say? It all seemed supernatural.

But my next sensation was that of my arms being pulled roughly behind my back; and my wrists being lashed together. Then my ankles. Then, an ungentle shove over on my side. I lay on it (my side). The gunfire began to peter out.

Eventually, I dared crack an eye. Some illumination had returned. An amber lamp nearby, LED torches sweeping the room. Just bright enough to make out a face – one wizened, markedly less serene than before. It was pressed, cheek-down, into the stone – six inches from my own. The Cardinal and I lay nose-to-nose.

We locked eyes. His were very pale blue; like mine. The silence grew awkward.

'Terribly sorry about all of this,' I ventured.

'Bless you, my child,' he said. But there was no affect in his voice. It was a reaction, a stored procedure, a tic.

To my immense relief, someone lifted me carefully to my feet. As I rose, unsteadily, I scanned the room in the dim light. Immediately, I saw great fields of other prone figures. All of the Swiss Guards, for starters. They all lay on their sides, as I had just seconds ago. All were bound at wrists and ankles. Guns and halberds lay willy-nilly. I turned, and found a similar tableau of Nagas and Qabbalists behind me.

Amongst all the bound bodies, in and out of the piles of weapons, stalked dark sinuous figures. I couldn't tell how many; they crossed one another, weaving in and out. They all wore black – soles to crown. They all had submachine guns or rifles to their shoulders, which they panned smoothly. They all had something on their faces, some kind of thick mask. Occasionally, one would pause to kick a gun away from a body.

And just like that, the standoff was over.

I raised my eyes to the figure who had pulled me up. He was one of the black-clad wraiths, a rifle held in the crook of one arm, his other hand on my elbow. His face was also covered. Close-up, I could see it was a night-vision device on his face. He reached up and pulled it away, onto his forehead. Underneath, he wore a black balaclava – a hood that covered all of his head but a band for his eyes.

But as those eyes smiled crinkily at me, I recognized them instantly.

'You,' I whispered through tears.

Thad.

Fifty-five

'Don't you get around,' I managed. I was trying to sound cheeky despite my half-swoon of relief, joy – and profound amazement.

'Yeah.' Thad turned and looked around behind us, particularly at the Nagas. 'Man. Those guys really are just dick-and-nuts naked, aren't they?'

'Thad!' I felt like Leslie, scolding him for being ribald in front of the kids.

More lights had come on now. The stalking shadow warriors followed Thad's lead and removed their night-vision devices. They seemed no less intimidating without them. Thad pulled his bala-clava over his head. He carried on looking around the room, seemingly in awe.

'Um,' I said. I hit him with my shoulder. 'Could you untie me, please?'

He turned back to me. 'Um. Technically, no. I'm supposed to get supplemental sign-off on friendlies. From our liaison guys. Oh, the heck with it.' He unsheathed a monstrous knife from his chest webbing.

But just then a tumult nearby grabbed his attention.

'Hang on,' he said, trotting off briskly. Looking past him, I could see two of the men in black – and, let's face it, I knew by now they were Delta Force soldiers – aiming their weapons unambiguously up into one of the elevated reliquary niches. I realized it was the alcove Basha had hidden in when we made our entry.

And as I thought it, none other than the woman herself emerged from behind the statue of St Longinus. She held her hands high – one of them gripping the Uzi by the very end of the barrel – and moved extremely slowly. As Thad trotted up, he shouted at the men covering her: 'Whoa, whoa! Stand down – one of ours.' With that, he reached up to help Basha down. They stood and exchanged words, out of my earshot.

I smiled and shook my head, now knowing that I really did have a guardian angel covering me from above. And as always, just when I'd needed her.

Then, belatedly, I remembered two things on the ground. One was the Artefact. I found it still lying at my feet. The other was Helen. I picked her out, twenty yards away – already getting to her feet as well. She was being helped up by two men. I'd seen neither of them before. Unlike the Deltas, they wore tan jumpsuits and light jackets – with no visible insignia. Neither was armed that I could see.

After helping Helen up, they immediately cut her free.

Thad trotted back up. He still had his knife out. But I directed his attention instead to the ground between us. He knew well what lay there. He leaned over and picked them up, then looked again at me. We shared a second of silent communion. He reached to his belt and pulled open a black duty bag.

'Sergeant.' It was a crisp address, tinged with warning – issued by one of the jumpsuited men. He'd walked right up to us, along with his companion – and with Helen.

Thad looked down again to the things in his hands wistfully.

The jumpsuited man shook his head slowly at him.

Thad held the Hands out, in offering – but Helen reached out and plucked them.

She turned to me and paused. My hands were still tied behind my back; my ankles crossed and bound. I might have fallen over. I looked into Helen's dark eyes. She didn't speak. She hit me with a very deep, very inscrutable look.

Then she turned on her heel. With one of the mystery men on her elbow, she strode briskly off towards the front of the basilica – towards the exit.

The other man backed away from me and Thad, watching us warily. I took a hop forward. He shook his head again, now for my benefit. I got his drift and stopped. He turned and trotted off after the other two.

I couldn't think of what to say. I felt Thad's hand on my wrist.

Gently, the plastic loop fell away. Then the one on my feet. I continued to stare at the three receding figures.

'Okay,' I said. 'Who the hell was that?'

Thad stood up again. 'Those were our liaison guys.'

'Liaison with whom?'

'With the people who sent us on this mission.'

I turned to him in puzzlement. 'The US government?'

'Presumably,' he said, a little sardonically. 'But, you know, honestly, I couldn't really swear to anything.'

I laughed out loud. I muttered: 'So that means Helen . . . Helen is . . .'

Thad sensed my disconcertion. 'Maybe they were arresting her. For working with the Qabbalists. Or with the Nagas.'

'I don't see any flexicuffs on her. Or any other kind of cuffs.'

With that, the three figures had disappeared into the gloom at the other end of the great hall. And Helen had gone.

Thad startled now from his reverie, hailed by another Delta nearby. The soldier stood over another prone form, holding a knife – and asking for Thad's approval.

'Yeah, yeah!' Thad answered, darting over. 'That one's good, he's good.' The man flicked his knife twice, and Thad leaned in solicitously to help him up. 'So sorry, your Eminence . . .'

'Why? How?' I asked, stepping over a body.

Thad and I were walking together toward the front door now. Around us, Deltas were piling up weapons, pulling satchels off Nagas, field-treating the wounded – and efficiently preparing to withdraw. Something on the ground, amidst all the other detritus of the battle, caught my eye.

I turned towards it; but Thad started to answer, and I was desperately curious to know what in hell he was doing here.

'They called and asked me,' he said simply. 'I said yes.'

'And why would they ask a decrepit old man like you?'

Thad grinned. 'Actually, you'd be surprised how old some of these guys are. It usually takes ten or fifteen years to get really good

290

at this stuff. Anyway, they asked me, firstly, because I know the layout of this building. And, secondly, because I know you, Helen, and Basha – and the details of what you were planning.'

'You sold us out!'

'No, no. Not that. They already knew. But they also said that so did your opposition, the Nagas and Qabbalists – and that they would be right behind you. In short, that you were walking into a trap and were going to need backup. And maybe a rescue op. That's why I agreed to go.'

We reached the vestibule. Thad turned and gave the basilica a long last look.

'Man,' he said, dazedly. 'When I decided to stop being Catholic . . . I never thought I'd end up taking down St Peter's.' He held the door open for me.

Outside, there were four large black helicopters set down in the middle of St. Peter's Square, rotors idling – but completely blacked out, lightless. Steering me toward one of them, Thad explained they were Black Hawks from the 160th SOAR (Special Operations Air Regiment): 'These guys land anywhere.'

We climbed in, followed by an additional half-dozen or so Deltas – as well as one Basha Levy. One of the men tried to hand her in; but she swung her legs over the lip and flopped down like she'd done it a dozen times that night. Empty-handed, relieved of command, along for the ride, she looked passive – almost a little melancholy.

The engine wound up and we ascended into the night. As we lifted off, I could see more members of the rescue force streaming out of the basilica, making for the other aircraft. When we had climbed above the height of the dome, and banked around, I found I could make out a fifth helicopter, ahead of us, in the distance. I guessed who was on it.

A cipher Helen Dolan had been the night she came into my life; and a cipher she remained going out of it. Really, I knew now that she had become a stand-in for everything I feared about other people: she and I could never really bridge our divide; I never really knew who she was; we worked at cross-purposes – except when our purposes happened to overlap. She was brilliant – but her intelligence led her to completely different places than mine. And, finally, and most tellingly of all: she was going away.

And at that moment, I was already beginning to understand that those were precisely the wrong lessons for me to have learned. I knew the time was coming for me to turn a major corner – to embrace my hopes, and show my backside to my fears.

One thing that made this seem so possible, in that moment, was: another blessed refrain of that rapturous chorus of individual cells of my body, singing their praise that I had survived another night. That I yet lived. That my singular spark of consciousness abided, was still simply here – here in the world. Once again, I'd experienced the near loss of my life, had felt its profound fragility and contingency; and once again I'd been left with a shuddering sense of the startling beauty and power of every bare sensation, every second, every breath.

And the other reason for my new optimism – this one so much more powerful, and resonant, and insistent on being explored – was: the presence of the two people sitting on either side of me in the swooping helicopter. Thaddeus Gottlieb and Basha Levy. These two other distinct sparks of consciousness, who – despite their near-infinite complexity and multifold motivations and idiosyncratic makeups – both had repeatedly demonstrated the arrestingly simple and infinitely endearing trait of . . . never having let me down. Not ever. Not once.

I couldn't possibly doubt that they loved me. Or that I loved them.

And they were both still right here. Right by my side.

I reached out to either side of me, found two hands, one twice the size of the other, and squeezed. For just a few seconds, I hung on – for life.

As we flew together through the dazzling night above the Eternal City.

Fifty-six

Yes, okay, I admit it: a night like that makes you a little sappy.

But my epiphanies from onboard the helicopter were not chased away by the morning light. To the contrary, they deepened, and clarified. They walked.

That is, Thad and I walked, together again, now on the banks of the Tiber; trying to hash out some of the lessons life had recently launched at our heads. Thad had his hands in his jeans pockets, shoulders rounded, face pointed down at our path. We both wore dark glasses. The wind played hell with my hair. It was just like any other day – only with Rome in springtime standing in for the soulless Silicon Valley office park.

In particular, I was trying to explain to Thad that all-consuming sensation of cellular joy I'd been left with after escaping from the shootout at the lodge – and then again, after surviving, seemingly miraculously, the standoff in the basilica.

'Yeah,' he said immediately. 'I know what you mean. I used to get that rush a lot, back in my days in the unit. At least, I think it was similar to what you had.'

'But here's the thing,' I said, growing animated now. 'The thing I realized on the helicopter. As I examined these feelings, I found them strangely reminiscent of something. Strangely familiar. I was reminded of our old nemesis the existential flu – and, specifically, of your existential despair. You know, that feeling that there is no point to existence, and no obvious reason to carry on.'

'Hmm. Why did the one thing remind you of the other?'

'Because of the sheer force of the feeling, its irrational insistence, its insusceptibility to reason. There I was, flying through the night air, watching the lights, feeling the wind, happy and grateful for every raw sensation, smiling out loud in my soul, my whole body kind of vibrating . . . and that's when I realized: *existential horror has an exact flip side.* It's . . . *existential rapture.* The sheer, awed, unlikely

293

joy at simply being alive in the world second to second. The absolute certainty that *life is its own point.*

Thad nodded and considered; thoughtful and respectful as ever. 'Yes, but . . . what if you're not able to arrange a shootout? What good does that rapture do you when you're stuck in the despair?'

'Just this,' I said. 'It gives you hope. Knowing that the state exists. That, out there somewhere, or perhaps somewhere inside of you, there is an urge to keep on living that is every bit as strong and implacable as the despair to quit. A feeling that is its own irreducible reason to go on living. And that it could come back at any time . . . Because the antidote to hopelessness is always hope.'

We turned to cross a bridge over the river – back toward the historical centre, where we were to meet Basha. We stepped out over the flowing waters in silence. Thad looked up and around, considering solemnly. Then he smiled.

'It's a great point,' he said. 'You do just never know how you're going to feel from one day to the next – or what life is going to bring. I certainly wouldn't have guessed I'd ever again be putting on a uniform and picking up a rifle. But I did. And it did give me a taste of that old feeling, that rush of life force. I'd almost forgotten it.'

'And how did it feel? To remember?'

'It felt good. But you know what? There was something else I'd nearly forgotten. That rush of survival, this thrill of being alive, however joyful . . . I don't think it *is* enough. There needs to be some sense of purpose, some larger meaning, attached to it. Underneath, holding it up. Back in the day, it was that belief I had that we were out there battling evil. Protecting people. Helping them. That used to be my undergirding.'

'And now?'

'That's the big question, I guess. Obviously, that old thing is gone. And aside from this little reprise – and, to a lesser extent, my work with the police – it's never coming back. But, starting when I flew out of the US, and coming to a head when I kicked down that door last night, and when the shooting started . . . suddenly I knew. I knew what my larger meaning was, incredibly clearly. It's Leslie and

the kids. That's it. My family, and a few close friends. Including –
and I mean this – dear Auntie Kate.'

And with that he turned and smiled at me, right in the middle
the bridge.

And you can probably guess what I was doing.

Around tears, I said: 'You know, I think you've found the missing piece.'

'And now you've just got to find your meaning. For you.'

I sniffed. 'Helen actually told me something I remember, something Sartre said. "For many, life begins on the other side of despair".'

And then Thad surprised me by being a lot more pointed than
he ever had before. He said: 'You don't need me to tell you, Kate, that
nothing is ever going to bring your brother back. And nothing will
ever make his loss okay, or fill up the place he had in your life. But
it kind of seems to me . . . that as long as what his life was con-
tinues to have *meaning* – for you, for your parents, for everyone who
loved him . . . well, that's one of the best things any of us could hope
for. To really touch the people in our lives. Yes, people go away. But
the good ones also stay with us for ever.'

I advanced smartly from weeping straight to sobbing uncon-
trollably. Thad put his arms around my heaving shoulders; and I
tried to burrow through his chest.

'From everything you've told me, his life was a great blessing.
But . . . and here's where I might be getting out of line . . . but it seems
to me that surely the lesson he would want you to take from that is
that you *should* continue to let people into your life. That you *should*
take the risk of giving your heart away again. And that you should
live as fully as you can. Which means loving people. Whatever the
risk.'

Basha had annexed an outdoor table for us, at Tre Scalini – world-
renowned gelato Mecca, near the centre of Piazza Navona. She sat
there looking all cool – sipping espresso and wearing a pair of sunglasses (the first time I'd seen her do that). She was also breezily
flipping through a large pile of the morning's papers.

295

'What's the good word?' I asked. I was still a little puffy-eyed when we walked up, but not really worse for wear.

'The word is mum,' she said, refolding the paper in her hands. It appeared to be *La Repubblica*. Beneath it I could see a copy of the *International Herald Tribune* peeking out. 'No gunfights. No break-ins. No black helicopters. Nothing untoward at all in or about the Vatican. Nothing all week.'

'Wow,' I said.

'Man,' Thad said. 'These guys are a cover-up *machine*.'

'Helen would be tickled,' I added, as Thad and I sat down.

'Helen might be behind it, for all we know.' Basha said. She paused and smiled. 'So. Thad. Do you not have to get back to work? To meet your Version 6.0 release date?'

'Do you break into the mail of everyone you know?' I asked mock-sharply.

Thad tried to look taken aback, but then quickly smiled. He said: 'Well . . . pardon me, but fuck Version 6. After working over the weekend, and getting shot for my trouble, I'm taking a few days off.'

I laughed. 'Perhaps now they'll understand your dim view of working weekends.'

Thad nodded. 'That's right. Probably everyone who works on the weekend gets shot. For all I know. Or care to.'

'Still,' I said, 'I've got to think you would have been safer at the office than bailing us out from the middle of that wild west show in the basilica.'

'Yeah, that was a pretty crunchy situation you got yourselves into.'

Basha spoke up – sounding slightly defensive. 'Oh, it was not so bad. And, anyway, you can only walk so far into the wilderness—'

'. . . before you're walking out again!' Thad and I sang in tandem.

'Dude,' I said, 'you are really going to have to learn to stop repeating yourself so much. If you want to make a go of it in the secret agent business.'

'You might also want to learn to use contractions,' Thad added. 'I found that a little bit of a giveaway. Personally.'

Basha clammed up. She smiled, shook her head, and sipped at her espresso. Thad and I ducked inside to get us all gelato.

On our return, we talked a little more about meaning. We told Basha about our various personal epiphanies. And for the first time, perhaps oddly, it occurred to us that the Pandora sequence might have some bearing on our relationship with meaning.

'What do you think,' Thad asked Basha. 'Could the sequence have given us meaning in our lives – in addition to all the other stuff?'

She looked very thoughtful for a moment, behind her glasses. 'No,' she said finally and firmly. 'Not meaning. Perhaps, in some way, our need for it . . . or some propensity to seek it. But no genetic sequence can tell us what we find meaningful.' She tossed her head toward the Bernini sculptures in the centre of the plaza – the spectacular Fontana dei Fumi (Fountain of the Rivers). She said: 'You could no sooner describe meaning with genetics . . . than explain the beauty of Bernini's marbles with geology.'

'Like the Cologne Cathedral.' Thad paused to put away some gelato *tartufo* (which he had immediately christened 'the best proof of God I've experienced in some time'). He added: 'We might know for sure, if it hadn't been for Helen.'

'God, I still find it hard to believe she was working for the Feds,' I admitted. 'I guess, though, that explains her issues with authority. One way or the other.'

Basha nodded. 'Her resentment did seem very elaborate.'

I laughed. 'I still can't believe it, though. I mean – she was so mysterious! What sort of secret agent would act like that?'

Basha grinned. 'But her act appears to have worked perfectly.'

'Great. Reverse psychology.'

'The tragedy, though,' said Thad, 'is that she has the Artefact.'

I let a couple of beats go by. I tossed my curls. 'No,' I said. 'She doesn't.'

'What? We saw her walk out the door – with the Hands right in her hands.'

'No,' I corrected. 'We saw her walk out with *some* hands in her hands.' I paused to spoon up some credulity-strainingly-great *nocciola* gelato; as well as for drama.

'Okay,' I elaborated. 'When we were walking out. There were people and things all over the floor. Thad's friends had emptied out some of the bags the Nagas were carrying. And something there caught my eye. Half-hidden under a piece of cloth, or something – another pair of hands. Just exactly the same. And also taped together.'

'You're kidding.'

'Nope. And that's when I also realized – I hadn't seen A'hib. Not since the first standoff. Even if he had fallen in the fighting . . . he was the only Naga wearing clothing. The Deltas had everybody, living, dead or wounded, near the centre of the room. And there was nary a *kurta* to be seen. I looked.'

'The mêlée in the argon cloud . . .' Basha said.

'Yep. He must have slipped out then. With the Artefact.'

'I had forgotten,' Basha said. 'He had it when they left us. In his bag.'

'But why would they have dummy Artefacts?' asked Thad. 'Fakes?'

'Most likely,' said Basha, looking impressed, 'it was to put them in place of the real ones. So the theft would go unnoticed. But we had already broken the case.'

'Clever boys,' I said. 'But why multiple pairs?'

'Just best practice, perhaps? Redundancy of any critical system.'

'Maybe. Or maybe for just this eventuality,' I mused. 'So they could pull a switcheroo if it became necessary – if they were way-laid, for instance.'

We finished our gelato, ordered coffee to follow it – and enjoyed the sunset on the beautiful and lively piazza. And, most especially, we enjoyed one another's company. It was a lot like our three-way email exchanges. Except much, much lovelier.

'So,' said Basha, removing her sunglasses in the last light, and lean-ing back in her chair. 'What now? For you?'

I was a little caught out by her question. But not entirely unprepared. 'I don't know, honestly. I guess . . . I don't feel as if I could just jump back into my old life – such as it was. Certainly not right away.'

'Whatever you do,' Thad said, 'Erasmus has a home for the duration.'

'Thank you.'

'Don't worry. Kennedy and Holden are in monkey heaven. They just monkey around all day long.'

I realized Basha was looking at me lingeringly, biting on the arm of her sunglasses. 'How do you think you might feel,' she finally asked, 'about living on a kibbutz for a while? I happen to know a very nice one, in the Galilee. The land is so beautiful there. And lots of nice Jewish boys – very muscular, and dutiful, and kind.'

'Oh, my goodness . . .'

'Also, I know they always need computer help – they forever trouble me about it when I am around. Speaking of which . . . I cannot promise that you will see a great deal of me while you are there. It depends on my duties. But I know you will like the others. And I know they will like you as well.'

Oh my. A real community. Something I'd known nothing of for ten years.

She left the matter with a *Well, take your time and give it some thought* shrug.

Fifty-seven

Basha had to fly directly back to Tel Aviv only a few hours later. Her holiday – not to mention her mission of the last year – cancelled. We knew where to reach each other. Thad, despite his healthy attitude of rebellion toward work, in the end wasted little time in flying back to San Francisco – where his family waited. And, of course, Helen was God only knows where – probably in a black helicopter on her way to the Pentagon.

I decided to stay in Rome on my own for a few days. Perhaps more than a few. It seemed a better place than most to think things through.

The first important conclusion I reached was that Thad was right – even glorious, cellular, existential joy wasn't enough. Pleasant as it was . . . it had to have meaning to underpin it. Life had to have meaning. And if meaning was neither a product of Darwinian evolution through natural selection . . . nor a gift from the 'gods' above . . . then that left only one alternative. We had to generate meaning for ourselves.

Obviously, I had known this beforehand – at least on an intellectual level. Recall my hastily enumerated suggestions to Thad, during our Existential Flu walk, for generating meaning in life. But, aside from the intellectual operation, there was no way to deny that my life had been pretty darned meaningless, for quite some time. And I also had to recognize that the reason for this was: I had been doing a crap job of generating meaning in my life. In fact – I had been energetically dodging it. For ten years.

Trevor's death had taught me that meaning – in the paramount form of meaningful relationships with other people – led inexorably to pain. Pain of the unendurable sort. But that, too, was precisely the wrong lesson. Thad was right – it was certainly not the lesson my brother would have wanted me to learn. Now, after all I'd experienced, I knew that the only thing more fragile than a flesh-

and-blood human being is the relationships between and amongst them. But this fragility . . . it only made both things all the more precious.

It was funny. This past year, the idea was that it was Thad who was in crisis, and me helping him through it. But the truth was just the opposite. I mean, at least Thad *knew* he was in crisis – and he was trying to make his way through. He knew that something important was missing. And he was trying to find it. All of which put him well ahead of me. I didn't even know, as the saying goes, that I was sick.

And as for who was helping whom: Yes, I had a lot of intellectual firepower to bring to bear on existential issues. But, obviously, all of my intelligence, and knowledge, and theorizing, availed me very little. I mean – my closest day-to-day relationship was with a chimp. And a monkey – basically a six-million-year-old model person – just wasn't enough. I needed to build relationships with my own kind, I needed to be part of a community. But until now, I never would face this.

In the end, I'm sure my philosophizing did much less for Thad than he did for me – with his kindness, his concern, his loyalty. With his unalloyed friendship. And also with his seven-year-old and his three-year-old.

Charles Darwin was all well and good.

But Holden Gottlieb was where it was really at.

Just before she left, I'd hit Basha with my last question for her.

'One final thing, Levy. Who was the phone?'

'Who was what phone?'

'Oh, come on. You must know – if it wasn't actually you in the first place. I've been thinking back – and you were never around when the phone called.'

'I genuinely have no idea what you are talking about.'

'Fine, then. It wasn't you. But you must know. Was it the Nagas? The Qabbalists? The Feds? It must have been the Papists. Trying to scare me off. Right?'

301

But I could not get her to give an inch – to admit that she knew anything.

In any case, I never heard from my phone again.

Except for just one last time.

I was sitting on the edge of the Trevi Fountain a little before midnight. The waters splashed winningly, the lights danced on the waters, and the young people flirted happily beneath the lights. A stellar scene. I felt very happy. And my phone beeped.

The text message beep.

I flipped it open. It said:

K8: I do believe ur finally getting the msg – & looking 4
the right things, in the right places, 4 once. 8^) O, and
about ur decision 2 save A & the Nagas. U were right; I
was wrong. – P

For the love of God.

And then it beeped again, just as I put it away. This time it said:

O, yeah – turn around.

I spun on my stone ledge. Behind me, smiling, was . . . A'hib Khouri.

I was obviously speechless, so he went ahead and spoke.

'I can't stay long,' he said with a gleam – as if I might imagine why he had to run. 'But I wanted to thank you. For helping us back there. And for finding it for us.'

He handed me a prettily gift-wrapped packaged. Since I still couldn't really find words, I went ahead and tore it open. It was a copy of the Bhagavad-Gita – the holy text (poem, really) of Hinduism. A hardcover volume, illustrated, and gorgeous. On the inside cover, an inscription: 'To Earth's foremost cryptologist, in gratitude, A'hib'.

I thanked him, but went silent again. The fountain, and the

302

lights, and happy crowd went on with their frolicking. A'hib took a seat beside me.

'God's trick,' he said.

'Sorry?'

'God's trick,' he repeated. 'Theologians refer to the *Deus Absconditus* – the God who went missing. And without explaining anything for us first. That disappearing trick is supposed to be why we never forget about Him.'

I got his drift. 'But someone finally caught him out.'

'You caught him out.'

'Do you really think of them as gods?'

'Without their intervention, it seems that we'd all still be apes. Fire-building apes, maybe. But without our consciousness. Our complexity. Our . . . ornate fountains.'

I stared at the fountain for a moment. 'May I ask you a question?'

'Shoot.'

'How did you even know about the Artefact? The Hands? That it was in the Vatican? And that we were planning to swipe it?'

'Honestly? We had a spy in the ranks of the Qabbalists. And they have a spy in one of the Israeli security services.'

'Jesus. Everyone sniffing everyone else's dirty laundry. Wearing it on their heads, more like . . . You know I'm going to want to tell Basha about that.'

'Be my guest. After this week, there's no love lost between us and the Cabal.'

'Point taken.' I remembered another question I had. 'Why did you cut and run from California? But leave us with the data?'

'It was getting dangerous. I felt I needed to bail out – and call in my cavalry. But I left you with the data in the hope that you'd solve the puzzle. Which you did.'

I sighed. 'Shouldn't this thing be in the hands of scientists?'

'You forget,' he said. 'India, which is the world's most populous democracy, also churns out more scientists and engineers than any other country. Just because a man is naked and smeared with ashes doesn't mean he's not a top guy in his field.'

I smiled out loud at that. 'Nonetheless, without the Artefact in the public domain . . . all of its revelations will just become more urban myth, whispered stories, conspiracy theories on dodgy websites . . .'

'I can't let you have it, I'm sorry. But I will make sure you learn everything about it we do. I know where to reach you.'

'Thank you.'

'No need. Like I said, it was your discovery.'

I softened a little, my sense of A'hib as an all right bloke still intact. As he rose to leave, I said: 'One final question: The Artefact. The Film, the User's Guide for Human Beings, whatever it is. Does it have anything to say about . . . meaning?'

'How do you mean? What sort of meaning?'

'I mean . . . what we're supposed to care about. What makes life worth living. The point of our lives here.'

'Well, we're only really beginning to interpret it. But so far . . . no, nothing.'

'You're sure?'

'Pretty sure. But I'll keep you posted.'

I smiled at this. Finally, I said: 'A'hib, I'm sorry I shot your guy . . . Did he make it? Did he survive?'

A'hib's countenance grew dim. 'Oh. Ravi. Right. Yes – he lives.'

'That's a great relief.'

'But . . . I'm sorry to have to tell you. He's sworn a death oath against you.'

'What?!'

'And your whole family. All your descendants, for a dozen generations. His family will never rest until they've satisfied the vendetta.'

I hung my head. 'Oh, God . . . you've got to be kidding . . .'

He put his hand on my shoulder. 'Yes, I'm only kidding. Sorry for that.'

He left quickly – before I could hurl him into the fountain.

Epilogue

So. Now.

It is almost exactly one year later – a year after the standoff in St Peter's. Which makes it nearly Easter again – or, I should say, nearly Passover. And here's where you'll find me: sitting in a small, somewhat humble, but nicely appointed and pleasingly air-conditioned, computer lab. The lab is inside a large communal building. The communal building sits nearly at the centre of a township of buildings – all of which have been built at the nexus of a number of great, rolling fields of olive trees.

I'm sitting here, and I'm checking email.

As well, I'm also slinging a little code. Nothing serious. Just some backup scripts. I decided the backup schedule should take into account the upcoming high holy days.

The fact that I'm not actually Jewish – rather conspicuously not, I can't help but think – has not turned out to be a big issue. Basha told me I'd be surprised what a secular society Israel is. And, as ever, she was right.

I did not join, become a member of this place, straight away. I made a couple of visits at first, just hanging out with Basha, meeting her friends and her (greatly) extended family. Then I spent three months as a volunteer; after which the kibbutz council officially voted to ask me on. In between all this, I mainly spent a lot of time back home, in London – with Mum and Dad. As well, going around the city, and the country, trying to reconnect with more distant relations. And with old friends I had let grow all too distant.

But, ultimately, I formally put an end to the glorious isolation I had arranged for myself in the Bay Area. Beautiful weather, beautiful natural scenery – and beautiful me, all alone in the middle of it. I know now that Thad saw through me perfectly – much, much better than I ever saw through myself. Instead of searching for real meaning, instead of connecting and growing roots, instead of living fully . . . I had run away, to the other side of the world, and nearly closed myself off. All this had to change. I guess I was just lucky to have seen it when I did. To have been granted that insight.

In part because life has become so much fuller for me lately, I don't spend as much time online as I used to. But I still stay in touch. And I read the news. For instance, I've followed a series of extremely exciting breakthroughs in behavioural genetics – coming from, of all places, a handful of biotech startups in India. They've found some very interesting genetic correlates of behaviour, consciousness, higher functions – off in the backwaters of 'unexpressed' DNA. Really shaking up the field. Shocking a lot of people. Albeit not me.

And it seems we've all kept our mouths shut about the Pandora sequence itself. At least for the moment. A true conspiracy. Of course, it's inevitable that someone else, some other biotech, some visionary grad student, will rediscover the sequence eventually. But, for now, the secret remains ours.

In another in an ongoing series of honest moments, I realized I wasn't the only primate I knew who needed the congress of its own kind. And so it was that the estimable Erasmus D found a community of his own, too (with a little human help). After a brief joyful homecoming, I tearfully took him off to apply for membership in a tribe of bonobos in Salonga National Park, in the Democratic Republic of the Congo.

Salonga is Africa's largest tropical rainforest preserve (14,000 square miles), established in 1970 specially for the protection of the bonobos. We met with some very nice scientists and field staff there – and who have promised to keep an eye on my simian beloved, and to try and ensure that his transition into bonobo society is a smooth one.

I plan to go and visit him one day. (He has a cute little radio implant that will allow us to locate him.) But not too soon. I think it would be a little painful for both of us. But he should live a great many more years. And, moreover, they should be years full of community, socializing, fruitful foraging, beautiful natural habit – and, of course, loads of constant, varied, and totally gratuitous sex.

Believe it or not, I still work for Complete and Total Ass-Kicking Entertainment. I just work off-site now, officially as a contractor. Basically, that means I put in about twenty hours a week – and draw about 80 per cent of my old salary. (Told you I was unfireable.) I fly back to the Bay Area, for meetings and whatnot, once a month, for about five days. I stay with the Gottliebs, and commute with Thad in his truck down to the ole cubicle farm in the fecund Valley.

With the rest of my week, I do most of the computer tech support around the kibbutz. You'd be amazed how many computers it takes to run a farming operation these days! Speaking of which, I'm also very pleased to have my own little miniature bit of olive grove. All mine. Farming is awesome. And digging in the dirt – in the Upper Galilee, right in the Holy Land – is *really* good for the soul.

On top of all that, I'm also on the committee for the dance club – where I DJ two nights a month. I'm on the technology resource planning committee. I'm a member of the philosophy club (of which Basha is a founding member). And I teach occasional programming classes for kids age six to sixty.

Like I said, life is fuller than it has been for a long, long time.

I also still put in a good bit of time at the gym. (We've quite a decent one.) Though, I'm happy to say I've kicked the diet supplements. And I've also developed a healthier relationship with food – and my own body. Let me tell you, after a day in the field, hunger is truly the only driving force behind eating. And, more importantly, I find I've got a lot less I'm trying to crowd out of my consciousness these days.

Oh, and get this, if you can: I'm pregnant. How's that for connection, for faith in the future, for putting down roots? The father's name is Ari. And he truly is muscular, and dutiful, and kind – just as Basha promised. He's also intellectual, and well travelled, and well read, and extremely hard-working, and deeply moral and compassionate. He recites poetry for me – in English, French, and Hebrew. He's a farmer, and a citizen soldier. And he's got very much the same face like deep, still, and very clear water that Basha does. (In fact, they're cousins.) We already know the baby is a boy. And that we're going to call him Trevor. This was Basha's idea.

Speaking of Basha: Her duties keep her away most of the time. But I really enjoy the time we do get to spend together. When she's not here, we swap an awful lot of email. Just like always. I've also had much to learn from her other friends and family (now my friends and family) about not worrying for her safety. The others all know that her work is terribly important; and they are all rightly proud of her for doing it. As am I.

As for the conflict itself, which is so much a part of everyone's worries: It's both saddening and terrifying. But I'm hopeful for the future. Only upon leaving it, did I realize that I'd spent fully a third of my life – the entire adult part – in America. And, in one regard, at least, I am truly American: I believe in progress. For me, for my loved ones, for the world; and for good old anomalous, artistic, language-using, consciousness-plagued *Homo sapiens sapiens* – the only living things on this damp, spinning stone standing upright and gazing toward Heaven.